A World Darkly

Wrath of the Old Gods Book III

John Triptych

ISBN (soft cover) 978-621-95332-5-6

J Triptych Publishing

Cover art by Deranged Doctor Design (http://www.derangeddoctordesign.com)
Interior formatting by Polgarus Studio (http://www.polgarusstudio.com)

For Beverly (AKA Polgara).
A gracious lady, good friend, and ever loyal fan.

Author's note:

Dear reader, I would like to thank you for purchasing this book. As a self-published author, I incur all the costs of producing this novel so your feedback means a lot to me. If you wouldn't mind, could you please take a few minutes and post a review of this online and let others know what you think of it?

As I'm sure you're aware, the more reviews I get, the better my future sales would be and therefore my financial incentive to produce more books for your enjoyment increases. I am very happy to read any comments and questions and I am willing to respond to you personally as quickly as I can. My email is jtriptych@gmail.com if you wish to contact me directly. Again, thank you and I hope you enjoy reading this book as much as I enjoyed writing it!

Please join my exclusive mailing list! You will get the latest news on my upcoming works and special discounts. Subscription is FREE and you get lots of FREE books! Just copy and paste this link to your browser: http://eepurl.com/bK-xGn

Down to a dark abyss my heart has sounded,
A mournful world, by grey horizons bounded,
Where blasphemy and horror swim by night.

For half the year a heatless sun gives light,
The other half the night obscures the earth.
The arctic regions never knew such dearth.
No woods, nor streams, nor creatures meet the sight.

-Charles Baudelaire, *De profundis clamavi*

1. Dastardly Doings

Texas Front Line

They officially called it the Dallas Line, though its more popular nickname was the Doomsday Defense. It was really nothing more than a series of observation posts strung out along the south of the city. The soldiers own nickname for it was the "string of no resistance". The military had now been so depleted, there was no way they could fully man the country's receding borders to the south. Although there had been a Federal order to evacuate the whole state, there were still significant numbers of native Texans who stayed behind. The US government had been making dire warnings that an invasion from the south was now imminent, but many people refused to become refugees. They just didn't want to pack up, they couldn't bear the thought of leaving the state that they had grown up and lived in for decades. If this would be their final stand, then so be it. The soul of the Alamo lived on in them.

Private First Class Tyrone Gatlin climbed up on the hood of the Humvee as he carried their dinner using both arms. Since the vehicle was parked facing the truck stop, all he had to do was place the container of food on the overhanging roof of the building. As he did just that, another soldier standing on top of the roof looked down on him and aimed his M-4 carbine at Tyrone.

"Halt, who goes there?" the freckle faced soldier said.

Tyrone snorted as he used his arms to pull himself up on the overhang. "It's me for chrissakes."

"Yeah? What's the codeword then?"

Tyrone shook his head as he picked up the paper bag again. "Jesus."

"Wrong. It ain't Jesus."

Tyrone sighed. "Okay, it's quarterback. Are you happy now? What's the countersign?"

"Sneak. Come on up then."

Tyrone took two steps until he faced the wooden façade of the upper roof. Then he placed the bag on top of the wall and pulled himself up once more. After climbing up a second time, he was now on the topmost roof of the truck stop as he walked towards his gear. The second soldier smiled and took off his ballistic helmet as he sat down on a folding chair. The night air was cool and the skies were clear as they could see the twinkling stars above.

"I can't believe you have to challenge me every time I make a dinner run for the both of us," Tyrone said as he placed the paper bag on the steel folding table. "Can't you see that it's just me?"

"Just followin' orders," Specialist Fred Novak said as he began rummaging through the bag and took out a styrofoam box. "What've you got this time?"

"Ribs and trimmings. One of the volunteers brought along a full barbeque kit, so it looks like the whole unit's gonna be eating good tonight."

They were both stationed in a small town called Carl's Corner, less than forty miles from the southern outskirts of Dallas. The place was really nothing more than a truckstop in between two highways. A famous country singer once had a museum in the compound, but hard times forced it to close. Now they were sitting on top of a building that had been abandoned ever since the crisis began. The area surrounding them was mostly flat grassland and highways, with occasional copses of trees out across the horizon.

Tyrone chewed on the last of his portion of ribs as he stared at the white water tank out in the distance. He had joined the Army just a scant eleven months before the Glooming happened. Before that, he'd worked at his parent's grocery store in Georgia. Even though his mother had encouraged him to go to college, Tyrone hated school and so he'd joined the military instead. It was just his luck that the world suddenly turned upside down and now he had the feeling that he was going to die soon. Many of the people he trained with were now missing since most of his training batch was assigned to US Army South, just before they crossed into the Mexican border and were never heard from again. That had been almost a year ago. Now they were hearing rumblings that whatever was down south of them was preparing an invasion. If an entire Army Corps was unable to stop whatever it was out there, what chance would an ad hoc unit of reservists and newly-trained recruits have?

"You seem to be zoning out again, Ty," Fred said as he drank from a plastic water bottle. He was a native of Dallas and had been with the Army for two years now. His father and grandfather before him had all served in the military, and Fred was prepared from birth to follow in their footsteps. Fred had already signed up for Selective Service even before his eighteenth birthday, just to show everyone how patriotic he was. While Tyrone had uneasy thoughts about the coming war, Fred was more than ready to lay down his life for his state and his country.

Tyrone got up and put his trash in the black plastic bag on the side of the building. "Just thinking about home is all."

"Where you from again?"

"Georgia, I thought I told you."

"I guess I forgot," Fred said as he too got up and walked over to the radio. The rest of their squad was at Hillsboro, less than four miles away to the south. The two of them had orders to report any possible flanking movements by the enemy. Their mission was not to engage but only to observe and report. A small group of civilian volunteers was over at Lovelace, a compound of houses just a couple of miles to the west. The military was hard-pressed, so any civilian who had a two-way radio and was willing to volunteer, was immediately sworn in as paramilitary support. Two brothers, who were former truckers, were now holed up in one of the houses at Lovelace with a CB radio tuned in to a military frequency.

Tyrone took one of the folding chairs near the table and placed it near the radio. "I haven't heard anything at all this evening. You sure that thing's working?"

Fred sat on the ground as he adjusted the radio settings. "Everything seems okay to me. Maybe there's just nothing to report."

Tyrone shrugged as he picked up his own M-4 rifle and checked it. "I'm just surprised Lieutenant Sabatini isn't doing one of his hourly radio checks."

"You're right," Fred said as he put on the headset and began transmitting. "Opie Four to Hillsboro, come in, over."

For the next few minutes, Fred continued to try and contact his commander in Hillsboro but all he got was static. He switched frequencies to contact the civilian volunteers at Lovelace and got a satisfactory response. Fred then went back to the HQ frequency and continued his attempts to contact Hillsboro once more.

Tyrone took out a sandstone medallion from one of his pockets and began to rub it. The symbol in the center of the pendant was that of an intertwined serpent eating its own tail. "Any kind of response?"

"Nothing, but at least we still got Lovelace, and they're reporting everything is a-okay," Fred said as he took off the headset and noticed what Tyrone was doing. "What is that you got there?"

"Ouroboros. It's a lucky charm."

"I can see that. Are you superstitious or something?"

"Not really," Tyrone said as he shook his head sheepishly. "Well, maybe just a little. This is a religious symbol to me, like a cross."

Fred smirked. "Oh yeah, what's your religion?"

"I was born into African Methodist Episcopal because my family was. But you know, times have changed. I started worshipping the Master of Breath a few months ago."

Fred laughed. "So that's what's the medallion for? You worshipping one of these old Indian gods now?"

"Muscogee and Seminole," Tyrone said. "I met a guy who said he saw the god Esaugetuh Emissee manifest himself to him. A lot of people in my home state are starting to worship him. They all say he's real, compared to Jesus being a myth."

"I read that news report too. It was about that giant maggot in New York City, right?"

Tyrone nodded. "No, I heard that was Ahone- he's a Powhatan god up in the Algonquin area- the people up in the tri-state area are worshippin' him from what I heard. I started to get strange dreams at night ever since this Glooming began. I couldn't quite figure it out until I met this guy, he was a supply sergeant and part Seminole. That guy told me all about this god, and when I heard it, I felt something inside of me stir up, you know? I bought the medallion from the guy. We don't know too much about him, but I think if we just say a prayer to him now and then, maybe he'll give us his blessing or something."

Fred rolled his eyes. "Yeah sure, go ahead and worship those pagan gods. I really don't care."

Tyrone looked at him straight in the eye. "You never thought about it? You never considered changing your religion since these old gods came back and proved to everybody that they exist now?"

"My parents were religious, they're Polish Catholics," Fred said wistfully. "I just never had the time to think about it. I just never felt a need to worship anything. I was too focused on the real world."

"Yeah I know. So was I. But these gods are in the real world too. If we go up against those Aztecs, I figure that if all else fails, maybe the Master of Breath will protect me, you know what I mean?"

Fred laughed again. "Well, if they come and we ain't stoppin' 'em, then I got my own get outta jail free card."

Tyrone was confused for a minute. "Say what? A get outta jail card? For reals?"

"Yeah, lookee here," Fred said as he pulled out a jade necklace from underneath his field uniform. "This is an old Aztec charm that I bought from a Mexican a few weeks ago when I told him I was being deployed to defend the border."

"What in the hell are you gonna do with that?"

Fred kept on giggling. "Well, if the worst happens, and I get captured or something, then all I'm gonna do is pull this out and show it to them. I'll tell them I'm one of them."

Tyrone shook his head in disbelief. "So you think they gonna just believe that crap? You crazy motherfu—"

The radio suddenly began to squawk. “US military, come in, over! Anybody! Help us! Oh God!”

Fred instantly turned his attention back to the radio as he put the headset back on. “This is Opie Four, we are reading you. Identify yourself, over.”

“This is Lovelace, we’re the ones in Lovelace! You gotta help us now! Heeelp!”

Fred took out a codebook from his fatigues pocket. “Lovelace, I need you to calm down. Please authenticate.”

“Oh God! Hang on, lemme get those codes! Hang on! Here it is … Echo Zulu Niner, over!”

Fred nodded. It was the right code. “We are reading you loud and clear, Lovelace. What’s the sitrep?”

“They’re coming! I can see ‘em!”

Tyrone was off his chair and crouched down beside Fred as he tried to listen in the conversation. “The Aztecs?”

Fred waived him away as he concentrated on the radio. Lovelace was just a few miles ahead of them, just beyond the abandoned airport. “Lovelace, calm down. We need more intel. Can you identify what you’re seeing, over?”

The voice on the radio was becoming more hysterical. “It’s a goddamn army of monsters out there! They’re headed this way! We don’t even need our scopes, we can see them with our own eyes!”

“Shit,” Tyrone hissed as he grabbed his binoculars and ran to the edge of the western wall of the rooftop. He began to quickly scan the area but all he could see was a mist beginning to form in the horizon. “I am not seeing anything, but visibility is getting worse.”

Fred continued to speak into the radio receiver. “Lovelace, can you get a headcount? We need to know how many of the enemy is out there and what type, over.”

‘I-I think I can see hundreds of them coming out of the fog,” the voice on the radio said. “No, it’s thousands, tens of thousands! Most of them are men, I think … they’re wearing those goddamn Aztec costumes and they’re carrying those goddamn sword clubs … oh shit, I can see one of those women demons, the ones who look like skeletons! We’re getting the hell outta here!”

Fred frowned as he keyed in the receiver once more. "Lovelace, can you give me their exact position? I can request close air support or some artillery, over."

Tyrone kept looking through his binoculars. Both men soon heard some gunfire out in the distance but it was very faint. Since Lovelace was behind the municipal airport, Tyrone wasn't able to get a clear view using his field glasses. The mist that had been a distant part of the horizon was now drifting towards them. It was like a grey wall that obscured everything behind it.

"Lovelace, come in," Fred said. "Lovelace, we need you to look at the map grid we provided to you and give us some coordinates for a fire mission, over."

The radio was still on but all they could hear was static. Fred tried calling the volunteers a few more times, but there was no response.

Tyrone was moving from one end of the roof to the other as he tried desperately to see if he could spot anything. He silently cursed to himself since their commander had failed to requisition any sort of nightvision equipment for them. He knew that the other squads in the platoon had them, but their observation post had somehow been overlooked. Both he and Fred had been clamoring to get at least just one night vision goggle for their helmets, but the Lieutenant kept saying that there was a shortage, and therefore a delay until they could issue any more of them. Now that the actual fight was on, they were caught with their pants down. It was a typical military screw up.

Fred was so frustrated, he almost threw the receiver down on the ground. "Goddamn it, they ain't answering! Those chickenshits must've run away the moment they got their last message in."

Tyrone didn't take his eyes of the binoculars as he kept observing the area. He could hear sporadic gunfire out in the distance. "Can you get Hillsboro then?"

Fred switched frequencies on the radio once more and then he tried to call in the rest of the squad. After listening to a few minutes of white noise, he gave up. "They ain't answering either, something's up."

Tyrone's jaw trembled a little. Maybe they were all alone now. "Try Dallas HQ."

Fred's head bobbed as he realized that he forgot about their main unit. He quickly shifted frequencies again. "Dallas HQ, come in over. This is Opie Four. Come in, over."

The calm voice that answered on the other end of the line was an immediate morale boost for both of them. "This is Dallas HQ. We are receiving you, Opie Four. Please authenticate, over."

"Authentication is Bravo Bravo Zulu One, over" Fred said. "We have a possible enemy contact at Lovelace. Our own squad in Hillsboro is not answering our calls, over."

"Okay, Opie Four, stay on the air. You are the only OP that we are in contact with. Can you confirm size and make of enemy units, over?"

"We lack long range optics and nightvision, but Lovelace confirmed to us that main Aztec body is on the move, heading towards us," Fred said. "Request reinforcements and immediate fire support, over."

Tyrone's jaw dropped as he saw a fellow soldier running towards them on Interstate 35. "Holy sheeit! I think I can see Stratton… yeah it's him alright, he's running towards us!"

Fred jumped up as he ran over to his side while carrying the radio. "What?"

"Look," Tyrone said as he pointed to the highway at the south of the building.

Fred didn't have a pair of binoculars so he squinted at first, but it was now obvious that Tyrone was right. Coming up from the highway was Specialist Hank Stratton, he was a former star running back in high school before he joined up several years ago. He had been part of their squad and was assigned with the lieutenant and the rest of the team over in Hillsboro. They could see that he had only one boot on and his combat uniform was torn up in several places. Stratton wasn't wearing a helmet and there was some blood on his buzz cut. He had a wild look on his face as he ran towards them as fast as he could.

Tyrone waived at him. "Stratton, over here! We're over here!"

Stratton gave them a quick glance before continuing his sprint down the highway. He didn't even slow down as he kept up the relentless pace. The swirling fog moved in and he was soon lost from their view.

Tyrone just shook his head. "What in the hell happened? He saw me. Why didn't he run over to us?"

Fred keyed in the radio receiver again. It was clear that Stratton must have chickened out. He wasn't sure if that guy was going to make it to Dallas or not since it was a long way off. No way could he run all the way there, not with one boot on. "Dallas HQ, we need to report that Hillsboro might be overrun, repeat, Hillsboro is believed to be overrun, over."

A different voice on the radio soon answered them. "Roger that, Opie Four. You have been transferred over to Divisional HQ. Can you confirm your grid coordinates, over?"

Fred crouched down and looked at the tactical map. He quickly gave the grid coordinates and then repeated it just to make sure. "We estimate that the enemy could be here any minute now, over."

"Roger that," the voice on the radio said. "Alamo is in play, stay on the air and report as soon as you detect enemy contact. Your orders are to continue to transmit as long as you can and report exact position of main enemy body. Please acknowledge, over."

"Mission order acknowledged, over," Fred said before taking his thumb off the receiver key. "Alamo is in play? What in the hell's that mean?"

Tyrone shrugged as he kept looking. "I've got no idea. You're from Texas, aren't you? What's the meaning of Alamo to you?"

"I don't see a big deal, I mean it's just a true story about brave Texans holed up in a fort against the Mexicans before we became a state. They were outnumbered like a hundred to one and they didn't surrender. The ol' boys from Texas all died and became heroes. That's pretty much it."

"So it's just about sacrifice then? Does that mean that maybe the Alamo would be like Dallas or something?"

"Dallas ain't no fort, it's a city."

Tyrone put down the binoculars and looked at him with wide eyes. "Oh my god."

Fred was still confused. "What is it?"

Tyrone hands started to tremble as he held onto the binoculars. "Alamo! They're gonna nuke this whole area!"

Fred's jaw dropped. "No way, are you kidding me?"

"Think about it! I've seen a number of trucks when we deployed down here with those yellow nuke markings on them," Tyrone said. "They must have seeded this place with nukes. I heard from Sergeant Smith that the corps of engineers was making all sorts of digs in this whole area!"

Fred started to look around frantically. "I don't like this, Ty. You're scaring me, dude."

Tyrone quickly ran over to where his gear was stacked up, then he started rummaging through his bags as he sat down behind the wall.

Fred just looked at him. He had a growing sense of fear and confusion. "What are you doing, Ty?"

Tyrone quickly unfolded his CBRN suit and began to wear it over his field uniform. Fred quickly realized his partner was putting on a special protective outerwear in an event of a chemical or nuclear attack. He quickly ran over, opened his own pack and began putting it on as well. Within a few minutes, both men had gotten into their suits and were putting on their oversized boots when the radio began squawking again.

"Opie Four, what's your sitrep, over?" the voice on the radio said.

Fred ran back over to the radio as he carried his gloves and mask. He gestured at Tyrone to use his binoculars again. The thin black man from Georgia had already put his gloves on and just needed to put his mask over his face, but instead he grabbed the binoculars that were lying on the ground as he looked out from the roof again. In less than a second, he made an audible gasp before ducking behind the wall of the roof again.

"Ty, what is it? I need a sitrep," Fred said.

Tyrone was shaking like a leaf. "T-they're here," he whispered.

Fred didn't get it. "What do you mean they're here?"

Tyrone's voice was like a squeal of a cornered mouse. "T-they're all around us. The Aztecs."

Fred inhaled deeply as a feeling of terror rolled down his spine. They were going to die. The one thought that came to his mind was the advice of his grandfather. *If you're gonna die, then take as many of the enemy with you.* That was when he slowly and deliberately picked up the radio receiver and keyed it in. "Dallas HQ, we're surrounded. Request all ordinance to be dropped or detonated on us, over." Then he repeated their grid coordinates.

The reply on the radio was terse. "Acknowledged, Opie Four. Stand by for Alamo detonation. Suggest you hunker down, over."

Tyrone whimpered as he placed the gas mask over his face. Fred didn't bother to put his own mask on as he felt that he was going to die no matter what. They could hear chants in a strange language in the parking lot down below. Fred slowly picked up his rifle and checked to make sure it was loaded.

And then all hell broke loose.

The constant squawking on the radio must have attracted them. Within minutes, a swarm of Aztec warriors, hard, painted men dressed in traditional loincloths and feathered headdresses, climbed up to the overhang and then started to hurdle the wall of the roof. Fred saw them first and began firing as the first Aztec warrior bounded over the divider. Tyrone also made a grab for his rifle as both men began to engage the unceasing swarm of warriors that tried to climb their way up to them. Fred was able to bring down over a half dozen of them before switching to semi-automatic fire in an effort to conserve his ammunition. The Aztec men they were facing seemed to be in some sort of weird trance as they moved slowly and advanced on them with their macuahuitls, an Aztec sword made out of wood with embedded obsidian blades along its sides.

In less than two minutes, they were both able to bring down three dozen assailants. They covered each other's backs as the horde down below had apparently wavered and no other warriors attempted to climb up on the roof. At that moment, something fell out of the sky and landed less than twenty yards away. As both Fred and Tyrone looked out over the roof, they saw that it was some sort of bomb, sticking out of the ground just at the edge of the highway.

"Opie Four, are you still there?" the voice on the radio said.

Both of them looked at each other. It was clear that the warhead was either dropped or launched from an artillery piece. But it hadn't detonated. Alamo was a nuke and it had proved to be useless.

Then things got even worse.

A creature straight out of myth suddenly leapt onto the roof. At first glance, it looked like a pale, naked woman wearing a metallic skirt. Its face was that of a fanged skull, with blank sockets that resembled an empty void of death, its long hair hung like black curtains over its flaccid breasts. The monster's skeletal body was just bones over dead flesh while its hands ended in razor sharp black claws. They called it the tzitzimitl, the dreaded Aztec demon from the stars.

Fred screamed as he began firing on it, but all he did was make the monster even angrier as it advanced towards them. The rifle rounds seemed to either pass right through the creature or did no visible damage to its gaunt body.

Tyrone had had enough. He dropped his rifle and sprinted to the other end of the rooftop before making a jump for it. As he landed on the concrete parking lot, he twisted his ankle. There were a few Aztec warriors that were yards away. They saw him but they didn't seem to care as they slowly made their way towards the city in the north. Tyrone grimaced as he stood up and started limping to a small building that housed the automated teller machine. He had seen an old sedan in the garage and he had hotwired it two days before, just in case he needed a getaway car. The Humvee was on the other side of the parking lot and it was surrounded by Aztec warriors, so this was the safer bet.

As he made it to the outskirts of the parking lot, something round landed just in front of him with a moist thud. The night obscured what it was, so Tyrone limped closer for a better look. As he got to within a few feet he cried out in sheer terror. It was Fred's head. The mouth was contorted in a silent scream and his eyes had been gouged out. A pool of blood had begun to form around it.

Tyrone made it into the garage as he got into the driver's seat of the sedan. His hands were shaking as he connected the ignition wires together. Several Aztec warriors slowly advanced towards him. The seconds seemed like hours as he kept fumbling with the wires. When he instinctively looked up, an Aztec warrior smashed the window glass right beside him with a wooden club, just as the car started up. The glassy-eyed warrior tried to pull him through the broken window, but Tyrone stepped on the accelerator and the sedan lurched forward. He drove the car into the parking lot now teeming with Aztecs. Another warrior tried to climb onto the hood of the car, but Tyrone stepped on the brakes at the last second and the Aztec was thrown off. A half dozen more of the enemy tried to rush the sedan but it plowed right through them and sped off into the highway. As the car headed towards the outskirts of Dallas, Tyrone didn't look back.

2. Reflections in the Flames

Arizona

When his neighbor suggested that he join them in moving into a bigger house, Brian said no. That was more than eight months ago, when the panic started and everyone was leaving the city. Now it looked like he was the only one left in the mobile home park. With so many abandoned houses in Phoenix, all the other people that once lived with him either moved into one of the wealthier digs, or they just decided to go away for good. He spent most of the day breaking into every single building and residence in the area, hoping to find a little food to keep him going. Whenever he found booze it was a cause for celebration. If it was a sizable cache, he would try to down a bottle before bringing the rest back to his mobile home. As the days went by, he was starting to find less and less stuff. He still had a half dozen bottles of the good stuff and several cases of beer he took from what was left of a liquor store, but now he figured it was best to ration his stash. Who knew how many days he had left before everything either went back to normal, or he would be dead.

He wasn't sure of the exact time, but the sun had already gone down a few hours ago by the time he woke up. Brian was so used to drinking, he hardly had any hangovers anymore, it was just one drunken binge after another. Every time he regained consciousness, he figured it was time for another drink.

The streetlamps had already gone out months ago, so he was fumbling in the darkness as he stumbled out of the front door. The moon above gave some illumination, but he was surrounded by shadows and he could barely make out any details. As he blinked his eyes, he noticed the large mound in front of him. At least he remembered to gather all the flammable junk before he passed out a few hours before. That was a good thing because the wind had picked up and he felt an icy chill cascading throughout his body.

With trembling hands, he was able to take the lighter out of his sweater pocket and he started to light the debris pile. When the fire instantly started and began to pick up in intensity, he realized he must have already poured the kerosene on it before his afternoon binge. So it looked like he didn't forget after all. It wasn't like the night before when he forgot about everything and just had to drink in the cold darkness with an old blanket wrapped around him. Even though the alcohol ultimately warmed him up, he woke up with a terrible cough the next day.

As the roaring flames began to intensify, the current of heat drifted in waves and he smiled as his body finally warmed up. Brian walked back into his mobile home but he kept the front door open so the heat would drift inside. He liked to just sit by the door so he dragged his old, beaten up easy chair until it was just facing the doorway. All he had left was gin and even though he hated drinking it, it was better than nothing. Brian sat down on the padded chair, opened the bottle and took a few sips. A part of him figured it might be more practical to move into another, much bigger house with a fireplace, but he preferred to just stay put. He had heard stories from drifters who came by, that those people who took over the larger homes in places like Scottsdale were ultimately found massacred in them. Brian figured that if he stayed put in his own house, then no one would bother him. No one ever did. Perhaps it was because his own neighborhood was run down and poor to begin with, but he never encountered any looters or bandits. He figured that if anyone was so foolish as to squat in one of the wealthier neighborhoods, then they would be a prime target for robbers. The best way to survive this ordeal was to stay beneath the radar, he figured.

He didn't get a whole lot of news since power had gone out of the city months ago. The last piece of information he got was from a group of former soldiers who had deserted their post in the south. He was walking along the highway with a sack of goods that he took from a house and they noticed him as they rode by in their Humvee. Brian thought they were going to shoot him, but instead they traded some of their military rations for two bottles of booze. Brian didn't really want to give it to them but he figured it was better to let bygones be bygones, so he gave them a couple of the cheap stuff. Just before they left, they told him the Aztec gods were on their way. The soldiers said they fought in a battle right at the border, just north of the Mexican town of Nogales and so many of them had died that they felt it was pointless to keep on fighting. They said that Tucson would probably be next and it was better for him to head north, like them. Even though they offered him a ride, Brian just gave them a toothy grin and politely declined, so they took off. That was over two weeks ago, so he figured those Aztec demons would have already conquered Tucson, meaning they could be here any day now.

Brian noticed a chilly draft coming from the inside of the house, near the back portion. He grunted and slowly got up from his chair as he carried the bottle with him. As he peered into the darkened, compact living room, he noticed part of the opposite wall had collapsed. That was when he remembered that he had tried to start a bonfire in the house about a month ago when the weather started to turn chilly. He was too drunk to realize that the back shelf wasn't a fireplace so he ended up wasting a keg of beer trying to put the fire out. He had been meaning to board up some plywood where the fire had torn a hole in the wall, but he always put it off for another day. Brian started cursing as he flopped back into the chair. He was hoping he would remember what to do about that hole when he would wake up the next day.

A shrill, cawing noise woke him up from his stupor. He noticed that the fire had died down a bit, but it still cast a goodly yellowish light across the trailer park. The cawing noise continued. It sounded like a bird or something.

Brian slowly got up as he realized that the bottle he was holding was empty. As he tried to move back into the house, he tripped on the front steps of the door and fell backwards, the back of his head hitting the gravel driveway. For a brief moment he just lay there as he cradled his throbbing head. The pain was pretty intense but he wasn't sure if it was the fall that hurt him or whether it was the onset of a hangover. After a few minutes he sat up, facing the bonfire as he rubbed the back of his head.

That was when he saw a raven perched on the roof above his doorway. So that was where the cawing noises came from.

Brian's voice was like a raw grumble. "Get outta there, you dumb bird! See what you made me do? You made me get up and so I goddamn fell, you stupid animal!"

The black bird started at him for bit before tilting its head and glancing around robotically. It hardly seemed to notice him.

Brian remembered that he once had a slingshot when he was a kid and he used to shoot birds out of the sky with it. It was a pity that the only gun he found when he was rummaging through houses didn't have any bullets. He was tempted to go back into the house and get the gun, but it was pointless without any ammunition. That was when the odor hit him. He hadn't taken a bath since God knows when, but he didn't want to keep sitting on the dirt so he slowly pulled himself up.

"Bravo, and here I was thinking that you were too drunk to get up," a voice said.

Brian looked around nervously. "What? Who's there?"

The voice sounded old but high-pitched. "Heads up, I'm right above you."

Brian looked up, but all he could see was the raven. He pointed at it. "You? Were you talking to me?"

The black bird looked at him. Its eyes seemed to glow in the dark. "Who else would I be talking to?"

Brian shrieked as he took a few steps backwards, but he quickly came forward as soon as his back nearly touched the leaping flames coming from the bonfire in front of his house.

"Be careful," the raven said. "The only liquid you got left is gin, it wouldn't exactly douse the flames if your back was on fire."

Brian's knees were wobbly but he was able to stand there and he pointed a finger at the bird once more. "A talking bird? You can't be real. I must be so wasted that I'm just hearing things."

"You are somewhat wasted, but not so much as a few hours ago," the raven said. "You may need another drink soon."

"Get outta here," Brian said as he picked up a small stone from the gravel driveway and threw it at the bird. The rock narrowly missed the raven as it bounced off the roof.

Another voice, this time coming from somewhere to his side, made him jump. "Daddy, where's Timmy?"

Brian turned. "Tara, is that you?"

Tara Weiss was standing near the side of the mobile home. The firelight made her reddish brown hair seem as if it was glowing. She was dressed in a brand new pair of jeans and wore a denim jacket over her pink t-shirt. It was his daughter alright, but there was something different about her. It must have been a year since he last saw her, when she was fifteen. He detected a certain confidence, a power within her he had never sensed before. "Yes, it's me. I'm asking you where Timmy is. Where is he?" Tara said.

By this time, his surprise had turned into contempt once more. He always felt that way about her. Tara reminded him of his wife. "I thought you were outta here, why did you even come back?"

"I told you, I came back for Timmy. Where is he?"

Brian scratched his thick stubble. He needed a drink. "It's none of your business. He's my son and I'm his legal guardian. I could do whatever I want with him. You're nothing. Go away."

Tara started to fidget. "I want Timmy! I'm the only one who cares about him. I want to take him out of here. I'm asking you again, where is he?"

"And I'm telling you it's none of your business where he is. He's my son and I can do whatever I want with him."

Tara's mouth trembled. "You're nothing but a drunk and a bum! I hate you! Tell me where is he is right now!"

Brian laughed. "You think you can come back here and insult me in front of my own house? You wanna start this again? I'm been pretty patient with you, but this is the last time I will allow you to talk to me like that! Now get outta here before I lose my temper."

Tara took a step forward. "I'm not leaving without my brother! Up yours, Daddy!"

A sharp flash of anger overtook Brian as he started moving towards her. One of his hands was held high so he could do an open hand slap once he got in close. "Why you goddamn little bitch! I'll teach you to talk to me like th—"

He suddenly stopped in mid stride, just a few feet in front of her. The hand that he raised up seemed to be suspended in the air and he couldn't move it. When he turned and looked at his arm, Brian noticed that another hand had grabbed a hold of his wrist. His arm was tiny compared to the huge fist holding it. It was thick and leathery, like the skin of an albino crocodile, and its fingers ended in black claws. As he twisted his neck even further, his anger gave way to sheer terror as his own eyes stared into the creature's blood red pupils.

Within less than a second, the pale creature twisted his arm backwards and threw him against the side of the mobile home. Brian's back hit the wall of his house with a loud crash and he slid down, groaning. His legs had buckled and he was sitting in the dirt with straightened knees, like a little child. He let out a short moan as the pain in his back shot up like a rocket to the front of his brain.

Patrick Gyle stood over him. He had been transformed by the last of the magical flower that once gave immortality to whoever possessed it. He was naked since he didn't need any clothes over his hairless, waxlike body. His armored skin was pretty much impervious to anything, so the cold night didn't bother him at all. His long, sinewy arms were unnaturally long, and his catlike feet had doubled in size. His genitals had sloughed off along with his skin a long time ago so modesty wasn't important to him anymore. "Stay down, and don't ever touch her again," he said softly.

Brian looked up at him with a blank stare. "W-what are you?"

Gyle's voice was guttural, like a cross between a foghorn and a lion. His grimacing mouth was full of razor sharp fangs. "Answer the question. Where's her brother?"

Brian took a minute to catch his breath. "H-he's not here."

Tara's frustration nearly boiled over. She was in near tears as she crouched down so their eyes met. "Where is he? What did you do with my brother?"

Brian looked away in shame. "H-he didn't want to stay here with me. He wanted to leave so he could find you. He kept crying and whining and just wouldn't eat. I-I couldn't stand it anymore."

Tara grabbed him by his shirt collar. "What did you do?"

"O-one of our neighbors," Brian said. "The O-Olsens. T-they said they were leaving and their son was Timmy's playmate. Timmy wouldn't shut up so I finally said they could take him with them. They weren't sure at first, but then they finally said yes. So they all left."

Tara let out a sob as her hands shook. "How long ago was this?"

Brian shook his head. "I-I don't remember. I stopped counting the days already."

"How long!"

"A few days after you left. F-five or six days after that, I think."

"That would mean that they left about the same day we found each other," the raven said as it continued to perch on the roof above them.

Tara was sobbing now as she stood up and took a step back. She balled up her fists but they wouldn't stop shaking. "Where did they say they were going to?"

"I-I think they were gonna go up to Kansas," Brian said. "They were gonna go and join up with that church up there I think. Yeah, that was it."

Tara took a deep breath. "They were going to the Rock of God Church? Are you sure?"

Brian blinked a few times. The pain and his hangover was making things look blurry. "Y-yeah, I think so. They got an SUV from somewhere. I'm guessing they might've stolen it since Mike Olsen's car was an old stationwagon. They packed it up with everything and they just took off. That was the last time I saw Timmy. I swear."

Tara wiped her tears away using the sleeves of her jacket. "Oh god, I was on my way to that place too. What kind of car was it?"

Brian placed a hand over his throbbing forehead. "I-I'm not sure, I think it was an Explorer. It was black with tinted windows. I didn't read the license plate."

"So that's it then," the raven said. "Now what?"

Tara turned and started to walk out into the darkness. Gyle glanced at her before looking back at her father. The raven flapped its wings and flew up slightly before landing on Gyle's shoulder.

Brian put his arms up in a gesture of peace and submission. "I've told you everything. Please don't hurt me. All I wanted to do was to be left alone. I-I'm not a bother to anyone."

Gyle snorted at him before turning around and began to walk in the same direction that Tara took. "You're pathetic."

Brian wanted to say something, but he wisely figured that keeping quiet would be a better alternative. Within a few seconds, Gyle's deathlike, hulking figure disappeared into the night and all he could see was the dying embers of the bonfire in front of him.

They were in an abandoned parking lot a few blocks away. The full moon cast vague shadows over them. The whole city seemed quiet other than the occasional howl of a coyote out in the distance. Tara was sitting by the curb as she buried her head behind her bent knees. Gyle stood a few feet away as the black bird moved around him, its claws hopping daintily along the pavement. For a long time, nobody said anything.

It was the raven who finally broke the stillness. "So, where do you plan to go next?"

Gyle looked at the trickster god. "You talking to me?"

"To both of you."

Tara stood up as she wiped the dust off the bottom of her jeans. "We go find my brother."

Gyle turned to look at her. Despite the darkness, he could see perfectly since his vision now extended not only into the ultraviolet spectrum, but in the infrared one as well. It was like daylight to him, but in different hues. "I get it. Your brother is the only real family member you got left. I would do the same."

Tara continued to stare out into the night. "Thanks for understanding. He's all that matters to me now."

Gyle nodded. "Then we need to hurry. Who knows where he's at right now."

"I can't believe how badly I screwed up!" Tara cried. "It's my fault he's not here. I should've stayed in the trailer park with him. Now he's all alone out there and I have to go find him. He's only six!"

"It wasn't your fault," Gyle said. "Your dad was beating on you and you had to leave. I would have done the same thing."

Tara let out a shriek. "But can't you see? I left my little brother behind! All I ever did was to think about myself. If I wasn't so self-centered, he would be safe and sound with me! Why did I ever leave the house, why did I ever get into the van with Larry, why did I ever meet that brujo?"

The raven hobbled over to them as it ruffled its wing fathers. "I told you when we met the first time that each of us chooses their own path, and each path chosen leads to other roads. Such is life. Once your path is forged in time, it cannot be undone. Some believe in destiny, others in chance. Once you tread on the road you've chosen, there is no reverse gear, so to speak."

Tara's tears were streaming down her cheeks again as she stared at the black bird. "I hate you! You're the one who kept leading me on like this, and all the while you made me lose my brother! You keep talking in riddles … a-and your stupid sayings but it is all just crap! You didn't even do anything when Ilya got hurt trying to rescue me! What kind of a god are you anyway? You're more like a devil than a friend!"

The raven showed no emotion as it titled its head from side to side. "You are the ultimate chooser of your life path. I am here merely to guide and advice. When we met the first time, I told you of the choices you could have made. It was not I who made you get into the van with Larry. That was all your doing. Every choice you made has ultimately led you to this parking lot and to this conversation we are having now. I cannot interfere with the choices you make. Ilya made his choice, just as Gyle made his choice. Now you must make another choice."

Deep in her heart, Tara knew the Trickster was right. "It's just not fair," she said softly.

"The world does not grant any special blessing on the weak," the Trickster said. "It is only through the power of mercy and compassion that determines the survival of those that are helpless. You have a good heart, but there may be times that your own kindness may abate you."

Tara stood up. "I'm going to find my brother. If you want to help, then I would appreciate it. If not, that's okay, I'll go look for him by myself."

Gyle remembered seeing his wife once more. "You both helped me to find Marie and I got to talk to her. That meant a lot to me. Alright, let's get this done."

Tara looked at him with a glint of determination in her eyes. "Then we need to hurry. When I rode with Larry, we took the northern route going out of state because of the flooding."

Gyle nodded. "That would be the logical way to get to Kansas. The other way would be through the south, towards Tucson. That would have meant getting close to the frontlines, and then going north through New Mexico. Then again, since their journey started months ago, if they succeeded, they would have made it to Kansas by now."

"Well, now we're getting somewhere," the raven murmured.

"We should go to Kansas first," Gyle said. "The separatists there seem organized and if we can find a source of information, we ought to locate them very quickly."

"That's assuming they made it there," the raven said.

Tara moved quickly until she stood over the black bird. She felt like grabbing the Trickster by the neck and throttling it. "I'm tired of your games! Do you know where my brother is?"

The raven looked up into the night sky. "The way it works is a little more complicated than that."

Tara hissed. Her eyes were dry and her patience was gone. "What do you mean? You're a god for chrissakes! I can't believe you have all these rules and limits to your powers. You're making things harder than it is!"

"I may be a god but I'm not all powerful or all knowing as you humans think we all are," the raven said. "I'm somewhat limited from what I hear. The animals speak and I can hear them for miles. Same with people. Even the trees, the rocks, and the rivers speak to me sometimes as well. From their voices I receive knowledge. As far as your brother, yes, your father did speak the truth. From what I have heard in this area, the Olsen family did take little

Timmy with them when they began their journey. In order for me to know more then, we must travel as well so I can hear more voices and listen to the tales that they tell."

Tara took a deep breath. "Okay. Then we go to Kansas first and have a look around."

"Agreed," Gyle said.

As the two of them started walking out of the parking lot, the raven looked around for bit before it started to preen itself once more. "Ah, here we go again. Our small band of stalwart heroes going off on another quest, with more soul searing tests until they reach their final destination. I haven't had this much fun in a long, long time," it said to no one in particular.

3. The Ritual of Skins

Tenochtitlan

Even though it was a special day, the constant rains and thunderclouds overhead gave it a gloomy mood. The day of the calendar was that of the 13th eagle, and the patron deity to be worshipped was Xipe Totec, the Flayed One. Of all the days that had begun since the return of the gods, this would be his most blessed day since it was to be the time that he would finally ascend the ranks of the priesthood, so this day meant more to him than any other so far.

He used to be called Ramon Miguel Ortiz y Cabrera. Ever since the great Aztec gods returned to their sacred valley near the capital, it was decreed that all the people within the city would revert back to their ancient, traditional Nahuatl names. This was not just a renewal of the old faiths, but as a living symbol that they would reclaim their lost destiny as an all-conquering people once more. Ramon's family used to be quite influential, and so when it came time to choose their names, he deferred the final decision to his very powerful uncle, who was now the chosen avatar to Xipe Totec. His uncle had decreed that the Cabrera family was no more. The new family name was Tlanextli Itztli, the majestic house of the Obsidian Knife. Ramon's true name was now known as Tepiltzin, which meant privileged son. Everywhere in public, he was to be referred to as Apprentice Tepiltzin, junior priest to the temple of Xipe Totec, the god of harvests and rebirth. When he returned to the house for rest though, his old mother still affectionately called him Ramon.

Apprentice Tepiltzin was almost thirty. His family had been so rich that he had spent much of his youth in equestrian riding competitions and maintaining the family haciendas at the valley foothills. It was his uncle who was the big moneymaker of the family, but they had rarely seen each other until recently. Ramon never married, despite the disappointment of his parents. He preferred to sort through half a dozen girlfriends and party the night away. It didn't help that he was spoiled by his uncle every time he came to see them. Ramon idolized his uncle, so much so that his own parents were jealous of their relationship. The only other person that Ramon did care about was his younger brother Jorge. Even though there was almost a ten year difference in their ages, Ramon always treated Jorge as his equal, and his brother loved him back for it. Even when their parents would chastise Jorge for being a spoiled teenager, Ramon would always back his brother. For many years they were inseparable. The only thing that disappointed Ramon was that his uncle didn't favor Jorge as much as him.

Of course, that all changed when the Aztec gods returned. At first, it was nothing more than a seemingly unending series of thunderstorms that swept into the valley of Mexico. The flooding in the city streets didn't seem important at first but as the days turned into weeks, it soon became dangerous, since a lot of the streets were now underwater. Days after that, much of the outskirts of the city along the edges of the valley were completely flooded. The ancient lake had once again risen up and Mexico City was now surrounded by water once more. That was when things took a turn for the worse. Less than two weeks after the rains began, a massive earthquake struck the city. Many buildings, especially the churches, had toppled and were completely destroyed. But for some strange reason, the most ancient of constructs such as the pyramids of nearby Teotihuacan stayed miraculously intact. By then, hundreds of thousands of people were either killed or injured but the strange events didn't stop. The Federal government of Mexico seemed powerless to do anything. For many days, people seemed to be struck by some sort of trance as a strange mist would seep into the city at night, making everyone forget their memories and responsibilities. Ramon could remember the time when the military swept into the city in an attempt to restore law and order, but soon they too were affected by the strange mists. Everyone would wander aimlessly in the rain drenched streets under some sort of psychotic daze that lasted for weeks.

By the end of the first month, everyone still living in the entire valley was trapped. The rest of the country was in a state of panic as the bizarre mists began to expand. Anyone from outside of the area who would dare to enter the zone was immediately overcome by its spell. That was when many people in the valley began to change. At first it was just a few individuals who claimed that the Aztec gods were speaking to them. Then these people started to gain followers, as each one professed an allegiance to a specific god and became very powerful priests. Slowly but surely, every living person soon began to take sides as the cults of their respective gods became stronger. Then the war began.

People called it the Second Flower War. It was a ritualized form of killing and capturing. Instead of guns, people began to fashion melee weapons made from obsidian and wood- the macuahuitl, the preferred ancient sword of the Aztecs. The toughest began to wear nothing but feathered headdresses and loincloths, telling everyone that their gods would protect them in battle. Fifteen separate factions exploded in open warfare, the Lords of the Night fought against the Lords of the Day. Of course, there were many gods who were worshipped in both nights and days, and so they were able to achieve a significant advantage over their rivals. Warriors who were not killed outright were sacrificed in order to hasten the gods return. Within days, two powerful factions achieved dominance over the others. The most significant turning point in the war was when the followers of the war god Huitzilopochtli negotiated an alliance with the followers of Xipe Totec. In the succeeding days, their combined armies defeated all the others in major battles all across the city. Their most significant victory was in wiping out the followers of Tezcatlipoca, the god of the smoking mirror. When the last high priest of Tezcatlipoca was sacrificed, it was the end of that particular faction. The only other gods that were powerful enough to threaten their alliance would have been Tlaloc the rain god and Quetzalcoatl. The followers of Huitzilopochtli and Xipe Totec were able to appease the followers of Tlaloc by decreeing an equal amount of sacrifices, and the construction of a temple in his name. As for Quetzalcoatl's followers, there were none. For some strange reason, the feathered serpent god never manifested itself in the thoughts of the people, unlike the other gods. By the time the Flower War had ended, most of the people in the valley were now worshippers of the god of war and the god of harvests.

A day after the end of the war, an even more miraculous thing happened. The center of Mexico City was torn apart by a series of massive earthquakes that reached all the way up to northern California. When the people woke up the next day, the Metropolitan Cathedral, the largest church in the Americas, had been completely swallowed up by the earth. Something gargantuan now stood in its place. As the people looked up, they saw two massive Aztec pyramids rising up hundreds of feet into the dark sky. They were made of black obsidian and had massive steps leading upwards that were carved from volcanic basalt. The people instantly rejoiced at the two new temples. It was from this point that a new class of people began to rule over the newly resurgent Aztec Empire. At first, the people thought they were nothing more than just ordinary priests, but when these prophets unveiled a stone idol of Huitzilopochtli that had been previously buried beneath the now destroyed cathedral, the people soon realized that they channeled the words of their gods. The city was now united and dissent had become minimized. That was when the next phase began.

By then, the entire country had fallen under the influence of the gods. The mists that had once been confined to the valley had now spread out far and wide. Stone causeways leading back to the city were constructed over the water and it brought about much needed trade and tribute. The resurgent armies of Huitzilopochtli began to expand their holdings as their mortal warriors were joined by demons and monsters to augment their power. The tzitzimimeh, demonic gods from the stars, soon became the shock troops of their armies as they continued their relentless advance. Men who learned the art of changing their shape into jaguars soon became the elite of the Aztec military as they had once again become unstoppable.

To north lay their greatest threat. Of all the nations of the world, America still clung solidly to their Twenty First Century civilization, as their high-tech military began to occupy the northern areas of Mexico in an effort to set up a buffer zone. No sooner had the Americans gone south across the border when they were instantly attacked and annihilated. All of their futuristic weaponry was no match against the divine power of the Aztec. Tens of thousands of American soldiers were captured and sacrificed during those months. If there were still any dissenters among the people of what was once Mexico, their incredible victory against US Army South had completely silenced them. As the celebrations ended, the avatars of the gods decreed that the people must unite even further, to prepare for an invasion of the American homeland, to destroy their powerful enemy once and for all.

Now that the invasion had finally begun, there was much work to do within the valley. Just a few days ago, his brother Jorge had finally completed his education in warrior training and he was now given the name of Yaotl, which meant warrior. Tepiltzin could not be prouder, his brother was now an honored warrior in the Aztec army. All that Yaotl needed to do now was to take as many prisoners as he could, the more Americans he captured, the faster his promotion in the ranks would be.

Tepiltzin made a short prayer at the shrine of Xipe Totec in his bedroom before he got up and dressed. Although most people in the city now preferred to wear the traditional loincloth and feathered cloaks that were common in the past, Tepiltzin still preferred to wear his raincoat and galoshes over them. Of course, he would don his priestly garb once he made it into the great temple, but he preferred to use his most practical clothes to walk through the rain drenched streets on his way over there. As he finally put on the plastic boots, he blew out the candles illuminating the shrine and walked out into the darkened living room. The house was once a ranch-style Spanish colonial abode, but the avatars had decreed that changes needed to be made in order to placate the gods. The first thing Tepiltzin did was to brick up the windows. Then he tore a hole in the wooden roof in order to allow the cooking fire to ventilate. After that, he had constructed a small shrine of his patron god in every room. Only after he did all these things was when they finally accepted him into the priesthood of Xipe Totec by his uncle.

Numerous town criers shouted across the city, telling the people of the rituals and sacrifices that were to be made today. Tepiltzin didn't want to be late so he hurried along the cobbled streets as fast as he could. There were a few instances when he nearly fell because the torrents of rainwater made the stone streets very slippery. When he finally got to the grand plaza overlooking the great temple, he had to maneuver past the crowds of commoners and the dancing troupes who had gathered to watch. Despite the rain, he could see that everyone was smiling and laughing. Proud fathers would have their small children sit on their shoulders while musicians playing flutes, trumpets, drums, and even guitars would constantly regale the crowd with victorious tunes. The people of the valley had now entered into a new, golden age.

By the time he made it into the foyer at the base of the great temple of Xipe Totec, there were a number of other junior priests who were already in their vestments. One of them walked over to him and shook his head.

"Apprentice Tepiltzin, you are almost late," the other priest said. "The ritual is about to begin."

"I know, I know," Tepiltzin said as he quickly took off his raincoat and opened a wooden locker situated along the sides of the chamber. Inside was his xicolli, a gold sleeveless jacket suspended on a hanger. A wooden box at the foot of the locker contained his feathered headdress, with white plumes and tiny golden chains and bells. He quickly put them on, just as he heard three loud trumpets coming from the outside.

The other priests quickly formed a line and faced the inner stairwell. Tepiltzin quickly joined them as he threw his raincoat back into the locker. Less than a minute later, they soon heard the chants coming from the top of the great temple. Now that the ritual had begun, they all started moving up the stairs in single file.

Each step they took was slow and deliberate, they were guided by the cadence of drums as they slowly ascended towards the inner heart of the temple. In addition to the top, the giant stone pyramid held numerous other chambers within its stone walls. These subterranean rooms were reserved for both the high priests, and for minor sacrificial rituals deemed not important enough for the public to see. It would be in these rooms that the apprentices would be giving their first sacrifice, as only the high priests would be allowed to sacrifice at the temple zenith. These hidden places would be their proving ground.

It took nearly an hour as they continued to slowly ascend up the stone steps. They were in complete darkness since light was not allowed in the stairwell. A single slip on the steps might mean serious injury since the stairs had no hand holds and it was now a long way down. By the time they saw a light up ahead of them, Tepiltzin guessed hey had climbed up over a hundred stories by then. He was thankful they were nearly there because his knees had begun to buckle from the strain.

The narrow stairwell led into a large hallway that had been built into the side of the temple. There were burning torches lined up along the wall while huge windows were open to the grey sky. There was a large stone table in the center of the room. They all saw one of the senior high priests come into the hall from a corridor at the far end.

"Welcome, apprentices," the senior high priest said. Tepiltzin recognized him as one of his uncle's assistants. "You are now at the final stage of your learning. There is to be one last test you must do and then you may be given the title of high priest of Xipe Totec, Our Lord the Flayed One. The empire is expanding rapidly, and there is a great need for clerics. Steel your resolve, because there is no turning back now."

All of the apprentices chanted in unison, their voice was one. "All hail Xipe Totec. He of the Flayed One. He who brings harvest and renewal. It is through his power that the Mexica are in ascendant once more. It is through his alliance with Huitzilopochtli and the banishment of Tezcatlipoca that has made all this possible. The Red Smoking Mirror and the Night Drinker are all in one, as he is the one in all. We praise Xipe Totec for the abundance of food we are given. We praise Xipe Totec for he shall show the way to our rebirth. It is right to give him thanks and praise."

"Amen," the senior high priest said as he stood beside the stone table. "Apprentices, take your knives and begin the ritual of Xipe Totec, the Flayed One. Even though these sacrifices are to be performed at the bowels of the great temple, do not be ashamed. Though the people will not see your sacrament, Xipe Totec will be there, and he will acknowledge your work. Do not listen to words of the condemned, for they are despicable men who cower in fear, rather than will themselves to glory that is our god. Go now and take your implement, for you shall know where to go. Let Our Lord the Flayed One guide you."

With those words, the senior high priest stepped aside. Each of the apprentices walked one by one over by the table and picked up a flint dagger. As soon as one of them had taken their instrument, the high priest whispered in their ear and pointed to a distant corridor at the other side of the hall.

When Tepiltzin walked over in front of the table and picked up his knife, the senior high priest took him by the elbow. "Your uncle, the avatar, has declared that you have been chosen to take the most cowardly of the prisoners," he whispered in Tepiltzin's ear. "He is in the farthest room of the corridor beyond. Do not grant him any mercy, for the Flayed One is watching."

Tepiltzin nodded silently as the senior high priest let go of his arm. This was a great honor. The one they once called Ramon then started to walk into the corridor beyond. He could see that the passageway was now made of polished, bright green obsidian. The stones seemed to reflect the light of the torches that lined along the corridor back all around him, it was like peering through a darkened glass bottle. After a few minutes, he made it in front of the final door. The entrance was made of deep lacquered wood, with sculpted human faces in all sorts of contorted agony carved on its surface. As he placed his hand on its surface, the door suddenly opened in front of him. As he momentarily recovered from that surprise, he bit his lip and stepped inside.

The room was smaller than he anticipated. The ceiling was low, just barely eight feet high. The walls were made of the same emerald green obsidian that lined the corridor. In the center of the room was an altar that resembled a stone bed. Lying on his back, a naked man was tied down on top of it. As Tepiltzin got closer, the door behind him suddenly slammed shut, as if it was closed by some unseen force. A narrow window provided the only illumination.

Even though he was restrained, the man jerked his head up and looked at him in terror. The sacrifice was on his back and he tried to pull at the chains that were wrapped around his arms and legs, but they held him fast. Tepiltzin walked past him and stopped until he faced the window. They both could hear the distant roaring of the crowds below.

The man kept twisting his head so that he could see him, as if by making eye contact he might somehow delay the inevitable by reasoning with him. When Tepiltzin finally moved away from the window and turned to face him, he could see that the sacrifice was drenched in sweat. Tepiltzin had kept the knife hidden in the back of his right wrist so that the sacrifice wouldn't see it.

"Do y-you s-speak English?" the man said. He was heavyset and balding. He looked to be in his mid to late fifties. There was grey hair on his chest, legs, and pubic region. He might have been formidable in his early years, but now he was nothing more than a featherless turkey, helplessly waiting for the slaughter to follow.

Tepiltzin was slightly taken aback. It was the first time in months he had heard another language besides Nahuatl. That piqued his curiosity. "Poquito. A little," he said, using both Spanish and English.

"Please, I-I beg of you," the man said in between nervous intakes of air. "I'm a g-general in the US Army. I know what you p-plan to do with me and I must ask you to reconsider it. My name is General Russell Benteen, and I'm one of the senior commanders for US Army North. Do you understand me?"

Tepiltzin merely nodded as he picked up a stone bowl from the floor and placed it near the altar. What a fool this man was, he either couldn't or wouldn't understand what was happening. No matter.

"Look, I-I'll do anything you want me to do. Just d-don't k-kill me, please," General Benteen pleaded. "I'm an important officer in the US military. I-I can help negotiate a p-peace treaty or something. Just spare my life, please."

Tepiltzin didn't reply. There was a small table by the window and it contained a number of glass jars. He took a crystal flask that contained some yellowish powder and poured its contents into the bowl.

The general had tears falling down his face as he kept trying to make eye contact. "Oh God, please! You don't have to do this! I'm telling you, you don't have to do this. It's against the Geneva Convention for chrissakes!"

Tepiltzin shook his head. "Your rules do not apply anymore. We have no need of treaties, nor of peace. We follow the will of the gods."

General Benteen let out a shrill groan. "For the love of God, please don't do it. Jesus is merciful and he will forgive your sins. If you spare me, he will look onto you as a righteous man and you will be in heaven with him!"

Tepiltzin sighed as he applied some of the yellow powder on his face and neck. "Jesus Cristo was a false god. He was not real. Xipe Totec is the real god. He has proven his existence to all of us and to you. Your cowardly actions have dishonored your fate. As a warrior, you could have gained great prestige by being sacrificed at the main altar on top of the pyramid temple. Your crying and complaining have made you a coward and cowards die here, deep within the temple chambers. You do not deserve the crowd's attention."

Trails of mucous were coming out through the general's nostrils. "Oh God, you don't have to do this! I will be your slave! I'll do anything, just don't kill me! Please!"

Tepiltzin now stood over the sacrifice as he placed the flint blade on the edge of the altar. He raised his hands, palms facing upwards. He tilted his head up so he could see the reflections of light on the low ceiling. "The Night Drinker, why must we beseech thee? Put on your disguise, your cloak of yellow gold. My Lord, you have descended upon the water. The cypress has become a quetzal bird. The fire snake is now a quetzal snake. Now they have left behind in our suffering. It may be, that I may be, I go to destruction and war. I, the tender maize plant, my heart is jade. But I shall yet see gold there. I shall rejoice if it ripens early. My God, let there be an abundance of maize, in a few places, at least. Thy worshiper turns his gaze to the mountain, toward thee. I shall rejoice if it ripens early. The war chief is born," he chanted loudly in Nahuatl.

General Benteen kept blinking his eyes as if it was some sort of terrible dream that he desperately wanted to wake up from. He shook his head violently from side to side, as if trying to dispel reality. "You don't have to do this. You don't have to do this. Have mercy!"

Tepiltzin took the knife from the altar and held it over his head. For the sake of the sacrifice, he shifted his language to English so the general could perhaps understand what he was doing, and what it meant for him. "O Flayed One, I offer you this sacrifice as a small gesture of my devotion to you. Do not look upon the cowardly pleadings as an insult to thee, o Night Drinker. Let his skin serve as the vessel for your renewal and rejuvenation."

General Benteen started screaming as the junior priest placed a hand on his chest. The American tried to shift violently from side to side but the restraints held him fast. An unseen force held him by the throat as his chest heaved upwards. "Help me! Somebody help me! Lord Jesus Christ, have mercy on my soul!"

Tepiltzin could now feel where the heart was. He had his free hand over the exact spot on the general's chest. Using his other hand, he made a deep cut just below the heaving ribcage. General Benteen let out a painful shriek and continued to plead for mercy but it was too late. Tepiltzin immediately used the knife to slice through the thoracic diaphragm. Using all of his strength, the apprentice priest pushed his right hand through the wound and began to dig through the chest. The general was now wailing and squealing like a crazed pig, his blood pouring through the wound and onto the altar. Tepiltzin's hand felt like it was burning due to the hot temperature inside the general's body. It was like sticking one's hand in a pot of hot stew. The apprentice priest had to push his hands underneath the lungs, past the thoracic aorta until he could finally feel the victim's throbbing heart. General Benteen screamed loudly for a few more seconds as Tepiltzin used all of his strength to grab hold of the still beating heart. His other hand used the blade to cut through the arteries. Gritting his teeth, the apprentice priest pulled as hard as he could, ripping the heart out of the general's chest, its valves opening up like gushing pipes as the outpouring blood stained his priestly garments.

Within seconds, the screaming had ended as the sacrifice rapidly lost consciousness. Tepiltzin held up the heart as he pivoted four times to face the four corners of the world, all the while saying a silent prayer to each one. Then he placed the throbbing heart on a smaller, adjoining shrine. As he put down the sacrificial knife, the still beating heart began to levitate above the stone altar, the blood pouring out of it seemed suspended in midair. Seconds later, the pulsing heart floated out through the window. Tepiltzin knew that the heart would ultimately keep flying away until it reached the sun. He started the next phrase, holding up a longer, thinner flint knife he took from the nearby table.

With mechanical precision, Tepiltzin quickly started the skinning process. He cut off the man's genitals and placed them in a clay pot sitting near the base of the altar. Then he quickly made a long cut from where the genitals were and made his way upwards, intersecting with the cut underneath the ribcage, then all the way to the throat. Tepiltzin had been practicing on animals before, but this was the first time he was skinning a human being, and so he wanted to make sure he didn't make any mistakes. The flint blade was very sharp, so he didn't have much of a problem as he sliced away the windpipe and took it out so that it wouldn't get in the way. Since he wanted to preserve the face, Tepiltzin made a cut around the edges of the dead man's cheeks, from the base of his chin and then he cut upwards, slicing at the side of the jaw and behind the ears. Taking the skin from the body was easier now that the chest was split open, so he just used both hands to peel the skin back from side to side. The legs he had to treat separately, so he cut along the inside of the legs and around the ankles until he could peel them all back.

It was hard work and it took hours. By the time he was done, he had a pair of leggings and a suit made from human skin. It took him a little bit longer for the face as he wanted to make sure that it would be a single mask rather than separate strips of skin. A few hours later, the blood on his body had started to dry and thicken as he took off his cloth jacket and put on the skin suit. He tied the loose leggings around his lower limbs using some fine silk thread. The general had been a large man and there was plenty of membrane left over. As he placed Benteen's face over his own, a loud trumpet was sounded from across the corridor outside. It was a signal for the final phase of the ceremony.

A few minutes later, each of the apprentice priests filed out of their respective rooms and walked back into the temple's inner hall. Each of them now wore a second skin over their own. The remains of the sacrifices would be cleaned up by a new batch of apprentices, who would simply throw the bodies out through the massive windows. As they lined up along the sides of the hall, three senior high priests came down from a nearby stairwell and stood in front of them. Tepiltzin recognized his uncle as the one who was standing in the center.

Avatar Tlazopilli raised his hands and faced the group of apprentices. "The Night Drinker smiles upon all of you. Xipe Totec has blessed us on this special day for we now wear the skins of renewal. While you performed your rituals in the chambers within the temple, myself and the other high priests performed these same ceremonies above, so that the citizens of our divine city can observe that our sacred ways are to be respected. I congratulate you all, for each of you shall now be given the title of high priest to the Flayed One. You shall be assigned to other cities in our growing empire, and you will train your own apprentices to the ways of Xipe Totec. Our great god grows stronger with each sacrifice, and with his alliance with Huitzilopochtli, it allows us more war captives to sacrifice with. Our ways are now unstoppable, and we shall be the vanguard for this new age."

The group of new high priests all raised their arms in unison. "All hail Xipe Totec, for he is the Night Drinker. He shall open the way to our eternal renewal. It is through his power and blessing that we have been gifted with a new empire for our people. Let our god walk through the streets of Tenochtitlan unimpeded, let our god traverse across the lands of the Mexica with all his power and might. Let our god smite our enemies and wear their skins. For he is the real god, for he is Xipe Totec."

As the ceremony ended, Avatar Tlazopilli walked over to his nephew and shook his hand using their respective second skins. "Well done, Tepiltzin, you have made your family proud on this day."

High Priest Tepiltzin bowed in reverence to his uncle. "I thank you for giving me this opportunity, uncle. It is a great honor to be a high priest to our patron god. I can only hope that I can continue my faithless service to the Night Drinker until my final days."

Tlazopilli nodded. "Xipe Totec has been observing you all this time. He has seen your loyalty and your dedication to his divine will. Even when that cowardly general was pleading for his life you did not falter. You are truly a child of the Flayed One."

Tepiltzin nearly recoiled with surprise. "But h-how did you know that the general was pleading for his life? Weren't you in the top part of the temple making sacrifices as well?"

Even though he wore a skin mask over his face that gave him two lips, his nephew could see that he was smiling. "Xipe Totec sees through it all. He is watching all of us. Did I not tell you how he came to me?"

"No uncle, I hadn't really spoken to you since you became the avatar. All I heard was stories and rumors."

"Then let me tell it to you now," Tlazopilli said. "A number of months ago, I was relaxing at my hacienda, my estate near Toluca. You see, I was celebrating my apparent victory over the Federales, the fools who used to run our former country. I had thought that I was the king back then. I had my own cartel and we were in the drug business. You remember what they all called me then don't you?"

"Yes, Uncle. They used to call you El Paco."

"Yes, that was my old name. Before the tzitzimitl came to my house and slaughtered all my men. I had thought they were going to kill me too, but they didn't. Instead, I was brought before Xipe Totec. He was a man of red skin and he already wore the golden hide of his victims above it. He showed me the way. The Night Drinker said that I was to be his avatar here on earth. His blood now flows through my veins. His commands are uttered through my mouth. And soon enough, the rest of America will soon be his as well."

4. Rivers of Voodoo

Louisiana

It was literally the end of the road, so Tyrone Gatlin stopped the car and got out. He stood facing what had once been the city of Shreveport. Now it looked like a swamp of half-sunken buildings out in the distance. It was dusk, and the sun was a fading yellow disk behind him. He could see where the road had ended and it was like standing in front of a pier. Dark, brackish water ebbed and flowed just a few feet in front of him. He was surprised that the skies were actually clear, since he had heard that the rains in the South had been nonstop when the Glooming began.

Tyrone crouched down as he rubbed his sore ankle. It had been less than two days when he ran away from the front lines in Texas and started making his way home. Dallas had been a nightmare. All he could remember were stop-motion scenes of panic and horror as the Aztecs swept in. He still couldn't believe how lucky he was to be able to get away from the demons and the half-crazed men who shot at everything. He drove nonstop and made it onto the deserted highway as he turned eastwards and proceeded into Louisiana. Now there was no way he could use the car anymore, since the land ahead was completely flooded. He needed to find an alternative way eastwards, or he would have to try and bypass the state entirely and go north, perhaps through Arkansas. He sensed that there was something here, something that he had to do, and that was what drove him to take this particular way. He didn't want to go up the northern route anyway, he knew for a fact that the roads up to Arkansas and Oklahoma would be jam-packed with fleeing refugees.

He turned around and sat in the driver seat of the car. As he took stock of his meager supplies, he decided to turn off the ignition. There was still some fuel left in the gas tank. Tyrone figured that if someone wanted to use the car to go the other way, then that person would be more than welcome to it. He took the backpack from the rear seat and rolled up all the windows. Tyrone had gotten rid of his Army fatigues awhile back. Now he was wearing a brand new pair of jeans and a t-shirt that he took from an abandoned department store in Dallas. Even though he had on a pair of sneakers, he stowed his army boots in the backpack, along with some canned food. He figured he could use some rugged footwear if he needed to do some long distance walking. The ouroboros medallion was now tied in a necklace that hung around his neck, the military ID tags that he once had were lying on the road somewhere. His Gerber Mark I boot knife was strapped to his right leg, underneath his jeans.

"Yo, mister. You need a ride?" a voice coming from out in the water said.

Tyrone turned around. He noticed a small boat with an aluminum hull at the edge of the water. Two black girls holding long wooden poles stood on it. One of them looked like a teenager and both had dreadlocks. They wore torn shirts, shorts and tennis shoes. The slightly older girl had a .38 snub-nosed revolver on her hip holster. Their facial features made them seem related. Both wore red colored plastic life jackets on their chests.

The younger girl smiled at him. "Is that your car?"

Tyrone smiled back. Even though he was from Georgia, he couldn't help but feeling somewhat safer among fellow black southerners. "Yeah, it's mine."

The older girl stared back at him. "Got any gas in it?"

Tyrone nodded. "About a quarter tank left."

The younger girl seemed friendlier. There was always something like a spark of joy and hope when it came to dealing with kids. "Where you come from?"

"Dallas," Tyrone said softly.

The older girl remained suspicious. "You from Dallas?"

"No, I'm from Georgia. I was just trying to make my way back home."

The older girl narrowed her eyes. She remained suspicious. "Did you live in Dallas before?"

"Yeah, I was in construction," Tyrone said. "I just needed to get the hell outta there now."

"Is it true what happened in Texas? Is it true that the Aztecs took over?" the younger girl said. Despite the seriousness of her question, her tone remained upbeat.

Tyrone nodded slowly. "Yeah, we got beat. That's why I left."

The older girl furrowed her eyebrows. "You fought them? I thought you was a carpenter?"

Tyrone rubbed the back of his neck. The older one was a pretty careful girl. Her caution would make sense since law and order was breaking down. You needed more than just words these days. "I was a civilian volunteer. I saw that fighting 'em was useless so I got outta there," he said.

The older girl seemed to accept that explanation. "You armed?"

Tyrone figured it was better to tell the truth. "I got a US army knife on my leg cuz they gave me one. That's about it. I lost my rifle during the battle."

The younger girl smirked. "You got anything to trade?"

"I got some food," Tyrone said. "Some cans of soup and corned beef."

Both girls whispered to each other for a few minutes. Tyrone looked around but he didn't see anybody else in the area.

"Okay," the older girl said as she looked at him once more. "We can give you a ride to our momma's shack and you can stay there for the night. It gonna cost you three cans of beef."

Tyrone let out a deep breath. That was a pretty high price to pay. "I'm gonna need the food if I'm gonna make it back to Georgia."

"Well we ain't giving a ride for free."

Tyrone pointed to the sedan. "I don't need my car anymore. How about I let you have it?"

The younger girl clapped her hands. "Yeah, we got us a car again!"

"Shush now," the older girl said to her sister before looking at Tyrone again. "How do you expect us to bring the car over to our momma's place?"

Tyrone dangled the car keys in front of her. "What I can do is to lock the car up and hide it in the bushes. If you want to use it, or if your parents would like to use it, then you can just come back for it. I don't think anybody else is coming along this here road anyway. They all seem to be making their way north, through Arkansas."

The older girl thought about it for a minute, then she nodded. "Okay then. Here are the rules, you help with the paddlin' on the boat and we both stay behind you. No funny stuff, mister."

Tyrone nodded. The girls were just being careful. He was okay with that.

It was dark by the time they finally set out. There was a kerosene lamp on the boat, so they could see that it cast a pale reflection in the water. Tyrone stood near the bow of the boat and did most of the pole work. The older girl, whose name was Moesha, stood at the stern and used her pole more for pushing away debris instead of making the boat go faster. The younger sister was Shani, and her older sister had placed the gun on her lap as she sat in the middle.

The water was calm and the clouds started to form in the night sky. Tyrone could see bonfires on top of a few of the building roofs. There were a number of wooden piers and huts that had been erected alongside some of the flooded edifices. Even though Shreveport was mostly underwater, tiny pockets of civilization were still surviving in it.

Although the revolver was on her lap, Shani knew enough not to play around with it as she kept her hands free. "Say, Mr. Ty, what's your religion?"

Tyrone glanced back at her briefly before turning back to concentrate on his pole paddling. "I worship Esaugetuh Emissee. The Master of Breath."

"Esau-get-uh E-miss-ee," Shani said, pronouncing the words slowly so that she could remember them. "Is he an Indian god?"

He nodded. "Yeah, he's a Muscogee Indian god. The Seminoles worshipped him too since they used to be from the same tribe."

"What kind of a god is he?"

"He created us all. There was a great flood and he climbed up the tallest mountain until the waters receded. Then he took some mud and he shaped the dirt like people. Then he breathed into them and created the first human beings of the world. That's why he's called the Master of Breath."

"So he's like a good god?"

"Yeah, I'd like to think so," Tyrone said wistfully. He still wasn't sure about what he believed.

"What made you believe in him?"

"I started dreaming about him first. Then one man showed me some stuff about him. I didn't believe at first, but then he kept coming up to me, in my dreams."

"What's your dream about?"

"I dreamt of a spirit, I couldn't really tell what he looked like since he was just a shadow. But he was friendly and told me to go this way instead of going north. He said I had a task to do for him. I think he sort of like saved me from the Aztecs too."

"You did say you fought the Aztecs in Dallas," Moesha said. "How close did you get to them?"

"About as close as you and me," Tyrone said. "One of those star demons- the tzitzimitl- could've killed me but she didn't. I like to think that it was the Master of Breath that saved me."

They passed by another boat that was out in the distance, about a hundred feet away. Tyrone could see a black man and two white men casting a thick fishing net alongside their boat. An old, pale woman stood at the bow of their boat as she shined a lantern at the water. They noticed Moesha and she waved at them. They waved back and smiled before going about their work.

Tyrone turned to look at Moesha. "What are they fishing for this time of the night?"

"They are looking to catch horned serpent babies," Moesha replied as she used her pole to push away a floating tree trunk.

"Horned serpent? I'm not familiar with that," Tyrone said.

Shani placed two upturned fingers on each side of her head. "The horned serpent started appearing a few days after the city was flooded. It's a magical creature that swims underwater. It's a sea snake with horns on its head. They want the large diamond that's in between its eyes because that gemstone has special powers. I heard the baby snakes got little gems on their heads too."

Tyrone's eyebrows shot up. "Special powers?"

Shani giggled. "Yeah, anyone who eats the gem can tell the future and it can be used for healing too. It's a good snake though, and my momma's been warning them not to try and catch it. You know people need stuff to barter these days, and gettin' that jewel on the serpent's head can get you a whole lotta food in return. The big momma serpent is bigger than all of us, bigger than the tallest tower, so I think they just tryin' to catch the little ones."

Their boat had now turned eastwards. They headed towards a row of wooden shacks that had been constructed on top of a series of adjacent concrete buildings, these places had platforms that connected on the waterline. Tyrone could see a few bonfires that were burning in sandpits alongside of the dock. As they got closer, he noticed two black men with rifles standing near the edge of the pier, watching him. He didn't want to stare, so he kept his eyes close to the water level as he helped to guide the boat closer.

Moesha waved at the two men. "Hiya, Antoine!"

One of the men waived back at them as they pulled up alongside of the dock. As he looked around, Tyrone saw a riverboat moored at the far end of the compound, its flat bottomed hull jutting out from the side of a red brick building, serving as a port for it. A tall black chimney protruded from its topmost deck, just behind the wheelhouse. He figured it must be powered by steam. Tyrone couldn't see the stern of the ship since it was behind the building, but he guessed it had a paddlewheel that was either made of steel or wood. What was surprising was they had somehow gotten a steam engine to work on it since most riverboats nowadays were supposed to have diesel ones.

There was a tap on his shoulder. It was Shani, and she held out his backpack for him. "You can go up now," she said.

"Thanks," Tyrone said as he slung the pack over his shoulder and clambered up onto the pier. He could see Moesha was tying the boat near the side of the dock. Shani had a little trouble climbing up the ladder so he helped the younger girl up. The two men who were watching them stayed at the other end of the wooden platform.

When Moesha finally climbed up on the dock, she pointed over to a wooden cabin on top of a rusted metal building. "You can head over there, my momma will wanna talk to you."

Tyrone thanked the two girls and started walking towards the shack. He noticed that Shani started running towards a group of children in an adjacent platform, while Moesha walked over to the two sentries and started talking to them. He could hear the beating of drums coming from the other houses as well as some chanting. The smell of roasting fish, along with the pungent muck of the water, was in the air.

When he got to the front of the cabin, he knocked on the rickety wooden door. The shack was a hodgepodge of different sizes of wooden panels and corrugated rusting sheet metal that were haphazardly nailed together. A dozen wind chimes were hung on top of the roof overhang, their tinkling melodies reverberating through the soft night wind blowing across the black waters.

"Come in," a voice said from the inside of the cabin.

Tyrone opened the door and then nearly tore it off since its hinges were loose. As he carefully used his free hand to push a rusted nail back into place to help support the door, Tyrone stepped inside and closed it behind him. The interior walls of the place were filled with shelves. The dividers had everything from glass jars to wooden boxes that were full of stuff. A number of charms and small, fist-sized dolls were hanging from the ceiling. There was a solid glass counter near the entrance that had assorted necklaces and beads on top of it. Along the wooden walls of the shack were masks in all sorts of grotesque styles, from red devils to grinning black and blue skulls. There were dozens of lighted candles in strategic areas all around the interior, their illumination giving off a constant yellow flickering over the entire scene. Standing at the center of the room was a thin black woman he estimated to be over six feet tall.

"Welcome, Tyrone Gatlin," she said. The woman wore an all-white duster dress and was barefoot. A solid black head cloth was wrapped around her scalp.

Tyrone nearly stumbled backwards but he was able to control his composure. "How d-did you know my name?"

She gave him a big toothy grin. "The loa tells me. They told me you would arrive at the end of the highway this day. That's why I had my two daughters pick you up and bring you to me. My name is Monique, by the way."

"Loa? What's that?"

Monique gestured towards an old wooden chair by the side of the door. "Have a seat. The loa are the invisibles, they are the spirits that serve as the agents of the supreme creator, Bondye. I spoke to them the night before and they said that you would come."

Tyrone frowned as he sat on the chair. Where they trying to swindle him? "Come on, lady. This must be some sort of trick. Did your daughter have a hidden cellphone on her or something? She told you my name using her cell, right?"

"Cellphones don't work in this part of the country. You know that."

He was still somewhat skeptical about trusting them. "Then is must be a walkie-talkie then, right?"

Monique sat down on the wooden floor facing him and crossed her legs. "No walkie-talkies here, Ty. We in this city drained almost every battery we had months ago. The only news we get are from traveler's tales and those windup radios, you know the kind that they used to distribute to the poor in Africa. Those things are highly sought after now."

"Assuming what you say is true, this loa you're talking about, what kind of religion is it?"

Monique laughed. "Boy, you must be dumb! Don't you know we here in Louisiana practice voodoo?"

Tyrone figured as much. Now it all made sense. "So y'all into these voodoo dolls and devil worship then?"

Monique kept giggling as she shook her head. "You have been so brainwashed by TV and such, you need a reeducation when it comes to our beliefs down here. We worship spirits and our ancestors. Our supreme god, Bondye, is distant and unknowable. He doesn't take part in human affairs and so we worship the loa, the spirits who serve him. We maintain a relationship with the loa through our offerings, our charms, and our ceremonies."

Tyrone was intrigued. He got off the chair and sat down, cross-legged on the floor, so he could see into her eyes directly. "What about these stories I heard? About devil worship and black magic and all that."

"Nonsense and misunderstandings. The European Christians always attribute what they don't understand to their concept of the devil. If it wasn't about Jesus then it was bad. As our voodoo evolved, we incorporated many Christian beliefs into our faith. Then again, I feel that we will devolve back into the olden ways again since the time of the Glooming."

Tyrone looked around. He wasn't too familiar with voodoo. "I dunno, those skulls and crossbones you have hanging around this place seems scary to me."

"The skulls are a symbol of our ancestors, they are not symbols of death in our religion. The crosses of bones represent the crossroads. It is the spiritual symbol of Papa Legba, the loa of the spirit world. He is the life bringer, he channels the power of Bondye to humanity, he serves as the bridge between the realms of spirits and men."

"What about possessions by spirits? And those voodoo dolls you people make to torture your victims with?"

"Voodoo dolls are not used for pain. Only evil practitioners would want to do that. The main purpose of the dolls is for healing. We don't really have much use for them. As far as spirits goes, we do not believe that spirits are evil, there are many good loa and these spirits can help the sick and the weak. It's a voluntary ritual and the practitioner must be willing to do it. Once the loa possesses a person, they can gain the power of prophecy or be healed through the channeling of energies from the loa to the body."

Tyrone nodded. "Okay, it's starting to make sense to me now, but you do admit that there are evil people who could use voodoo to do bad things, right?"

Monique sighed. "A year ago, when the Glooming started and the floods killed a lot of folks, there was a faction within the voodoo community that wanted to have power for its own sake. They called themselves the bokors. The rest of us didn't approve of what they wanted so we helped to drive them outta here. It was a tense moment but we prevailed."

"Where are they now?"

"I heard that they found a ship that would take them to Haiti," she said. "You wouldn't wanna go there."

"What's in Haiti?"

"It is said that over there they found something that made them even more powerful than ever before. They made the dead walk the earth again. A few of us wanted to go over there and right their wrongs, but we decided it's better to stay here and defend what little we got. Then I started to get dreams."

"So you mean there are zombies in Haiti now? They be like, eating people and all that?"

Monique shook her head slightly. "Lemme tell you something about zombies. They aren't like the ones you see in the movies, the ones where they eat the living and all that. Those kinds of monsters are just a creation of the entertainment industry. When someone dies, their body has two spirits in them, not one. When your body dies, the first spirit, called the grand angel, flies up to the afterlife. The second spirit is called the petit angel, it stays in your body for three days while it rots. If anything happens to the petit angel before it flies away, you might turn into a zombie. That's why many people in Haiti guard their dead for three days."

"So anyone whose body is disturbed before the three days are up just turns into a zombie, just like that?"

"No. That's where the dark voodoo comes into play. The bokors are the sorcerers, they can practice evil things and they can create zombies. They can trap souls in jars and they can steal spirits from people too. Once a dead person becomes a zombie they are like slaves, the bokor can order them to do tasks for him. The zombie will serve until their body rots away to nothing, then the bokor can keep the soul."

"So you can't kill a zombie by shooting it in the head then?"

Monique laughed a little. "Only on TV. The way to defeat a real zombie is to feed it salt. Because a zombie doesn't know he be dead, so giving them salt will make them aware of it. Once they realize they suppose to be dead, they will bury themselves in the earth and their petit soul escapes into the afterlife."

"Are there any zombies around here?"

"As of right now, I don't know of any. We practitioners here try our best to protect the land using our rituals to help the loa that protect us. Though our power is limited, as long as we are alive, we will protect the country from the evil ones. All this time we have been searching for someone who will give us the sign. Then, I started seeing you in my dreams."

Tyrone was surprised. "Me? But I'm not of the voodoo religion. I worship Esaugetuh Emissee, a Muscogee god."

"When I was possessed by a loa last week, it told me that the one I was seeking would be an outsider. He would be coming up from the borderlands and that I must help him on his quest for knowledge. That was when I saw your likeness in my dreams. The loa also told me of your name, Tyrone Gatlin."

Tyrone's whole body trembled. "There's n-no way you c-could have known my last name. I didn't even tell your daughters that!"

Monique winked at him. "Now do you believe?"

"I-I dunno what to believe. I only became a follower of the Master of Breath a few months ago. Surely there must be someone who knows more about him than I do. So why would I be chosen for anything?"

"You are a soldier. You fought the Aztecs and you survived. Very few people could say the same thing."

Tyrone looked down at the wooden floorboards. "I deserted. I ran away. I'm nothing but a coward."

"My loa Papa Legba told me you did fight them. Your side lost the battle and you left. There's nothing dishonorable about that."

"I'm still technically a deserter. I didn't report back to HQ. I'll be facing a court martial if they catch me."

"The Army has more things to worry about than you," she said softly. "The Aztecs have advanced across the southwestern states. They have swallowed up almost all of Texas now and are bringing their booty back to their great pyramid cities."

"Booty? What kind of booty?"

"Prisoners. So that they can make sacrifices to their gods."

Tyrone looked away. "I was that close to getting taken by 'em, but they seemed to ignore me. There were many times I was thinking I was a dead man, but they seemed to go right past me. I was in Dallas when they attacked it and they were either killing or takin' everybody prisoner. I still dunno how I got outta there."

Monique pointed at him. "That is because you are blessed by your god. He protects you. Papa Legba says the gods defend their own."

"How you know that?"

"I can sense an aura on you," she said. "I first noticed it on the docks. I figured one of the gods must be watching over you."

Tyrone sighed. "Why me though? What's so special about me?"

"Only the gods can tell you that. Did you not say that you were being led here?"

Tyrone closed his eyes so he could remember. "In my dreams. I didn't get much sleep in the past few days but when I would doze off, I would dream about this spirit. I couldn't really see what he looked like because he was all in shadow, but there was a bit of an outline like seeing that he had a head, two arms and legs. He would sort of point the way ahead to me. When I woke up it was like I knew which way to go, which roads to take. And it led me here."

Monique nodded. "Then that is your god speaking to you. Did he say anything about what you would do when you get here?"

"He really doesn't say anything, it's more like, he lets my feelings guide me. When I'm going in the right direction he lets me know it by making me feel that I'm headin' there. When I saw that riverboat docked by the building, I got that feelin' again."

Monique glanced up and took a deep breath. "The riverboat? You wanna join up with that crew?"

He knew he would have to join the crew. His dreams told him so. "I don't know. It was just a feelin' like I said. Why? Is something the matter with that boat? Who runs it?"

Monique's attitude had changed. She seemed testier now. "Papa Legba told me that crew up to no good and I warned the people here in this village. The captain of that boat is a man named Pillinger. I do not like him. He's a mercenary and his crew is just like their captain. They docked here a few days ago to stock up on supplies. They looking to hunt the beasts in the bayous and take them as trophies so they can sell them for money. They are bad men. I warn the others in the village not to join them, but a couple of the people here joined up with them anyway."

"Is hunting animals really bad? I mean, don't y'all need to hunt for food nowadays?"

"The gods allow us to hunt, but only for food, not for money or for sport. When you hunt like that, it disrespects the animal spirits. When you disrespect the spirits, you disrespect the gods."

"I guess you got a point there," Tyrone said. "Though I still gotta join 'em. My god is telling me to do so."

Monique frowned. "Then go ahead and join them, but you must not hunt the beasts of the forest or of the water. You must respect the spirits that dwell there, or you will be cursed and your god will abandon you. Papa Legba told me this."

"Then how can I join up with them if I ain't no hunter then? I don't think they accept passengers for this trip, do they? I don't have any money anyway so I can't buy my way into that boat."

"Find a way. I'm sure they could use some more deckhands."

"Okay, I'll try talking to them." Tyrone said. "What about you people? Are you just gonna stay here until the Aztecs come and take y'all?"

Monique seemed back in her usual calm self again. "Papa Legba told me that the Aztecs will not renew their push upwards to the north for at least a month in order to celebrate their latest victory and appease their gods. Our spirits have told us that the gods of this place will not allow the Aztecs to progress any further."

"Oh? So how will they stop 'em then?"

"The loa told me that the gods in this region will protect us. The first step is that a man will come from the south, they said. This man will be the key to protecting all the lands in the north, they say."

"And who would this man be?"

Monique smiled. "I'm looking at him."

Tyrone's was surprised. "Me? Like I told you, I'm nothing special. I got no idea what my god wants me to do for him."

"You will know when the time comes," Monique said. "The gods work in mysterious ways."

He just didn't understand it all. They were all telling him the same thing. Tyrone felt used, but whatever was going on was beyond his understanding. Maybe if he let it play out the meaning would become clear. It wasn't like he had anything better to do.

There was a knock on the door and then it opened. Standing outside were Shani and her older sister, who was carrying a metal cooking pot.

"Food's ready, momma," Moesha said.

Monique glanced at Tyrone as she stood up. "Remember what I told you. Now go help us set the table."

Dinner was Creole fish stew and cornbread. It was the first time in days that Tyrone had a hot meal and he ate heartily. They all sat alongside a folding table laid out at in front of the cabin. The only thing Tyrone didn't like was the foul tasting water that served as his beverage, so he took only a few sips at a time.

Shani giggled. "Doesn't seem you like our water, Mr. Tyrone."

"Hush now," Monique said to her youngest daughter before glancing back at him. "We have to use boiled river water nowadays, but I'm sure you know that."

"I'm not complaining, ma'am," Tyrone said. "This is the first decent meal I've had in weeks."

Moesha put a spoon down on her empty bowl. "You stayin' with us, Tyrone?"

"Nope," Monique said. "He will be joining the riverboat crew in the morning."

Shani's mouth was open. Bits of fish and soup dribbled down her mouth. "That boat? But momma, you said that ship is cursed!"

"I told you no shouting at the dinner table, Shani," Monique said. "Mr. Gatlin has to do something for the gods, and they will protect him while he is on that ship."

"I sure hope so," Tyrone said, muttering under his breath.

"No more talk of curses and such at the dinner table," Monique said as she stood up and started walking towards the open door of the shack. "I'll be right back."

Shani leaned over to Tyrone and started whispering. "I wouldn't go on that ship if I were you, Mr. Gatlin."

Moesha grabbed her younger sister's elbow and yanked it slightly. "Shani, stop scaring him like that."

"I was just telling him about momma's warnings," Shani said as she straightened up her body and resumed eating.

Tyrone smiled. "It's okay, your momma did tell me about it."

"Maybe she didn't tell you everything," Moesha said softly. "That Captain Pillinger is a scary man. And I don't mean scary just because he got a scar on his face either. The other people on the ship told me he has some sort of special prisoner in his cabin. He be trying to recruit all the greedy men who want to make a lot of money by hunting all the magical animals in the bayou."

Tyrone was intrigued. "He's got a prisoner on board his ship? What for?"

"It ain't no normal prisoner," Shani whispered. "We heard that he has some sort of magical creature that's gonna guide him through the rivers and swamps to find the most fabled creature out there."

Tyrone bit his lip. Was he getting into something over his head? "What fabled creature is out there? What kind of monster does he have locked away?"

"We don't know what kind of creature the captain has," Monique said. "He doesn't show it to anybody. We know about the great serpent of the swamps. Everyone around here knows that. It's the biggest horned serpent anyone's ever seen."

"I saw a big snake in my dreams," Tyrone said. "It looked like a giant-sized snake and its scales were glowing like bright light. It had horns growing out of its head, like deer antlers."

"That's it!" Shani exclaimed. "That's the great horned serpent everyone talks about! The one we told you about while you was on our boat. Everybody but my momma trying to catch it, the little ones anyway."

"Momma told us never to try and catch it," Moesha said. "It's a very powerful animal. Many people took their boats into the waterways around here and many of them didn't come back. Momma says that if you try to hunt the magic creatures of the bayou, it will be they who will be hunting you instead."

"Momma said anyone who goes on that ship will die," Shani added.

Tyrone stared out into the water for a minute. He was speechless. There was a rising fear growing at the back of his spine.

Monique walked back out along the pier. She was carrying a small bag made out of red cloth on her right hand. "Why is everyone so quiet all of a sudden?"

Shani giggled again. "We just scaring Mr. Gatlin."

Monique sat down and wagged a finger at her. "Don't scare our guest like that, Shani. Shame on you."

Tyrone shook his head and made a little smile. "That's okay, they told me a lot of useful things."

Monique placed the red little pouch on the table beside him. "Here, take that with you."

Tyrone picked it up. The red bag had a string tied around it. "What is it?"

"It's a gris-gris. A voodoo amulet bag," Monique said. "It will help protect you from the vengeful spirits of the bayou. Wear it over your neck at all times. I made that one especially for you."

"Thanks," Tyrone said as he placed it around his neck. "I hope my god will accept this."

Monique nodded. "He will. He and my loa Papa Legba are working together. You see, there is a growing darkness that must be stopped. And you will be playing a very big role in all of it. Remember my words to you, Tyrone Gatlin."

That night, Tyrone slept in the storage shack behind Monique's house. He dreamed of endless swamps and of mists rising from the waters. At one point, he could see himself standing on the bow of the riverboat as it cruised along the bayous of the rain drenched deltas of the south. There were other men with him, but they had a different sort of nature. While he was just a traveler, he could sense that these men were there for their own selfish reasons. That was when they all saw something darkening the grey sky above them. When they all looked up they realized it was a massive flock of owls, there were so many of the birds that the animals were now somehow all around them and he couldn't see anything else. Then the men beside him started screaming.

He woke up with a start. When he opened his eyes, it was already morning.

5. Minutes of the Meeting

Pennsylvania

By the time the small convoy had been cleared to pass through the sixth military checkpoint, it was already late afternoon and the skies had darkened. They were quite close to the state border with Maryland as the fleet of four Humvees turned into a seldom used asphalt road. In more peaceful times, the surrounding forest of great oak and hickory would have been an ideal place for a tranquil hike, but now the landscape had been marred by new construction works and heavy tracked vehicles.

Mary Arctor fidgeted slightly as she remained seated on the back seat of the third Humvee. Unlike previous people who held the title of Secretary of Defense, Mary was a civilian and had never served in the military. She had spent most of her career in the Defense Intelligence Agency. Mary had been one of their best analysts for over twenty years when it came to assessing potential worldwide threats from both rogue nations and terrorist groups. It was by pure luck she ended up as the United States Deputy Secretary of Defense, the previous two men who held the title of deputy had to bow out for two very different reasons. The first deputy had suffered a stroke while on the job and had to resign due to health concerns. The second deputy was involved in a scandal involving a prominent senator's wife and was disgraced. In order to placate a potential congressional investigation, the previous secretary of defense picked Mary out from a hat. She had a clean record and her accomplishments were spotless. The fact that she was a woman also helped out in the political arena. Her superiors in the White House figured that she would be allowed to serve as deputy secretary for a few years once the political firestorm had died down, then it was felt that she would quietly resign and someone more politically minded would ultimately take her place.

Then the Glooming happened. The world crisis deepened and the entire country had suddenly faced catastrophic losses in both the civilian and military spheres. The Secretary of Defense was killed, along with most of his staff, when the separatists from the newly self-styled nation of Christian Kansas detonated a nuclear device in Cheyenne Mountain. The president, who was attending a high level meeting at a nearby Air Force base, was abducted in a daring attack on his Marine One helicopters. Suddenly, Mary's once tranquil career had changed considerably. With the country's top leadership in chaos, she became the Secretary of Defense. The continuity of government was set in motion, and she was now the fifth most powerful person in the country. Although the president had been rescued, he was still incapable of assuming his duties. This made Mary's position even more critical than ever before.

Her assistant Sheila Giraud sat beside her. The NSA analyst spent most of the trip looking out of the window. "There must be a whole brigade of troops in this whole area," she said softly.

Mary nodded as the convoy stopped in front of the tunnel entrance. "I don't know what good it will do against the Aztecs, but it's better than nothing."

Sheila adjusted her thick framed glasses as she stared at the tunnel entrance. The mouth of the subterranean access way looked like it had been bored through a massive concrete ramp along the side of a hill. There were numerous defensive emplacements and bunkers that had been newly constructed all around them. M-1 Abrams battle tanks were stationed at the parking lot, ready to engage anything at a moment's notice. Numerous military soldiers with sniffer dogs and radiation detectors were in a constant state of alert as they made every effort to search them. "I wish I could take pictures, my dad would have loved this," she said.

Mary looked at her direction and smirked. "First time here?"

"Oh yes," Sheila giggled a bit at first, then she became serious. "Pity it had to be at a time like this."

Raven Rock Mountain Complex was a military installation built into the side of Blue Ridge Summit. Much like Cheyenne Mountain, Raven Rock had an underground nuclear bunker, designed to safeguard important persons in the government and would function as a command and control installation in the event of a major crisis. Now that the old gods had returned, the capabilities of this base would be put to the test.

The small convoy was led into the tunnel by military police. Mary could see that the underground passage was large enough to bring in heavy trucks. The tunnel walls were rough hewn and drilled directly through the monolithic rock, which meant that the designers had poked holes into a giant, underground boulder that now served as a critical juncture for the US government. The massive, thickened blast doors that they passed through were beveled to fit neatly at the tunnel entrance. Should the worst ever happen, the great steel doors would shut them all inside.

Sheila had to hold on to the side door as the convoy made several sharp turns while they travelled along the lit tunnel. Mary knew that the designers made deliberate choices to twist the passageway in order to angle away any potential shockwaves from nuclear attacks that could directly go through. As she remembered the details from the NORTHCOM briefing she had attended hours before, Mary knew that nuclear attacks would be the least of their worries right now.

After a few minutes, the convoy stopped in front of a smaller blast door that had a team of Secret Service agents guarding it. Mary and Sheila got out of the vehicle as the agents examined their IDs once more. Within seconds, they were guided through the second set of blast doors and into an airlock. As they waited for the atmosphere to cycle to its proper pressure, Mary straightened the collar of her office coat. The airlock opened after a few seconds and they were let into the heart of Raven Rock Complex.

Sheila could see a number of buildings situated in the underground caverns. Other tunnels led to the reservoir and the power plants at each ends.

There were cots with sleeping men situated at the sides of the rock walls. A number of soldiers were sitting on folding chairs beside makeshift tables of plastic crates, either playing cards or typing on laptops. It was a crowded place, but everyone felt safe inside.

One of the Secret Service agents led them past the command building and into a small meeting room situated at an adjacent bunker. Once they were ushered inside, the agent closed the door behind them. Sitting beside a narrow table were two men who were now the de-facto leaders of a battered country. Mary nodded to the two as Sheila stood slightly behind her.

Congressman Elias Baldwin was the Speaker of the House, and he was the older of the two. His silver hair was combed neatly to the side and he wore a dark blue suit. He pointed a finger at Sheila. "What's she doing here, Mary? This was supposed to be a private meeting."

Mary drew a deep breath before answering him. "Sheila Giraud is now the acting head of Task Force Omega since Dr. Paul Dane's disappearance. Since you both wanted an up to date assessment of the situation, I figured it's best to hear from the leader of my team directly. She has the proper clearances and she has a better grasp of the situation- that means she can provide direct answers to your questions. Is that okay with you?"

Senator Anthony Staley shrugged. He was the current president, previously holding the position of Pro Tempore of the Senate. Tall, rangy, with curly brown hair, Staley was supposed to be the next big thing in politics. He had plans to run for President of the United States at one time, but all this was before the Glooming. "I don't have a problem with her," he said. "Welcome, Mrs. Giraud."

"Thanks. And it's Ms. Giraud," Mary said as she sat down along with Sheila at the far end of the table.

Staley smiled. "My apologies. Now that we're all here, I think it's better we go by first names so that we can get to the heart of the matter."

"Fine by me," Mary said. Sheila smiled at them as she placed a stack of folders that she had been carrying on the table in front of her.

Baldwin seemed irritated as he drummed his fingers on the desk. With the president out of commission and the fact that a vice president had yet to be chosen, he was now running the country and was vice president in all but name. "Okay then, let's get to it. I called for this meeting because I need some answers to the crisis that's ongoing. My last meeting with the NORTHCOM commanders this morning wasn't very encouraging. Half of them want an all-out counterattack against the Aztecs while the rest want to nuke the separatists in Kansas. I need more options, and in order for me to have more options then I need more intel on what exactly is going on. Anthony has got his own questions too."

Staley looked at Mary Arctor. "Is it true that our nukes were useless against the Aztecs?"

Mary nodded. Paul Dane's predictions were right. If only they had listened to him. "It would appear so. Our nuclear failsafe option against the initial enemy advances have completely failed."

"How exactly did it happen?" Baldwin said. "Did the delivery systems fail to get the bombs to the enemy or did the devices fail to explode?"

"The latter. We used artillery with nuclear devices and we had planted nuclear bombs within likely areas where the enemy would be advancing through. For some unknown reason, each and every nuclear device failed to detonate," Mary said. "What we learned from the Israelis was that they attempted to nuke enemy forces in Jordan too. It didn't work there either."

Staley crossed his arms and leaned back on his chair. "So what happened then?"

"Exact same result as ours," Mary said. "Failure to detonate. For some reason, each and every device that has been deployed against these creatures has failed to achieve a nuclear chain reaction. To put it bluntly: nukes are useless against them."

Baldwin sighed. "Jesus. But we can't exactly fight them with conventional troops either. Every time we go up against them, we lose. These Aztecs seem to take plenty of casualties, but their numbers just don't seem to decline."

Sheila leaned over the table so that they would notice her. "The Israelis were able to win the first battle of Qasr Al-Hallabat by the use of golems."

All three of them turned to look at her. Mary said nothing. They couldn't fight these gods with what they had. She hoped that the two men sitting across from her would finally get that.

"Please explain," Baldwin said. "I thought we were out of communications with our overseas allies unless they send a ship with tons of letters on it."

"Before she begins," Mary said. "Let me just add that we're starting to put up a communications link with a number of foreign countries, but it's a slow process."

"How?" Staley asked.

"We're currently trying to set up a relay network of FM radio stations to pass information from one area to another. It's crude and there's plenty of interference from unknown sources, but it's the best we can do," Mary said. "We are also seeing if we could implement a semaphore line, which is an optical relay system but due to the undependable weather, we doubt it would work. The military is busy training a Morse code unit, but the only reliable means of getting word to the troops right now is using personal dispatchers."

"Let's keep at it, whatever works," Baldwin said before staring at Sheila. "Go ahead, Sheila."

Sheila cleared her throat before she started to talk. "As you well know, Israel has fallen to the Babylonians. There were hundreds of thousands of refugees that attempted to escape across the Mediterranean Sea to try and get to Cyprus, or Crete. Others attempted to go north, through Lebanon and to try and make it to Turkey. We know of a few thousand that made it through southern Jordan and into Saudi Arabia. The fate of most of these people is unknown. We don't know too much about what happened to the Israeli government, but we believe they attempted the initiation of something dubbed the 'Samson Option', which was the deliberate use of their entire nuclear arsenal against the advancing Babylonians the moment they smashed through."

Staley leaned forward. He was all ears now. "And?"

"No nuclear detonations in that region were detected, nor did we hear of one from all our intel sources," Mary said.

"So all nukes are useless against these gods then," Baldwin said ruefully. "Okay, please continue."

"Someone got through to one of our networks," Mary said. "He authenticated as one of our former CIA case officers in Iraq. It was a short message before he went off the air. Most of our intel in that region came from him." Mary looked at her assistant. "Sheila knows more about this. Sheila?"

"From what he told us, it seems that a rabbi in Israel was able to procure some sort of magical book and he used it to create mythical constructs of some sort. Our source called it a golem. He claimed that the Israelis were able to create up to a battalion of these creatures and used it successfully to stave off a Babylonian attack in Jordan. Though it was only a temporary measure, because these golems apparently suffered major losses. The source also told us that the Israelis sacrificed a large number of Palestinian prisoners in order to create those so-called constructs," Sheila said.

Baldwin shook his head in disbelief. "Sacrifice? How?"

"Human sacrifice," Mary said. "Our source claimed that in order to animate the constructs, the Israelis had to feed it with human souls apparently. It gave them some measure of defense but there must have been some sort of revolt, because the last intel reports claimed some sort of chaos erupted in the Palestinian internment camps."

Staley sat back on his chair, stunned. "Jesus. Human sacrifice?"

Baldwin scratched his head. "So it worked, but only temporarily. Did the Palestinians revolt or something?"

"Reports are sketchy from that point on," Mary said. "Our analysts don't believe the Palestinians could have staged a successful revolt by themselves since the Israelis would have outgunned them. We believe it might have been some sort of internal coup, perhaps a faction with either the Israeli government or military that rebelled against the treatment of the Palestinians. Whatever happened, it caused the whole house of cards to come tumbling down. Israel is gone, along with most of the Middle East."

Staley rubbed his chin. "All this was all made possible by a book, you say? Some sort of magical book?"

"That is what we believe," Mary said. "We're using all available resources to try and track that book down but we currently have no idea as to its whereabouts. The main piece of intel is that it is possible to at least temporarily defeat these gods, they are not invulnerable. I believe we cannot fight them using conventional means or with the use of nuclear weapons. The former head of our task force, Dr. Paul Dane, advised against the use of modern day weaponry against these gods, he claimed it would be useless. Based on all the evidence we've collated now, it seems he was right."

Baldwin nodded. "Yes, yes. I was there when he gave the briefing to the president and NORTHCOM a year ago. Is he still listed as missing?"

Mary looked down. "I'm afraid so. All we can surmise is that the same outer planar creature who sent us back the president took Dr. Dane along with his police liaison Detective Mendoza. As to where they are, we do not know."

"I read the full reports on it," Staley said. "Could it be possible that the so-called demon the Professor was able to call in, could it be possible that the demon exchanged him and Detective Mendoza for the president?"

Mary clasped her hands together in a prayer gesture. "You mean the demon took the president away from his captors in Kansas and replaced him with Professor Dane? I'm afraid that's highly unlikely. We have a number of assets operating in Kansas and they could confirm that the president was no longer held by the separatists. No sign of Dr. Dane over there either. Seems the remaining high value prisoner they have left is Admiral Zimmerman."

Baldwin looked at Staley. "We need Admiral Zimmerman back."

Staley returned his stare. "We are negotiating through backdoor channels, but the mood is pretty much that it's a fat chance the separatists will turn him back to us. They still feel they could use the admiral as a bargaining chip to prevent us from invading them."

"Bastards," Baldwin hissed. "I had to order our generals in NORTHCOM not to attack them, but I don't know how long we can keep the military leashed up like this. We're fighting a two-front war, what with the Aztecs down south. I'm surprised those goddamn Mexican demons haven't pushed up even further, our southern defense line is smashed. It's going to take months for us to reorganize and redeploy what's left. We've already lost about a million men and women in uniform and we're scrounging for replacements. I've been thinking about reintroducing the draft, but it'll be too little too late-we can't recruit, equip and train everybody in a month."

"We believe it's because of their gods, sir," Sheila said. "It seems that the Aztec armies like to blitzkrieg through our defenses, and then stop after each major offensive in order to bring their prisoners back to their cities."

Baldwin frowned. "Why would they do that? It doesn't make any military sense. If I were them, I would have pushed on till they got to Washington DC. They're giving us time to recover and set up a new defensive line. We're scrambling, and converting all non-combatant military personnel to frontline service, but it's still going to take awhile. At this point, I don't even know how we're going to equip them. We've got maybe less than two hundred thousand effective combat troops left."

"They feel it's important to appease their gods before doing anything else," Sheila said. "According to their beliefs, the most valuable thing in the whole universe isn't territory or material goods. It's blood."

Staley grimaced. "Blood? You mean they stopped their offensive so that they could bring American prisoners back to their temples and sacrifice them to appease their gods?"

Mary nodded. They knew so little about the enemy. "I'm afraid so."

Both men sat back on their chairs, stunned.

"We expect their celebrations to last for another month," Sheila said. "At that point, they will renew their offensive and push up north."

Baldwin looked away. "Oh my god. We've got to stop them somehow. Please tell me you have a plan. Anything to deal with this."

"There may be something," Mary said as she looked at Baldwin. She could see the tremendous strain he was under. "Sheila and I are working on an alternate plan. Though the chances are very slim."

"We're all ears," Staley said. "Right now we could use any help we could get."

Sheila adjusted her thick glasses before she started to talk. "Okay, based on the recordings that we took when Professor Dane summoned a demon in New York, we need to get in touch with a number of individuals who may hold or be keys to defeat these supernatural enemies we are currently up against."

"Yeah, I read that report and saw the video recordings," Baldwin said.

"That man Dane was actually able to conjure up a demon? I was skeptical, but now I'm close to being a full on believer."

"Professor Dane went on to ask quite a lot of questions to the creature he summoned," Sheila said. "Assuming that the creature was telling the truth, it named two individuals who happen to be American citizens. We've researched their names. One was attached with the CIA in Iraq, another happens to be a minor. We're getting some intel on them, but we believe they may be in the country."

Baldwin pursed his lips. "In the country? I thought your reports said that one of them was last seen in Iraq and the other one, the minor, was in Russia wasn't she?"

"We have their names. Patrick Gyle, a former Marine and current CIA officer," Mary said. "And Tara Weiss, a fifteen year old from Phoenix, Arizona. We pulled out all the records we could based on the demon's statements. We don't have much information on the minor, but Patrick Gyle's dossier is pretty interesting. He was part of the lead unit going up against the Islamic State when this whole crisis began. He disappeared at that time and was reported as missing. A few weeks later, we got a flash intel from the Green Zone in Iraq, stating Gyle had somehow made it into our embassy there just before it was overrun by the enemy. Then we received a final intel from that source in Israel which made the claim that Gyle had somehow been altered."

Baldwin took out a folder lying on the table and began to leaf through its pages. "Altered? What do you mean by that?"

"Altered as in enhanced somehow," Mary said. "His appearance has apparently changed to the point where he doesn't look human anymore. His abilities have also been … supercharged, as in being able to move with unbelievable speed. Patrick's strength was improved to the point where he can lift heavy objects with no strain. The source made a claim that his skin had become armored to the point where he can resist gunfire. His cellular regeneration has also increased exponentially and that means he can quickly recover from life-threatening wounds very quickly."

"Wow," Staley said. "So we could use him as an asset against these gods then?"

"We'll need to talk to him first," Mary said. "Assuming that he wants to be found, of course."

"What about the minor, this Tara Weiss?" Baldwin said. "What makes her so special?"

"This is where it gets murky and our intel veers into pure speculation," Sheila said. "We have unconfirmed reports we gathered from Russian radio intercepts, which some of our allies in Europe picked up and relayed over to us. It seems she showed up there somehow and was detained. A few days later, she was listed as missing in their records. We surmise she was somehow able to travel into another dimension."

Staley laughed a little. "Oh come on! First we're talking about demons and stuff, and now you're saying there are other dimensions out there?"

"It's the only plausible conclusion we can come up with," Mary said. She just couldn't believe the constant skepticism of these two men. It felt like denial. "With the disappearance of Paul Dane and Valerie Mendoza into thin air, the return of the president as if he just materialized from nowhere, and the last intel we got, we can only suspect that there are other worlds out there. We do not yet know how they travel back and forth, but we're working on it."

"If we can believe that mythical creatures from our fables are real, then why not the afterlife? Or at least the existence of the abode of the gods," Sheila said. "Since these ancient gods have been confirmed by the old myths and legends to exist, then these same stories also tell of an underworld or spirit lands. Every culture has it."

"Like a heaven and hell then," Baldwin said. "You think this is where those gods came from?"

"Professor Dane thought as much," Mary said. "He put his theory to the test and he was successful in summoning a demon, and he got back the president too."

"Looks like he paid for it, possibly with his life," Staley said. "Why hasn't your task force been able to summon this demon again?"

Mary looked down at first, then stole a glance at Sheila.

"We really couldn't find any volunteers that were willing to replicate what

Professor Dane did," Sheila said sheepishly. "I must confess I did try to dabble in it a little by following the steps he took in order to summon the demon again. It didn't work."

"I can understand the danger in doing it, at least you tried, and that was a brave thing to do. Nobody would want to screw up and get dragged off to hell or something," Staley said. "Why didn't it work when you tried it?"

"I'm not sure," Sheila said. "I must have either missed a crucial step, or Professor Dane did something that it wasn't in his notes. Or maybe I was just doing it half-heartedly. Either way, I will be assembling a new team of volunteers to see if we could attempt it again."

Baldwin put his right palm up. "Let's not be too hasty in trying that devil conjuring thing. Like Anthony said, one screw up and we could all end up in hell or something like that."

"That's what we're all afraid of," Sheila said. "The last thing we would want to do is to summon something and then be unable to control it. We're still sorting through the professor's notes."

"Do not attempt anything in that regard again without my express approval," Mary said to her. She didn't even realize Sheila had made the attempt.

"Yes, ma'am," Sheila said.

Baldwin kept scanning the reports that were laid out in front of him. "You mentioned something about having intel that both individuals are in the continental United States. What's the story on that?"

"Well, since we started looking into their names, we tracked down Patrick Gyle's family," Mary said. "His wife and children left Dallas months before the Aztecs attacked and resettled with her brother in Oregon. There were a number of survivalist enclaves staying in the forests there and that's where we found her. We were able to get a team of Federal agents up there despite the dangers, and they were able to interview her. She claimed to have seen him a few months ago but would not divulge any additional information. We wanted to bring her to one of our Federal offices in Portland but she refused. The team of agents also started to incur casualties so they felt it best to leave her where she was and return back to civilization."

"Casualties? What kind of dangers were up in those forests in Oregon?" Staley asked.

"We're not sure," Mary said. "Unconfirmed reports of ghosts and demons inhabiting the forests I think. A number of the prepper enclaves in the remote areas of the country have been found massacred, or everybody went missing."

"Jesus," Baldwin said. "Even without the threat of those damned Aztecs, we still got monsters in our own backyard."

"So Patrick Gyle is here," Staley said. "Why didn't he report in to CIA headquarters or something?"

"That we're not sure about," Mary said. "It's possible that his loyalty to the Federal government has been compromised. The only other thing his wife told us is Patrick wants to find a way to save the country somehow, so we can be somewhat assured he is working in our best interests, at least."

"Well, that's good news," Staley said. "Why doesn't he get in touch with us? We could help him and he could help us."

"Maybe he doesn't think we're part of the solution," Baldwin said to him before giving Mary a worried glance. "You don't think that he's going over to the Kansas separatists, do you?"

"We're not sure at this point, but it's unlikely," Mary said. "From his file, Patrick Gyle wasn't a very religious man, so we have that working in our favor, at least."

"I hope to god you're right," Staley said. "If he takes sides with the Kansas rebels, then we'll be in real trouble."

Baldwin's hands trembled a bit. So many things had already gone wrong. The last thing he needed was their only weapon going over to the enemy. "What about the kid, Tara? How do you know she's back in the country?"

"We were able to deploy a team of agents to Arizona," Mary said. "We met up with her father, who happens to be a drunk living in an abandoned trailer park. Seems he is just staying put while the rest of the city was evacuated northwards before the Aztecs get there. It seems that he met up with his daughter and possibly Patrick Gyle less than a few days ago."

Staley's eyes opened wide. "What? Why didn't the agents talk to the kid and Gyle directly?"

Mary looked away in embarrassment. "Seems they missed encountering them by only a few days. Our communications across state lines haven't been up to par, I'm sorry. By the time the agents got there, Patrick and Tara were gone. They interviewed the father and they were willing to transport him to safety, but he insisted on staying behind. We left a surveillance team in the city just in case Tara goes back there for him. Though based on what the father told us, it's highly improbable."

Baldwin was shocked at the recent news as well, but he maintained his demeanor. "Explain, please."

"From what the father told us, it seems Tara was extremely upset with him and that's why she ran away months before," Mary said. "She also has a younger brother named Timothy. The reason why Tara returned to the trailer park was because she wanted to take her brother away from him. But Timothy wasn't there. Tara's brother was apparently adopted by another family that set off towards Kansas."

Baldwin pounded the table with his fist. "Jesus H Christ!"

"We now believe that Tara is travelling with Patrick, since the father described being manhandled by some sort of horrible creature that fits Gyle's description," Mary said. "Our best guess is they could be on their way towards Kansas."

Staley rubbed his throbbing forehead. "Okay, what can we do? Are you sure they won't go over to the separatists?"

"We think Tara is only trying to get her brother back," Mary said. "Based on what we know, she doesn't come from a religious background either. What we're doing now is to try and use our assets in Kansas to try and locate her. If they made it to Kansas then we should be getting some intel on them soon."

Baldwin was taking shallow breaths now. So much information, so many things that could go wrong now. "Make sure that you tell our assets on the ground there that under no circumstances that those two individuals be allowed to go over to the separatist side. Use everything you can. If we can find her brother before they do then maybe we could have a positive outcome on this. We cannot fail in this, Mary."

"I understand the stakes involved, Mr. Speaker," Mary said tersely. "We're doing everything we can right now."

"Okay," Staley said, changing the subject. "What about the president? I understand you just came over from Camp David. How is he?"

Sheila pursed her lips. "Not much change in his condition. He alternates between Latin curses, speaking in tongues, and nonsensical English. We've brought in every psychologist and even had a neurologic specialist take a look at him. They are all saying he seems to be physically in good shape and there is normal brain function in his CAT scans. They seem clueless on how to treat him though. We also tried to ask a priest to exorcise him, but he failed as well-in fact the priest has been incapacitated."

Baldwin grimaced. "We need him back. My own doctors told me the stress of this office is getting too much for my own health to bear."

Staley didn't say anything. They all knew that important decisions concerning the presidential line of succession would have to be made soon. The Secretary of State, who was currently fourth in line after Baldwin, Staley and the president, was being held in seclusion in an undisclosed location just in case Raven Rock was in any danger. None of them could think beyond the issues that were affecting them all right then and there.

"If the president is really possessed by evil spirits," Mary said softly. "Then there is only one man who could possibly help him and that's Professor Paul Dane. The problem is that even if he isn't dead, he's probably trapped in his own hell right now."

6. Below the Mud

Otherworld

When she was a child, Valerie Mendoza was deathly afraid of going to hell. While her older brothers were never religious, Valerie and her sisters would always attend church with their mother, Josefina. She had grown up in a rough and tumble neighborhood, where gangs, drugs and robberies were common. The one thing that kept the girls away from the crime and the desperation was their shared conviction of Christianity. They would take turns reading the Bible to each other just before bedtime, and would discuss the finer points of avoiding eternal damnation. The apartment that they lived in was so tiny that Valerie would sometimes hang out in the nearby public library, just so she could get some peace and quiet to do her homework. She liked to browse and walk through the myriad shelves of books. The scent of old, moldy paper and leather bindings brought some pleasure to her otherwise mundane childhood. What she really liked were the paintings of Jesus and of the saints. The first time she saw the son of God on a cross, she let out a few tears after her mother told her the story. At night, after their mattresses were spread out on the floor and all the children snored away, Valerie would sometimes pray silently in the dark for minutes on end before falling asleep.

She could remember that one day that finally changed her life. Her parents had just received word that their eldest son had been killed in a gang war. While the whole family grieved at the news, she went away by herself and took her customary cubicle in the library. Lying on the desk was a book about an early Renaissance painter from the Netherlands. The previous occupier of the cubicle had evidently forgotten to put the photobook back in its shelf. Thinking that it would be just another art book showcasing the paintings of Jesus and his disciples, Valerie started to flip through its pages. The painter's name was Hieronymus Bosch. The strange, twisted images in the paintings both recoiled and fascinated her. It also reinforced her fear of ever being sent to a place of eternal damnation. At ten years old, Valerie made a vow that she would follow the core tenets of her religion. She would forever make sure that she would not fall prey to the temptations of the world that got her brother killed. When she came back home that night, her entire family was praying for her brother's soul in heaven. As she knelt down beside her grieving mother, Valerie clasped her hands together, closed her eyes, and made a different sort of benediction. She prayed that her brother would find a way to repent while his soul languished in hell.

Time had passed, and Valerie gradually moved away from her extreme religious fervor when she finally graduated high school. By then most of her older siblings had either gotten married, or were in prison. Even though she stopped going to church on a regular basis, Valerie still believed that she needed to live life the right way. She took a few classes in a local city college and worked part time as a library assistant for a couple of years. Then she applied for a job at the NYPD, and was accepted into the police academy after passing the tests. The hours and stresses of her job, along with her single-minded devotion to move up the ranks, took away most of her free time. Valerie didn't have a life, but she remembered the teachings of her religion. She had stopped thinking about hell and damnation, her mind was too preoccupied with case files and paperwork. Valerie figured that as long as she kept walking along the straight path, she would have nothing to worry about when it came to the afterlife.

Then the Glooming happened. Her first brush with the supernatural occurred when she and her partner were investigating a suspected assault on two men. Myron, the senior detective and her mentor was killed, and her attackers slashed her face with an obsidian blade. Although she eventually recovered, the attack left a long, jagged scar on her face. Through sheer strength of will, Valerie forced herself back on the job. She didn't have anything else to live for since her beliefs of serving the city had been shattered. The country was falling apart, but she redoubled her convictions, thinking that if she just did her part, the world would somehow come back together again.

Not long after that, she met Paul Dane. He had been the head of a newly organized Federal task force designed to deal with the return of the ancient gods. Valerie had always felt uneasy around academic types. She felt that they were somehow so smarter than she ever could be. But Paul's easygoing attitude and natural charm had put her at ease. The fact he had had enough sense to keep her as a commander for the police contingent during the raid on the museum had given her added confidence. Although she had barely survived when the god Okeus attempted to manifest itself as a gigantic worm, all her experiences gave her a newfound purpose in life. With Paul she had found a kindred soul, they both had survived a number of unearthly encounters with strange beings, and they slowly gravitated towards each other. Each of them had lost someone they loved, and it was through their mutual grief and experience that their attraction to each other grew even further. After Paul's return from Boston, he had realized just how much he needed her. For Valerie, the feeling had been the same. Paul was the man she had been looking for all her life, even though she didn't know it back then.

When the new Secretary of Defense reconstituted the task force after Paul had quit previously, the mythology professor had immediately demanded Valerie be his liaison officer. Within weeks, they had been able to piece enough evidence to put together a plan. Paul would decide to risk everything in summoning a demon that had once materialized in the museum, and they would try to find answers as to what was truly happening in the world. The operation had succeeded beyond everyone's wildest imaginings, when Paul successfully brought forth a demon from the netherworld. So much intelligence had been gained when the demon had answered their questions. But Paul hadn't been satisfied. Knowing that the president of the United States had been kidnapped by a separatist theocracy in Kansas, he had manipulated the demon into bringing back the country's head of state. Paul had succeeded in returning the president back, but in so doing he angered the demon Dantalion, and the infernal creature gained its revenge by taking him back to the dimension that it came from. Valerie of course, couldn't have let it happen. She had grabbed onto Paul's hand and struggled to pull him back from the abyss that the demon was sending him to.

She had failed, and now she was in Hell along with him.

The last thing she remembered was the darkness unfolding all around her as she kept a tight grip on Paul's hand, just as the demon dragged them both into the underworld. Both she and Paul were screaming in pain and terror. She tried to draw him closer but she could feel intense forces all around her, as if she was being buffeted through the air in the eye of a tornado. The fury of the howling winds all around her was so great that she was unable to keep her grip on Paul's hand. Valerie screamed out his name as she trashed about, her body spinning through the blackened vortex of nothingness. It felt like an eternity as the air was so full of fury that she couldn't even hear her own shrieks of despair.

When she finally recovered her wits, she realized that everything had gone quiet once more. Only this time, everything was so silent that she couldn't hear a thing, not even her own cries of anguish. The darkness all around her meant she couldn't see anything either. It was as if she was totally blind, deaf and dumb. The only feelings that were still operating were her touch and her sense of being. She could still think and move somehow but she couldn't hear or see anything.

Valerie could feel that she was somehow lying down on the ground, which seemed smooth to the touch. She very quickly got up and almost fell down again as she tilted forward and spread her legs out for balance. She could still sense the clothes she was wearing as she fumbled through the pockets of her jacket. When her fingers touched the hip holster that still had her Glock pistol, she felt an immediate sense of reassurance, but it was tempered by the fact that she still couldn't see. She felt neither hot nor cold and wondered if she was trapped in a room or something. Valerie ran her hands along her face and she could feel the thickened skin where her scar was. So maybe she wasn't dead after all. As she took out her smart phone, she attempted to activate it but she fumbled with the buttons and the phone dropped from her hand. Valerie cried out and knelt down as she tried to feel her way on the ground, trying to find her lost phone. The seconds seemed to turn into minutes as she kept running her hands along the smooth floor, hoping to locate her phone. After what seemed like an eternity, she was unable to find it using her sense of touch, so she cursed out loud and stood right back up again.

Almost by instinct, she started to walk forward. Although her first steps were slow and short, she soon figured out her stride as she began to walk briskly. Valerie hoped that there was a light source somewhere, the only way to find it was by moving and she would stumble upon it by pure luck. She could sense her eyelids blinking, even though there was nothing but a jet black, inky darkness in front of her.

This went on for a long time. Valerie just kept on walking, her movements had become almost like an exercise. She hoped that she was not walking in a circle as she used her sense of balance to try and walk in a straight line. On and on. Step by step. Place one foot forward, and then the next one. Keep going. Keep it up. *If you're in a darkened place, then it must lead to somewhere*, she thought.

As she kept on walking, her thoughts began to gradually metamorphosize into a gnawing pit of despair. Valerie kept trying to push the negativity away, but as time seem to pass on, the temptation to just give up and lie down began to manifest itself in her deepest subconscious. Her once long striding began to slacken. The seemingly endless darkness had begun gnaw at her very soul. Dark thoughts that she had seemingly thought she had suppressed now returned to the center of her mind in an unassailable fury of helplessness. By now, her rapid walking had become a slog as her feet became leaden, each step had become agony. Within moments, the despair had become so great that she finally stopped.

For a long while she just stood there, in the pitch-black space of oblivion. A sense of gloom permeated all over her body. The fact that she was in an endlessly dark place with no visible means of an exit meant that she was already dead. All she had to do now was just to sit down and stop thinking about it. If she cleared her mind, perhaps all the self-doubt, all the misery, and the pain would stop too. After all, she gave it all she got. There was no shame in giving up. She could forget about everything now. All her problems were over. It was time to stop struggling, since in the end it was all pointless anyway. If she could get some rest, then she would finally be at peace. Yes, there was no need to go on anymore.

Just as she was about to give in and lie back down on whatever surface this place had, a small kernel of thought had seemingly planted itself at the back of her mind. It started out as no more than a drop in the ocean, but it soon transformed itself into a wellspring of a memory. That was when she realized why she was here. The image in her mind began to coalesce.

Valerie let out a big sigh that her ears failed to pick up. She realized that even though she couldn't see or hear anything, she could think. She was aware that if she could think, then she must exist somewhere. The words and thoughts in her head began to form themselves into bright paintings in her imagination. Yes, she could think abstractly. She wasn't guided by instinct, but by reason and logic. The comprehension of her thought processes increased with a newfound awareness. Could she use logic and will to get herself out of this mess?

That was when she remembered her time with Paul. Even though the world had turned into a nightmare, the last few days before the summoning had been happy ones for her. Despite the gloom all over their heads, she still found some solace in his companionship. It was the little things that mattered after all. As Valerie's thoughts turned to Paul, she suddenly had a new source of hope. That was it! The reason why she wouldn't give in now was because of her caring for him. *Damn all the gods*, she thought. *I don't care if I die trying since I'm already dead anyway. Hell won't stop me.*

Valerie sensed that she was still on her feet. Her legs no longer felt like they were chained to giant boulders. She placed her right hand on her hip once more and felt the cool, reassuring touch of the gun still holstered there. *If I was put in here like some sort of prisoner, then there must be a way out*, she thought.

A crazy idea manifested itself in her mind. What if something was holding her senses back that kept her from seeing the exit? Could she will herself out of this place?

Valerie began to picture a door in her mind. It was like a rectangular opening, an aperture that led into a roomful of light. She tried to make a guess as to which direction it was. Valerie started to pivot her body clockwise until she sensed where the breach was. Then she started walking, only this time, instead of a desperate stride, it was on a slow but confident pace.

As the minutes of eternity passed, she soon noticed a tiny pinprick of light out in the distance. It looked like it was hundreds of miles away and her tiny pulse of hope almost flew away at the thought that it would take weeks or even months for her to reach it. Valerie immediately placed the darkening thoughts away and concentrated as she started to run towards it.

For long while, it seemed that she wasn't any closer as she kept on running. Valerie couldn't sense how much time had elapsed but she wasn't feeling winded at all. She could feel her legs moving underneath her torso but the point of light was forever distant, like a faint, twinkling star. It wasn't getting any closer.

"Come on!" she shouted as she started pumping her arms back and forth. Valerie gritted her teeth but it felt like she was running in place. She could feel her neck muscles tighten as she strained to get closer to it, but it didn't seem like anything had changed.

"Don't give up! Don't give up! We're almost there!" Valerie shouted at herself. The point of light wasn't any closer, but she could feel a shortness of breath now. Instead of discouraging her, that sense of hardship only made her running even faster. She realized that if she could feel her body working, it meant she was still alive. At that very moment, she could see her hands in front of her, as she parted a wall of dirt ahead and then kept on pushing until she was blinded by the light ahead of her.

Suddenly, her eyes opened wide as she stared out into a grey, overcast sky. Her vision had returned while she heard her own heaving gasps as she seemed to breathe for the first time. The next thing she knew she was on her knees. The ground was grayish mud. Everything around her was grey. Valerie had a sense that she had somehow been buried beneath the muck of this place and she had apparently clawed her way up to the surface. The whole area seemed like an endless sea of muddy hills. There were no plants, or trees or even buildings, just small mounds of drab clay.

As she stood up, she noticed some sort of movement stirring in the dirt beneath her. Valerie was confused for a moment before realizing that there were other people trapped beneath the mud. She cried out as she knelt down and started digging with her hands, but every time she pulled out a few handfuls of muck, the seemingly human faces that she had expected to find underneath had disappeared back into the ever shifting sludge.

Valerie looked around. She could see patterns of faces that would form in the dirt all around her, but they all seemed to fade away after a few minutes. At that moment, she felt a kindred empathy for them. She realized that they were in the same predicament she had been in. They too were trying to come out from the mud, but where they failed she succeeded. A sudden, terrifying thought manifested itself in her mind. What if Paul was trapped beneath the mud as well?

"Paul!" she screamed, hoping to find a reply. All she could hear was the occasional bubble of air that escaped from the endless puddles of muck.

Unwilling to give into despair, Valerie stood up. That was when she realized that the mud wasn't sticking to her hands, the liquid dirt seemed to just drop away back onto the soggy ground. Even her clothes were dry, when she would lift up her foot, the mud would just slide off her shoes and pants. The one thing that did bother her was the smell, the whole place reeked of an abominable filthiness, it was as if the gods were using this whole world as their cosmic toilet.

There was nothing to be gained by staying where she was, so she picked a landmark and started moving towards it. It was the highest hill that she saw across the horizon, but when she finally got close enough to make out its details, it seemed just like the other mounds of dirt in the entire place. Everywhere she looked, it was all a series of dirt hills overlooking puddles of mud. She kept on moving, even though she didn't know where else to go. That was because she felt a curious sensation every time she stopped, that was when her feet would start to become leaden and numb. Valerie sensed that if she stood still for too long, the unceasing mud would somehow swallow her up once more.

Her sense of time had pretty much waned. As she kept on moving, Valerie was no longer certain as for how long. The grey, overcast sky above her didn't change one bit, even though she was sure that she had been walking around for days now. The landscape stayed the same as well, it became a concern for her that she thought she might have been moving around in circles, though the fear of being sucked back into the mud was of an even greater worry for her. Since Valerie felt neither the need to eat or to rest, she just kept on going.

It was during one of these endless walks that she spotted something in the distance. What it was she couldn't be sure, but it was definitely not part of the landscape, so she started moving towards it. As Valerie got closer, she soon realized it was another person. It looked like a very corpulent man who was sitting down in the center of one of the mud puddles. When she got near enough, he noticed that his long dark hair hung low over his sagging shoulders. The man was naked. The folds of his fatty skin covered his body like a pink, fleshy coat. His large, sagging breasts were suspended above his rotund sides and bulging belly. He sat cross-legged in the middle of the quagmire of muck.

Valerie moved around until she stood a few feet away in front of him. "Hello," she said as she put one hand up. "Do you speak English?"

For a few minutes, the man didn't react. Then his sad, heavy lidded eyes looked up and focused on her. He tried to lift up his double chin, but the effort seemed so taxing that he gave up. His eyes kept trailing her as she shifted slightly to his right. His flabby arms stayed glued to his side. His whole body seemed rooted in the mud.

Valerie leaned forward so their eyes met. "Are you alright? Do you need help to get out of that puddle?"

There was a brief ray of hope in the man's eyes before he suddenly returned to his lethargy. When he finally talked, his voice was like that of a shrill parrot. "Who are you?"

Valerie smiled. At least she could understand him. "My name is Valerie

Mendoza. I'm with the New York Police Department. I don't know how I got here but you're the first person I've seen. Do you need help?"

The man's eyes shifted until they were downcast again. "I never heard of you. Or of that place. I once lived in the kingdom of Hungary. I was a nobleman. But now..." His voice trailed off.

Valerie bit her lip. "Okay, where I come from really doesn't matter. It looks like you're stuck there. Do you want me to try and help you out of that mud puddle?"

"Yes, alright," the man said slowly as he put up one of his hands, the drooping flesh on his arms wiggled as he tried to reach out, but the effort seemed to tax him greatly. In the end, he withdrew his hand, just before Valerie nearly clasped it.

"Come on," Valerie said as she kept extending her hand. "You were nearly there, just a bit more effort."

The man let out a deep sigh and looked away from her. "I think I'll just stay here."

She wanted to argue with him, but she could tell from his expression that it was ultimately pointless. The puddle of mud around him had already covered up his legs and it looked like it would ultimately sink into its depth completely. Valerie didn't want to see any more of it so she turned and started to walk away. As she kept on moving, she took one last glance behind her. The man was still sitting there. It was as if her offer of help was more of an annoyance to him than a benefit.

Valerie shook her head, and kept on going. It had been a pathetic encounter, but it did give her some hope. She had thought that she was the only one on the surface of this strange land, but she sensed that there might be others around after all. *All I have to do is to keep moving and sooner or later, I'll find another*, she thought as she rambled on.

"It is admirable that you try to help them, but they must get out of the mud on their own volition," a voice to the far side of her said.

Valerie pivoted sideways as her hand instinctively reached for her Glock pistol.

Another man stood a dozen feet away from her. His matted hair and grizzled beard were both unkempt. All he was wearing was a black, tattered cloak and she could see his bare, scrawny legs and skeletal feet below it. He looked anywhere between fifty and sixty years old. His bony, emaciated body seemed to barely hold onto his meager existence, even in this world. He gave her a gap toothed smile. "I come in peace," he said softly.

Valerie sensed he wasn't a threat. She relaxed as she let her arms fall to her side. "Who are you?"

The old man looked at the grey sky above them and squinted his eyes. "Just another wanderer in these wastes. I don't think my name is important anymore so I won't ask for yours either."

"Well, I'll tell you my name anyway," she said. "It's Valerie. My friend and me were kidnapped by a demon he summoned. This demon is called Dantalion, and the next thing I knew, I woke up here. I think I was buried in the mud of this place but I somehow got out."

The wanderer nodded. "Yes, most people arrive in this place from the mud below."

Valerie stared at him. "Did you arrive the same way? Through the mud too?"

The wanderer shook his head. "No, I traveled across the other worlds to get here."

Valerie was shocked. "There are other worlds? Worlds like this?"

"Yes, I suspect there is an infinite array of worlds that one can go to. I have been moving across these places for a long time now."

Valerie understood. "If I could ask, are we in Hell?"

The old man looked up at the sky again as he scratched his beard. "Hell? Oh you mean a place of torment. Well yes, this place could be called that."

"I've always thought Hell would be a pit of fire with demons and all that," Valerie said. "Not a depressing cesspool like this."

"The planes of damnation are many. I can no longer count as to how many I have traveled to. I'm sure there are more."

"Wait, there are many other worlds like this?"

"At the very least," the wanderer said. "This particular world has many names, for it is constantly being given new names by its inhabitants, and they all come from different places themselves. One of the most common names for this plane is Desidia, otherwise known as Sloth."

Valerie remembered the teachings of the Bible. "Sloth? As in being lazy? As in one of the seven deadly sins?"

"Ah, you are of that faith then? Yes, this world seems to coincide with that particular transgression. You see, the people trapped here in their own lethargy lack the will to struggle. Hence, they are swallowed up by the muck. Quite a few of them try to get out of it, but most of them fail. It is hard to overcome one's will of just doing nothing and of abandoning all hope and goals in life. Many of them are content to just stay in the mud," the wanderer said.

"So is that why I can sometimes see people's faces forming in the mud, but then they disappear after awhile?"

"Yes, that is about right. You cannot really help them. All you can do is to observe and hope that they overcome their own indolence and break free. But alas, very, very few ever do."

Valerie placed her hands on her hips and sighed. "This whole thing, it just isn't fair. What have I done to deserve being sent to this mud pit of a hell?"

"I asked myself that same question many times when I was stricken with illness and despair back on earth," the old man said. "You see, I worshipped all the gods, I always paid attention to their rituals and followed their commandments. Yet I was struck down by a horrid illness and I lost my job, and my possessions. I asked myself what had I done to deserve such cruelty. Ultimately, the wrongs done upon me were redressed but the central question remained."

"So you didn't get an answer then?"

The old man shook his head in disappointment. "No, not really. One of the gods rewarded me for my patience and will, but I still ask myself the question as to why they had done such wrong to me in the first place. That is why I wander across the underworlds after my death. I am seeking that answer."

Valerie sensed that the man reminded her of someone, but she couldn't pinpoint it. "I hope that question gets answered too but right now, I got bigger worries. There's a friend of mine, his name is Paul. He was also taken by that demon and I'm very afraid that he may be stuck in the mud here too. I need to get him away from there."

The old man closed his eyes for a moment. "Ah yes, I can sense your feelings. They are quite powerful and emanate from you. This is clearly a sign that you are not of the dead. You have been taken here not as a path in your afterlife, but rather because you have been imprisoned here."

"Is this why I'm still wearing the clothes that I wore when that demon was summoned?"

"Yes, you have been transported with not just your body and soul, but with your possessions as well. That gives you certain advantages over the other denizens of these worlds."

Valerie's heart began to race. "Then there's still a chance that Paul might still be alive somewhere! Please, can you help me find him? I'll do anything! I'll gladly give up my life for his!"

The old man placed a palm up in the air as a gesture of patience. "As much as I would like to help you, it is not up to me, for I have not known your friend during the time of my life. Only you can find him. For you are the one most familiar to him."

Valerie's lips trembled. She felt like retching due to the foul stench in the air, but she had to stay focused. Her whole world was only inches away from being shattered. She didn't want to live if she couldn't get Paul back. She had come through so far now to just give it up. That's what kept her going. "Please, kind sir. You've got to tell me how. How do I find him across seven worlds?"

"Close your eyes," the wanderer said. "I shall tell you a tale. I once had a lovely second wife. She was my favorite. I still remember her exquisite brown eyes and her addictive smile. She had this most profound laugh that still echoes in my mind. That is what you have to do. You must remember your love closely. You must recall the slightest scent of his breath. The warmth of his body on a cold, cold night. Every memory you have of him must be brought forth into your thoughts. You must remember what his aura is like. You must imagine him but standing beside you, ready to bask yourself in his protective embrace. You must feel him."

Valerie closed her eyes. She used her memories of Paul. Of their last few nights together, she remembered that he would constantly lean over the numerology charts as they pieced it together, in order to successfully summon the demon Dantalion. She remembered the little things, of how he would constantly adjust his glasses in a subconscious manner, whenever they were on a verge of a breakthrough. Of the coffee in his breath when he gave her a kiss on the lips, when the group finally got the circumference of the thaumaturgical circle right. Paul's ever confident smile when he would instruct the team of professional code breakers and mathematicians on how to seemingly solve an insurmountable problem. Most of all, of the time when they were both so exhausted that they slept side by side together on a cot in one of the storerooms of the museum. She could remember his quiet breaths next to her head as she snuggled up to him, his arms wrapped around her body. That was when she knew that she could sense his presence. She could even sense him calling out to her for help. Paul was clearly in distress. There was no doubt that Dantalion was tormenting him. All she needed to do now was to travel to the worlds of the mind and she was sure that she would find him.

When she finally opened her eyes, she saw that the old man was still standing there, smiling at her. "Did you finally sense him?" he asked.

Valerie nodded. "Yes. I can feel him calling out for help. He isn't in this world, though. I think he's in another. The demon hated him so much and it sensed Paul's affection for me. Dantalion wanted him to suffer by knowing that I would be worlds away from him and there would be no way for Paul to help me either."

The wanderer clasped his hands together. "Well done, mortal. You have taken your first steps in learning about these myriad worlds and of the paths you must take. That is exactly how I was able to track down my second wife in these wastes. I merely kept going until the force of her aura became stronger. The moment I could sense getting closer to her presence, I knew I was on the right track."

Valerie walked up to him and put her hand on his bony shoulder. "Will you help me? I am not familiar with these places and I could use a guide."

The old man laughed. "You are the first interesting person I have met in these dismal planes in a long, long time. I find your story to be most intriguing. Since I have nothing better to do I shall say yes to your offer for help. I have some knowledge of these worlds and that may prove useful to your quest. Yes, it is most interesting."

Valerie was so happy, she nearly hugged him. Tears of joy began to form on her eyelids. "I can't help but thank you enough—"

At that moment, she heard a large bellow in the distance. As she turned around, she saw the most grotesque thing she had ever witnessed. Towering above them, no more than a few hundred yards away, was some sort of gigantic being. It looked vaguely like a man since it had a head shaped like one. The creature must have been several hundred feet tall. It was walking on bird like legs that resembled gigantic tree stumps. The giant's body was shaped like a smooth egg and its human like head was perched above it. It had no arms to speak of and it looked like the stuff of nightmares. The monster twisted its face in their direction and stared at them with eyes the size of satellite dishes. The creature then turned until the rear of its oval torso was in front of them. At that instant, the egg-shaped rear that was the size of a small building developed a crack along its spine. The lower crack crumbled away like a torn shell and a gigantic hole was visible in the creature's rear end. Within seconds, a stream of nauseous, grey colored excrement began to pour out of the monster's anal cavity, and the pile of sludge moistened the low lying mounds nearby.

The wanderer merely thrust his lower lip forward in a gesture of bored resignation as the stench of the miasma cascaded all around them. "That is Peor. He is a creature who regularly replenishes the mud of this place from his own buttocks. He was apparently worshipped as a god once."

Valerie couldn't stand it any longer. She bent down and began to throw up, her own orange bile mixing in with the endless, grayish mud of the land.

7. Hearts of Darkness

Louisiana

It was just after lunch when Tyrone Gatlin would finally get the chance to board the riverboat. The rains had been falling hard over the dark skies since early morning. The mist shrouded visibility was not good enough to cast off today. Everyone on the boat except for the captain was apparently holed up in the inside of the main deck, so the coast was clear.

He had tried to get a chance to speak with the captain for the past few days, but the ship's first officer, a surly looking man named JJ Glanton, told him they weren't taking any new crew or passengers. Glanton then told him to shove off. Tyrone then tried to just walk across the plank from the pier to the side of the main deck just yesterday, but he was stopped by two men armed with AR-15 rifles. They "politely" told him if he took one step onto the deck, they would riddle him full of holes, so he turned around and walked back.

Tyrone had spent a few more days with Monique and her daughters. He later learned that her husband had left them years ago and she was working as a waitress to support Moesha and Shani before the Glooming happened. Monique soon experienced what she called a possession, when one of the loas entered her body and spoke to her soul. It was at that point when she became one of the voodoo queens in the community of survivors of the sunken city of Shreveport. The two girls took a liking to Tyrone, they soon confided their personal stories and invited him on their fishing trips to get food for the community. At the last dinner they had, Shani even asked her mother up front if he could stay with them for good. Tyrone smiled and thanked them for the offer, but his god had other plans for him. He could see that there was a glint in Monique's eyes, as if she was silently pleading with him to stay and live a somewhat safe life with them. But in the end, his restless dreams kept telling him to get on the boat. So by the third day, he was finally determined enough to either be accepted as part of the crew, or die trying.

It had already been a few hours since he stood behind one of the shacks beside the boat. Tyrone had wedged himself at the side of the wall, behind a few crates. It was an ideal spot to observe the actions of the ship's crew without being noticed. He could vaguely see the riverboat's name painted in black bold letters near the bow of the hull. The ship was called the *Nimrod*. Streams of rainwater continuously poured down from the corrugated steel overhang of the shack, as Tyrone looked out at where the boat was. He could see that the guard posted at the upper deck looked miserable. The man kept pulling at his raincoat to tug it away from his shivering body as he stood exposed to the elements. Tyrone pitied the guy for having to stand watch out in the pouring rain. The man's floppy hat was drooping down to the point where it covered his eyes, it clearly had been soaked all the way through. After fifteen minutes of just standing there, the guard shouted out a curse as he turned around and started to walk towards the cabin just underneath the wheelhouse.

That was it. Tyrone immediately made his way to the edge of the pier. After making one last check to make sure that the coast was clear, he rapidly moved towards the gangplank and started to stride across of it. The wooden ramp was slippery and he nearly fell into the water, but he flung his arms out in the air in order to right himself and barely succeeded. Just as he got on board, Tyrone then ran sideways along the rain soaked main deck until he got to where the white painted ladder was. He quickly made his way up before crouching down beside the railings. The upper deck looked clear so he sneaked around until he made it to the rearward side of the cabin. It was there that he saw another set of wooden ladders that led up to the topmost compartment of the riverboat, the wheelhouse.

Tyrone used his hands to climb up the second ladder. Just as he made it to the back of the wheelhouse, he realized there was a man sitting beside the rear door that led into it. It was Glanton. The first officer had been sitting on a stool just underneath the overhanging roof, so Tyrone was unable to notice him until he got up to the third level of the boat.

Glanton stood up. The front part of his poncho was wet but the rest of his clothes were more or less dry. He was a gaunt, sullen looking man and the first thing one would notice was his sunken cheeks and piercing blue eyes. Glanton's light brown, shoulder length hair was tied down in a pony tail at the back of his head. In his right hand was a .45 Kimber 1911 pistol, and he was aiming squarely at Tyrone's direction.

Tyrone let out a big sigh as he raised his hands in the air. The howling wind and rain had soaked his clothes to the point where he didn't even notice that he had started to piss down his pants. It looked like he was about to fail his god.

Glanton spat out a wad of chewing tobacco which almost hit Tyrone, but the falling raindrops intercepted it and the spit became a brownish puddle on the roof of the upper deck. "I told you, boy. I told you nevah to come on this boat. Are you deaf or somethin'? The men on this boat told you that if you ever step foot on it, you'd die. Looks like we get to make good on that promise, you dumb coon!"

"Glanton! Bring him in here," a husky voice from the inside of the wheelhouse called out.

Glanton turned and hissed, but he kept his gun aimed at Tyrone. "What do you wanna meet him for?"

The voice from the wheelhouse became louder in tone. "That's an order, goddamn it! Do as I say and put your gun away!"

Glanton grimaced as he stepped sideways, turned, and then opened the door to the wheelhouse. "Get in there, you stupid monkey," he said to Tyrone as he put the pistol back beneath his poncho.

Tyrone put his hands back down as he walked into the wheelhouse. The first thing he noticed was the ornate wooden ship's wheel. It was made of black lacquered wood and had beautiful carvings on its ten spokes. The wheelhouse was the second tallest structure of the riverboat, just below the smoke stacks. It was also the smallest building and looked like nothing more than a wooden booth. Tyrone stood at the foot of the door for a few seconds before he was rudely shoved further inside, so that Glanton could stand right behind him. Tyrone knew for a fact Glanton still had his gun ready in case of any trouble, so he didn't protest.

There was a man sitting on a high chair at the side of the cabin who had been looking at some maps on a small wooden table. The man swiveled the chair sideways so that he faced both Tyrone and Glanton. The captain was a bear of a man, Tyrone estimated him to be over six feet five inches tall if he stood fully upright. The man was barrel chested and wore a biker t-shirt. While his large arms had once been muscular, the advancement of age made them flabby. Tyrone could still sense that he had tremendous reserves of strength in those limbs, and he sure didn't want to be on the receiving end of any trouble that would arise.

Tyrone wiped off some of the rain on his head with his hand as he stood before the captain of the *Nimrod.* "Sir, my name is Tyrone Gatlin. I'm sorry for having to bother you like this, but I heard that you are headed east, towards the Deep South. I would like to request to join you. You see, I need to get back home to Georgia."

Captain Pillinger eyeballed the young man in front of him with his cold grey eyes. He had a .357 Magnum Ruger Redhawk revolver strapped to his side holster and wore alligator skin boots. Pillinger's silvery hair was long and tousled, his grizzled beard extended down to the top of his chest. There was a scar on his right cheek. "My crew is all set, Mr. Gatlin. I don't need another passenger either. This isn't gonna be a river cruise or a transport job. My men and I are in the middle of a hunting expedition," he said.

Tyrone nodded. "I understand that, Captain. My problem is that I need to get to Georgia as soon as possible and all the roads are flooded. I'll do anything that you ask me to do. I can bring my own food and help out as best I can."

"The captain told you we don't take in any more people, boy," Glanton growled in Tyrone's ear. "You must be stupid in not even getting that."

"I'm sorry, but I gotta go with you," Tyrone said softly. He felt like someone else was putting words in his mouth. "Like I said, I'll do anything."

Glanton pulled out his pistol again. "Captain, this here black dog obviously won't take no for an answer. I can easily get him outta here right now."

Pillinger held out his hand, signaling Glanton to stop before looking at Tyrone once more. "That true, boy? You won't take no for an answer? You do realize that we can kill you anytime you're here on this boat. The new rule is that there are no rules now. The ones with the guns make the law. I don't want to get into a conflict with the community here since I trade with them every few weeks or so. But it won't stop me from killing you the moment we are on our way. I don't need anyone demanding anything on my ship."

"I'm making no demands, sir," Tyrone said. There was a compulsion in him now, something that wouldn't take no for an answer. "I'm actually just beggin' you to be a part of your expedition. I promise I won't be a burden to you at all. If you'll just have me. I can sleep anywhere and do anything you want."

Glanton held the pistol at the back of Tyrone's head. "Just lemme shoot this stubborn son of a bitch right now."

"Put the gun away, Glanton," Pillinger said.

"But Captain, he—"

Pillinger placed his own hand on the butt of his Redhawk revolver. "I said put it away!"

Glanton cursed as he safetied his Kimber before placing it underneath his poncho for the second time.

"Just give me a chance, Cap'n," Tyrone said. He felt his heart had stopped beating a couple of times in the last few seconds. He thought he was going to be dead for sure. "Anything you want I could do."

Pillinger snorted. He could easily have the man killed but he was feeling somewhat charitable today. Perhaps the gods could clear the weather for them so that they could finally get going. "We could use another deckhand, the ship's got enough spare room anyway. What part of Georgia are you headed to?"

"My folks live in Macon, sir," Tyrone said. Maybe if he could just get there, maybe the dreams would stop. "If I could get anywhere near that part I could make my own way after."

Pillinger crossed his arms as he leaned back on the pilot wheel. "The ship is only gonna skirt around Georgia. We will head into Columbus for a fuel run before we head southwards towards Florida."

"Columbus would be fine, sir," Tyrone said.

Pillinger waved a stubby finger at him. "Remember, I am captain of this ship. My word is law. If you get in the way of my crew I will personally execute you myself. You screw up and it's gonna be your ass. Is that clear?"

Tyrone couldn't help but smile. Whatever was eating him up from the inside finally stopped. "Clear as day, sir."

Pillinger looked at Glanton. "JJ, get the man set up with a bunk. Tell Eight-Ball he has a new assistant in case he needs help in the engine room."

Glanton couldn't hide his disgust as bits of chew dribbled from his mouth. "We don't really need another coon on this boat, Captain."

Pillinger's demeanor changed almost instantly. His face reddened and his grimace was like the face of death. He didn't say anything but instead just stared deep into Glanton's eyes. Despite not being the focus of the captain's anger, Tyrone was also terrified.

Glanton immediately took a step back as his chin started trembling. "Okay, Captain. Whatever you say," he said before turning around and walking back out into the pouring rain.

After a few tense moments, Pillinger calmed down again. "Looks like my First Mate took an instant dislike to you."

"Sorry 'bout that," Tyrone said. He hated Glanton too but it was best not to say so. "I'll see if I could earn his trust."

"You do that," Pillinger said. "Just remember that him and me have been working as a team for months now and I trust him a lot more than I trust you. Don't force me to choose again, because next time you will lose."

"Understood, Captain."

Pillinger kept staring at him. "You're a deserter, aren't you?"

Tyrone was instantly surprised. "I'm sorry, what—"

"Didn't you hear me the first time, boy? I was asking if you was a deserter."

Tyrone blinked rapidly in confusion. "H-how?"

"It's the little things that gave you away," Pillinger said. "Your haircut, your build, and especially those Army boots you wearing. I was in the Marines myself, but that was a long time ago. You a coward, boy?"

A sense of shame washed over him. "I-I ain't no coward, sir."

"Yet you ran, didn't you? Why else would you be stuck in this shithole. Did you even fight the Aztecs at all?"

Tyrone straightened his stance. It felt like he was standing in front of a military tribunal. "I did fight them, sir. I used everything I had but it wasn't enough. My unit was wiped out so I figured it was time to leave. The enemy coulda easily captured me but they didn't. It felt like they were just ignoring me as I walked right past 'em. I did fight. I ain't no coward and I'm willing to prove that."

Pillinger scratched his beard. "We're gonna see if you're a coward or not. If you desert my crew during battle, I will put a bullet in your head. There won't even be a court martial here. I gotta have a crew that's willing to fight as a team and willing to kill for each other. If you are going to stay with us, you better be ready to do just that. There can be no hesitation, we will be up against some very dangerous beasts out here."

"I gave you my word, Captain," Tyrone said. "I'll stick with it no matter what happens."

"We'll see about that," Pillinger said. "Do you know why we're out here, boy? Do you know where we going?"

Tyrone shrugged. "Not really, sir. I think you're the head of some sort of expedition. I'm not really sure about what it's all about."

"Have you been back to your home state lately?"

"No, sir. Not since this Glooming started. Last time I was in Georgia was right after basic training. After that it was mostly at Fort Irwin."

"Then you don't know what you're heading into," Pillinger said wistfully. "The South is now a bunch of islands and peninsulas surrounded by bayous and waterways thanks to the Glooming. I gotta update my maps daily. All sorts of strange animals have popped up and the investors that hired me want their hides. This is the second expedition I'm mounting. Do you know how many of my men I lost in the first one?"

"I dunno, sir."

Pillinger looked out of the window. The sheets of rain hitting the glass of the pilot house created cascading shadows on his face. "I lost half of my men. We got hit by something really bad just east of New Orleans. Out there in the new lakes. Things just in came at night and started plucking my people as if they were sheep for slaughter. Strange flying creatures I can barely even describe. A few of my crew were screaming for help as they were being carried away into the darkness. But there was nothing we could do. Even with all our guns, we emptied 'em, mostly into the air since we couldn't see 'em. The crew was pretty much on edge after that, but I insisted we keep on going. You know what? Them flying things wasn't even the worst thing we encountered on that last trip."

"What coulda been worse than that, sir?"

Pillinger looked down on the wooden floor. "It was that damned snake. Biggest son of a bitch I ever seen. Came out of the water and it was bigger than the boat. It had a glowing hide, like having diamonds for scales. Its head was huge, like the size of a small car and it had horns growing out of it. We tried to bring it down but we didn't have much ammo left after the fight with the flying things. The giant snake just picked us off, man by man and just swallowed 'em whole. Then for some reason, it just sunk back into the dark water as if its belly was full. I learned an important lesson that day, that one must always be prepared for anything."

Tyrone didn't say anything. He just nodded.

"That goddamned snake killed my son," Pillinger said softly. "So I spent everything I had in order to repair this boat and find new backers as well as hiring more crew. This time I got me the meanest, nastiest people who are willing to do whatever it takes to find that snake and bring its head back to my investors in Tennessee. You must have noticed that the crew we have for this boat isn't much and there seems to be plenty of room for passengers, right?"

"Yes sir. I was wondering why don't you wanna ferry more people. I'm sure you could make a lot of money doin' it. You got enough space for it."

"Our displacement isn't that low right now since the ship is mostly empty," Pillinger said. "I'm gonna need the space if we're gonna find that snake, kill it and chop it up. I made sure we stocked up triple ammo loads for everyone. At this stage, you don't get a gun. You need to prove yourself as a part of this crew first. Is that clear?"

"Yes sir."

"After all that you heard, and what happened and where we're going, are you sure you still want in on this?"

Tyrone didn't bat an eye. "Yes sir."

Pillinger narrowed his eyes. He suspected something. "You must be really desperate to go this way if you are going with us, son. If you really wanted to just go back to your family you could have gone up north towards Missouri, then head east until you got to the government controlled areas in Virginia. I heard they still have a transport system for refugees so you could have gone south towards Georgia from there. Since this direct route is more dangerous, why don't you tell me the real reason you want on this boat, boy."

Tyrone looked away for a bit before meeting the captain's eyes. He wasn't even sure of himself. "Because my god told me so."

"Your god? Who's your god?"

"The Master of Breath, he goes by the name of Esaugetuh Emissee. He came to me many times in a dream. All I could feel was being on this boat and meeting a giant snake in a swamp. Then my dream ended and I would wake up."

Pillinger seemed unconvinced. "So you're headed into a pretty dangerous journey and it's all because of a dream? Hell, boy, you're either your god's shaman or you just plain crazy. Right now, I dunno what to think of you."

"I'm here, sir. I don't wanna be anywhere else. I'll see this through."

"So you were dreaming about this snake? Tell me about it," Pillinger said.

"The snake is called estakwvnayv in Muscogee, otherwise known as the horned serpent. The Choctaw called it the sinti lapitta, while others call it the Sint-Holo. It was a powerful monster and would bring men to their doom if they fought it, but sometimes it would appear to a few of the tribe's chosen.

That's all I know about it."

"So you do know something about these legends then," Pillinger said. "Maybe you might be useful after all."

Tyrone grinned. "Thank you, Captain!"

"Don't thank me yet, boy. Right now you just a deckhand, the lowest of the low. You need to gain everyone's respect. Especially Glanton's. We're going to cast off as soon as the rain subsides and the visibility gets better. You need to say goodbye to anyone?"

"Just the family I'm stayin' with, sir."

"Well go on, get to it then. Say your goodbyes and stow your gear onboard," Pillinger said. "Just remember one other rule on this ship and this one you ought to never forget."

Tyrone was about to leave the pilot house before he turned his head. "What rule is that, Captain?"

"Never enter my cabin unannounced. If I ever see you in there, I'm gonna put a bullet in your head."

8. Thunder Run

Kansas City

Steve Van Dyke used his binoculars as he stood on the roof of the now abandoned concrete building. He was looking past the freeway to his right and into the outskirts of the city beyond. It was late afternoon and he was checking if there was any sort of activity east of the Kansas River. Crouching beside him were two men with portable radios. They were part of an advanced observation team from the Soldiers of the Lord, the official designated army of the newly independent state of Christian Kansas. While the SOL radiomen were dressed in US Army combat uniforms with their universal tan and green camouflage patterns, Steve still wore his dark blue Dallas SWAT uniform. The one thing they did have in common was their badges: there was a black patch with a white cross where the American flag was supposed to be. Although Steve had been given a new pair of fatigues by the SOL logistics corps, he preferred to wear clothes from his old vocation. The fact that he was not officially a member of the Kansas Armed Forces meant that he preferred to look the part of an outsider instead. He was to serve as nothing more than a civilian observer for this mission, and so he felt that wearing military fatigues would only confuse the men even further. The other reason was pride. Steve's reputation had grown and he wanted to be distinct from the others. The men of the SOL constantly referred to him as the "SWAT general" even though he wasn't even part of the officer corps. That kind of status only made his head swell even bigger.

Straddling the border between the states of Kansas and Missouri, Kansas City was the largest metropolitan city in the region. When the State of Kansas declared its independence, the new country immediately claimed everything up to its state borders. Since Kansas City was still considered part of Missouri, the city itself remained as a part of United States territory, despite the fact that a number of its suburbs were thought to be a part of the new country. In time, the city's namesake had become an obsession with the new theocratic government in Christian Kansas, and plans were soon made to bring the city under its control. Even though this very mission might spark a violent conflict, Pastor Erik Burnley, the newly styled president of Christian Kansas, decreed that the city itself must be taken so that it could be part of the new holy country they were building to resist the pagan gods all around them.

Steve looked over at where the Interstate-670 was. He could see that the convoy of SOL vehicles were sitting idly by as they waited for the signal to advance across the freeway that spanned the river. The SOL brigade had been slowly deploying over the past few days as they prepared to storm across the bridges and into the heart of the city. The metropolitan center of Kansas City was straddling between two rivers, the Missouri and Kansas waterways, and it was roughly in the shape of a Y. The western side was part of the state of Kansas while the northern and eastern sides were officially part of Missouri. Steve figured that if the SOL forces could advance past the River Market area, they would be able to cut off the northern part of the city and that would enable them to keep the rest. *If we can get to the edge of Sugar Creek and to the east side in the south, then the city would be ours*, he thought.

The radio that the two SOL soldiers were manning started to squawk. One of the men listened using his headset before looking up at Steve. "Sir, it's General Teller on the line, he wants to talk to you."

Steve sat down and took the headset and receiver from the radioman. "Van Dyke here."

General Chuck Teller's booming voice was on the other line. "Steve, have you seen anything so far?"

Steve keyed in the receiver. "Nothing from my vantage point. Central Industrial District seems deserted. Any intel from our choppers, over?"

"Negative, they saw a few civilians running down the street, but nothing else when they made two passes over the metropolitan area, over."

Steve looked up at the clear blue skies above them. It seemed like a perfect day. It was pity that there could be bloodshed the moment they began their advance. Yet there was something gnawing at the back of his mind. Everything had been too peaceful lately. It was highly probable that the Feds in Virginia knew they would make a grab for the city, yet the place seemed pretty defenseless. Either the Feds were totally incompetent, or something was going on. "It's your call, General," he said over the receiver. "In my opinion, I just don't like it, over."

"What is it that you don't like, over?"

"The whole set up, it seems too easy," Steve said. "I think the Feds might be planning something, over."

"I've had both of my gunships doing recces for the past couple of hours and all they see are civvies, over."

"Like I said, General, it's your call, over."

"Okay, I'm taking in two companies for a thunder run, over."

Steve frowned. A thunder run meant that the lead tanks would go for a full speed dash into the center of the city before heading back towards friendly territory, in an attempt to provoke a reaction from any potential resistance. It was a bold gamble that could give them control of the city within just a few hours against a disorganized, poorly led enemy, but it could easily backfire into a military disaster if the adversary was prepared for it. "You sure about this, General?" he asked over the radio.

"We're good to go," Teller said tersely. "If we run into any resistance, Colonel Jones will proceed with the rest of the brigade using Highline Bridge, and come in from the south and also using the railway bridge beside the Six-Seventy, over."

Steve sighed. When General Teller made up his mind, there was no stopping him. Since he was just acting as an observer, there was really nothing he could do anyway. "Roger that."

Within minutes, a platoon of M1A2 Abrams battle tanks began to rumble across the Interstate-670, white crosses painted on their sides. The four tanks were going along a single line as each of their turrets were pointed in different directions. A second platoon of Abrams followed soon after. Steve heard on the radio that two more platoons of tanks started their advance over the Lewis and Clark Viaduct Bridge just below the northern edge of the city. He bit his lip in anticipation as two SOL Apache gunships flew overhead.

Lieutenant Deon Brown rubbed at the thick top of his close-cropped hair before putting his ballistic helmet back on. He was in charge of the forward observation unit hidden in an abandoned warehouse in the Garment District. Brown had been called up in the Missouri National Guard as soon as the Glooming began and he had been in active duty ever since. He had been a star linebacker in college before he tore up his ankle, so it spelled the end of his dream of joining the National Football League. Soon after he graduated he became a salesman, using his savvy communications skills to sell medical equipment while spending most of his free time helping in charity programs for the local black community. Brown also liked to play soldier and he was content to serve on weekends as part of the state National Guard. When the old gods started reappearing all over the earth, Brown kept to his Christian faith and refused to convert to the myriad pagan religions that were now sprouting up all over the place. Besides, he had more important things to worry about as he started rising up the ranks. Brown had been totally mystified that a church in Kansas had seemingly taken over the entire state almost overnight, it was as if the fanatics of that church had received some sort of diabolical aid or something. He just couldn't bring himself to believe that his fellow Christians could be as bloodthirsty as to nuke their own countrymen in Colorado, just in order to gain independence. *Surely there was a better way to go about doing that*, he thought.

"Sir," One of his radio operators said. "Remote cameras are detecting movement across the Six-Seventy Freeway and the Lewis and Clark Bridge. Estimate enemy strength is one … no, two companies of tanks, sir."

The man standing next to Brown looked like a civilian since he wasn't wearing military fatigues. He was something else entirely. The man had white hair and a pale moustache. He also was missing the lower part of his right leg so he walked using a cane. Even though he wore thick glasses, he was respected by Brown and the other soldiers as well. The man's name was Gerald Sykes and he was a former four-star general of the US Army. Sykes was very soft-spoken, but his words carried an air of experience and authority. "It's a thunder run. Just like what we did in Iraq. Let their advance units go all the way in until they pass the Financial District, then initiate Operation Blowback."

"Yes sir," Brown said as he started relaying orders to his communications team.

General Teller rode in a Stryker, just behind the second platoon's fourth tank, as they made their way into Kansas City. Unlike the tracked M1A2 Abrams tanks, the Strykers were wheeled armored vehicles capable of greater speeds with less noise, but it came at the cost of having less armor to protect the crews inside. Teller's Stryker was the M1130 Commander variant. Instead of a tank gun, it had two M2 .50 caliber machineguns mounted on remote turrets and a vast array of communications systems. Aside from the driver and the two gunners, General Teller also had three communications operators to keep him continuously updated.

One of his radio operators placed his hands over his headset as more information started pouring into the vehicle. "General, Captain Alexander reports that both companies have made it into the city limits. Second Company is now north of West Bottoms and heading towards the Garment District. Our company is now nearing the outskirts of Mulkey Square Park, sir."

General Teller adjusted the straps on his seatbelt as he took off his helmet and placed it in the empty seat beside him. "Okay, looks like there isn't any resistance. Contact Colonel Jones and tell him to get the rest of the brigade to—"

At that moment, they all heard several explosions in the distance.

"What in the hell was that?" General Teller said rhetorically as he grabbed his helmet lying on the seat beside him and hurriedly began to put it back on.

As the lead Apache gunship began a lazy turn back towards the west, it passed above the Air Line Junction at the northeastern edge of the city, as a warning alarm began sounding in the cockpit. The Apache pilot cursed as he realized that the warbling tone meant that the helicopter was being tracked using infrared lock on by an unseen enemy. Just as the Apache began to dive for cover, several man portable Stinger anti-air missiles were launched towards it. The Apache immediately began to jink and dive while activating its electronic countermeasures. While a few of the Stinger missiles veered off as they lost their lock on it, two more missiles stayed the course and continued to streak closer to the evading gunship. At the last moment, the Apache immediately deployed several dozen flares from its rear as it pulled yet another high-g turn, hoping it would evade the final two missiles. Another Stinger missile was confused by the flares and veered away, but the final missile's built in dual-detector seeker was able to distinguish between the brightly burning flares and the airframe of the Apache. Within less than a second, the last missile impacted near the rear rotor of the Apache and exploded. The helicopter soon lost control and crashed just near the northern banks of the Missouri River, less than a mile from the Charles B Wheeler Downtown Airport.

The second Apache gunship wasn't so lucky as both its pilot and gunner were completely blindsided by half a dozen Stinger missiles that came in from underneath it. Just days before, there was a glitch in the software for the electronic countermeasures on the helicopter, and it had yet to be serviced. As a consequence, the alarm failed to sound when the Stingers were locking onto it. The surface to air missiles had arrived almost at the same time and the second gunship exploded into millions of pieces as it flew over the sky above the city.

Just as the lead M1 tank of the first armored company rumbled down Interstate 670 and crossed underneath the deserted Grand Boulevard overpass, two FGM-148 Javelin anti-tank missiles flew just above it and detonated. Since the shaped charges exploded over the tank's thin top armor, the turret of M1 Abrams instantly separated from the rest of the vehicle as the body of the tank exploded in a huge column of fire. Almost immediately, the three other tanks that were right behind it suddenly stopped. As the rest of the platoon's tanks tried to turn around, several more Javelin missiles came in from above and detonated on the top of their respective turrets. In less than a minute, the entire platoon of SOL tanks was burning on the deserted freeway.

The second platoon following instantly saw what had happened. The four tanks pulled to an immediate stop and began to reverse. Their turrets began to turn and they started to fire indiscriminately in the general direction the attack had come from. Several dozen smoke canisters began popping out at the sides of their turrets as they desperately sought a means to cover their retreat. But it was too late, more than half a dozen Javelin missiles were already on their way.

While he kept his eyes on the freeway, the driver of the command Stryker apparently didn't notice what had happened and barreled right into one of the reversing Abrams tanks. Both vehicles stopped momentarily from the force of the collision as the front part of the Stryker was now tilted upward thirty degrees, and its two front wheels were now on top of the rear of one of the tanks. Just as two more Abrams tanks reversed past them, the Javelin missiles flew in and detonated the moment they impacted the tops of their vehicles.

General Teller somehow got lucky. The force of the rear end collision with the tank had pushed the Stryker's front up so the Javelin missile ended up hitting the front part of the vehicle instead of its top. Nevertheless, the Stryker's frontal armor wasn't quite as heavy as a tank's and the entire front section was instantly destroyed. What saved the SOL general were the large amounts of communication equipment located just at the front of the passenger compartment. The radios and workstations were completely destroyed. Two radio operators, along with the front cabin crew, were instantly killed.

Smoke had filled the rear compartment of the stricken command Stryker. It had the most awful smell, the stench was a combination of burning rubber, alloy, plastics and flesh. General Teller could feel his hand burning as he choked on the noxious fumes, his eyes were flash blinded and irritated by the opaque gas swirling all around him. Within a few seconds, the rear door suddenly opened and he could feel hands grabbing him, unfastening his seatbelt, then pulling him out into the welcoming sunlight of the outside.

The M2 Bradley fighting vehicle had stopped just behind the command Stryker. The enemy had apparently not been targeting it since it was beneath one of the freeway underpasses when the attack started. Its crew instantly reacted by getting in a few dozen feet behind the Stryker just as the missiles came in. Right after the Stryker was hit, four SOL soldiers came out of its rear compartment and tried to get the wrecked vehicle's rear door open, hoping to find the general. It was just the right kind of luck that saved General Teller's life. He was pulled out of the burning Stryker and placed inside the rear compartment of the Bradley before the crew reversed back underneath the overpass once more.

To the north, the second armored company of the SOL advance force also ran into a heap of trouble. Only this time, it was the second platoon following behind the lead group of tanks hit first. Within seconds, all four M1 Abrams tanks of the second platoon were burning on the Interstate 35 when they were hit by another half dozen Javelin missiles. The lead tank platoon reacted differently. Instead of reversing, the M1 tanks in the first company accelerated to full speed as each one of them drove off in a different direction. The lead tank made a sharp turn to the right and drove up the ramp that led up to the Heart of America Bridge. The second tank turned left and smashed through the concrete dividers in the middle of the freeway, before running into a small parkland situated between the turnabouts. As soon as the second tank made it underneath a copse of thick oak trees, the tank instantly stopped as its crew began to bail out. The third tank just continued to accelerate in a straight line, its driver was somehow hoping that the speed would parhaps shield them from an attack and give it enough time to get to the eastern edge of the city limits. The fourth Abrams tank made a rapid turn to its right, it rumbled through a grassy incline on the side of the freeway until it got to the adjoining street. From there, it began to move rapidly along the boulevards of the seemingly deserted city.

As the first tank began to race across the Heart of America Bridge spanning the Missouri River, its luck ran out. Just as it made it past underneath the northern bank of the river, a large barricade loomed up ahead of it. Abandoned school buses had been placed to block off any advance from the southern end of the bridge. Just as the driver cursed and began to reverse the tank, a TOW wire-guided missile emerged from somewhere near the barricade and impacted its rear engine block. The armor protected the crew, but its engine was disabled as a small fire started in the rear of the vehicle. Minutes later, four crewmembers exited the stricken tank, their hands up in the air.

For a few tense minutes, the third tank rumbled at full speed as it made it to Independence Avenue, a long stretch of road that ran across the northern part of the city's suburbs. The tank commander had been speechless ever since the attack started and the rest of the crew just kept looking at the driver. Just up ahead of them were a series of roadblocks and they could see bunkers with infantrymen, some armed with rocket launchers. The gunner had instinctively sighted the main 120mm gun, but the commander grabbed him by the shoulder and pulled him away from the optical sights. After a few minutes, the tank stopped and everyone got out as well, while the multiple infrared tracking sights of the Javelin anti-tank missiles were trained right at them.

The fourth tank wasn't so lucky. As it rumbled down southwards along the city streets, the M1 Abrams tank had inadvertently moved into the killing zone of the unit that had ambushed the first armored company. One team noticed the tank rumble past them as they stayed hidden on top of a building overlooking Holmes Street. They quickly deployed their two Javelin missile launchers, locked them onto the tank and fired. A few seconds later, the fourth tank was nothing more than a smoldering bonfire of composites, rubber, plastic, metal, and exploding ordinances.

Steve cursed loudly as he heard the reports that were coming through his radios. He knew that this was a bad idea. The Feds had planned and executed a stiff resistance in urbanized terrain, just as he sensed they would. Deep in his heart, he realized that the whole cause had gone too far. They were pushing their luck to the point where a setback was inevitable. This was more than just a defeat for the SOL and Christian Kansas, this was an absolute debacle. Now they would be on the defensive.

He turned to his radio operator. "Patch me in to Colonel Jones."

The radioman was fiddling with the switches. "Sir, his commo operator says the colonel's too busy to talk to you."

Steve raged. His face began to turn red. "Goddamn it! Tell them to pull back, right now!"

The second radioman with them looked up at Steve. He had a concerned look in his eyes. "But sir, General Teller's trapped out there."

Steve slapped the younger man's forehead so hard, his helmet flew off. "I don't care about one goddamned general, we could lose the entire brigade! Tell them to pull back right now!"

It was too late. Half of the elements of Colonel Jones's brigade were already across the bridges. Just as a company of M2 Bradleys started to cross the middle part of the railway bridge south of the Interstate 670 causeway, a series of loud explosions began. Steve and his men watched in horror as the entire span of the railway bridges collapsed into the Kansas River, taking out nearly a company of soldiers and vehicles along with it.

More explosions reverberated across the city, as numerous bridges that spanned the Missouri and Kansas rivers collapsed. Just weeks before, US Army sappers had planted C-4 explosives on almost every bridge in the city bordering the state of Kansas. As soon as the SOL moved in substantial amounts of troops into the heart of the city, these charges were detonated, thereby cutting the enemy off from any sort of organized retreat. Minutes after the bridges collapsed, Colonel Jones and the remaining men in his brigade came under attack from all sides, as US soldiers came out of their hiding places and began firing Javelin and TOW missiles at his exposed troops in the streets. As the colonel's lead armored company attempted a breakout at West Bottoms, they came under withering fire from anti-tank teams that were hidden in nearby buildings. In a span of less than ten minutes, over half of the vehicles in the brigade were either disabled or on fire.

General Teller woke up beneath the shade of the underpass, as men around him were screaming on the radios and at each other. His right hand was being bandaged by a medic and his uniform smelled of smoke. His ears were still ringing as he turned and saw the burning wreckage of his Stryker, less than a hundred feet away. A Bradley IFV was sitting idle behind him as it covered the road on the western side. They were in the sunken part of the freeway, the main streets of the city were more than twenty feet above them. They were exposed from at least three different sides and couldn't move without coming under fire. *Oh my god, we're like fish in a barrel here*, he thought.

That was when they saw brief glimpses of men hiding, up in the roofs of the nearby buildings as well as the crackling, popping sounds of gunfire. They were clearly surrounded as they could see the top of the helmets that the enemy wore. One of the soldiers got down to one knee on the ground and started firing single shots at the suspected targets using his red dot optical sight. A split second later, he instantly fell backwards as a high velocity rifle round entered just below his left eye and exited through the back of his head.

The other soldiers started hollering as two of them started to drag General Teller towards the back of the Bradley. One of the men was hit in the leg and he fell down beside the general, clutching his knee as his terrified screams reverberated along the sides of the freeway walls. Teller used his other arm and dragged himself backwards, even though he knew it was of no use. The overhang above them was too narrow and there were too many vantage points for snipers to use.

Just as he got close to the Bradley, the infantry fighting vehicle suddenly lurched forward, throwing Teller off balance as he fell to its side. The driver of the Bradley had evidently panicked and decided to leave them all behind. The Bradley rapidly accelerated out from beneath the underpass and tried to use the two burning vehicles in front of it as cover. The men who were still on the road screamed at the driver to bring the vehicle back, but the Bradley kept on going, its rear doors were still open and swinging back and forth as it raced around the burning tank. All that Teller could do was to prop himself up on one of the support columns of the underpass as the fleeing Bradley disappeared from view because of the smoke.

The other men who were with him knew the cause was lost as they placed their weapons on the concrete road and put their hands over their heads. Only the medic kept on going as he knelt by the man who was shot in the leg and began to administer first aid.

A loudspeaker started booming nearby. They knew it was directed at them. "All of you that are still on the freeway, drop your weapons and put your hands over your head! Now! If you do not comply you will be shot!"

Teller knew it was all over. Any SOL trooper that made it past the bridges and into the city would most certainly be either captured or killed by now. It was all his fault. He had been nothing more than an unassuming captain in the US Air Force until he threw his lot in with the Kansas separatists. He was a man of God himself and he felt that the Federal government just wasn't doing enough to fight against the chaos that unfolded around the world the moment the old gods came back. The newly organized SOL didn't have a whole lot of senior, active duty officers and so he got quickly bumped up through the ranks, even though he had no formal training or experience to command an armored unit of this size, much less a brigade. Now it looked like his whole unit was wiped out. Just hours ago he had several companies of main battle tanks, along with numerous support vehicles. In just a matter of minutes, it was all gone. He wanted to bury his head in shame. Teller anticipated what it would be like during a formal inquest as to how his unit was destroyed. He could imagine himself making all sorts of excuses why it wasn't his fault, but in the end it would all be lies anyway. He did screw the pooch on this one, and he would be man enough to admit it.

As the minutes passed, he could see groups of soldiers from the US Army were now above them, in prepared positions on top of the overpass. With the exception of the soldier who was wounded in the leg and the other one lying dead on the ground, the rest of them started walking back westwards with their hands in the air, were there was an onramp that would take them off of the freeway. The Federal soldiers stayed along the sides of the elevated walls, their M-4 rifles carefully pointing at them with triggers on the ready.

One of the Federal soldiers in the overpass above started shouting at him to get his hands up. General Teller stayed where he was, still sitting behind one of the support columns. He didn't want to get captured. He knew the drill. They would treat his wounds before interrogating him. Then they would lock him up and formally charge him with treason. Teller was aware that they had a file on him. After all, he was the one who played a pivotal role in hijacking that convoy full of nukes to give it over to the Christian cause.

There was really no other way out and he knew it. Teller remembered what the Romans used to do when their side lost. They would go out with some dignity. Teller was a proud man. What he couldn't live with was the shame of it all. In the end he wasn't really that religious, he just figured that siding with the Christians would give him a little insurance if he made it into the afterlife. After all, he figured that as long as he believed in the Lord, then he would go to heaven no matter what he did.

Ignoring the shouts that were telling him to put his hands up, Teller drew his Beretta M9 pistol from his side holster and placed its barrel at the back of his head. He was blinded momentarily when somebody aimed a laser sight on his face, but he kept his resolve as he thumbed the safety off before pulling the trigger.

Lieutenant Deon Brown placed his hands over his hips while his communications crews were giving each other high fives. He turned to look at Sykes. "Well, that's it then. Looks like this operation was a success. Kansas City is still in government hands and we kicked their ass too. My mean have a new nickname for the SOL, we're calling them the shit outta luck army now. I'd like to thank you for your advice and all that. You really ought to get back to active duty, sir."

Gerald Sykes just smiled. *Score one for the good guys*, he thought. It was amazing what a few missile teams could do against an armored brigade if deployed properly. "I'm much too old, Lieutenant. But since my country needed me, I'm more than willing to lend a hand when it comes to planning and coordination. Let's see what those darned rebels do now."

9. Journey to Mictlan

Teotihuacan

Tepiltzin, the newly-christened high priest of Xipe Totec, climbed out from the idling minivan and stared out into the new city. It was early morning, and the short drive from the capital had barely lasted thirty minutes. The small convoy that he traveled with would have made it sooner, but the newly-built roads leading out of Tenochtitlan were still under construction. Once the main elevated highway was fully rebuilt to bypass the constant flooding of the valley, more and more people would be coming here. For even though their imperial capital lay thirty miles to the southwest, Tepiltzin knew that the true power of their empire originated from here, and he was glad to be assigned to this post.

When the ancient Aztecs began to dominate the valley some seven hundred years ago, they discovered a lost, ruined city in the jungle to the northeast of Lake Texcoco. They named it Teotihuacan, or the birthplace of the gods. It was here the Aztecs believed the sun and the stars were created, and that all the gods once lived there. They revered its forgotten temples and fashioned their own city after it. Now that the new Aztec Empire had once again become dominant, so too did the increasing importance of this city become.

Tepiltzin stretched his legs before looking around. The minivan had been parked just at the entrance to the Avenue of the Dead. In the past few weeks, the modern buildings surrounding what was once the archaeological center were torn down. The great temples were rebuilt almost overnight and there was gleaming white plaster on the pyramid walls. Tepiltzin noticed that the white plaster of the largest temple, the Pyramid of the Sun, had already been stained with blood, but it was not to the extent like the temples they had back in Tenochtitlan. *That will be remedied soon enough*, he thought. *Once we have more sacrifices brought here and more priests trained, these white temples will become carmine and brown very quickly.*

A troop of forty eagle warriors came out of a nearby building that had once been the museum and started walking towards Tepiltzin and his small group of apprentice priests. Dressed in brightly feathered costumes, these elite soldiers of the new Aztec Army also carried assault rifles that were slung over their shoulders. Tepiltzin knew that the warriors preferred to capture their enemies rather than kill them on the battlefield, so that meant that they used their modern firearms to aim for the legs rather than the enemy torsos. Rubber and plastic bullets were now very popular amongst the warrior class, and also made it harder for their enemies to die right away.

The lead eagle warrior wore a beaked helmet that resembled the head of a giant bird. His brown face was just underneath the top part of the protruding beak. He also had feathered wings protruding from his rear harness. A holstered pistol and his macuahuitl, the Aztec wooden sword, were strapped to his side belt. The soldier moved towards them and stopped until he came face to face with the high priest. "Welcome, High Priest Tepiltzin of the House of the Obsidian Knife, I am Commander Huemac of the House of the Blood Sky. My Eagle Knight unit is in charge of the garrison and training of the city militia. The avatar of Xipe Totec has sent messages of your impending arrival and we welcome you to your new post. We are to escort you to your newly built temple."

Tepiltzin made a slight bow. "Thank you, Commander Huemac. It has been a great honor to be assigned as the new high priest of this city. Have the children been assembled?"

Huemac nodded. "Yes, all the boys and the young warriors from the House of the Youth have been mustered and are in assembly. They are currently waiting for your speech at the Plaza of the Moon."

"Very well," Tepiltzin said. "Can my apprentices go ahead of us so that they may prepare the altar near the rack of skulls?"

Huemac pivoted slightly as he gestured towards the avenue ahead of them. "Of course, I shall send one squad of my Eagle Knights as a ceremonial advance guard."

Tepiltzin snapped his fingers. Almost immediately, his apprentice priests took out their gear from the back of the minivans and started to make their way down the stone avenue. Two of the youngest priests in training grabbed a sacrifice from the back seat of the van and started to drag him along with them. The prisoner was another American whom they had taken when the city of Dallas was sacked. The bound and gagged man wore a policeman's uniform, he struggled for bit, but one of the apprentices hit the back of his head with a wooden club that momentarily stunned him. Now that the prisoner was unable to resist, the apprentices half carried him down the street.

Now that the formalities were over until the ceremony began, Tepiltzin smiled as he stepped forward and shook Huemac's hand. "I wanted to ask you a favor, Commander. You see, I have a brother and he was assigned here for training and—"

Huemac let out a short laugh. "Do not worry. I know of your brother. He is Yaotl and he is doing quite well. He was able to participate in his first battle when we advanced on to Dallas. That young man acquitted himself quite nicely. He was able to capture a cop, I believe."

Tepiltzin grinned as he held his palms open to the darkening sky above. "Ah, praise Xipe Totec! Praise Huitzilopochtli for his safe return! The gods are truly looking after my family!"

"Yes, your brother has been reassigned here," Huemac said. "He will now be one of the combat instructors in the House of the Youth. He has earned his increase in rank."

"Excellent. May I make a request for a private meeting with him after the ceremony?"

"Of course, we are in between battle, and the warrior castes are here to serve the high priests, after all."

"Wonderful. Then let us proceed with the ceremony. The day is still young and we have much to do."

The youth of the city were dutifully assembled in the Plaza of the Moon. Every boy over the age of twelve had been silently standing in orderly ranks as they awaited the new high priest. Many of them were thankful that the heat of the morning sun was now obscured by the ever darkening clouds in the sky. On the opposite side of them were the ranks of the Aztec warriors, these men were in elaborate animal skins and fully armed as if they were ready to go on parade. Many of the children would continuously stare in awe at the soldiers, as the older boys would keep their assigned squads in line using their batons.

At the center of the plaza was a slightly elevated stone platform. In the middle of the stage was a small altar made of polished green obsidian. A small group of priests stood just behind it. Within minutes, Tepiltzin's entourage of priestly apprentices made their way to the altar and placed a small wooden chest behind it. Trumpets and drums began to sound as the new high priest walked slowly towards the center of the plaza. The apprentice priests quickly opened the chest and began to prepare the sacrificial tools while the prisoner was held down, just near the side of the stage.

It was a slow walk that took nearly half an hour, but Tepiltzin knew that all Aztecs must adopt an elegant, leisurely pose while walking down the street during a ritual. Commander Huemac and his eagle warriors followed him closely as they stayed in a tight formation. By the time he had reached the foot of the stage, the music became even louder, until it finally ended in a cacophony of trumpet blasts.

Tepiltzin walked up the stage, then turned around so he could face the audience gathered in front of him. "Welcome, people of the sun. Young citizens of the new Aztec Empire, and our brave warriors. I have come here as your new high priest for a momentous occasion. This ceremony will mark the beginning of the newly built temples of the Triple Alliance. In order to understand why we are here in this sacred city, and why we celebrate our victories with ritual sacrifices, we must first go back to the beginning of time.

I shall first explain to you the events that happened in the Popol Vuh, the Book of the People. In order for you all to understand the purpose of our new Aztec society, you must first understand how the world was brought into being."

He cleared his throat before continuing. "In the beginning there was only darkness. Then came forth the dual god Ometecuhtli, the primordial one, it was he who split into two gods, one man and one woman. It was from these two separate beings of the One that gave birth to the four Tezcatlipoca who would create our world. Like the four points of the compass, each one of these new gods would take their turn to create a new world, a new sun. The first Tezcatlipoca was the god of the smoking mirror. He kept the name of Tezcatlipoca, unlike the other three that had their own, unique names. The second son was Xipe Totec, our lord of the Flayed One, the Night Drinker. The third son was Huitzilopochtli, the hummingbird of the south, the god of war and patron of our mighty warriors. The fourth son was Quetzalcoatl, the feathered serpent, he of wisdom and magic. As with all brothers, they fought for control of the world. The four of them created fire, then men, then the underworld. After that they created the heavens and the waters."

Tepiltzin paused for bit before continuing. He had noticed that the priest that he was supposed to replace wasn't part of the assembled group at the rear of the stone platform. It was a slight concern, but he needed to finish his teachings first. "Then came the cycle of the five suns. It was of this time that the four gods attempted to create a new world, only to have each one end in destruction. The first sun was presided over by Tezcatlipoca. This was a time when giants walked the world. Quetzalcoatl was jealous, and he overthrew Tezcatlipoca and sent jaguars to consume the planet, thereby destroying it. The second sun was now ruled by Quetzalcoatl but Tezcatlipoca gained his revenge by turning people into monkeys and destroying the second world with hurricanes and wind. The third sun was then governed by Tlaloc, the god of rain. But Tezcatlipoca, ever the trickster, seduced his wife and stole her away. The rain god was furious, and he first stopped all the rains from falling on the ground, then he cast sheets of fire at the world until there was nothing left but ashes. Then came the fourth sun, which was ruled by the water goddess Chalchiuhtlicue. Yet that world was also destroyed when the jealous Tezcatlipoca made the goddess cry from his lies. When he had told her that the love of her people for her was false, she became saddened. Her tears flooded the world and the surviving humans were turned into fish. Finally came the fifth sun, when the minor god Nanahuatzin sacrificed his body to become the new sun. The other gods were moved to pity by his selflessness and they sacrificed their own blood in order to make him move around the earth, so as not to burn it."

As he paused once more, he noticed that the high priest that he was to replace was in fact standing high up above them. The other man was at the top of the Pyramid of the Moon, directly behind them. Tepiltzin sensed that he would have to deal with him later. In the meantime he had to continue his story. "So it came to be that our forefathers, the ancient Aztecs of the First Empire, were living under that fifth sun, before Quetzalcoatl returned under the guise of a Spanish Conquistador and destroyed that world. Now that the gods have returned, their words to us now tell of a new purpose. Huitzilopochtli and Xipe Totec are now working together to bring about a sixth sun, this will replace our now dying world with a new one, reserved for the new Azteca as their chosen people. To achieve this, the two creator gods have entered into a truce with Tlaloc and with his mutual consent, we have defeated Tezcatlipoca's faction and sacrificed his followers, and now that god's influence is no more."

Tepiltzin raised his hands and held them up to the sky. "Now we make sacrifices for a different purpose. Now we offer our most valuable essence, the blood of our people, and that of our vanquished enemies, as gifts to the new alliance of Xipe Totec, Huitzilopochtli and Tlaloc. May these three gods protect us in battle, may these three gods defeat our enemies, and may these three gods protect us against the return of Quetzalcoatl and Tezcatlipoca. May those two exiled lords never return, for as long as we give our blood to the Triple Alliance, so shall they watch over us and defend us against the other gods of the world. With this new pact of creation, the new priests who speak directly to the gods will now prove their divine powers."

With those words, four apprentice priests immediately grabbed hold of the prisoner and carried him to the altar. They quickly stripped him of his uniform and held him down as his back lay on top of the polished stone slab. The storm clouds above coalesced into a dark wall that covered the sky. Lightning began to strike near them but not a single person was hit by it.

Tepiltzin turned around and took off his feather cloak, letting it drop onto the base of the stage. One of his assistants handed him a flint knife, butt first. As he moved over to where the sacrifice was lying, another apprentice priest used a silken cord to pull down the victim's throat. The American was screaming, but the roaring thunder drowned out his desperate pleas for mercy. Tepiltzin worked quickly as he ripped open the skin just underneath the victim's ribcage before working the knife through the inner chest membranes and slicing around the heart. Within less than ten seconds, he held up the still beating heart above his head so that everyone could see it.

Almost immediately, a hole opened up horizontally in the center of the Avenue of the Dead. It looked like a rip in space. Everyone turned and some of the younger children actually fainted. The older youths and the warriors had seen this before. In fact, it was the third time it had happened this week that it was now becoming a common occurrence. They could not see what lay on the other side of the hole, it was nothing but an inky blackness that stretched up to twenty feet high, it was as if someone had placed a black hole in the middle of the street and suspended it vertically in the air with invisible hands.

Soon enough, there were things that started to come out from the hole. Tepiltzin knew it was a portal from Mictlan, the Aztec underworld. What came out looked like ordinary Aztec warriors. They were still wearing the bloody costumes that they had died in their last battle. A few of them were missing arms and legs and so they just hopped or crawled out of the opening. One Aztec warrior came through carrying his head in his arms. There must have been tens of thousands of them.

Tepiltzin let go of the still beating heart. The pulsating organ began to float in the sky and it started to drift towards the portal. As the bleeding heart passed over the resurrected Aztec warriors below, its crimson drops seemed to heal their wounds as shattered bones become whole, separated limbs were magically reattached and missing ones grown back. By the time the floating heart was swallowed up by the portal, there were now a fresh batch of close to thirty thousand Aztec warriors who had previously died in the past few months, now back in the land of the living once more. Soldiers from the Eagle Knights recognized some of their fallen comrades as they walked over and embraced.

"See the power of our gods!" Tepiltzin roared from the top of his lungs. "Witness their devotion to our people! For even Huitzilopochtli goes forth to the underworld just to bring back his fallen children, so that they can fight for him once more! Our new empire cannot fail, we will not fail! For our armies are now endless, our warriors will return from the land of the dead to continue the fight until all our enemies have been vanquished! Nothing will stop the sixth sun from beginning!"

Later that afternoon, Tepiltzin had the previous high priest summoned to the temple. The former high priest Coaxoch came into the main hall wearing a suit of dried human skin. The husk was beginning to flake off, but it was still thick enough, Tepiltzin couldn't recognize the man beneath it. The new high priest was tempted to order Coaxoch to strip away his skin suit, but there had been strict orders from Xipe Totec's avatar that the suit must either be voluntarily removed by its wearer or just be allowed to flake away naturally.

"I greet you, High Priest Tepiltzin. Welcome to Teotihuacan," Coaxoch said.

Tepiltzin was sitting on a stone chair. He could feel the palpable hostility between them. He figured it must be due to jealousy. "Why did you not attend the morning sacrifice?"

"I had other duties to perform and I figured you would not need my help," Coaxoch said nonchalantly.

"I am disappointed in you," Tepiltzin said tersely. "I had expected a better display of respect coming from a high priest whose position I was to take. Though I understand your feelings. If you disagreed with the avatar's decision to be replaced, then why did you not speak with him about it?"

"That is a matter I shall be taking up with him when I travel back to

Tenochtitlan now that my position here is finished," Coaxoch said before making a slight bow. "My apologies if you thought my absence in your ritual today was a sign of disrespect."

Tepiltzin nodded. "Very well, you may go. Feel free to spend the night here before you go back to our glorious capital."

Coaxoch already had his back turned and was walking away when he answered. "I have no intentions of staying in a city in which I am no longer a high priest of." With those words, he had already left the room as he moved into the passageway beyond.

Tepiltzin said nothing. His assistants silently looked at each other with quizzical glances as they stood nearby.

The house of the high priest was once the palace of Quetzalcoatl. With the new alliance between the three other gods, all temples and houses to either the feathered serpent or the god of the smoking mirror were converted to other things, so as to suppress any memory of them. Since Teotihuacan had just been newly rebuilt, the façade of these ornate buildings looked very distinct with their white plastered walls. The carved representations of Quetzalcoatl had been removed and replaced by the stone idols of Xipe Totec.

Tepiltzin really didn't have time to admire his personal quarters, even though the newly painted walls were elaborately designed with myriad frescoes of Aztec daily life. He simply had too many rituals to do for the rest of the evening despite having already been exhausted from the ceremony that afternoon. He had already given orders to his assistants to summon his brother so they could have a private chat just for a few minutes, for that was the only time he had for his family. The rituals of appeasing the gods and the affairs of running a temple would take up the rest of his time for the next few weeks, at least. Unlike the ancient Aztec Empire of centuries ago, there was no emperor to rule over them all. In this new version, all the power was centered on the avatars and high priests of the Triple Alliance, it was through them that the gods spoke and ruled over all their lives. Even though there was now an Aztec aristocracy that oversaw the warrior castes, they were still subservient to the avatars of Huitzilopochtli, Xipe Totec, and Tlaloc. The new Aztec Empire was a literal theocracy.

Since he felt that he needed to enact the ritual before his brother came to see him, Tepiltzin took off his feathered cloak and placed it near his cot. Then he slid the loincloth down to his ankles and knelt in front of the small stone altar of Xipe Totec. Even though he was a high priest, it was still a sacred duty for him to sacrifice his own blood in order to appease his god. Since there was a mat of thorns he had placed in front of the altar, his knees started to bleed. When he had first enacted his personal bloodletting, the pain was so intense, he almost screamed in agony during the first dozen or so times when he tried it. Ever since he became high priest, he could feel the power of Xipe Totec coursing through his body and that gave him a much higher tolerance for pain. The magical incense that he had thrown over the burning brazier illuminating his chambers also had an anesthetic effect, since it numbed the nerves in his limbs as he inhaled its sharp, flowery fumes.

Tepiltzin then took a carved stingray barb lying on top of the altar. Using his thumb and forefinger, he bent down and pierced his left scrotum while using his other hand to place a small ivory bowl in between his knees. The trickle of blood soon cascaded down his upper leg as he scraped every drop of the thick, crimson liquid using the bowl. The pain was intense, but he gritted his teeth and concentrated until he had a fair amount of blood on the bowl. After placing the bowl and needle back on the altar, he grabbed a handful of green leaves from a wooden bucket beside the shrine, stuffed them into his mouth and began to chew. The plants were bitter, but they took the edge of the pain away. He spat out the pulp in his hand and rubbed it on his bleeding wound. As the pain began to subside, he stood up and pulled the loincloth back over his genitals, then rubbed more of the plant pulp on his skinned knees. Tepiltzin then crumpled some parchment inscribed with the symbol of the Flayed One and placed it on the ivory bowl. As he watched the crumpled paper absorb the blood on the bowl, he took a burning candle from a nearby side table and stuck its burning end at the bloody parchment. Almost immediately, the blood stained vellum disappeared in a puff of smoke.

"O great Xipe Totec," Tepiltzin chanted. "I humbly offer you this small sacrifice. May my blood mingle with yours. May my sacrifice satiate your need. May my sacrifice honor thy name. May my sacrifice strengthen thee. Amen."

Just as he finished his chant, the wooden door to the outside corridor opened and his brother stepped inside. Yaotl was dressed in an elaborate feathered harness. His red loincloth had strips of metal on it. The wrapped headband over his forehead had jaguar and eagle designs. Tepiltzin grinned as he walked up to his younger brother and embraced him for a whole minute.

The high priest continued to smile as he stood back and admired his brother's uniform. "You look like a proper warrior, Jorge. Thank you for taking the time to see me."

Yaotl giggled. "I should be the one to thank you for allowing me a break from my training. It has been hard, but just seeing you, even for a short time, makes it all worthwhile."

Tepiltzin gestured to a wooden table and chairs at the far end of the room. "Let's sit down and talk for a bit, it's been a long time since I've seen you, Jorge."

Yaotl followed his brother over to the table and sat down on the opposite chair. "I'm surprised you still call me by my old Spanish name. I thought we all have to go by our Nahuatl names now."

Tepiltzin grinned as he poured some wine from a glass bottle into a wooden cup and handed it to his brother. "We are alone and I have just finished enacting my bloodletting ritual. That ought to alleviate any sort of rule break. So I figured a little talk about the old times would be good for both of us. Have you been back to the farm to see our mother lately?"

Yaotl shook his head. "No, I haven't. I've been busy all this time. As soon as I finished my training in the House of the Youth in Tenochtitlan, I was immediately assigned to a training unit, just days before we attacked Dallas."

"I prayed to the gods to see you weren't hurt," Tepiltzin said. "Thank goodness you came out of that battle in one piece."

Yaotl laughed. "There is no need to pray for my safety, Ramon. Our gods always protects us in battle. In fact, it doesn't even matter if I die. Since our war god Huitzilopochtli always brings the dead warriors back from the underworld, death has become meaningless in our empire. I shall gladly give up my life in our wars."

Tepiltzin frowned. “Don’t say such things. You must promise me you will look after yourself. Even though our sacrificial rituals can bring you back from the dead, I would prefer you not to have to go through it.”

Yaotl was confused. “Why don’t you want me to die? What’s wrong with coming back from the lands of the dead to do battle once more?”

“Have you not spoken to the warriors who’ve returned from Mictlan?”

“Yes,” Yaotl said. “One of my batchmates was killed in Dallas and he returned from the underworld just a few days ago.”

“And? Was he still the same person after he returned?”

Yaotl rubbed his smooth chin as he thought about it for a moment. “Actually, now that you asked me that question, it does seem he is somewhat different. His name was Nelli and he was particularly good at sketching and painting. After he returned, all he could do was stare at the blank canvas and he couldn’t even pick up his paintbrush anymore. We all wondered about it. When we asked him, he just said that he couldn’t think about what to draw or paint anymore. We all thought that maybe it was just because he was no longer interested in it.”

“That is what I mean,” Tepiltzin said. “I’ve noticed that the warriors who have been killed and returned a number of times have already forgotten about their wives, their family and friends. It is as if every time they come back from Mictlan, the underworld takes a piece of their life essence and memory. I shudder at the thought of those that have been killed over a dozen times. I have a feeling that if you die enough times and come back, your body will be nothing but an empty shell. It is as if the gods exact a price every time you return from the dead. The constant resurrection strips away one’s very soul.”

Yaotl had a quizzical look on his face. “Then why has this not been discussed amongst our caste then? Surely we should make this part of our training so that less of our warriors would be so foolish enough as to charge in the face of enemy fire?”

His older brother’s response was in a half-whisper. “This is not a subject that is openly discussed. Some of the higher ranking nobles have talked about it, but we have all agreed to keep this bit of knowledge from the rank and file. We must keep up the faith that our warriors are invincible because they always return from the dead.”

Yaotl hissed. This was sobering news for him. "Can I at least tell my batchmates about it? I heard that we are assembling new raiding parties to cross the American lines to capture more sacrifices. If they are more careful, then we can incur less casualties."

Tepiltzin shook his head. "No, this knowledge cannot leave this room."

"But why, Ramon?"

Tepiltzin let out a deep breath. "I am telling you of this because you are my brother and I want you to be careful. We have won many great victories but I cannot afford to lose you. You must also not play in any official tournaments of ullamaliztli. I heard that you are a good player in it, but I must order you to stop playing."

Yaotl almost stood up in shock. "What? But it's just a ballgame! It's a game that our ancestors have played for thousands of years. All we do is hit a rubber ball with our hips, elbows and head! What is so wrong about that?"

"Yes, it is just a game. Yet what happens to the team when they win an official tournament again?"

"They are sacrificed. So what?"

Tepiltzin's hands shook with rage and frustration. "Yes they are sacrificed! Can't you see? I do not want you to end up winning an official match and getting sacrificed for it! Unlike warriors who die in battle, we do not bring back the ones who are sacrificed. You must promise me to stop playing in it."

Yaotl crossed his arms. "But being sacrificed is a great honor though. The winners are always remembered in that game."

Tepiltzin closed his eyes and grimaced. "Jorge…"

His younger brother started laughing. "You are really strange, Ramon. First you tell me not to get killed in battle because I'll lose a part of my soul when I return, now you don't want me to play a game of ullamaliztli! You're supposed to be a high priest that does sacrifices all the time! It doesn't make any sense to me. You're supposed to encourage sacrifice, not discourage people against it."

Tepiltzin grabbed Yaotl's hand as it lay on the table. He stared into his brother's eyes. "Jorge, I beg you. You are my one and only brother and I love you. I have always loved you since you were a child, and I will break if I ever lose you. Promise me. Promise that you do as I say!"

Yaotl was surprised at his brother's intensity. Then he smiled. "Alright, Ramon. I will do this for you. I will be careful in battle and I will stop playing ullamaliztli. Just for you."

Tepiltzin leaned back and sighed. It was as if a great weight was lifted from his chest. "Thank you, Jorge. I know you are giving up a lot but this means so much to me. I'm sure it will mean so much to Mama as well."

Yaotl took a sip of wine. "You are such a bearer of bad news to me. I had a plan to charge at the enemy ranks at the next battle, but now I must stalk like a jaguar to take my captives and gain an increase in rank. Do you know that one of my batchmates charged a barricade in Dallas and he was able to capture four of the enemy without even being wounded? They made him an Eagle Knight the very next day. I was so jealous of him because I have been dreaming of becoming an Eagle Knight too. They are the best in our army, the power of Huitzilopochtli enables them to fly and attack from above like a real eagle. Have you ever seen them personally in battle? They are a glorious sight to see. They are led by Commander Huemac, the greatest warrior in the empire- he's never been killed in battle and he's captured so many of the enemy, he's lost count. I hope to be like him one day."

Tepiltzin couldn't help but smile. His brother's eagerness was infectious. "Just take it slow and careful, you'll get there. The Jaguar Knights are better in my opinion. The eagle warriors may get all the glory but the true elites are the jaguars."

"Yes, yes, they are very good at what they do as well," Yaotl said. "Though they tend to be too slow and careful when they capture. The Jaguar Knights tend to change shape and attack when the enemy isn't looking. I prefer the way of the eagles- it's far more honorable."

"The Eagle Knights take a lot of casualties because of the way they fight, the jaguars rarely take losses. Be a jaguar. It's better."

Yaotl snorted. "That's easy for you to say. Right now, I have only notched one captive taken. It's gotten me a promotion into the blooded ranks of the warrior caste, but here I am stuck as an instructor for children! I will do as you ask, but you must use your influence as a high priest to get me reassigned."

Tepiltzin's eyebrows shot up. "Reassigned? Back to the front lines?"

"Yes. I need to get more captives so I can increase in rank and qualify for the jaguars or eagles. I can't do it as an instructor at the House of the Youth."

"You don't want to stay here close to me? You're safe here and under my protection. I pretty much run this city now."

Yaotl looked out the window and stared at the clear evening sky. "I appreciate all that you've done for me. But I need to strike out on my own. I cannot keep living beneath your shadow all the time."

Tepiltzin looked down at the crumbs on the table. His younger brother was right. "Very well, I shall see to it and have you reassigned. I know Huemac and I'll see what I can do."

"Thank you, Ramon! Huemac is the best, it's my dream to serve under him," Yaotl said enthusiastically before he saw his brother's worried demeanor. "Is there something else that's bothering you?"

Tepiltzin nodded. "It's not really something I should be telling you."

"You're going to tell me anyway. I know you and I know that look."

Tepiltzin drummed his fingers on the table. "The high priest that I replaced here, Coaxoch."

"What about him?"

"I think he is trouble. He did not participate in the ceremony today. That is a gesture of disrespect to me since he should have done a ritual handing over after the sacrifice was made. He dishonored me. Instead, he just stayed at the altar in the Pyramid of the Moon. Our avatar has forbade us priests to harm each other, but I must find a way to bring him under my heel."

"I see what you mean. I have met him a few times and I think I know why he doesn't like our family."

Tepiltzin was shocked. "What? He knows our family? Who is he?"

"His original Spanish name was Marcelino Morales. He was the son of Francisco Morales. Remember him?"

"Old man Morales? He was just a gardener in our estate as I remember."

"Yes."

Tepiltzin's eyes narrowed. "I see. So it's not just professional jealousy. He blames our family for what happened to his father then. Alright, that is good to know. I just can't imagine how our great uncle could have chosen him as high priest after you told me this."

"You know our uncle. I don't think he even remembers all the people who once worked for us. Maybe you should ask him to remove that troublesome priest."

Tepiltzin shook his head. "He won't do it. He never dismisses anyone that he makes a priest. Our uncle is the avatar of Xipe Totec. I don't even think he's fully human anymore since the Flayed One speaks directly through him. And that bothers me."

"What bothers you?"

Tepiltzin looked away. "That it may not have been our uncle who made Coaxoch high priest. Maybe it was Xipe Totec who made the decision himself."

10. The Stranger Cometh

Kansas

It was mid-afternoon when the silver bus number 160 drove into downtown Wichita. Tara Weiss was sitting by herself near the back row. In contrast to the constant rains of the South, the weather here was bright and sunny. Tara was surprised there was a free transportation service operating throughout the city. They had observed a number of buses going to and fro from designated stops that started from the outskirts. All one had to do was to sit in the bus stop and wait. A shuttle would drive by every few hours and she hopped aboard the one that said DOWNTOWN WICHITA on its front. Tara tried giving a few dollars to the driver but he just waved her off the moment she stepped on board. Since the vehicle was half-empty, Tara was pretty much by herself throughout the whole journey.

On their way towards the center of the city, the bus made a fuel stop at a local gas station. That was when she got a little bit scared, seeing armed SOL troopers and military vehicles standing by outside. The few passengers that had gone out of the bus were approached by the soldiers and it looked like they were being asked some questions. Tara had thought about getting down onto the concrete pavement to stretch her legs, but then decided that she didn't want the extra hassle of being interrogated, so she just stayed put. One soldier looked up at the vehicle windows and stared at her. Tara just made a faint smile and looked away. After about half an hour, the driver got back on the bus and they were off again.

Much of the city seemed quiet, almost peaceful. It was as if the Glooming had never touched this part of the country. Other than the occasional military patrols and the small groups of soldiers on every other street, Tara felt that this might just be the safest place in the entire world. Then she noticed a number of people being rounded up. The bus had stopped on an intersection and that was when she witnessed a heavily armed police unit bust down what looked like the front doors of a warehouse. As traffic was halted by a convoy of empty school buses that parked near the building, Tara could hear screams coming from the inside and the sounds of fighting. A few minutes later, a number of people were led out in handcuffs and were pushed into the waiting school buses. Once the three vehicles were filled, they were then escorted by a small convoy of Humvees and normal traffic was resumed. Since there weren't a lot of cars on the streets, the shuttle was able to make up the time as it drove to the next bus stop and picked up more passengers.

Just as they halted at the third stop, a large group of soldiers began to board the vehicle. That was when Tara decided to get off. She got up from her seat and made her way to the front. She walked past a number of military types that were busy chatting with each other as they carried around their olive green duffel bags. Tara figured that they were just using the bus to go someplace but being around so many of them made her nervous. The driver didn't seem to notice her as she got off while a number of soldiers were still getting on board.

As the bus drove away, Tara started walking down the street while she looked around. Even though there was a façade of normality, she could see that many businesses in the area had been boarded up and shuttered. A lot of billboards and advertising posters had been torn up and replaced with banners for the Rock of God Church. She remembered listening to the pastor's radio broadcast as she travelled the southwest with a man named Larry. Even though it had happened almost a year ago, to her it seemed like a distant memory. Larry was dead, murdered by another man who soon died at the hands of mythical creatures. Not long after that, she met a brujo, who then instructed her on how to conquer her fears and self-doubt. Then she learned how to travel across the other worlds with the help of the trickster god.

The streets were mostly deserted. A few small groups of people would sometimes gather at the intersections before they were broken up by a passing police car. As she kept on walking, Tara could sense a palpable fear in the air. The people who she passed would look at her nervously before going about their business. Nobody seemed to be smiling. It was as if they were all waiting for something terrible to happen. A few clothing and convenience stores were open, and she noticed they were manned mostly by older folks. Most of the younger ones were either in the military or were somewhere else that she didn't know about. The whole city seemed to be one big lie, and yet everybody believed in it.

A loud cawing coming from across the street momentarily surprised her. As Tara turned, she noticed a raven perched on top of a nearby diner. Although it seemed that every one of those black birds all looked alike, she sensed that it was the trickster and it was leading her onto something. As per the plan, it was keeping her under watch, just in case she got into trouble. Thrusting her hands into the side pockets of her denim jacket, Tara waited until two cars drove by before crossing the now empty street. She looked up at the black bird for a brief moment before pushing the restaurant doors open.

It was a typical fifties-style diner. Streamlined white plastic furniture and stainless steel molded in Art Deco style. Imitation red leather padding on the seats and stools. Checkered marble flooring. Glass walls so that the whole place could be seen from the outside, like an aquarium. An antique vinyl jukebox sat unplugged near the door. The place was nearly empty, except for an old couple at the far side of the restaurant. She saw a heavyset cook with a crewcut come in and out through the port-holed double doors that evidently led to the kitchen.

A middle aged woman in waitress attire approached her with a smile. She had blond curls and wore a bright blue dress with a white collar. There was a small white cap on her head and a black cross hung on the base of her neck. A white apron was tied neatly in front of her uniform, just like in the movies. She was carrying a large brown tray with a pot of coffee on it. "Good afternoon. Feel free to sit wherever you want, we've got plenty of room. I'll be right with you in a minute."

"Thanks," Tara said as she smiled back. She thought about picking a booth to sit in, but then figured it would be less of a big deal since she was by herself. In the end, she just sat on a stool by the counter instead. There was a metal stand with a half dozen menus on it so she just picked one out and started to read it.

A few minutes later, the smiling waitress walked up to her from behind the counter. "What can I get for you today?"

Tara squinted her eyes as she pored over the menu. "Um, how about a milkshake? A strawberry flavored one, please."

The waitress bit her lip. There were a lot of wrinkles at the edges of her mouth and her makeup looked old and worn. "I'm sorry, hon. All I can get for you is a vanilla milkshake. We haven't been able to update our menu since you know when."

Tara kept smiling as she nodded. "Okay, a vanilla milkshake is fine by me."

"Coming right up, do you want anything else?"

Tara shook her head slightly as she put the menu back with the others. "Not right now, thanks."

"Okay, be back in a jiffy."

As the waitress walked back into the kitchen, Tara looked around again. The old couple at the far end seemed to be minding their own business. As she tried to look over to where the kitchen was, she noticed that the cook was staring at her through the stainless steel shelves that separated the cooking area and the counter. Trying to give herself something to do, Tara picked up the menu once more and pretended to read it, hoping that the man would stop looking at her. She didn't like being stared at and it was making her self-conscious.

After a few minutes, the waitress came back with a tall milkshake and set it on the counter in front of her. "Here you go, enjoy."

Tara thanked her before picking up the long spoon set on the counter. She scooped up the cherry sitting on a bed of whipped cream and popped it into her mouth. Although the fruit obviously came from a can, Tara couldn't help but close her eyes as she chewed on it, her taste buds enjoying the tart, sweetened juices of the cherry. The plastic straw that came with the shake looked like it was reused, but she didn't care at this point as she started to slurp the thick contents down her parched throat. It wasn't the best milkshake that she had ever tasted, but it had been a long time since she had a treat like this and she sipped at it slowly, enjoying every bit of the creamy, sweet goodness that, for a brief moment, took away her worries and problems. Even though the ice cream tasted like it came from a powdered mix and the whipped cream smelled funny, she still enjoyed the heck out of it. The next few minutes were a complete ecstasy for her as she slurped it all down to the bottom of the parfait glass.

When she had finished, the smiling waitress came back. "That was good, huh? Can I get you anything else? A cheeseburger maybe?"

Tara was tempted, but her concern for her brother was at the forefront again. "I'm good, thanks. How much for the milkshake?"

"That'll be ten dollars. I know it's expensive, but that's pretty much the way things are right now."

Tara suppressed her surprise as she started rummaging through her pockets. It was a good thing she didn't order anything else, or she might have trouble paying this bill. She took out two crumpled five dollar bills and placed them on the counter. "Okay, here you go."

The waitress frowned as she held up the old bills. "These are Fed dollar bills, you don't have any of the newly issued Kansas dollar bills?"

Tara's heart sank. A few days ago, both she and Patrick Gyle rummaged through several abandoned houses to find some expense money. She had thought they hit the jackpot when Gyle tore open a wall safe in an abandoned office that still contained some wads of cash. Now it looked like it was all but useless. "Oh, I'm sorry. I'm kinda new here."

The waitress was becoming suspicious. "Didn't you go through the processing center? When you register as a citizen of Christian Kansas, they give you an identity card and exchange all the old dollar bills into the new currency. Can I see your ID?"

"I don't have one yet, sorry."

The waitress narrowed her eyes. "Where are your parents?"

Tara shifted uneasily in her stool. She was never a good liar. Her friends and father always figured it out when she did. "They're uh, over at the processing center right now. They just gave me ah, some money and told me to go get something to eat. Then they told me to come back to them right after. I'm sorry, I didn't know about the new dollar bills."

The burly cook came out from the kitchen and stood beside the waitress. He had a white collared t-shirt and a long cooking apron that covered his torso. "Something wrong, Laurie?"

"Nah," the waitress said. "This girl just came in to pay with the old dollar bills. The deadline to turn in these bills was supposed to be last week, but I figure Bob over at the bank ought to still accept this."

The cook stared deeply into Tara's eyes. "You new here, honey?"

Tara blinked. Her palms started to get sweaty. "I-I, yes. My parents are over at the processing center and they're waiting for me. Is it okay to pay you with those bills?"

The waitress smiled again and nodded. "It's okay, hon. I think we can accept this. Which processing center is your parents at?"

Tara's throat was pretty tight. She didn't know the answer to that one. "Um, the big one. I forgot what it was called."

The cook's eyebrows began to furrow. "There's two of them. The Century Convention Hall and the Intrust Arena. Which one is your parents at?"

Tara nodded. Thank goodness they gave her a choice so she could make a guess. "Ah, the first one, the Century Hall. I need to head over there right now."

"Okay, hon," the waitress said. "You can head over to the bus stop at the end of this street and take the number eleven bus. That should get you over there in a few minutes."

Tara grinned as she got out of the stool and headed for the doors. "Thanks, I hope to see you again."

"You too hon, bye," the waitress said to her just as she went through the doors.

Tara walked briskly as she moved towards the opposite direction from where they told her to go. That didn't go well. Gyle told her to keep a low profile and she just screwed up. She didn't look back even though she knew they were staring at her from the glass walls of the diner. What she could do was maybe get some distance before boarding another bus so that she could get lost in another part of the city. Just as she rounded an intersection, Tara heard a siren to her right. She stopped in mid stride and slowly turned.

It was a police car sitting idly by the road. Two uniformed men were sitting in the front and stared at her through the windshield. The police officer on the driver's side gestured at her to come closer. Tara swallowed back the rising bile on her throat and moved towards him.

"Hi there," the officer closest to her said. "Can I see your ID?"

Tara shrugged. "I'm sorry, officer. I don't have one. My parents are still being processed at the Century place."

The officer nodded and looked at her with dead serious eyes. "Uh huh, no one is allowed to wander these streets without proper, state-issued identification. I need you to come with us. We'll take you over to the processing center."

Tara looked away for bit before looking back at them again. "Look, I can go there by myself. I'm sure there are others you can help."

The other officer got out of the front seat. "I'm afraid that wasn't a request, girl."

Tara sighed. This was going to take longer than she thought.

The drive to the processing center near the banks of the Little Arkansas River took only a few minutes. The two policemen escorted Tara until she was past the entrance and handed her over to Immigration Security. A uniformed security guard then ushered her into the main processing hall. The Century II Performing Arts Center once held concerts for theatres and orchestras, but ever since the State of Kansas had declared its independence, its exhibition and expo halls were laid out with cots for the growing number of people who needed to be sorted through. A number of folding tables were set up in the center of the convention hall and were manned by immigration officers to process the tens of thousands of refugees from the other states. It was in these centers that they would be weeded out and only the most religious of Christians that were loyal to the ROG church would be eligible for citizenship.

Tara was sitting down on a metal folding chair. The security guard that met her in the building lobby was hovering by her side. Sitting across from her and writing on a clipboard was a processing officer.

The processing clerk was a rotund woman who wore thick glasses and was dressed in office attire. A black wooden cross hung on her neck. She kept her eyes on the form that she was filling with a blue pen. A laptop with a long, snake-like cable was on the table beside her. "Can I have your name and age, please?"

Tara sighed and crossed her arms. Might as well get this over with. "Tara Weiss. Fifteen."

"The names of your parents?"

"Brian and Claire Weiss."

The clerk just kept on writing, it was as if she was talking to a computer. She didn't even bother to make eye contact. "What city and state are y'all from?"

"Phoenix Arizona," Tara said softly.

"What is your parent's religious affiliation?"

Tara frowned. She was getting antsy. "Look, I'm here to look for my brother. His name is Timothy Weiss. He was in care of Matthew and Melissa Olsen. Can you check on them? The last information I had was that they were on their way here."

"I still need your parent's religion."

Tara rolled her eyes. Might as well lie about it so she could get this done faster. "They're Christian, okay? Now could you please check on Timothy Weiss? We got separated. I need to know if he's here somewhere."

The processing officer adjusted her glasses for a bit before writing down what she said. "I need to know the church that you and your parents belonged to. What kind of denomination is your Christianity too."

Tara shook her head. She noticed that the security guard had already walked away. That made things easier. "Look, I don't know what church we belong to. But we're Christians. Isn't that enough?"

"So your family doesn't go to church? How do you know you're a Christian then?"

"I just know," Tara said. "We would study the Bible every evening."

"Where are your parents now?"

Tara shrugged. "I don't know. We got separated just as we got here. Can I check your registry? Maybe they already signed up or something."

The lady sighed as she turned slightly to her right and started typing on the laptop's keyboard. Then she started clicking on the computer mouse before looking up at Tara. "I can't find your parent's names on our database anywhere."

"What about my brother? Timothy Weiss."

The processing officer shook her head as she kept staring at the laptop. "Nothing on that name either."

Tara thought about it for a few seconds. "Maybe they changed his surname to Olsen. How about Timothy Olsen?"

The woman typed on the laptop again. "There's a Tom Olsen, but he's a senior citizen. That's about it. I'm sorry."

Tara sighed. "Are you sure about this? Is your list complete?"

The lady crossed her arms and stared at her. "Look, I have a link to our national database on all the citizens we have at present. It looks like none of them are here. Since you're a minor and a Christian, then we can still process you. I can see if I can match you up with a family that's willing to take you in, but that might take a few days. It will take a few more weeks once we get approval, but I'm pretty sure I can make you into a citizen. In the meantime I'll assign you to a cot here. There are bathrooms just outside the auditorium and there is some food near the lobby area. It looks like you could use some rest."

"There's still families that are willing to adopt?"

"Of course there are. Pastor Erik says it is our Christian duty to care for all wayward children. I'm sure I can find a family who would be willing to adopt you. If your parents make it here at a later date, then we can reintegrate you back to them without a problem. Either way, you're safe here. Those pagan devils won't touch you because we are protected by the power of Our Lord Jesus Christ here."

Tara nodded slightly. Yeah right. More religious crap. She was tempted to roll her eyes but thought better of it. "Okay."

The lady smiled as she typed on the laptop again. After about a minute she gave Tara a slip of paper. "Great. I'm assigning you to cot one hundred seventy, that's over at the expo hall. I'll have one of the volunteers bring you a pillow and blanket. In the meantime, if I get a flag on my computer if your parents show up, then I'll let you know."

"Alright, thanks," Tara said as she got up and walked away towards the other hall.

As she made her way into the expo hall, she noticed there were around two hundred people either lying in cots or just hanging out. A few kids were running in between the folding beds as they noisily played with an inflatable ball. A small group of people were on the far side of the huge convention center as they all knelt down in a semi-circle, their hands clasped together in silent prayer. Tara's assigned cot was there but she didn't feel like resting, so she moved right past it and walked out into the corridor. All over the walls were billboards, along with lists of people that were evidently either missing or dead. There were metal folding tables near the end of the corridor that had trays of paper wrapped sandwiches and small plastic bottles of fruit juice. Tara took a sandwich, tore off its wrapping and bit into it. It was mostly bread with mayonnaise, as well bits of ham and tomatoes. After taking a few more bites she threw it into a nearby trashcan. Tara then took a bottle of orange juice and walked back over to where the billboards were. Many of the letters were handwritten. There were a few pictures of families that were pinned on the board, from casual photos to formal portraits. Tara just kept going through the printed lists of dead or missing, hoping that she would find any clue as to where her brother was. That was when she noticed a short, thin man with brown hair covered by a baseball cap. He was standing beside her as he too scanned the names on the board.

Tara glanced at him before looking at the lists again. "You're trying to find a missing relative too?"

The man wore slightly tinted glasses and had a plaid shirt on. His voice was in a low whisper. "Just checking to see if they finally executed my brother and put his name up here."

Tara half turned and stared at him. "What?"

The man looked around to make sure no one was staring at them before answering her. He looked to be middle aged and had tanned skin. "Didn't you know? Some of these lists are for the people who were executed by the new Christian government they got here. The lists says they died due to accidents, but I know better."

Tara took in a deep breath. "No. I-I just got here. I'm looking for my brother. We got separated and I heard he left my home state with another family. I was told they were on their way here. He's only six."

The man nodded. "Yeah, I figured you were new to this place. I saw you talking to the processing officer. Your parents not here?"

"I ran away from my dad. He used to beat me and he gave my little brother away. My mom moved away years ago. I don't even know where she is."

The man held out his hand. "Sorry to hear that. My name's Aaron."

Tara shook it. "Tara. Did you just come in recently too?"

"Yeah," Aaron said. "Just came in as part of a convoy from Wyoming. My family and I used to live in Dubois, near the Shoshone National Forest. About a week ago the whole town was attacked by giant monsters. Just smashed the whole place to bits. Thankfully my wife and kids survived, so I packed whatever we had left and took the truck towards this state. I'm not what you'd call a hardcore Christian, but I'm a believer. Now that I got here, I ain't so sure."

Tara frowned. "What's happening over here? When I took the bus going into the city I saw the cops rounding up a whole bunch of people."

"Those are the morality councils. Anyone who isn't a white, straight member of the church is going to get arrested," Aaron said. "I've been here for a few days now and I've talked to a lot of people. Some of us are gonna leave. You're free to join us if you want to."

"Where you going to after this?"

"We'll try to make it back to the Federal territories over in Virginia and maybe New York after that. I heard New York is peaceful and they tolerate different types of people there. The ones over here are too cruel for my tastes. Anyway, I think there's gonna be a full scale war between the Christians here and the US government soon."

Tara looked down on the carpeted floor. "I've been away. Do you really think there's gonna be a war between Kansas and United States?"

"There will be for sure," Aaron said. "The Christians got whupped when they tried to take Kansas City over at the Missouri border. Just heard rumors about it but I think it's true. Everybody's nervous because they all think the Feds are gonna counterattack. The way the leadership here is going, I think they may be desperate enough to try something crazy, like using one of their nukes or something."

Tara shook her head in disbelief. "This is all so crazy. I can't believe they're going to fight each other while the Aztecs are coming up from the south."

"Yeah, well the fundamentalist Christians here think the apocalypse is happening anyway so they figure they got nothing to lose by resisting to the very end," Aaron said. "I still care for my family and I want to keep them alive as long as possible. That's why me and some others are gonna get outta here in a few days."

"Let me think about it," Tara said. "But I have to find my brother first. If he's here I got to get him out before I leave. I talked to that processing lady and she told me that his name isn't on the database, so maybe he isn't here."

Aaron pressed his lips together. "The names on that list that she has only contains the people who are citizens. The other ones that don't belong get sent to camps."

Tara was shocked. "Camps? What kind of camps?"

"Internment camps," Aaron said. "I heard they made Leavenworth into an internment camp for undesirables. They don't allow people to leave anymore, that's why we gotta sneak out in order to leave the state."

"My brother is around seven by now. You think he could be in those camps?"

"I dunno about your brother," Aaron said. "If he's that young maybe they had another family adopt him and change his name. I'm pretty sure the ones they can't brainwash are in Leavenworth."

"Why are they keeping all those people prisoner? Why don't they just let them go?"

"Bargaining chips in case the Feds attack," Aaron said softly. "Hostages and human shields, maybe. That's what I heard, anyway. Nobody talks out loud in public here, so it's all hushed rumors, but word gets around."

"I can't believe they would stoop that low," Tara said. "It's disgusting. Cowardly."

"It is. That's why we're leaving."

Tara scratched the top of her head as an idea formed in her mind. "If that processor clerk only had a list of the current citizens that they had, do you think there's another list somewhere with the original names of the people who changed their names?"

"I bet you there would be," Aaron said. "I don't know where you could access that kind of a list though."

Tara stuck her hands into the pockets of her denim jacket as she tried to think. "There must be a place here where they would have that list. But where…"

Aaron smirked as their eyes met. "The morality council headquarters. They must have the complete lists of everybody because they would need it to find people. I bet they would probably have a list of people in the camps too. I mean, they run them camps anyway."

Tara smiled a little. For the first time in as many days there was a tinge of hope. "Okay, where is this headquarters of theirs?"

"They've got several," Aaron said. "They took over all the FBI offices in the city, that's for sure, and probably all the other Federal buildings as well. I wouldn't know the exact place, but I bet it's the one with the most lights on at night."

It was close to midnight when Tara sat up from her cot. She was too nervous to sleep, but at least she was able to close her eyes and rest her body for a bit. After lacing up her sneakers, Tara put on her denim jacket and walked out into the adjoining corridor. There were still a few people milling about, mostly volunteers who were vacuuming the red carpeted floor of the theatre hall. When Tara walked over to the entrance foyer, she saw two uniformed church security guards were standing outside of the glass doors.

The two guards were facing the outside parking lot, so they didn't notice her standing behind them. Tara saw that the raven was perched on the roof of a pickup truck parked nearby and she gestured at it. One of the guards sensed something and turned to see her silently waving her arms in the air. The man was shaved bald and he had thick, muscular arms, evidently after working out using heavy weights at the gym. The guard seemed confused as he tapped his partner and they both turned to face her. As he came down from the top of the roof, Patrick Gyle landed behind them, then threw a series of lightning fast punches to the back of their necks. Both guards crumpled and fell face down. Tara pushed open the glass doors as Gyle dragged the guards to the side of the entrance. The raven landed and perched itself on a nearby guard rail.

Tara stared at the results of Gyle's handiwork. She thought his methods were brutal, but effective. "Did you kill them?"

Gyle kept moving until he was behind a column. With the parking lot's streetlamps active, his pale, naked body stood out like a sore thumb. "Nope. At least I don't think so. They may be concussed though."

The raven blinked as it turned to face Tara. "Did you find any clues as to where your brother is?"

Tara started buttoning up her denim jacket. There was a chill wind in the night air. "We need to find a building that's sucking up a lot of power. It ought to have a computer where we can search through a list of names."

Gyle poked his head from out of the shadows. His pale red eyes glowed from the reflection of the streetlights. "I think I know just the place."

The William Donovan Federal Building was brand new. It had been constructed just two years before and was designed to house a new department for the NSA. As such, the eight story building near the banks of the river was one of the standout landmarks since Wichita had very few skyscrapers. What made the design of the building so remarkable was that it had very few windows, most of its façade was tan-colored concrete. The Federal government had hoped to put up one of its core databases for the PRISM surveillance program there. Most of the rooms within the building were composed of nothing more than sterile housing for internet web servers. A minimal staff was to be assigned to maintain its massive database and keep unwanted intruders out. Then the Glooming happened.

When Kansas declared its independence, it threw the NSA into a panic. With no clear instructions from the government, the NSA leadership did its best by shutting down all the servers and evacuating its personnel. As soon as the Rock of God Church took over the city, a number of former NSA contractors had already defected over to the separatist side, and within a matter of days had restarted the database, this time with the aim of using the records stored in it as part of a new counter-intelligence apparatus to defend Christian Kansas against outside attack. In addition to that, another part of the database would also serve to keep the most intimate secrets of the newly independent state. Several months after the Glooming, the building now served as the official hall of records for the separatists, and it was administered exclusively by the ROG morality council.

Tara and Gyle stood on the roof of the building and looked down below. They could see several Humvees with machine gun turrets stationed at the parking lot. Several squads of heavily armed soldiers were milling about, completely oblivious to them. Two soldiers were lying inside the back of the vehicles, asleep.

The raven was sitting on one of the generator units that dotted the roof. "Must be a whole platoon guarding the entrance down there. Funny how those people didn't even station any guards up here."

Gyle turned and started walking around, looking for a way inside. "There are no nearby buildings of this height. If a helicopter tried to land up here, they would notice it. I guess they didn't expect anyone to materialize out of thin air to appear on the building roof."

"If I could laugh, I would," the raven said. "No surveillance cameras either. So how do you suggest we get inside?"

Gyle stopped in front of the door that led to the stairwell. He ran his clawed hands along the sides of the door. "I can feel the electrical current along the frame and the lock. If I break it down, it will trigger an alarm."

Tara walked over and stood beside them. "How about through a ventilation shaft or something. I saw that in a movie once, I think."

Gyle pointed to a nearby exhaust vent. "You mean that one? It's too small for me to squeeze through."

Tara looked around, then she pointed at a slightly raised concrete platform. "What's that?"

Gyle walked over until he was standing beside it, then he ran his hands along its base, feeling for any electrical currents. There was none. The top of the platform led down into the main elevator shaft. "Yeah, this will do."

Dave Reeder zoned out a couple of times as he stared blankly at the server uptime, disk usage and network traffic on the monitor screens. He wore a thick wool sweater in addition to his leather jacket as he sat in front of a number of consoles. The temperature in the entire seventh floor was maintained at a slightly chilly 68 degrees Fahrenheit to make sure that the servers wouldn't overheat. Most of the upper floors in the entire building consisted of large, air conditioned rooms that had nothing but rows and rows of plastic and metal boxes and their attached cables. Out of all the buildings still operating in the city, this particular one had the most priority when it came to electrical use. There were reserve diesel generators in the basement levels, ready to kick in automatically should the metropolitan power grid would ever go belly up.

As he sipped the last of the lukewarm coffee from his paper cup, Dave got up from his office chair and yawned. He hated these lonely nights, but he felt that he had a duty to his new country. Only a few months before, he had been a systems administrator here as the company he worked for had a contract with the NSA to maintain the database for its organization. After the Glooming began, Dave refused to heed the call to shut down the servers and head east. He was a devoted Christian and he felt that the words of the great Pastor Erik Burnley were the only possible way he could save his soul. His wife disagreed, and she took the children with her and went back to

California. But Dave's faith was unshaken. He fervently believed that Kansas was the one true sanctuary against the demons and devils that had suddenly appeared throughout the world, and he was determined to stand with the church against them.

Dave shook his head rapidly from side to side as he tried to fight off the combined effects of a lack of sleep and fatigue. His eyelids felt heavy as he took off his glasses and rubbed them with his hands to put some life back into them. He knew that from experience, the only thing that could keep him awake until the morning shift would relieve him were the constant, almost endless cups of coffee that he drank all night long. Since the entire department was short-staffed, he had to cover for his subordinates too, so that meant even longer hours. The church deemed that it was imperative that their records were constantly updated in order to make sure that their citizens remained loyal, as well as to identify any potential subversives that could possibly be a threat to them. To that effect, the servers had to be running constantly, day and night, seven days a week, without any interruption.

Time for another cup, he thought as he walked out of the office and headed towards the pantry at the end of the corridor. While the server rooms and offices had dimmed lights, the adjoining corridors had bright overhead illumination that had the effect of daylight, so Dave squinted for a bit as his eyes slowly adjusted. The church had been training a new systems administration crew, but they were still weeks away from being assigned here because of other priorities. Dave felt his frustration growing, but his loyalty to the church kept his dissatisfaction in check.

When he got to the gleaming white pantry, he noticed that the pot was empty again. As he poured water into the percolator to boil a new batch of coffee, Dave suddenly felt a slight jolt. The overhead lights in the pantry dimmed slightly for a few seconds before returning back to normal. It felt like a slight tremor, as if the whole building was hit by a small earthquake. As he waited for an aftershock, there was none so he shrugged and took out a can of instant coffee from an overhead cabinet. Almost immediately, he heard a distant grating noise, like the sound of metal being bent or crushed. Dave placed the coffee can on the countertop and nervously looked around. It didn't sound like it was coming from nearby, it seemed more like it was coming from inside of the building somewhere. Dave stood still for a few minutes as he wondered what could have caused it. Then he heard the sound of glass breaking from somewhere close by.

Dave immediately ran out into the corridor and looked around, but nothing seemed amiss. Since the security office was just one floor below him, he decided to head over there and would ask them what was going on. So he walked over to an adjoining corridor, stood in front of the elevator doors and pushed the down button. After a few minutes, nothing happened. Dave frowned as the buttons to summon the elevator didn't seem to be working.

Shaking his head, he walked over to the stairwell, pulled out his keycard, then slid it over the electronic lock. As soon as the door was unlocked, it immediately swung open and hit him in the face. Dave cried out in pain as he was sent sprawling backwards onto the tile flooring of the corridor. He ran his hand along his face and felt a bruise on his forehead. As he readjusted his now slightly bent glasses to find out what just happened, a teenage girl stepped out into the corridor from where the stairwell was.

"Sorry about that," Tara said to him.

Dave was wide eyed as he pulled himself up. "W-who are you?"

Tara shook her head slightly. "My name doesn't really matter. I need to access your database."

Dave clenched his fists. "You are not authorized to be here, little girl. Who do you think you—"

His words were cut off in mid sentence as Patrick Gyle came into the corridor carrying the unconscious security officer over his pale shoulder. Dave's mouth was wide open in a silent scream.

Gyle placed the stunned security officer down onto the floor as he started to walk towards the goggle-eyed systems administrator. "Don't do anything stupid. We just want access to the database."

Dave started to piss in his pants. He pointed a trembling finger to the door leading to his office.

Tara pushed the office door open and peered inside before glancing back at him. "Is there like a password or something?"

Dave shook his head slightly. "N-No, it's a-already o-open."

"Okay," Tara said before ducking into the office suite. She quickly sat down on the padded chair and noticed that the administrator had left a query search running. She was pretty familiar with computers at school since she always stayed after dismissal and did extra studies in the computer lab. She typed in Timmy's name but it came up with zero results. She then tried different variations of his name along with the Olsen surname but she still didn't get anything. When she searched for six year-old male orphans that were adopted by families she ended up with several thousands of names. After sighing out loud, she got an idea and started going through other databases. That was when she noticed a file marked Valhalla. When she opened it up and did a search, it immediately got a hit on Matthew and Melissa Olsen. They were listed as internees in the Fort Leavenworth camp compound. Her heart started to race. Timmy was close. She could feel it. They would be reunited soon enough.

The urine that had stained Dave's trousers had already cooled and it was uncomfortably chilly when Tara walked back out and into the corridor. Gyle just kept standing there like a monstrous statue, as he kept staring at the terrified man with his lidless, bloodshot eyes.

"Okay, I got something," Tara said as he looked over at Dave. "Where is Leavenworth Camp Number Two?"

"T-that's a-a n-new camp they s-set up at Fort Leavenworth. At t-the woods n-near the national cemetery," Dave said nervously. His urine had a sour, acidic odor and it made his nostrils flare.

Tara looked at Gyle with concerned eyes as she gripped several pages of printed paper in her hands. "I couldn't find Timmy in the database, but I found the Olsens, and that's where they are. Maybe they could help me pick my brother out from the names on the list I printed."

"That's good enough. Let's get going," Gyle said to her, before turning to look at Dave once more, as he pointed to the unconscious security guard lying on the floor. "I took out this guy when he wasn't looking and turned off the video cameras in the security room. So that means he won't remember me. But you will. If you tell your superiors what happened here, I will come back for you. You will erase our queries from your records and you will not talk about this ever again. You get me?"

Dave nodded. His shrill, squeaky voice was now like that of a scared little child. "Yes. I-I p-promise n-not to t-tell."

Tara figured he was too scared to tell the others. There was a sudden blur, and both the teen girl and the creature were gone. It was as if they never even existed and it was all just a figment of his imagination. The only thing that hinted it wasn't a dream was the unconscious guard and an ice cold, sticky coating covering his crotch and legs. Dave's mind just couldn't take it anymore.

He fainted.

11. Lord of the Lies

Otherworld

The landscape was an endless expanse of dried lava flows, like the undulating bark of a smooth, black tree. Gigantic mountain peaks could be seen in the distant horizon, their jagged, vertical walls of black basalt seemed like an insurmountable barrier to the damned that inhabited this blighted place. The sky had a reddish glow that cast its accursed illumination on the ground, as if the heavens itself was on fire above.

The old man gripped his tattered cloak closer to his frail body as he pointed a bony finger at a nearby mountain range. "There is a pass near that base, I believe. That is the one spot where we can get to the river and onto the next layer."

A gust of wind tousled Valerie Mendoza's dark brown hair. She neither felt cold nor warmth from it. "It seems like we were walking through that pile of crap and then all of a sudden, the ground changed and now it looks like we're in a totally different world. What is this place?"

"This layer is called Gulam," the wanderer said. "The realm of the gluttons. Come on."

They started walking. Valerie could not get a sense of time, it was as if all the clocks in the universe had stood still, and yet it felt as if all the seconds, hours, days, and years were all happening at once. She sensed it would take forever for them to get to the base of the mountain, since it never seemed to get any closer, yet it somehow felt like they had been steadily moving towards it for days on end. Time and distance seemed meaningless now.

Although the landscape didn't change much, they started to pass by a number of extremely large people that seemed to be imbedded in the lava, only their fat faces were protruding from the solidified rock. A number of creatures that seemed to look like a nightmarish combination of animal and human corpses were hunched over them, as these monsters would vomit over their victim's open mouths and would use their claws to force the bile down their throats. The unfortunate men and women were trapped, and they would plead at the demons to stop forcing their puke on them, but to no avail.

Valerie forced herself to look away as she kept a tight grip on the pistol by her side holster. "Oh god, I can't bear to see all this anymore."

"You must pay them no mind," the wanderer said as he kept on a steady pace. "They have been condemned for their excesses and this is their eternal punishment."

Valerie shook her head in disbelief. "This just isn't fair! So what if they ate a lot while they were alive? Nobody deserves this kind of punishment, not for pigging out!"

"I have the same questions as you," the old man said. "That is why I wander these other lands. I search for the answers."

"Did you find out anything?"

The old man shook his head. "No. All I have witnessed is an endless stream of cruelty and malice."

Valerie grimaced as she sidestepped away from a screaming woman who was embedded in the dried lava. She had nearly stepped on the sinner's face. "Why do you keep traveling to this sick place then?"

The old man turned his head slightly at her and smiled as he kept on moving. "Something called hope. It is what keeps me from becoming one of the denizens of this blighted land. I like to feel that there will be an answer and I shall find it one day."

Something huge almost ran into her as she kept her eyes on the wanderer. Valerie cursed as she nearly collided with an onrushing demon. She almost drew her gun but the creature shifted sideways and narrowly avoided her. It was hairless, had a bear-like body and a head of a gigantic, misshapen vulture. The demon barely seemed to notice her as it concentrated on the helpless souls on the ground, using its pawed feet to stomp on their pleading faces, leaving bloody pulps on the igneous rock.

"Pay them no mind," the old man said. "They are tasked to punish those that have been sent here. Since we do not belong in this place, they will ignore travelers as long as they are not interfered with."

Valerie saw the same demon run ahead of them and smash its foot on one helpless soul's face, breaking the man's nose and teeth as it kept pounding at its victim. "That thing's killing them!" she screamed.

The old man shook his head as they walked past. "The souls here will get hurt, but their bodies will heal in the blink of an eye. No one can die if one is already dead."

"So they just get tortured and killed endlessly? That's insane," Valerie hissed. "What kind of a justice is this?"

"A kind of judgment of the gods," the old man said. "It is accepted by the people who dwell here."

They soon came upon an infinite procession of people. Like the other souls in this world, they were all naked and crawling on the ground on all fours. As they got closer, Valerie realized that each victim's mouth had been attached to the buttocks of the person ahead of them. It was like seeing one horrific, multi-limbed creature. The excrement that they produced would pass through an endless loop. A number of eyes locked onto hers, pleading for some sort of respite or release from this unimaginable procession of cruelty.

Valerie nearly put her hands over her eyes. "Oh my god, this isn't happening!"

The old man took her trembling hand as they got closer. "We must stride over them. Come."

Valerie shrieked as they both stopped in front of the moving, caterpillar-like mass of souls. The old man gently put one foot up in the air and strode over the column as it kept moving. Just as Valerie tried to do the same, a woman who was part of the gruesome procession, tried to grab at her. Valerie cried out as she got entangled on top of the woman, who kept trying to pull her down to the ground as she kept moving. The old man reached out and held onto Valerie as they both were able to pull away. The two of them ran for a bit until they crested a blackened dune and were soon out of sight.

Tears were streaming down Valerie's face as she knelt down on the solid rock. "Oh my god. How can all of this be real? This is the most disgusting thing I've ever experienced!"

The old man stood over her. "I have felt like you when I first ventured to these wastes. We must look beyond the cruelty, beyond the suffering, and we must ask ourselves if this serves a purpose."

"An endless amount of pain and suffering serves no purpose," Valerie sobbed. "This is like a world of horror that never ends. No god, no matter how evil, could possibly condone all this."

"I have had the same thoughts as well," the old man said. "The more I pondered the problem, the more it seems the purpose of gods may not be to lord over men, but to guide them."

Valerie looked up at him. Her tears of sadness were now tears of frustration. "Guide us? What kind of a guidance is this? People make mistakes, we're not perfect. That's what makes us human. If we're like children then we should be taught, not punished for all eternity over something we did that lasted for a few moments!"

The old man pointed to another man trapped in the ground. "It seems to me that the demons of this place serve the souls here rather than the other way around. If you look at them, all those damned men, you can see that they feel that they do deserve to be here. You will notice that none of them seem to want to escape from the dried rock that traps them. It seems to me that they chose to be here."

Valerie got up and wiped her tears away. "That can't be true," she said as he walked around until she saw someone's face embedded in the ground.

The face in the ground had been smashed into a pulp, most probably by a wandering demon. It looked vaguely like a man, but the nose was crushed and bloody so she couldn't be sure. Bits of teeth were lying in a small puddle of blood near its side. One eye was evidently gouged out, but they could still hear the groans of agony coming out of its mouth.

Valerie knelt down so that the soul would notice her. "Hello. Can you hear me?"

The face opened its bloody mouth and coughed up bits of blood. "Please, don't hurt me anymore!"

"I'm not going to hurt you," Valerie said. "Do you want to get out of there? Can you move your arms?"

"I just want to be left alone here."

"You don't have to be stuck in there. I know it must be torture but, maybe we can find a way to pull you out of there. Don't you want to get out?"

The single eye's pupil kept moving round the eyelid, like a rotating brown planet in a sea of milky whiteness, surrounded by crimson. "I'd rather just stay here. Let me sleep. I don't want to eat any more vomit and excrement. I feel so full, I'm going to burst!"

Valerie placed her hands along the side of the face and started to pull. Her eagerness to help overcame her revulsions. "Nonsense, here, let me help you."

The face started screaming. "Noo! It hurts, it hurts, it hurts!"

Valerie grimaced as she squatted and tried to pull the head out, at least. She could feel a slight shifting in the ground. There was a gap between the embedded face of the soul and the solidified lava, all she needed was a bit more effort. "Almost there," she gasped as she pulled harder.

The soul in the ground was screaming incoherently now as it slowly began to regenerate its missing eye. Valerie sensed the creature's agony was more due to irritation than pain as she felt the floor underneath it begin to give way.

As she put a little bit more effort into it, the soul's head suddenly popped out and Valerie fell backwards as she cradled it in her hands. But instead of a neck, the creature had a worm-like, segmented body two feet in length. Valerie fell on her back and the squirming giant maggot with its human face landed on top of her.

Valerie screamed in terror as she quickly threw the thing onto the ground beside her. The soul continued to spout gibberish as it crawled away, its bloated, tube-like body wriggled on the ground. She looked at her blood and pus covered hands and wailed in frustration and disgust.

The old man bent down and helped to pull her up. "I have tried that before and it ended the same way. That soul is damned no matter what you do. It will crawl into another hole and embed itself there," he said.

Valerie grimaced as she looked at the black fissure where the creature once lay embedded in. "This whole place. It's too sick. Oh god, I can't stand another minute here."

The old man began to walk again. "Then we must keep moving."

Valerie let out a deep sigh and followed. "I can't sense Paul here, we need to go faster."

"Then you must concentrate," the old man said. "The journey from one part of the otherlands to the next is a matter of will."

"Okay," Valerie said. She remembered the time that she was trapped in the muck of the previous world. She had been able to get out by sheer concentration. Valerie gritted her teeth and tried to picture Paul's face as she kept moving. In a time like this, it would be her memories of him that would be the key to get through this hellish landscape. She needed to stay focused and not get distracted by all the horrific scenes that were occurring all around. If she let all the pain and cruelty affect her, she had a feeling she would become a denizen of this horrific place.

As she sensed Paul's distant cries for help, the effect was almost instantaneous as both she and the traveler were suddenly walking through a gap across the gigantic mountain walls that towered above them. It was as if their combined wills carried them past the endless dried lava flows and they were now nearing the borderlands to the next world.

"Oh my god," Valerie said in astonishment. "This is amazing. It's almost as if we can get from one point to the other by simply concentrating and if—"

She stopped in mid-sentence. The mountain pass was at least several hundred miles wide in between the gargantuan cliffs that nearly blotted out the sky. Once again, they were not alone.

Valerie could see an endless array of circular stone tables that seemed evenly spaced in front of them as they kept on walking past. Several naked people were tied down in chains and were forced to sit on stone benches, as they faced the pale, marbled tables. There were massive stone bowls on the tops of the tables and they were filled with all sorts of monstrous, squirming toads and insects. These vermin would crawl out of their bowls, making their way to their victims, then crawling up their bloated bellies, where they tried to force themselves into the mouths of the unfortunate souls that were tied down. The human sufferers would try to twist their heads away or clench their teeth to prevent the bloated little creatures from forcing their way in, but the toads and the worms would bite, and chew their way through their victim's lips, even break teeth just to get in. From there, the assorted vermin would wriggle and eat their way through the intestines, then force themselves through the anal cavities, and then finally through a hole at the bottom of the stone bench, only to crawl back up towards the stone bowls, in order to begin their terrible, endless cycle all over again.

"I find it best to look away," the old man said as they moved around them.

Valerie's teeth were chattering. She kept trying to look away, but some strange force kept making her view the unending suffering, it was a sort of combination between disgust and fascination. That was when she drew back into her palace of memory and thought about Paul. As she remembered his gentle smile and the warmth of his arms around her, the recollection of their love allowed her to finally concentrate on moving past the endless, tormented feasts of the damned. Within moments, they were finally moving away from the mountain pass while the ground underneath them became softer, as the dried lava became little sand pebbles.

"*Ah, wanderer, it seems your latest companion is one of the stronger ones of late. She was able to remake her thoughts and was therefore not easily swayed by my sumptuous banquets*," a not too distant voice said. The sound seemed to carry itself through the air.

Valerie started to look around. "What was that?"

"*I am right behind you, mortal*," the voice said.

Both Valerie and the old man turned. High above the mountain cliffs, a dark, cigar-shaped figure emerged as it buzzed its wings and landed a short distance away. Valerie gasped as she stood looking at it. The creature was the size of a skyscraper, its squat, insect-like thorax must have been hundreds of feet long. Along its soft, segmented back sprouted a pair of gigantic, feathered wings that couldn't have possibly belonged to it. At first glance, it resembled a monstrous, misshapen fly with angel-like wings. What was most horrible were its limbs, resembling colossal, human-like arms which ended in hands that crawled along the ground. Trillions upon trillions of flesh eating maggots were crawling all over its body. The creature stared back at them with its pair of large segmented eyes that shined like multitudes of door-sized yellow mirrors.

The old man placed his hand on Valerie's shoulder as he stood beside her. "That is Beelzebub, the demon prince. Beware its honeyed words."

Valerie nearly gasped, but she maintained her composure.

"*Welcome back, wanderer,*" Beelzebub said. Its voice was like that of a million buzzing flies. "*And who do you bring into my abode?*"

The old man frowned and shook his head. "I'm sure you already know that, o lord of the lies."

"*I do indeed,*" the demon said. "*Is it not a courtesy when visiting my kingdom that proper etiquette is at least followed?*"

Valerie crossed her arms. "I'm Valerie Mendoza. We're just passing through, thank you."

The demon's segmented eyes were like little mirrors as an infinite array of their own reflections stared back at them. "*What do you think of my realm so far, mortal? Do you not admire the exquisite beauty in my lands, or with my servants?*"

Valerie's lips curled in anger. "You have the most disgusting, most horrible kingdom in all that exists in this universe! How you can even justify the unlimited suffering in this shit hole is beyond me! You are a loathsome monster!"

The demon's incessant buzzing became shrill. It seemed like it was laughing. "*My realm is but a reflection of human wants and desires. This endless array of food and plenty is merely the eventuality of where their hungers and passions leads to. If one is hungry, then one eats, then eats even more. An endless hunger demands an infinite amount of sustenance. A human being's hunger for food and other things is never satiated, therefore I must supply them with even more variations of my cosmic feasts. Human wants and human emotions last forever and are infinite in number. You demand, and I supply.*"

Valerie shook her head. "No! You've gone overboard! I curse at whatever god put you up to this! If you're behind all of this then screw you!"

The demon shifted sideways slightly as its gigantic body smashed against the side of the mountain pass, bringing down tons of jagged rock and crushing a few souls underneath it. "*Ah, just like their desires, so too does humanity have an endless array of curses and words for bodily orifices, insults and jeers. This is what I love about human beings. They always seek others to blame for their misfortune. Whether it's other humans, or bad luck, or the gods, humans will never be able to point fingers at their individual selves. This is why beings like me exist. We demons are also but a reflection of your most subconscious desires. For in the end, we are the ones who serve at your pleasure, not the other way around.*"

Valerie snorted. "You call all this pleasure? This is suffering! It's nothing but pure torture! Pain!"

"*When you have lived as long as I,*" Beelzebub said. "*You will soon realize that pleasure and pain are all but one, a mere shard that is part of the same gigantic mirror. One cannot exist without the other. A life of infinite pleasure would be meaningless.*"

"That's easy for you to say," Valerie said. "You're not the one getting tortured here. Where the hell is the pleasure in all of this?"

The demon laughed once more. "*Hell indeed! The pleasure is in seeing others suffer. The pleasure is in the anticipation of the pain. The pleasure is in the endurance of the pain. The pleasure is in the overcoming of the pain.*"

Valerie looked away. "You're insane, do you know that?"

"*Who is more insane? The father that tortures his own children like whipped dogs? The men who murder for the sake of their gods? The people who preach false words? The one who eats while others starve? The things that are being done here are no different than what is being committed in your world, even before the gods returned,*" Beelzebub said.

Valerie looked at the old man. All this pain. With no real hope. She suddenly felt fatigued. It was as if nothing mattered. "Let's go. All this isn't getting us anywhere."

"*Perhaps we shall meet again, Valerie Mendoza,*" the demon said as its wings started flapping. The air around it began to swirl as it somehow was able to lift its monstrous body up into the air. "*But beware, next time, it might very well be on my terms.*"

As the demon prince flew away, the old man turned around and started walking again. As Valerie followed close behind, she noticed that they had now come upon the edge of a vast, flowing river. She couldn't see anything on the other side. The lapping waters were dark and opaque, it was if the liquid was made out of the substance of darkness itself.

The old man placed a gentle hand on her wrist. "Do not touch the water."

Valerie stood at the river's edge. "Why? What kind of river is this?"

"We are on the banks of Lethe," the old man said softly. "This is the river of forgetfulness."

12. Repel Boarders

Mississippi

By the second day, the *Nimrod* had made it to the Big Black River as it headed in a northeasterly direction. Ever since the rains began, almost every single dam in the state had burst. Unlike Louisiana, the central parts of Mississippi had a much higher elevation, so this meant that the riverboat would be going upstream until it could get to the flooded city of Canton. The plan after that was to go south along the Pearl River, then get to a connecting waterway and make a beeline to Mobile, Alabama, for a fuel stop. In this part of the journey, the diesel engines would be going close to full power, in order to make it past the downstream currents. The ship's paddlewheel would be doing most of the heavy lifting until they could make the cross over at Canton, after that, it would be smooth trip going downstream.

Tyrone Gatlin wiped off some of the water stains on the solid oak bar counter using a damp rag. It was a clear, moonlit night and everybody was getting a few drinks at the bar before turning in for bed. They were getting close to Canton and Captain Pillinger had assigned a few of the men on guard duty. There had been rumors that marauders had begun to use the flooded city as a base of operations, so everyone had a two drink limit when it came to beers for the evening. The captain wanted everyone to be alert just in case of any trouble, so almost everybody had rifles slung over their shoulders. Since Tyrone was the all-around deckhand for the ship, he was assigned as bartender after every dinner, and he had to work the counter until everybody turned in.

As he placed the empty beer glasses in the sink behind the bar, Tyrone couldn't help but feel a pang of regret. The moment he had been accepted as a deckhand on the ship, he went back to Monique's shack to get his things. Monique had been there along with her eldest daughter, Moesha. The voodoo queen hadn't say much, all she did was to place her hand on the gris-gris that hung around Tyrone's neck and told him to take care. Moesha had remained totally silent and her younger sister Shani hadn't even been there. A part of him had wanted to stay and build a life for himself back in that flooded city, but the dreams had compelled him to join up with the crew of the *Nimrod.* It was as if he hadn't had a choice. The gods clearly had plans for him, his dreams told him that. It wasn't exactly something he wanted to do. A sudden urge washed over him, it was a sense of defiance. Maybe he ought to get off in the next stop and make his way back to Shreveport and screw the gods, forget their plans- it was his life to live for, not theirs. Then he realized that if it wasn't for them, he would have been dead by now, and the brief pangs of rebellion soon left his subconscious.

"Hey, gimme another beer. And I wanna shot o' that moonshine," a voice behind him said.

Tyrone turned. Sitting at the edge of the bar was JJ Glanton, the ship's first officer. He was wearing a sleeveless denim tank top and flanked by two of the hunters. The first guy to his left was Bear Mattingly, he was a huge man with unkempt, fiery red hair and a beard that extended down to his chest. Bear had a hunter's vest over his exposed chest and wore khaki pants. The second man to Glanton's right was called Mohawk, he was part Creek from what Tyrone heard and like his moniker, had a Mohawk hairstyle to go along with his leather bike outfit and boots. All three men had been hanging out in the bar for hours, laughing and swapping stories to each other. The only other people left in the room were another group of hunters jamming guitars and banjos on the old, unused stage over at the far end of the saloon.

Glanton seemed to be in a good mood but he was starting to get irritated. "Well? What are you waiting for, boy? Gimme another beer."

Tyrone glanced at the two empty bottles of beer in front of the first officer.

"Sorry, sir. You've already had your allotted two bottles. Captain's orders was for everybody to have a two beer limit this evening."

Glanton's turned to his buddies and laughed before looking back at Tyrone. "I'm the first officer, boy. I'm second in command of this here vessel. That limit doesn't apply to me."

Tyrone shook his head. "I'm sorry, Mr. Glanton. But the captain told me there would be no exceptions."

Glanton's grin quickly turned into a grimace. "What did you say, boy?"

Tyrone stared blankly at him and shrugged. "Captain's orders, sir."

Glanton crooked a finger at him. "Come here."

Tyrone walked over until he stood face to face with the first officer as he stood behind the bar counter. Glanton quickly leaned over and grabbed his shirt collar as he pulled the deckhand closer so their eyes were only inches away from each other. Tyrone was ready to knock the first officer's hand away, until he noticed Glanton was holding a Marine Ka-Bar knife with his other hand and kept it a few inches away from Tyrone's neck.

"Don't you ever refuse an order from me, boy," Glanton hissed. Tyrone could smell the moonshine in his breath since their faces were so close to each other. He had evidently been drinking more than his fair share tonight.

Tyrone blinked a few times. Beads of sweat began to pour down his forehead. The night air was still and very humid. "I've got orders too, sir. I gotta follow 'em. I made a promise with the captain."

Bear Mattingly leaned forward so his face was parallel with Glanton's. Unlike the other two, the big man was still grinning. "Looks like the rookie has guts, JJ. At least he follows captain's orders, I'll grant him that."

Glanton bared his teeth as he brought the knife closer. "I'm gonna cut your throat open, boy. I don't like your lack of respect."

"I'm not disrespecting you, sir," Tyrone said softly as his hand gripped an empty beer bottle out of sight, behind the counter. "I gotta follow my superior's orders."

Mohawk took out a pint-sized bottle of clear liquid he had underneath his leather vest and placed it on the counter. "I still got some moonshine left, JJ. You can have it. The last thing you wanna do now is to kill another deckhand.

Remember the last time? The captain almost plugged you."

Glanton's eyes shifted towards the small bottle of moonshine that had been placed on the counter before staring back at Tyrone again. The former soldier noticed that Glanton had Aryan Brotherhood tattoos all along his arm. Tyrone figured he must have gotten them in prison, which explained Glanton's hostility to him.

Bear just kept on giggling as he drew back and started to walk behind Glanton. "If you're not going for that bottle of moonshine, it's mine."

Glanton quickly let go of Tyrone's collar and swiped the bottle from the counter before Bear could get his hands on it. He opened it and took a sip, just as Tyrone backed away from the counter and wiped the sweat off his forehead. As their eyes met again, Glanton pointed a finger at Tyrone. "Don't you ever refuse me again, boy."

As Tyrone glanced away and said nothing, the alarm bell sounded. Everybody started running as they took their positions. Glanton shouted at the other hunters to follow him and they all ran out of the room. Tyrone quickly gathered the empty bottles and glasses at the bar counter and set them aside before locking up the cupboard. Since he didn't have a weapon, his job was to go down to the engine room to see if help was needed there. It was important for the ship to have engine power in order to maneuver in the event of a confrontation.

Since the *Nimrod* had a flat-bottomed hull, the engine room was also at the main deck, so Tyrone just ran towards the back, past the kitchen. The moment he got through the double doors that led to the engine room, he could see the massive pistons of the engine just chugging away as it pushed and pulled at the huge paddlewheel at the rear of the boat. Eight-Ball was there, still dressed in his overalls as he stood by while looking at the pressure gauges. Tyrone wasn't quite sure how the engines worked, so he just made certain the ship's engineer saw him as he stood around, waiting to be told what to do.

Eight-Ball Jackson was the only other black man in the crew. He was short and thin, with a grizzled scalp and white stubbles on his cheeks. Tyrone had heard that he had been working as a ship's engineer for over forty years, and he was the captain's most trusted man on the ship, just slightly ahead of Glanton. Eight-Ball was like a savant, he lived and breathed in the engine room so much that he even ate his meals there. Tyrone knew that Glanton was jealous of him, but there was nothing the first officer could do, since the captain had told the entire crew that the engine room was Eight-Ball's exclusive domain and his word was king there. Tyrone had tried to spend time with engineer to get to know him better, but Eight-Ball politely kept him at arm's length. The old man's passion was the ship's engines and he wanted no distractions when it came to maintaining and running it.

Although the sound of the engines drowned out most of the noise from the outside, Tyrone could hear faint popping noises. He knew then that guns were being fired. A loud ringing noise began, as the ship's bell was being sounded. Eight-Ball walked over to the antique intercom system and picked up the receiver. Tyrone thought it looked like an old rotary phone as he saw Eight-Ball looking at him while speaking into it.

After talking for a few minutes, Eight-Ball put the receiver down and shuffled over to Tyrone. The old engineer cupped his mouth as he spoke into Tyrone's ear so he could be heard over the noise of the engine. "Captain needs you, right now."

Tyrone nodded as he turned around and headed out of the engine room. As soon as he walked onto the main deck, he could see that the captain had turned off the ship's lights. The hunters were spread out as they huddled behind the sandbags that were placed just behind the ship's wooden railings, their rifles on the ready. When Tyrone looked around, he noticed the ship was passing by a number of half sunken buildings, like giant concrete boxes that jutted out of the dark waters.

As he just stood there, someone whispered to him. "Get into cover, you dumbass."

Tyrone realized he was totally exposed just standing out there on the main deck. He quickly ran until he got behind the sandbags. There was a hunter with an M-14 crouched down beside him. Tyrone recognized the guy, his name was Peter Johnson, but everybody called him Pete. An Army veteran, Pete had been discharged a few years ago and was living off the land from his hunting lodge in Colorado. He had moved his family to the south for protection when the Glooming began. Pete joined up with the expedition so he could cash in on the lucrative demand for the skin and furs of creatures once thought to be mere legends.

Tyrone turned to look at Pete. "I need to get to the wheel house, the captain's been asking for me," he said softly.

"Wait a bit," Pete whispered as he used the night vision scope mounted on his M-14 while scanning the waters beyond. "I think there might be snipers on top of those buildings. Wait till we pass 'em, then you can go on up."

Two popping noises came out in the distance as Tyrone heard a bullet whizz nearby. He peered out slightly, just above the sandbags, but he couldn't see anything. "Who's shooting at us?"

"My guess is that it must be marauders."

Tyrone gulped. It was another word for pirates. "Marauders? What the hell are they doing here?"

Pete kept looking for targets with his scope. "My guess is that they think this is a transport ship. They might want to try and take it."

Tyrone made a hopeful smile in the darkness as he kept crouching behind the sandbags. "We're going at a pretty rapid pace. Unless they got a ship of their own, I doubt they can catch us."

Several more popping noises could be heard in the distance. Tyrone could see that there were more hunters in the upper deck behind the sandbags there. He saw Glanton and Bear pop their heads up from one pile of sandbags before disappearing out of sight again. A few more minutes passed as the ship finally got past the half sunken buildings as it headed to the outskirts of Canton.

As soon as the buildings were behind them, Tyrone got up and ran to the stairs, then ascended towards the upper deck. He noticed Glanton looking at him with calculating menace as the first officer huddled with a group of other hunters behind the barricades. Tyrone didn't pay him any notice as he ran up the second flight of stairs and then headed towards the wheelhouse. Just as he got up to the back of the entryway, he knocked rapidly on the door.

Captain Pillinger's voice was loud as it reverberated through the wooden paneling. "Get in here already!"

Tyrone meekly opened the door and stepped inside. The captain was still standing in front of the ship's wheel as he kept glancing at the open laptop sitting on the nearby table. There were a number of sandbags that had been placed just below the windows but the area around the ship's wheel was fully exposed because of the glass windshields.

Captain Pillinger turned and looked at him. "Get over here and man the wheel."

Tyrone bit his lip. If someone was going to get shot, it would be him. He was the expendable one. The wheelhouse was totally out in the open since it was the tallest compartment in the whole ship. He walked over and grabbed hold of the lacquered wooden handles, just as Captain Pillinger moved over to the side before sitting down on a stool. The captain started looking at a topographical map on the laptop.

Pillinger cursed. "I didn't want to make the crossing at night, but we ain't got a choice now. There's a sunken highway overpass somewhere ahead and we gotta make sure we get over it. If we cross over the wrong part, the boat could get stuck."

Tyrone gulped. That was when he realized that the sniper fire was meant to make them veer towards where the sunken overpass was. If their displacement wasn't shallow enough, the ship's hull would end up sitting on top of the underwater highway. Once that happened, they would be at the mercy of whatever the enemy had in store for them.

Pillinger had his eyes glued to the laptop, but he would periodically look out of the forward window of the wheelhouse, just to make sure he got his bearings right. "Okay, at my command, turn the wheel thirty degrees starboard."

Tyrone blinked as he glanced at the captain. "I dunno what starboard is, sir!"

Pillinger let out a deep breath. "Port is left, starboard is right. Got it?"

Tyrone nodded as he kept his eyes straight ahead. He was a bundle of nerves now. "Okay, sir."

Shouts were heard coming from the decks below. From the corner of his eye, Tyrone could see that the men were running around the main deck and screaming to each other. He heard footsteps coming up the stairs from behind the wheelhouse.

Glanton opened the door. "Captain, we're seeing a couple of airboats coming up behind us. They're a couple miles away but closing in fast."

"Then get ready for 'em," Captain Pillinger said tersely. "Make sure everybody's armed."

"Yes, Cap'n," Glanton said just before he closed the door behind him.

Pillinger got up and locked the door behind them as he pulled out a Remington 870 shotgun from a cabinet underneath a side desk. He rummaged through one of the top drawers until he found a box of 00-buck shotgun shells, then he proceeded to load the gun. He pumped the weapon to place a round into the barrel chamber, then loaded another shell into the magazine tube. Pillinger then placed the shotgun on the table where the laptop was before sitting down again.

"At my command," Pillinger said as he looked at his laptop again. "Turn thirty degrees starboard… now!"

Tyrone was about to turn the wheel left, then realized that starboard as right as he turned it a few notches to his right. The *Nimrod* was now going at 15 miles per hour, its diesel power plant driving two traction engines, which pulled the rear paddlewheels via two forty-foot long chains as it cruised along the black waters near the sunken town. The enemy had apparently expected them to veer to the side of the supposed sunken part of the overpass. Just as the ship began crossing near the sunken onramp that lead up to the overpass, its flattened hull slid just underneath two school buses that had been deliberately sunk vertically, with their front sides embedded in the bottom of the flooded highway. The *Nimrod* angled up slightly, but the moment the center part of its top heavy hull passed over the upright school bus underneath, the ship immediately shuddered to a halt as the top part of its hull was nearly raised above the waterline. The enemy had also placed underwater steel poles that lined around the sunken buses. These thirty-foot long metal rods immediately were made from lamp posts and they broke pieces of the ship's rear paddlewheel as one of them was torn loose and imbedded itself onto one of its spokes.

In the engine room, Eight-Ball immediately realized what had happened as he pulled the lever to shut down the engines before any more damage was done to the paddlewheel. The ship was suddenly idle.

Captain Pillinger cursed as he reached for the ship's telephone box. Loud whizzes were heard all around the wheelhouse as holes suddenly appeared in the glass panels. Pillinger and Tyrone immediately ducked down beneath the sandbagged part of the room as bullets started peppering it. One bullet tore off the top of one of the handles of the ship's wheel while another punched a hole into the wooden telephone box of the ship's intercom.

Tyrone crouched up and stared out from the lower edge of the windows as he shifted from one vantage point to another. He could see at least three airboats that were modified with armored canopies circling the stricken riverboat. Shots continued to ring out as the *Nimrod* crew continued to engage the circling craft from their sandbagged positions. One of the hunters stood up like an idiot in order to get a better shot and was instantly shot through the neck. The doomed man fell over the upper deck railings and into the murky waters below. As Tyrone shifted his vantage point to the stern of the boat and tried to look behind them, he let out a gasp.

Pillinger was breathing hard due to the stress and frustration. He noticed Tyrone's shocked look as he cradled the broken rotary telephone system in his arms. "What is it?"

Tyrone pointed at something out in the distance. It was an object that moved in between the two partially sunken buildings that they had passed by just a few minutes earlier. When it finally revealed itself as it came closer, Pillinger let out another curse.

It was a black-painted SURC, a small unit river craft used by the Navy. An armored patrol boat that was fast and could easily withstand small arms fire, this was very bad news for all of them. Tyrone could see that the bow of the SURC had an armored turret on it and it looked like it was equipped with a machinegun. He now had a sinking feeling he should have never left Shreveport. There was a good chance that the ship would be taken.

As he sensed his hopes slipping away, Tyrone felt a rough hand clenching his left shoulder. Pillinger got close to his ear and Tyrone could feel the short, desperate breaths coming from his mouth. "Time to prove you ain't the coward everybody thinks you are, boy," the captain hissed. "I need you to head over to Eight-Ball and do what you can to get the engines restarted. Otherwise, I'm gonna shoot you myself. Ya hear?"

Tyrone nodded. He didn't feel like they had much of a chance. He preferred to do something instead of just surrendering to those pirates. He quickly got up and got the back door open. Just as he was about to make a run down the white painted stairs, he heard a whistle behind him.

"Here," Pillinger said as he threw the Remington shotgun at him. "You might need it!"

Tyrone caught the barrel of the shotgun and he cradled it in his arms as he waited for a lull in the firing below. He had been trained with rifles in the army but he figured that there wasn't much difference, just point and shoot. Tyrone immediately sprinted past the doorway and was down the first stairwell the moment one of the airboats passed behind his line of sight. Just as he started running towards the second stairwell, the SURC began to open up with its machinegun turret as it finally got into range. He saw the heavy machinegun tracers streak by like laser beams, as they punched multiple holes in a nearby group of sandbags. One man who had been hiding behind it with an AK-47 instantly fell to his side and stopped moving, the rifle clattering on the deck. Tyrone kept on running and dodging from one spot of cover to the next as he headed for the stairs leading down. The almost continuous machinegun fire began to throw wood splinters all around as it chewed up the ship's walls and railings. People were screaming and cussing all around him.

Instead of running down the side stairwell, Tyrone slid down its steps using his buttocks. It was painful, but it gave a little bit more cover than running down the stairs in an upright position. By the time he reached the level of the main deck, his butt as well as his lower back was in acute pain. He would probably have bruises in the morning, but it wouldn't matter unless they got the engines restarted.

The main deck was in chaos. One of the airboats was foolhardy enough to get within ten feet of the starboard side of the *Nimrod.* As the pirates lifted up their armored canopy to try and get onboard, a group of hunters lying low at the upper deck instantly stood up and poured several dozen rounds of full automatic and semi-auto fire into them. The four men in the airboat died almost instantly as they were shot full of holes. The turret gunner on the SURC saw what had happened and began to return fire, just as the hunters were able to get back into cover once more, although he was able to wound two of them.

Tyrone crouched and then sprinted through the double doors of the main deck saloon as he started to run past the bar. Several bullets tore through and broke the glass portholes of the doors just as he sprinted through them. As he twisted to his right in order to run towards the engine room, he noticed another hunter lying face down on the barroom floor. It was Mohawk, and he had a small hole at the back of his head. A puddle of crimson was forming on the wooden floorboards beside him. Tyrone looked away and then opened the engine room door. As he stepped inside, he quickly saw that Eight-Ball was pinned along the steel railings that housed one of the pistons for the engine. One of the pirates was able to board and he had a knife that he was slowly pushing towards the chief engineer's throat. Eight-Ball had his hands on the pirate's arms to stop the blade, but he was losing the battle.

"Hey!" Tyrone said as he aimed the shotgun.

The pirate was startled as he let go of Eight-Ball and turned around. He wore military fatigues but his hair was long and unkempt. The blast from the shotgun caught him square in the stomach as he doubled over with a grunt. The pirate writhed on the floor for a few seconds, then he stopped moving altogether.

Tyrone grimaced from the pain on his shoulder. He hadn't anticipated the recoil as he pumped another round into the shotgun's chamber. Then he looked at Eight-Ball. "Are you alright?"

Eight-Ball just stood over the dead pirate as he was busy catching his breath. "Thank you, I was hidin' in here when he burst through the door. I was able to knock his rifle away with my wrench but then he pulled out a knife and almost gutted me."

Tyrone quickly moved over to him. He could hear the clanging noises as the gunfire would sometimes hit the outer steel casing of the engines. "We've got to get moving again! If we don't then we're all dead!"

Eight-Ball turned around before pointing at the gap in the rear where the giant paddlewheel was. "There's that long steel pole that's stuck in the wheel. We gotta get that thing out before I can restart the engine."

Tyrone handed the chief engineer the shotgun before scrambling up the idle paddlewheel. It was like climbing on a wooden, slippery Ferris wheel. Tyrone's feet nearly slid out from under him as he made his way to where the steel rod was sticking out, but he managed to hang on using his arms and got himself into an upright position. By the time he got close to the pole, he was already fully exposed outside. Fortunately, nobody noticed him in the dark as he climbed to the upper part of the paddlewheel. As he gripped the metal rod, he realized it was jammed fast, the pole had bent and was now stuck in between two of the steel spokes.

At that moment, one of the airboats noticed him and it started to maneuver to go around to the stern so that the marauders on it could get a clear shot. The SURC continued to get closer as it kept raking the upper deck with withering machinegun fire. Tyrone sensed that they were now out of time. As he locked his arms along the top part of the spokes, he used one leg to brace himself. Then, with all his strength, he started kicking at the rod with his free leg. Tyrone could hear the grinding sound of metal as the rod began to give way. Just as he was about to deliver a final kick to jar the pole loose, a bullet ricocheted off one of the steel spokes and hit him in the side of his arm.

Tyrone screamed as the pain in his right arm made it go limp and he nearly slipped off the paddlewheel and into the water. He could hear more bullets whizzing by as one of the airboats was concentrating their fire on him. From the corner of his eye he could see that the SURC was less than thirty feet away from the ship. Gritting his teeth for one last try, Tyrone ignored the pain on his arm as he willed it to grab hold of one of the spokes. His sense of time and place narrowed down to this single instant as his whole life flashed before his eyes. He was like a hamster in a wheel, hanging on for dear life, while men around him were trying their best to kill him.

Screw it, he thought. Tyrone didn't care anymore. If he was to go down then let it be this way. With his remaining strength, he kicked at the steel rod with both feet, just as another bullet grazed his skull. The pain disorientated him and he let go with his arms and the added weight finally pushed the steel rod loose from the spokes. Tyrone's shoulder bounced off of one of the spokes as he fell into the dark water.

Eight-Ball had been watching the whole thing from the gap at the rear of the engine room. He immediately saw that Tyrone was able to get the rod loose from the paddlewheel. The chief engineer quickly ran over to the controls and placed the throttle on full. Since the engine was merely idle, the paddlewheel began to turn almost immediately. The extra force from the engines was able to shake the rear part of the undersea school bus loose as the *Nimrod's* hull tore through its rear body.

Just as the SURC started getting in close, its machinegun jammed. While the boat's gunner started to clear his weapon, two of the *Nimrod's* crew members stood up and threw a pair of Molotov cocktails that hit squarely on the deck of the attacking boat. The incendiary bombs instantly ignited, and the river patrol boat was now on fire. The captain of the SURC immediately went to full throttle as it veered away. The two remaining airboat crews were so demoralized, they too turned and fled away from the battle.

When Tyrone regained consciousness, he realized that he was lying on the barroom floor. He felt a bandage over his forehead where the rifle bullet had grazed it. His right arm was aching but he could feel it was whole. As he raised his hand to test its grip, he noticed Captain Pillinger and Eight-Ball were standing over him.

"Looks like you got real lucky," Pillinger said. "We saw your big black head floating on the water so we just had to reverse and pick you up."

Eight-Ball had a smile on his wrinkled face. "You did good, brother. Your injuries are pretty minor too, the bullet to your head merely grazed it, and the bullet that hit your arm only tore a little bit of skin and muscle off of you. I say that you're either the luckiest sonuvabitch on this earth or there must be a god looking after you."

Pillinger was holding the Remington. "You've earned this." He placed the shotgun beside Tyrone along with a box of 00-buck shells. "Rest up. We're now along the Pearl, in a few hours we make the turn into the Leaf River. Then we ought to be in Mobile in a day or two."

As the two men walked away, Tyrone couldn't help but smile a little. Looks like he earned their trust, and about time too. Then he shifted his gaze to the side of the room and he saw half a dozen men being treated for gunshot wounds.

13. The Dream of the Smoking Mirror

Teotihuacan

Unlike the temple area, the outskirts of the city were being constructed along more modern means. High Priest Tepiltzin could see that the factory had steel roofing and the walls around them were concrete. The newly installed machinery was humming as the factory workers were busy churning out weapons for the resurgent empire. It had taken weeks to install the new electric grid, but it was absolutely essential in order for the city's industry to work.

The factory manager that was showing him and his assistants around no longer wore the traditional Aztec loincloth and feathered cloak. Instead, this man was wearing overalls underneath his embroidered robe. The fashion seemed strange, but it was a new way of combining the old with the new. As high priest to the Flayed One, Tepiltzin could have easily ordered all city workers to stick to their traditional clothes, but he had been distracted by strange dreams in the past few days.

As Tepiltzin pretended to listen to the factory manager's boasts and salesmanship, his mind began to wander again. Less than a day after his brother Yaotl had been reassigned at his request, his once peaceful nights were now being inundated by dreams of a young, fair-haired boy holding a small mirror made of black obsidian. At first, he dismissed it as nothing more than the dreams of a distant past, when he was addicted to watching telenovelas on

TV while still living his previous life as a rich playboy. For some strange reason, the dreams continued and in fact, began to intensify to the point where he would wake up in the middle of the night, drenched in sweat. Even when he increased his personal bloodletting in order to appease the gods so that they would give him a more restful sleep, the dreams were unabated by it. In the past week, he had hardly been getting any sleep. Tepiltzin would stay awake all night, using the painful spines of the manta ray to bleed himself, fearful that he would see the boy in his dreams if he dared close his eyes once more.

The plant manager smiled as he gestured at the finished piles of bullets that were lying in white plastic crates in front of them. "This is the end product, High Priest. As you can see, our quality control has increased exponentially. We had a problem at first because our warriors preferred to be issued rubber bullets over the lead ones. The reason, of course, is because they prefer to wound their opponents rather than kill them. We all know that is so because the empire needs captives for sacrifices. So it was a bit of a problem when we took these machine parts from an ammunition factory in Dallas and then set it up here. The calibration for rubber bullets is slightly different and we needed to find the right kind of rubber too."

Tepiltzin continued to pretend he was still interested. He smiled back at the clueless manager who stood beside him. "Fascinating, please continue."

The plant manager nodded as he gestured at the small group to follow him to his office at the far end of the plant. "Yes, as I was saying. It took us weeks to find a good source for the rubber. In the meantime, our quality control suffered and our warriors took more casualties due to misfiring of the bullets. But since our brave soldiers always return from the dead lands anyway, it was really more of an annoyance than a problem because they were forced to use lead bullets for a short time afterwards. This meant that the number of captives taken had gone down and they were not too happy about that either. Thankfully, that has all been rectified now."

Tepiltzin just nodded as his group of priests and assistants were led into an air conditioned office with plush chairs and imported tables. The manager all bade them to sit as a secretary hovered nearby carrying a silver tray.

The secretary was dressed in a traditional Aztec dress as she beamed at him. "Would you like a cup, High Priest?"

Tepiltzin was momentarily confused for a moment, then he looked up at her. "I'm sorry, what did you say?"

"She was asking if you would like a cup of xocolatl, High Priest," the ever grinning manager said as he sat down with them. "Our cacao beans were harvested just yesterday and we make our chocolate here in the traditional way: with no sugar, just freshly crushed chili and vanilla. Of course, if you prefer the modern Spanish version, she can prepare that for you very quickly as well."

Tepiltzin's head was pounding due to the lack of sleep but he forced himself to smile as he looked at the worried secretary. "The traditional Aztec way is good. Thank you."

The secretary quickly poured him a cup and set it on the coffee table beside him. The junior priests accompanying Tepiltzin had slightly concerned looks on their faces. They had hoped the high priest would admonish this plant manager for returning to modern colonial ways, but they were surprised because Tepiltzin hardly said a word during the entire tour. Since there were no emperors in this new empire, it was the priests who determined the ways in which to live. Tepiltzin's pale demeanor and tired looking eyes gave them a feeling that something was not right.

As Tepiltzin raised the cup of chocolate near his mouth, his wrist began to tremble slightly, spilling a few drops of chocolate onto the padded couch. His assistant acolyte Chipahua sensed something was very wrong as he made sure his hands were free.

The plant manager didn't seem to notice as he just continued talking. "The cacao beans come from the farmer's plantations just a few miles from here. If you have the time, I can take you there for a tour this afternoon. So far, the gods have doubled our crop yields ever since we increased the number of sacrifices to them. Praise Tlaloc!"

Right when he heard those words, Tepiltzin's head started to swim. The room began to whirl around him as he lost his sense of balance. The creeping pain at the back of his head had suddenly thrust itself until it exploded just behind his eyes. Tepiltzin started to see bright flashes as his body swayed back and forth. The cup of chocolate fell from his hand. Chipahua instantly caught his master before he fell to the floor. All Tepiltzin could hear were shouts of alarm as everything suddenly turned dark.

The next thing he knew, Tepiltzin was standing near the banks of a small stream. As he looked up, the sky was of glowing mauve and pewter. He couldn't see the sun, but based on the light all around him it seemed like either the early morning or mid-afternoon, he wasn't quite so sure. The brook was at the base of a series of hills and soft, green grass was growing all around. Across the horizon, he could see a gargantuan structure that covered the surrounding lands all the way towards the distant, mist-laden mountains at the far edge of his vision. It looked like a haphazardly built series of overlapping wooden walls that stretched upwards to over a hundred feet in several places. He could see large, ornate carvings of runes and serpents along its façade. The whole construct must have been hundreds of miles long. The structure was completely roofed by multitudes of overlapping metal shields, it was as if millions of warriors had suddenly raised their round circular shields up to blot out the sky. A number of black birds could be seen circling around the place, they were either crows or ravens, but he couldn't really tell.

"The Lord of the Near and Far isn't too happy with you, mate," a slightly high-pitched voice said.

The high priest of Xipe Totec turned around. Standing at the top of the small hill behind him was the young boy that had been in his dreams. The kid looked to be around twelve or thirteen years old and wore a blue hooded sweatshirt and jeans, but with a curious pair of pink striped sneakers on his feet. He was fair-haired, with sky blue eyes that seemed to stare right into Tepiltzin's soul. The boy was casually holding a small, circular mirror made of polished black obsidian in his right hand.

Tepiltzin's eyes narrowed. "Who are you?"

The boy just shrugged casually. "Well, I could tell you my name is Steve and I'm from England, but it doesn't really matter, does it? I think you already know who I am."

Tepiltzin frowned. He realized that he was still speaking in Nahuatl and the boy answered him back perfectly in the same language. This had to be a dream. "I have been to England in my previous life before the rebirth of our empire. Where we are right now is surely not that place."

Steve rolled his eyes. "Duh, I said I'm from England. I never said this place was England. You haven't been listening very well, have you?"

"Perhaps it is because of our language," Tepiltzin said. "I am speaking in Nahuatl- an ancient language of my people, and yet a boy from England can speak it as well? There is something unnatural about all this."

Steve tilted his head up and started laughing. "Unnatural? Oh, that's really funny! With all the gods coming out all over the place and all these monsters and creatures that are suddenly all around us, and you make a complaint about something so trivial as not being natural? You are such a funny man."

Tepiltzin grimaced. "You are a disrespectful little child! How dare you speak to a high priest of Xipe Totec this way! I can have you flayed alive for insulting me like that!"

Steve shook his head as he kept on giggling. "Sorry, but I had expected better questions coming from you. I mean, you did say you were a high priest and all that."

Tepiltzin hissed. The boy was insolent. But he sensed that he was merely a visitor and it was Steve who held all the power here. He needed to be patient and control his own temper. "Very well, let us begin again. I am High Priest Tepiltzin, of the temple of Xipe Totec in Teotihuacan. If I may ask, where exactly am I?"

"That's better," Steve said. "Well I can tell you that you are in a dream. So you're definitely right about that, mate."

Tepiltzin looked around. "So all this is just a dream? Then why does it seem so vivid? I could have never dreamt of all of this by myself."

"You didn't," Steve said. "Since you're a high priest, then you should also know that the gods sometimes visits their chosen ones in the form of dreams. This particular place is the land of Valhalla. It's where the honored warriors of the Vikings go when they died on earth."

Tepiltzin was confused. "Valhalla? But my god is Aztec. What would this place have to do with him?"

The boy held up the black mirror. "Do you know what this is?"

"An obsidian mirror," Tepiltzin said. "We have many of those back in my city."

"Do you know what it represents?"

Tepiltzin drew in a deep breath. "Yes, Tezcatlipoca. He is the god of the smoking mirror."

Steve grinned. There was a mischievous twinkle in his eye. "Correct, it looks like you're getting warmer now."

Tepiltzin's eyebrows shot up. "Wait, are you a manifestation of Tezcatlipoca?"

"Not quite," the boy said. "I am a real person and I actually do have his mirror, I think I've been attuned to it somehow. This sort of explains why you're here in Valhalla. It seems that our dreams and thoughts are overlapping."

Tepiltzin crossed his arms. "I am a high priest of Xipe Totec. The god of the smoking mirror has nothing to do with me. Why would Tezcatlipoca use you to enter my dream state? What is all of this for?"

"To give you a message," Steve said. "Tezcatlipoca is quite angry with you."

"Angry with me? Why?"

Steve looked away for a bit. "He says your colleagues killed his priests and wiped out his followers. As you well know, Tezcatlipoca is a very dangerous god and it was he who created the first sun."

Tepiltzin nodded. "Yes, I am aware of our creation stories. I have memorized the entire Tale of the Five Suns by heart. That is part of my responsibilities as high priest. Going back to your message, are you saying Tezcatlipoca is angry at me personally, or is he angry at the entire Aztec people?"

"At all of you," Steve said softly. "He has asked me to convey this message that he has been wronged and he will seek redress. It was not right for your people to slaughter his followers and desecrate his temples. He told me he intends to return and to punish you all for your insolence and betrayal."

Tepiltzin bit his lip. He had been warned by the avatar of his patron deity that the god of the smoking mirror would attempt to return soon and that they must be vigilant. "Tezcatlipoca may try and gain revenge against us, but we are now a united people. There is no dissension among our ranks and we are protected by the Triple Alliance of Huitzilopochtli, Tlaloc and Xipe Totec. Our three patron gods will protect us from the likes of Tezcatlipoca. How can he expect to defeat us when we have the might and the advantage of numbers over his nonexistent power base?"

The boy pointed a finger at him. "Through you, mate."

Tepiltzin took a step backwards and nearly tripped over as he staggered for a bit. His eyes went wide in both shock and surprise. "Me? But I am a loyal priest to Xipe Totec. My uncle himself was chosen as the avatar of the Flayed One! I shall never betray my position as high priest! I would rather die!"

Steve gave him a blank look. "You will know the power of Tezcatlipoca soon enough. Then you will realize that you gave false allegiance to the Flayed One. After that, you will be given a choice. Yet as you weigh in on these alternatives, you will experience pain and suffering. You will need to endure the crucible of despair. Only after that will your eyes be truly opened."

Tepiltzin shook his head violently. "Never! I deny the god of the smoking mirror! Xipe Totec will protect me! I will warn my uncle of this and we will take steps to make sure Tezcatlipoca shall never return!"

The boy held up the black mirror until it was just above his head. "The god of the smoking mirror has many aspects. He is the night wind, the enemy of both sides, and the possessor of sky and earth. He can assume many forms, has many names and an infinite number of manifestations. Tezcatlipoca cannot be stopped. His mirror is the all seeing, the all knowing, and only he shall foretell the future. Of all the things that shall pass, Tezcatlipoca knows them all, mate."

"Nooo!" Tepiltzin shouted as he opened his eyes and sat up from his bed. That was when he realized that he was back in his personal chambers in the palace of the high priests in Teotihuacan.

His assistant Chipahua had been sitting beside him. The junior acolyte placed a caring hand on Tepiltzin's chest and gently coaxed the trembling high priest to lie back down on his back. Chipahua stood up as he took out an ice pack from a cooler that had been lying nearby and placed it on Tepiltzin's forehead.

Tepiltzin blinked a few times as his breathing started to slow down back to normal. "H-how long have I been out?"

"Since late morning, High Priest," Chipahua said. "You collapsed in the manager's office so we took you back to your quarters here in the temple. You were trashing about and you had a high fever. You were talking in your sleep so we called High Priest Coaxoch back from Tenochtitlan. He arrived this afternoon and he did the dusk ritual in your place. It is now early evening. How are you feeling?"

Tepiltzin frowned. Coaxoch was Marcelino Morales. So they recalled his enemy back to his city. "Why did you not make some incantations to wake me? Who gave you the order to call Coaxoch back here?"

"High Priest Eleuia from the temple of Tlaloc came by," Chipahua said nervously. "He took a look at you and said that you were in a dream trance, it was best not to disturb you. So we went ahead and called the main temple at Tenochtitlan and Avatar Tlazopilli said he would be sending High Priest Coaxoch to take over your duties while you were in your dream state. We were instructed to care for you but not to disturb you."

"Yet I am awake now and finished with my dreams, there is no need for Coaxoch to be here any longer. I will resume my position as head priest of Xipe Totec here in this city."

Chipahua briefly looked away before answering in a low voice. "B-but the orders from the avatar was clear. Coaxoch would be high priest in this city until further notice. He said even if you awake from the dream, Coaxoch would still be in charge of the temple."

Tepiltzin gritted his teeth. "But… what about my position here?"

"I-I do not know, sir," Chipahua said. "I was instructed to care for you in this chamber until you recovered. High Priest Coaxoch will be staying at the guest quarters until you were well enough to travel, I was told. Then I was to take a report from you as far as what your dreams meant, and then send my findings back to Tenochtitlan. T-those were my only orders."

"You were not told anything else?"

Chipahua shook his head as he started to rise. "I'm afraid not, High Priest. I will send for a meal and then we can talk about your dreams tomorrow."

Tepiltzin placed a hand on his assistant's arm. "You may stay. I am ready to talk about my dreams right now."

Chipahua smiled as he reached over to take a ballpoint pen and a pad of paper from the night table beside the bed. Then he sat down beside him once more. "I was told that when a priest goes into a dream state, that is when their god speaks to them. I had heard stories about Grand Priest Tlazopilli and his dreams. One of my favorites was when the tzitzimitl visited him when he was still living as an ordinary man. I heard they even brought him directly to Mictlan, the underworld where all the dead go to, and he stayed there for a whole season before they brought him back to our world once more."

"Yes, those were good stories," Tepiltzin said. "He told me quite a few more when Xipe Totec would appear to him in a dream. He said that the dreaming of the gods were more important than even the sacrificial rituals, because it was the messages in those dreams that would determine the fate of our people."

"I hope he will grace me the honor of being able to hear it from him personally one day," Chipahua said wistfully.

Tepiltzin couldn't help but smile. Despite his ordeals, his assistant always found a way to cheer him up, if only for a short while. "I'm sure you will, Chipahua. You have the makings of a future high priest in Xipe Totec's temples. All that remains is for you to dream about him."

Chipahua grinned at the imagined anticipation until he realized he was holding things up with his small talk. "Okay, sir. I'm sorry but we might as well begin the report then. This way we could finish early and you can get your rest. So tell me, High Priest, did you meet our patron god Xipe Totec in your dream?"

Tepiltzin laid his head back on the pillow and closed his eyes. "Yes, I was in a dark, smoke-filled land. The next thing I knew, he had appeared in front of me. I immediately fell on my knees in respect."

"What did he look like?"

"Like he always does. He was wearing an old husk that slowly rotted away, piece by piece. The flayed skin near his wrists had completely rotted away and his hands were bare. His exposed hands had red skin. His face I really couldn't see the full features of, but it had a skin of gold. I couldn't see his eyes."

Chipahua nodded as he kept writing on the pad. "Did he say anything to you?"

Tepiltzin nodded as he kept his eyes closed. "Yes, he told me that the god of the smoking mirror would attempt to return. It was my duty to root out his hidden followers… and destroy them."

Chipahua gasped as the pen nearly fell from his trembling hands. "Tezcatlipoca! Did Xipe Totec say as to where these followers of the smoking mirror would be at?"

Tepiltzin paused briefly before answering. "He told me there is a traitor in his own temple. That I must find whoever it is. Then I must flay that traitor and wear his skin until it would naturally flake away as it dried in the sun."

Chipahua was writing furiously now. "Did he say who the traitor might be?"

"No, but he did give me some clues as how to find out and prove it."

"What clues were these?"

Tepiltzin opened his eyes and looked at his assistant. "That I cannot tell you. Xipe Totec told me that it must remain a secret between me and him. If I am to divulge it, then the traitor might be alerted and on guard."

Chipahua was shocked. "Huh? I must make a complete report to our Grand Priest back at Tenochtitlan, I am required to include every single detail!"

"I'm sorry but I cannot give that away."

Chipahua had a worried look on his face. "Oh dear, if I am not to include that bit of information and if the avatar finds out, I might be offered as a sacrifice for dishonoring the temple."

Tepiltzin placed a reassuring hand on his assistant's arm once more. "Do not fear. When I uncover the traitor and sacrifice him, I will make an after report to the avatar myself. In it I will mention you as an invaluable ally. I am sure you can become a high priest with that kind of recommendation. And not to mention that Xipe Totec himself will be indebted to you for your unswerving loyalty to him."

14. Escape from Purgatory

Kansas

The camp at the back of the Fort Leavenworth National Cemetery had only been constructed a few months before. Several acres of forest were bulldozed over, and the barbed wire fence was erected first. The inmates lived in tents as they constructed their own cabins from the felled trees over a three month period. Since there were plenty of empty housing in Fort Leavenworth, the camp guards tended to have their own individual houses nearby and would report to work their shifts as if going to a factory. An outer fence and thirty-foot tall guard towers were soon put in place. Soon afterwards, the camp was split in two. The first camp would house the men, while the women and children would be in the other. Many of the sinners that were deemed to be too degenerate to live as citizens of Christian Kansas were interred there. In the beginning, there were less than two thousand of them. As the threat of an all-out war with the Federals grew, more and more undesirables were soon interred within it. The camp had no official name, just a number: 2241. The guards had their own nickname for it. They called it Camp Purgatory.

The Fort Leavenworth area was right up to the border with Missouri, and the river served as a natural boundary between the two sides. The Federals in the eastern portion had already evacuated most of their citizens from nearby Weston, but the separatists were sure that there were military units stationed on the other side, waiting to cross the Missouri River if there was any sign of weakness. Most of the SOL troops were spread out in a defensive position near the military airfield, at the base of the salient. Both sides were in a quiet stalemate and nobody wanted a conflict to start. Nevertheless, the reason why the separatists placed an internment camp so close to the Federal border was as a show of force. The latest intelligence reports had stated that the separatists would be using their prisoners as human shields in case they were invaded.

The clouds had obscured the night sky, so most of the illumination at the camp ground were from the roving searchlights that were mounted on the guard towers. Patrols with military dogs would regularly sweep the outer perimeter, just in case there was a foolish attempt at an escape. Although there was electricity within the wooden cabins of the camp, it was only for a few hours in the early evening so most of the inmates got by using candles and kerosene lamps. There was a guard barracks nearby, but most of the off-duty sentries preferred to drive off to the nearby housing areas after they had finished their shifts.

Julius Jones got up from his cot and put on his shoes and coat before stepping out of his cabin. When the camp was first organized, there used to be a curfew and all prisoners were confined to their cabins after the evening meal. Ever since he started a prisoner's committee to demand better conditions, there was a noticeable change in the enforcement of the rules. The fact was that a former friend of his had become the new commandant of the camp, and this also played a role in the relaxation of the harsh order that had once made the conditions almost intolerable. Now the prisoners were allowed to cultivate vegetable gardens to supplement their meager rations. At night, people were allowed to visit other cabins in groups of two or in singles. Julius was also able to set up an occasional arrangement for the prisoners to visit the other camp, for married men to see their wives and children, and for conjugal visits as well. The new commandant had also proclaimed that these kinder, gentler conditions would be quickly revoked if there was any attempt of escape, or if any kind of revolt happened. Julius had every intention of escape, but he counseled the others that it must come at the right time, and not before.

As he stretched his back while standing just outside of his cabin, Julius drew in a deep breath and then exhaled, the vapors from his mouth made a fine mist as it reflected off of the nearby lights from the other cabins. The nights were starting to get chilly, and the camp commandant still hadn't approved his request that they be given more blankets. He wondered just how much longer this stalemate would go on. Julius had been thinking the Feds across the border would have to move against Kansas sooner or later.

As he rubbed his cold hands before sticking them back into the pockets of his wool jacket, Julius noticed some sort of commotion in the other cabin. He could see two shadows in the blurry window and one of them was wildly gesticulating, though no sound could be heard. He figured it must be some sort of animated discussion. Julius knew the camp guards in their towers wouldn't be able to see the cabin's windows from their vantage points, so unless there was a significant amount of noise, then they wouldn't be alerted. He had told the other prisoners to make sure that they did everything as quietly as possible in order not to get any suspicions up. If those two of the prisoners were fighting, then they would do it quietly, or else they would be ostracized.

Julius figured he might as well try to find out what it was about. He hunched his shoulders forward and started walking towards the other cabin. As he got closer, he could definitely hear someone arguing inside, it was quite animated but it was hushed enough so that anyone not listening intently wouldn't really notice. As he got to the front of the door, he knocked lightly in separate raps of four.

The muted arguing stopped immediately. He could hear footsteps walking up to the door and it opened slightly with a creak. A man with a dark beard and broken eyeglasses peered outside. It was Mike Thomas and his voice was a faint whisper. "Who's there?"

"It's me," Julius said softly. "What's going on?"

Mike had to blink a few times because his eyes just weren't any good anymore. He had been badly beaten by the morality council a number of times and his broken glasses were never replaced. It took a while for him to adjust between the dark and the illumination of the cabins. The worst thing about it was that he could barely read anything and it gave him a constant, melancholy disposition. "Julius, is that you?"

"Yeah, are you okay?"

Mike's response was terse and to the point. "Get in here, quick."

Julius stepped inside before closing the door behind him. Mike's cabin was just like the others. There were crude bunks and old secondhand furniture like tables and chairs that were donated by the commandant. There was an old, wood burning stove at the end of the room, it had a small chimney that poked out from the roof. A small kerosene lamp was suspended on a hook in the center of the room. Standing beside Mike was Jacob Neely, a young man from Wichita. Julius had known Mike when he was holed up in his church, right before the authorities raided it and arrested them both. Jacob was a recent internee. He had spoken out against the harsh treatment of non-Christians and was soon considered part of an underground movement dedicated to overthrow the leaders of the Rock of God Church. Once he was deemed as a potential traitor, Jacob's family disowned him and they completely agreed with the authorities to ship him away to the camp.

Mike instinctively rubbed the soft part of his skull, at the top of his head. That was where an enforcer from the church had hit him with a baton several months back. He was in the prison hospital for weeks with a skull fracture after that. "Did you hear about what we were saying?"

Julius shook his head. "No, all I could see was the shadow of one of you guys waving his hands around. That brown wrapping paper you put on those windows isn't a hundred percent opaque, you know."

"Sorry, that was me," Jacob said. "I guess I was just excited after what happened."

Mike looked around nervously. "Do you think the guards saw us?"

"No, the angle was such that they would have to be at ground level to see that," Julius said before turning to look at Jacob. "So what happened?"

Jacob grinned. His winter cap was still somewhat new but his second hand tweed coat had rips and patches all over it. "We found a girl in the mess hall."

Julius's eyes opened wide. "What? She sneaked in from the other camp?"

Mike shook his head. "No, nobody who's been to the other camp recognizes her and she says she came from the outside. She's pretty young, looked like a teenager to me."

"Yeah," Jacob said. "She must be around sixteen I think."

Julius adjusted his own pair of glasses. The men were allowed to visit the other camp for a few hours. But if the guards found out that there was a girl in the men's camp, all of their privileges would be revoked. "Who else knows about this?"

"Just us and Albert over at cabin eighteen," Mike said. "We had cleanup duty after dinner so we figured we'd do it just before midnight. As we started to clean up the place we saw her, she was just standing there, like hiding in the shadows between the windows."

"Where is she now?"

"Still there," Jacob said. "She said she would wait."

Julius rubbed his forehead. This was really unexpected. "What did she want?"

Mike kept fidgeting. He was clearly nervous about any potential punishments. His wife Alice was in the other camp and she had been beaten badly too. Although he was still defiant, he would now back off when it came to anything involving physical confrontations. "She said she wanted to speak to the leader of the prisoners."

Julius shrugged. "We don't really have an official leader or anything like that."

Jacob smirked. "You are, Julius. You pretty much speak for everyone here and in the other camp, and we always do what you suggest. We were going to tell you about this, but it's all making us nervous you know… since she said she would free us if we gave her some info."

Julius's eyes narrowed. "Free us? By herself? No shit?"

Mike shrugged. "That's what she said. Seemed pretty confident about it, calm even."

"You said we would plan an escape when the time was right," Jacob said as he looked at Julius. "This could be an opportunity if she's telling the truth."

"If she's telling the truth," Julius said, putting an accent on the first word. "You say she's a teenager? How on God's green earth will she be able to free us? The whole two camps are close to twenty thousand men, women and children. Even though we're close to the border, there must be a brigade of Kansas troops between us and the river."

Jacob bit his lip. "That's what she said. I know it sounds like bullshit, but what if she's telling the truth? Maybe she's part of an advance team from the Feds or something."

"She didn't look like a soldier to me," Mike said. "Way too young. Looked like she just came from high school."

Julius took a deep breath. "Either way, this is trouble. If the guards catch her then we're all in for it. If she's telling the truth then she better have a good plan because we've only begun to talk about it amongst ourselves and we're totally unprepared as of right now."

Mike was breathing heavily. "So what do we do now?"

"Let's go talk to her first," Julius said.

Tara Weiss saw two men enter the mess hall. Both of them were wearing glasses. She was leaning on a wall at the far end so that anyone looking in through the windows wouldn't see her. One of the men she recognized had been in the hall earlier when he was one of the cleaning crew. His name was Mike. The other one was a black man and was wearing some sort of priest's outfit. She hoped that the prisoners didn't squeal on her. Since she didn't hear any alarms, she figured that the other man must be their leader.

The black man walked up to her and held out his hand. "Good evening. I'm Reverend Julius Jones. I'm the spokesperson for the internees here."

Tara shook it. "I thought the people in this state respect priests. Why are you a prisoner in this camp?"

Julius sighed. "Let's just say that I was helping a number of people that the authorities in this newly self-proclaimed independent country deemed as undesirable. So here I am. May I ask what your name is and how you got inside?"

"My name is Tara and how I got inside is going to have to remain a secret for the time being. I need your help in finding someone."

Julius looked at her solemnly. "You want us to find someone here? Why couldn't you just have spoken to the guards and made an inquiry with them?"

"Because I don't like them," Tara said. "I don't appreciate what they've been doing. It's not right to put people in prison just because others don't believe in the same god as they do."

"Well, it's a pretty risky thing you did, sneaking into this camp," Julius said. "If they catch you then they will most probably put you in the other camp, the ones with the women and children."

"I've been to that other camp already," Tara said. "They won't get to me. I have friends helping me out."

Mike took a mop from beside the wall and pretended to clean the floor when a wandering searchlight passed through the windows. "Friends? You mean the Feds? Are they launching an operation to rescue us?"

Tara shook her head. They didn't know the truth and it was better that they didn't. "Not really. My friends are something else. They can definitely get all of you out of here. But I need to find somebody before we do the rescue thing."

Julius took a rag that was lying on the table and pretended to do some cleaning. "Who are you looking for?"

"I wanted to find my brother, but it doesn't look like he's in the other camp. I looked for him there but didn't find him. There doesn't seem to be any kids his age in that camp," Tara said. "I'm also looking for a Matthew and Melissa Olsen. They were a family from Arizona who came up to Kansas when the whole god thing started. They took my brother with them, I think. I tried to find Melissa in the other camp but no luck there."

Mike looked up. "Olsen? I know of a Matty Olsen. He's in the infirmary though."

Tara's hopes started rising. "He is? Oh my god, I need to get over there and talk to him. He would know where my brother is!"

Julius placed his palms up in the air. "Calm down, girl. Don't shout or you'll alert the guards. We can walk over to the infirmary, but only in pairs. The guards might see you and they will sound the alert."

Tara started moving towards the door. She was so close, there was no stopping her now. "I'm sorry but I have to go see him now."

Julius ran over to her. "Wait, maybe we could disguise you somehow," he said as he gestured to Mike. "Mike, give me your coat and cap."

Mike walked over slowly as he started taking his coat off. "Are you sure this is going to work, Julius? I'm almost a foot taller than she is."

Julius took the coat from him and handed it to her. "There's no guards walking inside the camp at night, they are all in the towers. If they look down on us, they might not notice the height difference too much. Anyway, it's a short walk to the infirmary. How did you know about this Matty guy, Mike?"

"Pablo is the registered nurse who works in the infirmary and I go there to visit every now and then," Mike said. "Since both camp infirmaries share medical records, he keeps me updated as to Alice's condition. One of the guys they have in one of the beds is a guy named Matty Olsen. He's the only guy with that name on the camp so I figured it might be worth the shot to see if that really is the guy she's looking for."

Tara put the coat on. It was several sizes too big for her but she figured it was enough to get her to where she wanted to go. "Why's he in the infirmary?"

Mike looked away as he took off his cap and handed it to her. "When he heard his wife died, he took it pretty badly. He tried to rush the guards I think and they took it out on him."

Julius placed his hand on the doorknob. "Okay. Mike, stay here and pretend to keep cleaning. Tara, just walk casually and don't make any sudden moves. Just follow me and I'll get you to the infirmary."

Tara nodded. "Okay."

Julius opened the door and they both stepped out. The searchlights from the guard towers were constantly moving and would occasionally shine over them as they made a slow walk towards the infirmary. Tara had tucked her long hair into the head cap so the guards wouldn't notice that she was a girl. Julius deliberately led the pace as he took one step at a time. He knew from experience the guards would notice sudden movements in their field of vision since they had thermal gear up in their towers. A slow, deliberate walk was the safest way for them.

As they made it halfway towards the infirmary cabin, they were both suddenly engulfed in a blinding white light. One of the guard towers had put a search light directly on them. Julius instantly stopped. *Oh no, they got us,*

Tara thought as she just stood there beside him.

"Hey Julius, where do you think you're going?" One of the guards up in the tower above them said.

Julius pointed towards the infirmary. "I'm just taking Jesse here over to the clinic. He said he's got a fever."

"Jesse? I thought from his clothes it was Mike. Who is Jesse again?"

Julius squinted his eyes as the searchlight's ultra-bright intensity made it more powerful than daylight. He pointed to Tara. "It's Jesse Bowen. You remember him don't you? He's the nineteen year old from Topeka. He's got a sore throat, I think he's coming down with something."

"Why isn't his dad bringing him then?"

"His dad is out sick too," Julius said. "He's in bed at their cabin."

Tara tilted her head slightly and waved at the guards in the tower. At that moment a raven flew into the searchlight's projector and landed on top of it. The guards tried to swat it away but it flew into the first guard's face and started to claw at it. The first guard screamed as he fell backwards and the searchlight swiveled upwards, its light now illuminated the roof of the tower. The second guard tried to kick at the bird but the animal flew up and he hit his own colleague with a boot to the face. The first guard angrily got up and both men seemed ready to kill each other. Tara started walking away as she tugged Julius by the elbow. They both made it into the infirmary without further incident.

The lights in the infirmary were brighter compared to the other cabins since the electricity wasn't turned off there. Pablo Fuentes had been a nurse at University of Kansas Hospital for almost a decade, but was interned in Camp Purgatory because he was openly gay. He was checking off his medical logs when Julius and Tara walked through the door.

Pablo stood up. "Can I help you guys?"

Julius walked up to him and shook his hand. "Pablo, do you have a patient named Matt Olsen here?"

Pablo looked at Tara for a minute until he realized that she was a girl. Then he turned and pointed to a bed at the far end of the room. "He's over there. They brought him in over a month ago and he's still recovering."

Julius nodded. "What happened to him?"

"They beat him pretty badly when they brought him in here," Pablo said softly. "Concussion, multiple arm and leg fractures. The poor guy can hardly move his hands, much less talk. I think he suffered a stroke a few weeks ago, so there's also a possible intracranial injury. I have begged them to bring him to a proper facility since we don't have any CT scanners or advanced medical equipment here, but my requests have been ignored."

Tara stood over the hospital bed. The man who was lying in it was partially in shadow, his head and arms covered in old bandages. She could smell the sweat, along with the pungent odor of stale antiseptics and urine. The man seemed to be awake as his one eye was moving back and forth along the edges of his eyelid. He looked like he was in very bad shape. Tara soon realized that it was indeed Matthew Olsen, her one-time neighbor in the trailer park in Phoenix. She didn't know him very well but they always said hi every time they bumped into each other. His son Tyler was eight. Tyler was Timmy's playmate and they were always running around the neighborhood together. Tara's heart was now at full throttle. If there was anything she could do to help Mr. Olsen, she would.

As she placed her hand on his arm, she instantly drew back when he let out a shriek. His eye stopped wandering around and locked onto her. Tara smiled a little and stayed silent, hoping that he would somehow recognize her.

The words that came out of him were half formed. It was as if he knew what to say, but his mouth and his brain wasn't working too well for him to say it properly. "T… ara?"

Tara's smile became bigger as she nodded excitedly. "Yes, it's me, Mr. Olsen. How are you doing?"

"No..t goo."

Tara looked down at the wooden floorboards. "I'm sorry. I tried to look for Mrs. Olsen in the other camp, but I couldn't find her. I tried to look for Tyler but he wasn't with the other kids there."

A single tear rolled down Matthew's cheek as his eye began to rapidly shift back and forth. "Mel..sa, she…g- on, hey bea… he-r. Ead."

Tara bit her lip. She really didn't want to bother him when he was in a state like this but she needed to know. "My daddy said you took my brother Timmy with you when you left Arizona, do you know where he is?"

"Heey… too..kk, my… oy."

Tara frowned. "They took your boy? You mean they took Tyler away?"

"Esss."

"Did they take Timmy too?"

"Esss."

"Do you know who it was?"

"Ouncil… he… ame.. e… sen."

Tara leaned closer. "Who?"

"E… se-n."

Tara tried to figure out what he said but she couldn't be sure. "Esen? Did you say Esen?"

"Esss."

Julius walked over and stood beside her. "I think he's saying Eason. It must be Charles Eason. He was the former assistant to the commandant of this camp."

Matthew lifted up a finger. "Esss. E… se-n."

Tara smiled as she lightly placed her hand on Matthew's arm a second time before turning to look at Julius. "Where is this Charles Eason guy now?"

"He left the camp about a few months ago," Julius said. "Eason was a sadist, he used to beat people up for looking at him the wrong way. I think I remember that there was a commotion in the women's camp when Eason ordered some of the younger children to be transferred out of it. A lot of women protested and I heard one of them died while trying to protect her kids. When the men over here heard about it, some of us tried to rush the guards. It was awful and half a dozen of us were killed, a few others were beaten so badly they ended up here."

Tara shook her head slowly. All this cruelty, it was madness. "What did he do with the younger kids?"

Julius snorted. "That Eason was a talker and a braggart. I always heard him say that he wanted to grow his family and he needed to adopt more children. To instruct them to be proper Christians in the eyes of the Lord, he said. Since he was being transferred out of here, I guess he decided to take some of the kids in the other camp with him. I don't know where he is now though."

Tara nodded. "I will find him and he will lead me to my brother. Now, I need you to organize everybody because you're all going to escape from here."

Pablo walked up to them with a surprised look on his face. "Who exactly are you? How do you expect us to escape from here just like that?"

"We checked out this whole area earlier today before I got in here," Tara said. "There's a barge that's been tied up along a small pier just across from Sherman Avenue. You ought to be able to fit a lot of people on it to make the trip across the river and into Fed territory."

Julius crossed his arms. "That's easier said than done. First of all, there are like eight guard towers, and that's just on this camp. Each tower has at least two guards with automatic weapons. There's also dog patrols moving along the outer walls. If we can somehow get past all that, there's more guards that are sleeping in the houses nearby. Then after that, I heard there's a whole army of tanks and those armored jeeps in Fort Leavenworth proper. So unless you got the Feds right behind you, I don't think any of us are getting out of here in one piece anytime soon."

Tara had a blank expression. "I was able to get in here with no problem."

Pablo looked at her closely. "How did you get in here?"

"By magic," Tara said.

Julius let out a deep sigh. "By magic. Oh great. Maybe you can cast a spell to make all these guards disappear too."

"I wanted to do it quietly," Tara said. "Though Patrick wanted to do it his way. He said he wanted to teach the separatists a lesson. So we're using his plan to get out. He'll deal with the guards so you can escape."

Pablo crossed his arms. "Who is this Patrick and what is his plan?"

Tara took out a red and yellow colored tube from beneath her jacket. "Patrick is my friend and I already told you the plan. All I gotta do is fire off this flare and we're on."

Julius held out his hand. "Wait a minute, so all we gotta do is just start running after that flare goes up in the air? Are you kidding me? How many is there of you?"

"Just me, Patrick and my pet bird," Tara said. "That raven who distracted those guards, he's with me too."

Pablo was incredulous. "So it's just you, one guy and a bird? Are you crazy or something? There's about five thousand internees in the other camp and another eight thousand here."

Tara nodded confidently. "I know. All I'm saying is, you need to get organized and run as a group towards that barge. Just wait when all hell breaks loose. All you have to do is get everybody ready."

Julius took his glasses off and rubbed his tired eyes. "And if nothing happens? What then?"

"Then you can all go back to sleep," Tara said. "But can you please give me the benefit of the doubt?"

Julius thought about it for a minute. He first thought the whole idea was nuts. Yet deep inside of him, he sensed that this teenage girl was telling the truth. She exuded a feeling of confidence. He knew that she wasn't telling him everything. The fact that they somehow made it this far was a sign. Finally he nodded. "We've got nothing to lose anyway. I set up a way where we can get the word out quickly, just relay it from cabin to cabin. You'll need to give me about half an hour to get the word out. Once the fireworks or whatever it is you've got planned starts, we can start getting out of there, assuming that the fences go down somehow."

"Don't worry, they will," Tara said before turning to look at Pablo. "Can you get these patients out of here too?"

Pablo pointed to Matthew. "Other than him I got another guy who can probably walk with some assistance. There's an old wheelchair stashed in the back so I can take Mr. Olsen."

Tara nodded. "Okay then, go ahead and start spreading the word. I'll stay here and I will fire off the flare in about half an hour."

In the dark woods surrounding the camp, the raven flew along the trees until it spotted something pale and manlike standing in the upper branches of a huge oak. The bird made a steep dive and fluttered its wings as it settled on a branch beside the creature.

Patrick Gyle turned his head and looked at the bird, just as the animal began to preen itself. "Well, did she get into the camp?"

"Yes, she did," The raven said. "She nearly got caught by the camp guards but I was able to distract them enough."

"Okay then," Gyle said as he looked out towards the outskirts of the camp. "I don't think it's going to be a problem taking out the guard towers and the fence on this side, but if they bring in reinforcements from their units stationed near the river, I will be hard pressed to take them all out while I'm protecting the escapees."

The raven looked up at the darkening sky above them. "Don't worry, I have a friend coming over. He said he's going to take care of the SOL units watching the river."

"Whoever this friend of yours is, I hope he comes packing," Gyle said. "I counted three platoons of tanks, and at least two dozen Humvees and Bradleys for support. They've even got artillery pieces dug in near the airstrip. They are expecting an attack by the Feds from across the river so I hope he attacks from the west. Otherwise he might be in big trouble."

"Oh, I have a feeling it won't be much a problem for him," the raven said.

"Once Tara pops that flare we all need to move," Gyle said. "How long will it take your friend to get here?"

The raven kept glancing at the clouds above them. Distant sounds of thunder could be heard nearby. "Oh, I think he's already here."

Gyle was about to say something, but then a bright red flare appeared above the camp. It burned brightly in the sky, like a red beacon that signified a fight was about to start. Gyle crouched his legs to increase his strength, then made a mile high leap towards the guard towers. The raven flapped its wings and took off, just as the alarm began to sound.

The guards in Tower Six never knew what hit them. Gyle landed feet first on the tower roof and collapsed it as he drove down into the base of the stilts. The tower crumpled into the ground as if it was made of matchsticks, taking out a wide swath of the surrounding chain link fence along with it. Gyle quickly leapt out to the next tower as if he was a flea. One of the guards saw him but the speed of his jump never gave his enemy time to react as he tore into them with his clawed hands. After he was done, Gyle leapt down onto the ground beside the tower and lifted it up as he tore its foundations from the ground. Gyle then swung the tower as if it was a pole as he started tearing the rest of the fence down.

A military dog patrol with two German Shepherds and their handlers chanced upon him. Instead of attacking, the two dogs began yelping in sheer terror and ran away, their leashes dangling behind them as the two terrified soldiers tried to bring their weapons to bear. Gyle shredded them both before they could aim their rifles.

Tara began to direct the fleeing prisoners as hundreds started to run past the torn down fences. Julius and the others began to lead them as they ran past the tombstones of the cemetery and towards the abandoned golf course. The ones who were too infirm to run were carried by the others as they continued to flee towards where the barge was.

Gyle was constantly leaping from one end of the camp to the other as he continued to kill any of the guards who attempted to stop the escape. He ignored the ones who put down their weapons and ran away. Within ten minutes, most of the guards in the camp were dead and the prisoners were halfway towards the river bank. As he leaped ahead of them to clear any resistance, Gyle noticed several Humvees making their way south towards them. What happened next surprised even him.

From out of the sky came a gigantic, monstrous black bird. It was the size of a small building. Every time it flapped its wings it generated a thunderous shockwave that staggered Gyle, even though he was several hundred feet away. When the thunderbird opened its colossal beak, a forked bolt of lightning emanated from it and struck several of the vehicles that had been dispatched to the area. Two M-1 Abrams battle tanks were hit by the direct force of the lightning bolt and both vehicles instantly exploded, their own ordinance detonating after being exposed to the superheated sheets of plasma. Within less than a minute, an entire platoon of tanks was completely destroyed. Two SOL helicopters that tried to take off from the airfield were sent crashing back onto the tarmac, their main rotors shredded by monster-like claws.

The SOL forces in Fort Leavenworth were caught completely by surprise.

Many of them dropped their weapons and ran for cover as soon as they saw the thunderbird up above them. The others that tried any sort of resistance were quickly crushed.

As the escapees began to board the barge, they could see the Federal troops waving at them on the other side. Most of them made it past the river and were safely in US government territory a few hours later.

Back in Wichita, Dave Reeder glanced nervously as the intel reports of the debacle that had occurred in Fort Leavenworth began to filter through the network. As he started reading through the details, the descriptions of a pale creature with supernatural strength made him shudder. It had described something that he had been suppressing when his superiors interrogated him after they found a hole in the building's roof less than a week ago. He told them that he didn't see anything. He had blacked out, just like that security officer who had been found unconscious lying next to him.

"Hi," a voice behind him said.

Dave's eyes went wide as his mouth hung open. He knew it was them again. He turned around slowly as he swiveled the office chair.

Standing at the doorway was Tara and Gyle.

"Sorry, but I need to use your network again," Tara said. "Can you locate a Mr. Charles Eason for me?"

Dave just sat there as he promptly wet himself for the second time that week.

15. The Guilty Ones

Otherworld

Valerie Mendoza sat at the bow of the boat as she continued to stare into the murky waters that surrounded them. Not long after they reached the riverbank, a small wooden boat had approached them. It looked like a rowboat made out of gnarled, rotting bark. A being stood at the back while it guided the boat using a long wooden pole. It was a man and looked very similar to the wanderer, with his unkempt beard and tattered black cloak. For a brief moment Valerie almost thought they were identical twins. The wanderer produced a silver coin from the folds of his cloak and offered it to the ferryman just as the boat touched the shore. Soon enough, they were helped onboard and were now travelling slowly across the calm, dark waters. Time had seemed to pass, but Valerie was unsure since the river drifted endlessly onwards as the distant mists obscured the surrounding lands.

She turned and took a look at the old man who was sitting behind her. "The ferryman, is that Charon, the boatman who travels the underworld?"

The wanderer shrugged. "He goes by many names. Though your description is correct, so I must assume that you are right."

"Where is he taking us now?"

The old man looked out into the fog shrouded horizon. It was not quite daytime, but it wasn't night either. It seemed like a perpetual, grey twilight. "This river travels and branches out in multiple tributaries, it is probably the best way to travel the wastes."

"Where did you get the coin to pay Charon with?"

The old man smiled slightly. "Oh, one does find coins and other things every now and then. Sometimes these things just get washed up on the shores since the ferryman throws them over the side once his service is done. He really doesn't have much use for coins or other riches, you know."

Valerie stared past the old man and looked at Charon. "He seems to look just like you. You're not brothers or anything?"

The old man giggled a bit. "Once you've been here long enough, everybody starts to look the same. The people that you see are nothing more than mirrors to your mind's eye. You may recognize a few souls here that you may have met in your previous life, but it may very well be your mind that projects an image of someone that you want to know."

"So all the people here might be someone else, depending on who is looking at them?"

The wanderer nodded. "Correct. Many have drunk the waters of Lethe, the river of forgetfulness. They lose all memories of their past lives, but there is a spark in them that retains some sort of primordial essence, a small piece of themselves that remembers what they have done to deserve eternal punishment. It is what motivates them to relive their own suffering as they are constantly killed and then resurrected in order to renew the cycle."

Valerie looked away. "This is all just so insane. I worked for the police when I was back on earth. I enforced the law. I brought criminals to trial and then the judges mete out their sentencing. But it's nothing like the masochism that dominates this place. Every single punishment here is totally cruel and unusual. That would be against the very laws I swore to uphold."

"You are correct," the old man said. "The endless punishments here are worse than anything beyond imagining. Perhaps there is a purpose to all of this."

Valerie frowned. "You said it yourself. A punishment cannot be endless or else it really serves no purpose other than continuous torture. Where's the purpose in that?"

"Perhaps it is a reminder to always obey the gods, yes?"

Valerie shook her head in frustration. "Don't you see? These people are all dead. Whether they deserve punishment now is pointless since they can't affect the living on earth. Maybe if they were born again, but if they forget all the memories from their previous lives then how can they possibly learn their lesson? Punishment ought to be temporary and it ought to mean something."

"One must look at the nature of suffering," the old man said. "One must ask if suffering is caused by the gods, and if it is true, then one must ask why. In my life, we were taught to serve the gods. We were instructed to keep quiet lest our noise bring upon another great deluge that would kill us all. My people would enact many rituals on a daily basis to placate the gods. We believed that the gods created us in order to serve them. There were many times that we would pray to the gods for a bountiful harvest or to spare us from the ravages of disease. The gods served us just as we served them. When I was struck down by illness and all my friends turned against me, I asked if I had done anything wrong. One of the gods answered me and brought forth a sorcerer to heal me. It was then that I praised Marduk."

Valerie as confused. "Marduk? So I guess that means you aren't Job after all."

"Job? Who is he?"

"I read the Book of Job a long time ago," Valerie said. "It's about a kind old man who had a big family and lots of possessions. God makes a bet with the devil to see just how righteous Job is. Then God kills Job's family, kills his animals and puts a disease on him but Job never falters, he refuses to denounce his god. In the end, God restores Job's possessions and gives him a new wife and family."

"This God you claim to be in this story, what kind of god is he?"

Valerie pointed to herself. "In my religion, there is only supposed to be one god. He is lord and ruler over everything."

The old man shook his head. "Oh no, the story of my life is a little different. I worshipped many gods and I thought I placated them all equally. It seemed that I offended Marduk and he cursed me with an affliction and made me lose my job, among other things."

"What city were you from?"

"I was born in Sumer."

Valerie's eyebrows shot up. "You're Sumerian then? When you first told me your story, I thought you were Job, because your story is so similar to his own. Paul told me that the Sumerians were considered to be the world's first civilization. Many stories from the Bible were transplanted from Sumerian sources, he said. I guess it makes sense then."

"What makes sense?"

Valerie sighed. "That the story of Job was copied and then changed over the centuries. So I guess you're the original Job. Or the Sumerian version, at least."

The old man stroked his beard. "Yes, I can see the similarities in the story. It seems that these Hebrews you mentioned changed the story so that instead of multiple gods there is only one. But that begs the question, why would a single god inflict that kind of cruelty to his most loyal worshipper?"

"Like I said. It was a bet. A wager."

"So in this story my entire family was killed over a wager? That seems even more cruel and pointless."

"Yeah," Valerie said softly. "It just shows that the gods can do whatever they want and we just have to keep suffering for it."

"In my world, we have many gods," the old man said. "We can pray to one god if another is cruel to us. We can ask another god to intercede on our behalf in order to right the wrong. Yet if there is only one god, then it is he who is responsible for everything. Tell me, what did this Job learn at the end of his story?"

"Nothing," Valerie said. "God tells Job to suck it up and that's it. Yeah, it's a pretty sad story. If there is just one god behind all of this I can see that he isn't a just god at all. He's just a brutal and evil monster."

The old man pursed his lips. "Yes, that is indeed a very cruel tale. That brings us back to the nature of suffering. Cause and effect. When I suffered, I asked myself many times and I assumed that I was guilty of some sort of offense against the gods. That there must have been a cause as to why these cruelties were afflicted on me. There were no signs as to what kind of offense I had ever done, and as to which god I had done it to. I had thought perhaps that I had offended Marduk since it was he who sent a healer to cure me. As I think of it further, perhaps it may be another god that I had offended and it was Marduk who took pity on me, that it was his magic that overcame the curses of the other. In all my time travelling these wastes, I have never found the reason for the offense. It is all a mystery to me, the ways of the gods are ever mysterious, their own motivations impossible to understand. If you look at it from the point of view of our own existence, then it becomes clear."

"What becomes clear?"

The old man pointed to her. "People can be evil and good, because the gods made us this way. Perhaps the reason they made us is because we are so much like them. You see, the gods need us too. They need someone to worship them, to placate them, to acknowledge their presence. They are prideful creatures and that is their weakness. Without us, they are but forgotten and pitiful. They may have the power to rule the earth, but to rule over nothing is not in their nature. Perhaps that is the reason why these hells were created. To fulfill our own inner desires."

"What do you mean?"

"Do you remember what Beelzebub said? He said that his world is a reflection of human desires," the old man said. "Perhaps it is not the gods who want to inflict the endless cruelty on us. Perhaps it may be just us."

Valerie looked down at the wooden floor of the boat. She thought about it for a minute. "Are you saying that all this, all this unlimited torture is being done on these sinners because they feel that they themselves deserve it?"

"It does make sense if you think of it this way," the old man said. "Almost every one that I encounter in these forsaken lands doesn't want to leave. A part of them seems to think they deserve to be here. Could the gods have created this blighted place to serve their worshipper's innermost desires for self punishment? Perhaps they must go through an endless cascade of pain in order to experience something before they are reborn again? Or perhaps as a way to cleanse the stain on their souls?"

"You're saying that it's humanity's collective guilt that's created Hell? Surely people don't want this. I just can't believe that."

"Perhaps they say they don't want it, but deep in their hearts, they feel it is what they deserve," the old man said.

Valerie snorted. "That doesn't answer why the righteous ones suffer though."

"Perhaps the righteous ones were never fully righteous."

Valerie looked at him blankly. "So even the most pious of people still deserve punishment because of some deep down desire of being guilty of something? What about children? They get killed all the time. They don't know any better, yet they suffer as much as adults. Where do you draw the line?"

The old man looked down. "I'm afraid I don't have the answer to that. That is why I am still journeying across these planes."

Valerie crossed her arms. "Good luck. If you haven't found the answer by now, I really have doubts that you'll ever know."

Loud clanging noises could be heard out in the distance. The sound of banging metal and trumpets were punctuated by howls of derision and screams of pain. They could see there was a riverbank in the distance. The fog had given way and an endless shore of blackened sand revealed itself. The far horizon was an infinite wall of fire, it was as if they were inside a gigantic furnace with walls of flames.

Not far from the riverbanks were endless armies of half dead creatures. They looked like blackened, burned out corpses but they were clearly alive as they moved and screamed like men. Each of them were armed with swords, spears and every weapon known to man. Hordes of them would continually form up and attack each other, using their blades and clubs to tear into one another. Valerie gasped as she saw one of the creatures get decapitated by another, only to see the headless creature bending over to pick up its severed head and place it back onto its shoulders before turning around and fighting once more.

The wanderer stared blankly at the carnage by the shore. "We have now passed into Acheron, the river of woe. This is a place of endless bloodlust, of constant battles between armies of what were once men."

Valerie shook her head in disbelief as she kept staring at unceasing butchery that unfolded. "My god, what are they fighting for?"

"They fight for the sheer pleasure and anger of it," the old man said softly. "The ones who die will be reborn in a vast smoking pit of ash not far from here. After that, they will try to find weapons before rejoining the battle. There are plenty of armor and swords lying around. The ones who lived and ruled by violence are condemned here."

"None of them ever want to get out of this?"

"A few," the old man said. "Occasionally, one does lose their nerve and tries to get away. When the others sense the cowards in their ranks, they will torture the victim for a long time before killing them. Once the victim returns to the pit, his memories have been forgotten, and the seasons of murder shall begin again for him."

High above them was a stone city that seemed to float in the air, hundreds of feet above. Valerie could see smooth walks of black basalt that formed a sort of outer wall. The city seemed to be attached on top of a gigantic boulder that was several hundred miles across as it lay suspended in midair. Valerie immediately had a tingling sensation at the back of her neck as she stared at the city above them.

"Oh my god," she said. Valerie could feel his presence, his very soul was calling out to her, like a beacon in the endless night. "Paul's up there! I can sense him! We need to get to shore so we can find a way up there!"

"That is the city of Dis," the old man said. "It is a place of torment for those with malice in their hearts. Cruel words and malignant lies all have their place within those floating walls."

Valerie's heart began to beat rapidly. Sweat started to form on her forehead. "We've got to get up there! I have to get to Paul!"

"If we get there, you will be subjected to the cruelty of words. These will be like daggers of sound aimed at your heart. You will be consumed by despair and guilt," the old man said.

Valerie grimaced. "I don't care! All this, this whole nightmare of a trip is nothing if I can't get to Paul! I'm not leaving Hell without him!"

The old man gestured at Charon to take them closer to the shore. "Your dedication to your loved one is admirable. I felt the same way when I searched for my second wife here."

Valerie kept staring at the shore as they got closer, her determination building up. "Oh yeah? Did you find her?"

The old man nodded slowly. "I did, though it was too late. She had drunk of the river Lethe and had forgotten about me. She didn't want to travel with me, despite my insistence. So in the end I let her go and moved on. It was the hardest thing I ever had to do."

As soon as the boat touched the shore, Valerie immediately jumped out and started running towards the floating city, only to stop in mid stride. She realized that she had no idea on how to get up there. Valerie turned and looked back at the old man who slowly placed one foot onto the sandy shore and then another. Valerie's impatience nearly caused her to lose her temper but she was able to hold it in check. She had managed to calm down by the time the old man got closer to her.

Valerie kept looking up at the city in the sky. "Please, we have to get up there."

"Very well," the old man said as he started a low whistling tune that she didn't recognize.

Two black dots appeared in the ash colored sky. Within moments, these objects started getting larger. Valerie saw that they were creatures that vaguely resembled men, but they had bat-like wings and naked, muscular torsos. Their man-like faces were twisted and deformed into perpetual fanged grins of hatred. What was most horrifying of all was that they didn't seem to have any eyes, just a blackened depression beneath their skull-like foreheads. The two demons landed less than ten feet away. Strange, glowing symbols that signified some sort of infernal writings were magically suspended at the top of their heads, as if they were written on air. Every time the creatures moved, the luminescent symbols would follow.

"Ah, who is it that calls upon us but our old acquaintance, the Righteous Sufferer!" the first demon said.

Valerie turned to look at the old man. "Is that what they call you?"

"In this world, yes," the old man said. "I do have many names. These two beings standing before us are the Malebranche, part of the order of the fallen ones who attend to the souls in this plane."

"What is it that you wish of us, o' Sufferer?" the second demon asked.

The old man pointed to Valerie. "My companion here has a loved one that is trapped in the city above. I must ask you to take us there."

"A task requires a price," the first demon said. "And we are sick of gold coins."

Valerie took out a small plastic bottle of holy water from her jacket and offered it to them. She had been keeping it with her ever since the demon Dantalion pulled her and Paul into the underworld. "Here, maybe this would be worth something."

The first demon took the bottle into the palm of his clawed hands and laughed. "Ah, water from the earth! How foolish is it that men think that the fallen would be vulnerable against such a liquid. Very well, I shall carry you up to the city of Dis."

"Don't forget to wait there for her, for she will come back down once her task is completed," the old man said to the demon before turning to look at Valerie. "I am sorry, but all I have is another gold coin, meaning I shall have to stay here and wait for you."

Valerie nodded. "I understand. I'll be back soon."

"Now it is time for us to depart to the walled city of Dis," the first demon said as it grabbed Valerie by her shoulders and leapt up in the air. Valerie shrieked at the suddenness of the demon's flight and nearly pulled at her gun before she was able to calm her nerves. The demon laughed maniacally as its flapping wings made them both ascend hundreds of feet in the air in a matter of seconds. The second demon waived at them from the ground before it began to converse with the old man. As Valerie and the first demon flew higher up, the ones on the ground soon became nothing more than dots on the landscape.

Within moments, the demon had flown parallel to the dreaded black walls of the floating city. Valerie thought that the city walls were featureless at first, but as they got closer, she could see human like forms and faces etched on the façade of the rock itself. Valerie immediately sensed they were lost souls of the damned that were somehow embedded within the rocks.

The demon that carried her sensed her curiosity. "The foundation of these walls are what we call soul slabs. The city of Dis had its walls carved out from the souls of doomed men. It is through their suffering that allows the city to float above the lands below us."

Valerie pointed to a distant black tower that looked like a stone skyscraper. "Over there, take me there."

The demon laughed as it shifted its body so that they changed direction as they headed for the tower. "Oh, you will like that one, mortal. Your agony will help power the city."

"We'll see about that," Valerie said as they hovered above the tower. "Put me down slowly on the top level."

The demon giggled, letting go of Valerie as they floated thirty feet above the apex of the black tower. Valerie screamed as she fell but she was able to hold out her arms to angle herself. She landed at the edge of the top part and her momentum nearly made her roll off the side of the roof. Valerie grimaced as she dug her fingers into the blackened stone so she wouldn't slide off. The demon continued to laugh as it circled above her. Valerie stood up and gave the creature her middle finger before looking around the roof for a possible way inside.

Sure enough, there was an opening in the middle of the top floor. It was a smooth hole with steps that led downwards. Valerie hunched her shoulders and started to make her way down. The stone steps were winding and it made her dizzy as she descended deeper into the building.

As soon as she made it inside, the very walls around her suddenly shifted and merged into each other and she soon found herself in a small room. The walls seemed to be made of mud and brick. It was daytime, but she couldn't tell where the light was coming from. As Valerie looked around, she saw that she was in fact standing on where the ceiling was. Her shoes crunched the dried straw roofing as she took a step forward. Up above her was a wooden table and two chairs that seemed to be stuck up at the top. A bowl of fruit was on the table, but it was suspended above. It seemed like a part of some ancient house, but everything was upside down.

Valerie saw a wooden doorway and she made her way towards it. As she entered the adjoining room, it looked like a sort of bedroom. A rickety wooden cot was suspended in the ceiling along with a small table and crude blankets. Sitting in the middle of the room above her was a man. He had his back turned to her as she could see he was wearing a modern day sweater. His thinning hair had streaks of grey in it. That was when she knew.

"Paul!" she screamed out loud. As she tried to reach out to the top of his head, her hands were too far. She tried to jump but it seemed that she couldn't launch herself. Her feet seemed to be stuck.

"Paul!" Valerie said again. "It's me! I'm here!"

Paul Dane looked up at her briefly before turning away. He had been sitting on the edge of the cot. His arms were crossed over his chest. His face seemed expressionless, his body language had an uncaring sense about it. "Go away," he said softly.

Valerie was confused for a moment. "Why? What's wrong, Paul?"

Paul just stared out in the distance. "Elizabeth will be coming back soon. I have to wait for her here."

Valerie sighed. Something was affecting his mind. It had to be his guilt. "Paul, Elizabeth's dead! You're still alive!"

Paul shook his head. "No, you're wrong. She's nearby. I saw a glimpse of her every time I turn my head. It's like she's hiding from me, just around the corner of my eye."

Valerie frowned. It looked like he was under some form of spell. She needed to break him out of it. "Paul, you've gotta listen to me. Elizabeth is dead. She died a long time ago. You and me, we got sent to Hell because of that demon. This place is playing with our minds. It somehow increases the guilt we feel and turns it against us. That thing you're feeling about your dead wife is part of the power in this place. You've got to free yourself of it."

"Go away," Paul said softly. His face was a mask of stone, unyielding, lifeless. Without hope. "Just leave me alone."

A sudden sense of despair swept over her. She was about to lose him forever. Valerie tried her best to get those dark thoughts out of her mind. For that brief moment, she sensed Paul was already lost and she might as well give up on him. The times that she remembered being with him kept her strength up, and fueled her will. It was like a lone figure facing off against an uncountable horde of gloom, but it was enough and it thrust her back into the present once more. "Paul, I know it's hard to think about anything else but you've got to try. You need to let go of the past and focus on what's happening now. You remember being pulled into the darkness don't you? Right after you summoned that demon. You remember now?"

"It pulled us in and it killed us," Paul said. "It sent me into this place. There was fire all around me and I was in pain. It's over. We tried and we lost. Time to let it all go."

"No! We can still fight this! You're a mythology professor for chrissakes! If there's somebody who can find a way out of Hell, it's you," Valerie said.

Paul seemed to be in a daze. "Dante. When he described the inferno it gave me nightmares. Now that I'm here, it's worse than I ever imagined. If this is where we end up, then what's the point of it all?"

"We're not dead yet, Paul! I came from another part of Hell just to find you! I traveled across so many different worlds, along a river pulled by Charon just to get to you! If I can do this, then so can you!"

Paul just stared blankly into space. "It's all hopeless. In the end, we will be here again. So what's the point of going on? The only guarantee in life is death. That will bring us back to square one."

"The point is that we keep fighting, Paul! People are depending on us! The whole country is in big trouble and we can help them," Valerie said. "You remember the two kids that you saved from that wendigo? They're with my mama and they need us. They need you."

Paul shook his head slowly. "I…I remember. But what good am I to them? I haven't done anything to help anybody. Everybody is dead because of me. Sometimes they come into this house to visit me. All of them. My graduate assistant, that professor I met in England, even those two guys from the embassy. Let's not even mention all the cops and soldiers that were under me in the museum. All gone. Because of me."

"That wasn't your fault," Valerie said. "You tried your best with the limited facts that we had at the time. It's not too late yet. We can still help the country out."

Paul looked up at her. Hs mouth began to tremble. "I-I can't do it, Val. I don't want the responsibility of having all those people risking their lives for something I may get wrong. Then once the crap happens, the blame will go to me. It always does."

"All we can do is try," Valerie said softly. "You won't bear this burden alone. I'm with you. I didn't come all this way to give up now, and I wanted to tell you something."

"What?"

Valerie smiled at him. "That I love you. I will go to wherever you are just to find you and be with you. Not even all the demons of Hell could stop me from doing that."

A spark of hope was in his eyes. She could feel it. Paul smiled back as he stood up. Valerie pushed her heels as high as she could go and stretched out her arms. Paul hesitated at first, but somehow he was able to summon his inner reserves as he pulled himself up from the cot and reached out to her. The moment their hands clasped, the room began to swirl around them. The wind suddenly picked up and a monstrous howl seemed to come from everywhere. Valerie grimaced as she used all her effort to pull herself closer to him. Paul sensed her devotion as his own willpower picked up and he held on tighter. This time, they would not be separated, he swore to himself. The vortex intensified as everything around them began to lose cohesion. By the time they both were in each other's arms, their love had developed its own kind of power that shielded them from the increasing chaos all around.

When they both came to their senses, they found themselves lying on a white sandy beach. Paul got up first as he pulled Valerie to her feet, their clasped hands never loosening their grip. The sky above them was a multitude of colors that swayed like a daytime aurora borealis. They both could feel a soft breeze that came from somewhere in the endless blue skies above.

"I must congratulate you," a voice behind them said. "I have never witnessed this before."

They both turned. Valerie realized the old wanderer had been standing behind them. The old man's bony hand held his tattered cloak closer to his body as he smiled at them.

Paul still wore his glasses and he adjusted them slightly as he stared back at the old man. “Who are you?”

Valerie giggled as she hugged Paul tightly. “Now that’s a long story.”

16. The Secret Prisoner

Alabama

Like Shreveport, much of the city of Mobile was now underwater. After the rains and floods had sunk most of the metropolis, the remaining survivors attached wooden platforms on the sides of the high-rise buildings in the city center to form a continuous pier. The waterline had reached up to the first five floors of many of the hotels and bank buildings, and the river wharf had become a part of the Gulf of Mexico. Much of the country's coastline had been changed irrevocably. All along the South, half-sunken cities now dominated the area.

Tyrone Gatlin got up from his cot behind the bar counter and looked out through the glass windows of the riverboat. The night sky was dominated by the torch lights that ringed the city wharf. The *Nimrod* had been docked for two days, as the crew made repairs and new recruits were brought in. This would be their final supply stop, before the ship headed northeast along the twisting currents of the Alabama River, then finally up into Georgia. He had heard stories that something strange happened to the Talladega National Forest north of Montgomery. News reports stated that the forest itself had experienced an unprecedented plant growth. Giant trees had suddenly appeared overnight and swallowed up the surrounding towns. Anyone who dared to venture into its vast, overgrown terrain never came back. Rumors about ghosts and monsters inhabiting the forest began to circulate from refugees that had abandoned that whole region had become commonplace.

As he got to the front of the bar counter, Tyrone buttoned up his plaid shirt and put his boots on. His wounds were pretty much superficial, but he was given light duty after the pirate attack. The resupply and repairs had been completed and most of the crew were busy enjoying themselves in the numerous bars that dotted along the sides of the wharf. They were having one final night of fun since the *Nimrod* would be casting off at dawn. Tyrone was still being inundated by strange dreams, and as they got closer to Georgia, he could no longer get any proper rest. There were many times when he would just lie in his cot and keep his eyes open. He was too fearful to sleep now. Images of snakes swimming across the flooded lands and flocks of owls that covered the sky crowded his mind every time he slumbered.

Tyrone walked towards the back of the hall and into the engine room. Eight-Ball Jackson was still there as he leaned beside one of the wooden columns while talking on the rotary intercom. Tyrone smiled to himself. Eight-Ball wasn't into booze or women, and he almost never left the engine room either. It was almost as if he was married to the diesel engine of the ship. The paddlewheel spokes had been patched up and the *Nimrod* was all set to go.

Eight-Ball placed the old phone receiver back in its vertical cradle. "The captain wants you."

Tyrone nodded. "He's up in the wheel house, right?"

"That he is."

Tyrone smirked. "Eight-Ball, do you have a family?"

"Nope. Why?"

Tyrone grinned and shook his head. "Just asking is all. Seems you care more about this engine than human beings."

Eight-Ball looked away from him. "I had a wife, kids and grandkids once. They all be dead now."

Tyrone looked down. "I'm sorry. I-I didn't know 'bout that."

"S' okay," Eight-Ball said wistfully. "It was the floods that killed 'em. I was working in another riverboat at that time when all hell broke loose. It must have rained for forty days and forty nights. That was when a tsunami hit my home town. Killed pretty much everybody. Never even found them bodies. After that, I went back to the only thing I knew about. The captain had heard of me and sought me out. Been with him ever since."

"Thanks for telling me," Tyrone said softly.

Eight-Ball took a wrench from a toolbox lying nearby and started tinkering with the engine block. "You better get to the captain now. He be waiting."

"Right, okay. See you around."

Tyrone walked out of the engine room, went past the main hall and started running up the stairs. The wound in his arm had torn part of his triceps, but it was more or less still functional. There was also a pink scar on his forehead but he felt he was luckier than the ones who didn't make it. Two crewmembers were so badly wounded, they had to be helped off the boat, and another four men had decided to quit the moment they got to Mobile. JJ Glanton and the others were busy recruiting in the bars for their replacements.

When he opened the door to the pilot house, he saw Captain Pillinger hunched over a map. Just like Eight-Ball, it seemed that the captain never left the helm of the ship. Tyrone sensed that both the captain and the chief engineer were the heart and soul of the vessel. Without either of them, the *Nimrod* would be doomed.

Captain Pillinger glanced at him before turning his attention back to the map. "You feeling better now, Gatlin?"

'I've been okay for awhile now, Captain," Tyrone said sheepishly. "Anything you need me to do, I'm up for it."

Pillinger turned to face him as he leaned back on the table. "If you think those pirates were bad, this next bit is gonna be the most dangerous part of the journey. I've got faith in you since you proved yourself to everyone on this boat. So far, we've only encountered other men. Now we will be going up against things that aren't part of the natural order."

Tyrone scratched the back of his neck. "I've fought the Aztecs and their demons. I've been hit by these dreams every time I close my eyes. I think I'm pretty much ready for anything now."

Pillinger had a surprised look on his face. "These dreams you are having, tell me about them."

"Can't really tell you much," Tyrone said. "I just could remember moving along the waterways, seeing the stunted trees and the fog coming out of the black waters. Then I sense some sort of spirit guiding me on as I seem to float deeper into the woods. Once I'm surrounded by trees I could sense something big making its way towards me. Then, the next thing I know I'm face to face with a giant snake. Even though I oughta be scared, I'm not. I try to reach out to it and it seems to want to guide me somewhere. Then a flock of owls come out of nowhere and fly all around us like a swarm of bees. Then I wake up. It's just a stupid dream that keeps on repeating itself, Captain."

Pillinger nodded. He had a serious look in his face. "I'm going to tell you the real reason why I accepted you as a deckhand on my ship. Two days before you went and confronted me in this cabin, I had a dream of my own."

"You, Captain?"

"Yeah," Pillinger said as he looked down. "I actually dreamt of you."

Tyrone was surprised. "Me?"

Pillinger crossed his arms. "Yeah. Ever since my last expedition, I kept dreaming about the time I lost my son. Just a few days before we met, I dreamed about my son again and in it, he told me to make sure a black man was part of the crew. I thought he meant Eight-Ball but he corrected me. He told me that a younger man, a deserter from the Army, would beg me for safe passage on my boat, all the way to the swamplands. When I woke up, I thought nothing more of it until you came up here and did exactly what my son had told me would happen."

Tyrone exhaled loudly. "I-I didn't know 'bout that."

"I never told anyone about my dream," Pillinger said. "Not Glanton and not Eight-Ball, or any of the other crew. I nearly had to shoot my first officer just to stop him from killing you. It was against my better judgment, but I had a feeling you were the one that my son was talking about. Now for some strange reason, it's all coming together."

Tyrone didn't say anything. He just nodded.

"The things that have been happening in this world has convinced me there are other things out there I just don't know about. That there may be life after death. I asked about you before we left Shreveport and a little black girl told me you were a shaman. Is that true?"

Tyrone shrugged. "I-I don't know, Captain. All I know is I'm getting dreams from what seems to be an Indian god so I decided to worship him. I've been pretty lucky so far since I ain't been killed yet."

"You've gotta be a shaman," Pillinger said. "What other explanation is there?"

"Maybe I am. I dunno for sure, Captain."

"I've gotta ask you a favor," Pillinger said. "Do you think ...you could find a way to reach my son?"

Tyrone looked away. "I-I dunno, Captain. I don't think I've ever dreamt about your son. I dunno what he even looks like."

Pillinger moved towards him and clasped his shoulders with his large hands. "Promise me that if anything happens to me, at least tell my son I loved him. If you can find a way to contact him for me, tell him daddy always thinks about him."

Tyrone stared back at him blankly. "I-I'll try, Captain. It would help if I know what he looks like."

Pillinger took a step back as he pulled out a set of keys from his pants pocket and gave it to him. "Go to my quarters. My son's picture is on the table beside my bunk. Take a look at it and bring it up here for me."

"Okay, Captain."

Tyrone turned around and walked out of the pilot house. As he made his way down the stairs to the upper deck, he felt confused. The captain clearly thought he was a shaman of some sort, even though he had never thought of himself as such. Now he had a dilemma. Should he try and just fake his way up to the captain's good graces by pretending to be in contact with his dead son? The only other alternative was to try and find a way to actually make contact with the dead, but he had no idea on how to go about it. As he got to the door of the captain's cabin, he placed the key in the lock and twisted it. The door gave way without any resistance and he went inside.

The captain's personal quarters had white painted wood paneling, just like the other staterooms in the ship. A large bunk bed lay to the side, near the window. The rest of the room was dominated by tables and cabinets. As

Tyrone moved over to where the bed was, he noticed a small picture frame had been placed on top of a side table. He picked it up and took a look. The still portrait was that of a young man with chestnut brown hair and high-boned, freckled cheeks. Tyrone tried his best to remember, but he couldn't recall having recognized the man in any of his dreams.

"Hey," a tiny, high-pitched voice within the room said.

Tyrone nearly dropped the picture as he juggled it in his trembling hands. He looked around nervously but he didn't see anyone else in the room. "Who s-said th-that?"

"Down here."

Tyrone instantly looked down. Underneath one of the side tables was a large wooden box, it was the size of a small trunk, around two feet high and a foot and a half in width. There was an antique golden lock at its front. The edges of the box had gold linings. The black lacquered wood had ornate carvings of distorted faces and animal symbols that were evidently done by an exquisite craftsman.

"I'm in here," the voice said. "You need to let me out, Tyrone."

Tyrone took two steps back and instantly fell on top of another table. Papers, pens, books and assorted bric-a-bracs fell to the floor. There was something weird inside the box and Tyrone was speechless with a sudden fright.

The voice coming from the box was slightly muffled. "Come on, Tyrone, you have to let me out. The Master of Breath doesn't like it when one of his servants is trapped like this."

Tyrone blinked several times. "W-what are you?"

"As I said, I'm one of the people of the lands."

"How did you get into that box?"

"I was caught in a net by one of these greedy humans. Then I was placed in this box by a magician. Only a shaman who serves the Master of Breath has the power to release me. So hurry up."

Tyrone held up the keychain and began to sort through the numerous keys to see if there was one that matched the ornate lock on the box. "I don't know which key to use."

"It's not part of that bunch," the voice said. "The golden key is with the captain. It's around his neck. You must take it from him."

"What? Look, he trusts me now. He even asked if I could somehow communicate with his dead son," Tyrone said. "He gave me a chance to join his crew. I can't just betray him like this because a voice in a box tells me so. This has got to be some sort of trick."

"No trick, I'm a real being, and I'm trapped in this box."

Tyrone rapidly shook his head. "You can't be human if you're in a small box like that. You could be anything."

"I dwelled in the forests when the world was young," the voice said. "I instructed many children of the tribes in the ways of healing and knowledge of the land. Now I am being used to hunt the horned serpent for greed. This ship is cursed, as all who are in it. You should do well to heed my warnings, Tyrone Gatlin."

Tyrone was still breathing rapidly. He was too nervous to think properly. "You know my name. But how do I know this ain't a trick? Maybe the captain has you trapped in there for a good reason. You could be an evil creature that needs to be imprisoned for all I know."

The voice inside let out a muffled laugh. "Ah, for a shaman of the one who sits above us, you are easily deceived by the greedy others. In due time you will learn who is telling the truth. Let us hope that by then it will not be too late, for your sake."

Tyrone just stood there silently for a minute. He wasn't sure about what he was going to do. The captain seemed like an honorable man. He was now a trusted member of the crew and he had risked his life for them. Now all of a sudden, a creature inside of a box was telling him something else. Who could he believe?

Biting his lip, Tyrone made his decision. He placed the keys back in his pants pocket and gripped the portrait of Captain Pillinger's son. As he turned and twisted the knob on the door, he heard a bit of laughter coming from what was inside of the box, then it fell silent. Tyrone glanced at the container for one last time before opening the door and stepping out.

Tyrone closed the door and locked it. As he turned to head down the corridor towards the stairs, he realized that JJ Glanton was standing there, leaning on one side of the passageway, looking at him. The ship's first officer had his hand placed on the hip holster that had his Kimber 1911 pistol. Tyrone stayed rooted as Glanton walked over to him and made eye contact.

"Just what the hell were you doin' in the captain's quarters?" Glanton said. He smelled of whisky, tobacco and sweat.

Tyrone instinctively kept his feet close together as his arms lay at his side, as if he was still standing at attention back in the military. "The captain told me to get a picture and bring it up to the pilot house. He gave me the keys."

Glanton nodded sarcastically. "Is that right? Then why did I hear talking in there? Answer me, boy."

"You were just probably hearing things," Tyrone said as he turned and started to walk away.

Glanton placed a restraining hand on his shoulders. "Don't you walk away from me, boy."

Tyrone used his arm to knock away Glanton's hand as he kept on walking. Glanton cursed as he ran up in front of Tyrone and tried to block his way. Tyrone used his arm to gently push the first officer aside as he kept on going. The stairs were close.

Glanton nearly drew his pistol, but then realized he didn't have much of a backing if the captain questioned him about it afterwards. "You think this is finished, boy? Well it ain't! I'm gonna get you one of these days, and not even the captain is gonna be able to save you!"

As Tyrone made his way up the stairs towards the wheel house, he regretted not having the shotgun with him. *You're right, asshole. Next time it'll be different,* he thought.

17. A Child to the Mother

Tenochtitlan

At the center of the new metropolis stood two gigantic stepped pyramids, one facing the other. Both were of identical height, signifying the equality between the two patron gods of the empire who were now allied with each other. The façade of the great temple of Xipe Totec had now been stained red with the blood of its sacrifices. On the other hand, the grand temple of Huitzilopochtli's walls took on a bluish tinge, as befitted the god's other name, that of the Blue Tezcatlipoca. In the complex mythology of the Aztec gods, their titles and names would sometimes overlap with the others. It was as if one god had assumed many names and guises, or that each of the deities could become like the other. Every god had different aspects to their personality, so each had to be placated.

High Priest Tepiltzin ascended the interior stairs of the grand temple. He had been slowly making his way upwards for the past twenty minutes. The stone steps that were carved on the outside of the pyramid were reserved for public sacrifices, while the priests that attended private matters came up from the inner chambers of the temple. An occasional warrior passed him on the flight of stairs and he acknowledged them with a nod. He was now in the main temple dedicated to Huitzilopochtli, the Aztec god of war and of the sun. Even though the interior layout of this place was very similar to the great temple of Xipe Totec, he soon realized that it was markedly different in scope and intent. For one, he noticed that there were other passageways in the ground floor that led underneath the pyramid. No such passageways existed in Xipe Totec's temples. Tepiltzin had heard rumors that the passageways underneath Huitzilopochtli's temple led directly to Mictlan, the underworld of death. That would pretty much explain why the place was filled with warriors who had come back from the dead.

It took nearly an hour, but Tepiltzin finally made it to the upper chambers of the temple. The constant exercise of going up these pyramids made his legs stronger, but he still wished that they could have installed modern day elevators, in order to make it easier for all of them. Even though he was used to the workout, he was still exhausted by the time he made it to where he needed to go. As he rubbed his aching legs, Tepiltzin lowered his breathing as he stood at the base of the upper stairwell. He could see a corridor that led to the personal chambers of the avatar of Huitzilopochtli and that was where he was summoned to. Steeling himself, he walked out of the stairway and into an adjoining passage.

As he went past another stairwell that led to the top of the pyramid, he came upon the entrance to a large, interior hall within the pyramid. Two acolytes stood at the side of the stone doorway, they wore the brightly feathered headdresses that differentiated Huitzilopochtli's priests from that of the other gods. The polished obsidian walls around him seemed to glow with a faint bluish fire. He was not in his element, and it made him nervous.

One of the acolytes gestured at him to proceed, so Tepiltzin drew a deep breath before entering the great chamber. Unlike the halls of Xipe Totec's pyramid, there were no openings out into the sky, the whole place was hemmed in like a shadowy cave. Without the yellowish light of the numerous burning torches placed in set areas, the room would have been completely dark. The hall was large enough to house several twenty-foot tall stone statues that depicted the war god Huitzilopochtli in various poses. As Tepiltzin looked up, he could see glowing orange spheres that helped to illuminate the upper recesses. He wasn't sure what those were, most probably some sort of magic from the underworld that helped provide some light in this otherwise stygian place. The sacred stone idol of the war god was in a nearby alcove on the east side of the chamber.

"Those glowing balls of light are a gift from the tzitzimimeh," a voice coming from the far end of the room said. "The goddesses of the stars welcome our alliance with Tlaloc, and it is through his good graces that we are so fortunate to have them as part of our invincible armies."

Tepiltzin turned. Standing at an alcove near the far end of the hall was a man wearing an ornate feathered headdress. He had an embroidered loincloth and a harness fashioned from bright plumage over his shoulders. His face was painted blue and he had glowing, yellowish eyes that seemed to bore right into Tepiltzin's skull. For a brief moment, Tepiltzin felt a twinge of fear rising from his stomach and making its way to his heart. He had heard stories the avatars to the gods could see through a man's soul and would know if they were lying or not. Tepiltzin began to calm down after he realized that he would have already been killed if they had found out that he was lying. The fact that his uncle, the avatar to Xipe Totec, had instructed him to go to the temple of Huitzilopochtli instead of meeting him personally still gave Tepiltzin a sense of dread. Had they seen through his façade? Was he to be punished by the war god instead of the Flayed One instead? No, he couldn't allow his fear to overcome him.

Grand Priest Ixtli beckoned him with a single finger. "Come here, I would like to speak to you about your dreams."

As he tried his best to hide his unease, Tepiltzin casually made his way and stood facing the war god's avatar at the edge of the alcove. The high priest of Xipe Totec made a slight bow, acknowledging his respect and honor to be granted for such an audience. Everyone knew that Ixtli had been possessed by the very essence of Huitzilopochtli, and it was through him the war god spoke. "I am honored to be called here to the grand temple of the Blue Hummingbird of the South," Tepiltzin said. "To be in direct contact with the great god Huitzilopochtli is a privilege that is bestowed on only a few, and I am grateful for it. How may I, a lowly priest of Xipe Totec, be at your service?"

"The avatar of your patron god, Xipe Totec, has spoken to me," Ixtli said. "He has stated you have dreamed of the smoking mirror, our enemy

Tezcatlipoca. He has said you are aware of a powerful traitor within our empire. Is this true?"

Tepiltzin nodded slowly. He needed to keep up with the lie. There was no turning back now. "Yes, Avatar Ixtli. I have been having visions of Tezcatlipoca. My patron Xipe Totec has been appearing to me in my dreams as of late. He has warned me that the Lord of the Near and the Nigh is set to return, and it would be my duty to stop him."

Ixtli looked away briefly, as if he was staring into the darkened recesses of the alcove. "It is strange why Huitzilopochtli would be silent about this. Of the times I have spoken to him, he has not mentioned the god of the smoking mirror at all. I have also spoken to Grand Priest Tlazopilli, and he says that Xipe Totec hasn't said a word to him about it either. I find it strange the Flayed One would not discuss a portent like this to his avatar, and instead would relay it to one of his high priests."

Tepiltzin shrugged. "I too find it strange. Maybe it is perhaps because of my position. Since I am just a high priest, it would allow me the time and the way to find the traitor and kill him in order to prevent a wider conflict. If Xipe Totec had communicated through his avatar instead, the whole city would be aware of it. This way, our patron gods can keep it quiet, so I may find the avatar of Tezcatlipoca and deal with him."

"If the avatar of Tezcatlipoca has manifested himself here," Ixtli said. "Then he may already be too powerful for you to overcome and destroy. This is most peculiar."

Tepiltzin was about to say something, but then he heard rapid whispering coming from the darkened sides of the alcove around Ixtli. Were there other people hidden nearby? It seemed that the avatar of Huitzilopochtli had hidden advisors that he was talking to. Ixtli seemed to nod his head as if he was listening to the nearby voices. Tepiltzin couldn't quite make out what they were saying so he just stood there quietly. Ixtli moved slightly to his left and a figure moved out of the shadows as it stood beside him.

A sudden sense of terror gripped Tepiltzin. The creature that stood next to the avatar of Huitzilopochtli looked like a pale, emaciated old woman wearing nothing but a jeweled loincloth. The creature stared back at him with hollow eye sockets that had a faint blue light in them. Its fleshless, skull-like face had a fanged mouth and long strands of limp black hair covered the top part of its head. Deflated breasts draped over the creature's skeletal ribcage. Long, sinewy arms and legs ended in black talons. Tepiltzin knew that he was facing a tzitzimitl, one of the great star demons from the Aztec cosmology. These female monsters served as the literal shock troops of the Aztec armies. No mortal could stand against their fangs and claws. Tepiltzin knew he could be torn apart by this demonic hag— he had no defense against her whatsoever. He had seen one of these demons literally tear apart American battle tanks with their bare hands. They were the true reason why the United States was losing the war.

For what felt like an eternity, Tepiltzin just stood there as the tzitzimitl seemed to be examining him closely. Beads of sweat began to pour down his forehead. It seemed the Ixtli might be testing him by using a star demon to gauge whether he was telling the truth. Since his hands were clasped behind his back, Tepiltzin hoped they wouldn't notice his trembling. The creature swayed back and forth, but it didn't make any sudden moves.

Ixtli crossed his arms as he glanced at the creature at his side before turning his gaze back to Tepiltzin. "It seems that the star goddess cannot see into your aura. That too is strange, for the tzitzimimeh are supposed to see through all. It may be perhaps that Xipe Totec has extended this protective cloak over your soul in order to give you some defense against the avatar of Tezcatlipoca, should you find him. I myself have tried to peer into your mind, but I cannot either. Since you are a high priest of Xipe Totec and a trusted member of his servants, I shall give you my trust."

Tepiltzin slowly exhaled and made a short bow. "I thank you for your faith in me, Avatar Ixtli. It will be my sacred duty to find Tezcatlipoca's avatar and defeat him."

"I must confess," Ixtli said. "Your uncle, the avatar of Xipe Totec, cannot seem to examine your aura either, and that is why he asked me to send for you. He told me he expects great things from you, that hopefully you will replace him as the new avatar when it is his time to go to Mictlan."

Tepiltzin bowed again. He was out of danger and it looked like they trusted him to do the right thing. He was now free to go after his enemies. "My uncle honors me with his confidence in my abilities. I will make sure that I do not let him down, and neither will I fail the empire."

Ixtli nodded. "That is good. We need more men of your confidence and ability. You are doubly blessed since your god is watching over you. Now what are your plans on how to find this avatar of Tezcatlipoca?"

"In my dreams, Xipe Totec gave me some clues," Tepiltzin said. "He mentioned to me that the traitor has a flint knife with which to make sacrifices and that he is someone very influential in the temples of either this city, or in Teotihuacan."

Ixtli frowned. "From what you are saying, it seems the avatar is already a priest. Did your god tell you as to what order does this priest belong to?"

"No, Avatar Ixtli," Tepiltzin said. "My god simply said that I shall know him when all is revealed. To this end, I must visit all the temples and talk to the priests in them. I am confident that when the time comes, Xipe Totec will reveal to me who the traitor is and I shall kill him before he brings back Tezcatlipoca."

"Very well," Ixtli said. "I shall draw up official documents that will state that you will be given the authority to question any priest and from whatever temple they belong to. You shall also be allowed to enter their private quarters to examine their possessions. As you well know, we are still waiting for the avatar of Tlaloc to manifest itself in his temple, so you must tread carefully and take steps so as to not to upset his high priests. Remember that our alliance is still not solidly built, at least not until the main temple of the rain god is completed in Teotihuacan, and his avatar has been chosen. It is through Tlaloc's generosity that the tzitzimimeh are helping us win the war against the hated Americans. So if one of his priests is a traitor, you must not act until you discuss it with me first, is that clear?"

Tepiltzin nodded. "Yes, Avatar Ixtli. I swear on my family's honor I shall not act rashly. Only when I have all the evidence shall I then proceed with the traitor's execution. The new Triple Alliance will not unravel. Together we shall banish Tezcatlipoca's essence back to Mictlan."

"I am proud to be allied with your order," Ixtli said. "Now you may go."

Tepiltzin bowed for the third time before turning around and walking out of the hall. He could hardly suppress a smile as he passed through the outer doorway and headed for the stairwell. He couldn't believe that his ruse was working. The moment the tzitzimitl appeared, he thought he was dead for sure. Now it seemed that even the gods were with him. It looked like he was being protected by one of the gods since they all had failed to sense his deceptions. That must have been final proof that he was right after all. All he had to do now was to make sure that any evidence he uncovered would lead right to Coaxoch, his enemy in Tenochtitlan. As Tepiltzin descended down the narrow stairway, he was practically grinning. *So this accursed high priest thinks he can usurp my position in my own city? He was just a stupid son of one my servants before and now he thinks he can disrespect me? Just wait until I have him lying on the stone slab so I can take out his still beating heart. After that, I'll wear his skin for a whole month until it falls off*, he thought.

His assistant priest Chipahua had been waiting for him at the foot of the temple and they took a pedicab out of the central plaza. They crossed the eastern causeway and were soon traveling into the residential neighborhoods along the lakeshore. A light, afternoon rain had begun to pour so they drew up their cloaks since the pedicab had an open top. Although there were still cars around, fuel was now rationed since there had been management problems with the nearby oil refineries. Many of the foreign workers had abandoned the oil platforms out in the Gulf of Mexico and the oil production across the empire had suddenly ground to a halt. There had been a proposal to enslave a number of American oil workers to make them work at the wells and the fuel production plants, but the high priests couldn't come to a consensus. It seemed that each temple faction wanted exclusive control over the oil production in the empire and no one was willing to compromise. So far, each bloc had their own exclusive responsibilities. The priests of Huitzilopochtli had exclusive control of the Aztec Army, while the temple of Xipe Totec had the run of the inner workings within the empire, which included most aspects of running the state. The Tlaloc faction was still in the gestation stage, their high priests were waiting for one of their own to become

Tlaloc's avatar, but so far the god spoke only to them in vague dreams. Nevertheless, both the priests of Huitzilopochtli and Xipe Totec courted the members of Tlaloc's clergy as consensus builders when it came to deciding on state matters, so even though their faction was weak, it still wielded tremendous influence throughout the empire.

It took forty minutes for the pedicab to drop them off at the entrance of Tepiltzin's ancestral home. His mother, Carmencita Cabrera, would be meeting him for lunch. Unlike most other women, Carmencita eschewed her Nahuatl name and insisted that everyone address her by her original Spanish name. Even the house had not been rebuilt to Aztec standards, it still retained the old Spanish colonial style, with an inner courtyard ringed with rooms all around it. The fact that Carmencita was the sister of the avatar to Xipe Totec gave her a certain type of immunity from harassment by her neighbors. She even used her influence to her advantage, securing goods that were normally no longer available to the general public. To that effect, she wielded considerable power within the neighborhood.

Tepiltzin paid off the pedicab driver before walking up to the front gate and pushed the doorbell button. Unlike most other houses, his mother's home still had electricity. Chipahua stood by his master's side as he carefully folded the letter of authority that had been vested to Tepiltzin into a leather folder.

The front gate opened and a servant let them in. The two men walked into the courtyard and noticed that Carmencita was sitting near the open living room with another woman. Tepiltzin immediately recognized the guest as Isabel Rivero, one of their neighbors. He remembered her before the Glooming had started, but he didn't know her new Nahuatl name. As he stood underneath the overhanging roof with Chipahua, his mother got up from her leather chair and walked towards them.

"Buenas tardes, mi hijo," Carmencita said, still using the old Spanish greeting before switching to Nahuatl. Unlike the Aztec women of today, she still wore a blouse and her imported jewelry along with makeup. Her deep black hair was perfectly coiffed. She was rich enough to afford a hairdresser. "We have already had our lunch, but the food is still laid out in the dining hall. You and your assistant may go ahead and eat now."

Tepiltzin gestured to his junior priest to go on ahead. Chipahua made a slight bow to his mother before excusing himself to head over to the dining room. They had been staying as guests here for the past few days while Tepiltzin finished up his business in the city. He had to admit that this old house, with all of its colonial furnishings, was still a very comfortable place to live when compared to the retrofitted Aztec houses that now dominated the empire.

"Everything went well, Mama," Tepiltzin said as he kissed his mother on her cheeks. "I now have the authority to hunt down the traitors to the empire. I will teach that Morales bastard a lesson he soon won't forget."

Carmencita nodded. "I don't know why old man Morales's son is so angry at you. We always treated them well even though they were just servants. I even paid for extra schooling of some of the kids in our old hacienda. And now this is how they repay our generosity? They don't deserve any mercy."

Tepiltzin rolled his eyes. "It is the new empire, Mama. Anyone who is touched by the gods can become a high priest and I guess Coaxoch just got lucky. Now all of a sudden, he thinks he is somehow equal to me now."

"What a fool," Carmencita said. "Doesn't he realize your uncle is the actual avatar of Xipe Totec? That makes him one of the two most powerful men here. The only one who is equal to Paco is the avatar of Huitzilopochtli, but I forgot his name."

"Ixtli," Tepiltzin said. "He was the one I spoke to at the grand temple this morning. He gave me full authority to deal with traitors."

Carmencita grinned as she hugged her eldest son. "Oh that is so wonderful! This means that you now have the confidence of both avatars! I see a very bright future for you, mi hijo. Our family is so blessed!"

"Thank you, Mama."

"Tell me," Carmencita said. "Have you seen your brother Jorge lately? It's been months and I have not heard from him. I am awfully worried about him."

"He doesn't want to be called Jorge anymore, Mama," Tepiltzin said. "His name is Yaotl, which means warrior. I spoke to him a few weeks ago and I was able to get him transferred to the front line unit. He hopes to be an Eagle Knight soon."

Carmencita looked away. "I know that our armies cannot lose since our warriors can come back to life, but I'm still worried for him. What if the Yankees destroy his whole body with a bomb or something? There would be no way our war god could bring him back from the dead, right?"

Tepiltzin laughed a little. He was also somewhat concerned but he needed to show an air of confidence to his mother. "Do not worry, Mama. Yaotl is sure to return. There was one jaguar warrior who was torn apart by a missile I think, yet Huitzilopochtli made him whole again and he returned from Mictlan to keep on fighting. I'm confident Yaotl knows what he is doing."

"I hope so," Carmencita said. "I always found your brother to be a little slow ...and somewhat naïve when it comes to the world."

Tepiltzin crossed his arms. If there was one thing that made him angry, it was people condescending his brother. "Mama, don't talk about him like that. Jorge will make you proud soon enough."

Carmencita smiled and placed a reassuring hand on his arm. "Oh alright, you know him better than me and I trust your judgment. I remember when your brother was picked on at school, you would always come to his aid."

"Of course, he is my brother after all," Tepiltzin said before glancing over at the living room. "Is that Isabel?"

Carmencita took him by the arm as she led him towards the lounge by the courtyard. "Yes it is. I think it's been a long time since you two saw each other, come and greet her. She came to me because she has a problem and I think you can help her."

As Tepiltzin and his mother moved over to where she was, Isabel stood up and walked up to them. She bowed a little before extending her hand to the high priest. "High Priest Tepiltzin, it is an honor," she said softly as she shook his hand.

Tepiltzin was surprised. "Oh, you know about me?"

Isabel nodded. "Who doesn't know you? I have heard many stories about your exploits. They say you could succeed your uncle as avatar of Xipe Totec in the years to come."

Carmencita smiled as she gestured to the nearby chairs and sofas. "Why don't we all sit down? Isabel, you ought to tell him of your problem."

Isabel's fidgeted nervously as she sat down on a brown leather sofa. "He hasn't eaten yet? Perhaps he should have his lunch first?"

Tepiltzin smiled as he sat down on a chair beside her. "I ate a little before I came back here. Lunch can wait. It's been a long time since I've seen you, Isabel. I'm sorry if I am not addressing you properly, but I do not know your Nahuatl name."

"It's Nenetl," Isabel said. "Don't worry, you can still call me Isabel." She tried to smile but her lips startled to tremble and she looked away in shame.

Tepiltzin leaned forward. "Is something the matter?"

"I-it's my son," Isabel said softly. She was fighting back tears. "He is only nine years old and he is the darling of my life. The priests of Tlaloc came to his school yesterday and chose him. They said I must present him to their new temple in Teotihuacan in four day's time."

Tepiltzin leaned back and sighed. This was indeed a serious matter. When Tlaloc's priests chose a specific child, that kid would be their chosen sacrifice. It was said that when the child's tears rolled down their cheeks just before they were killed, it would signify good rains for crops. Unlike the other gods of the Aztec pantheon, Tlaloc's sacrifices were exclusively children. Tlaloc the rain god had been an important deity in the old Aztec Empire because his rains that would determine either a good harvest or a drought. The old Aztecs were highly dependent on a steady season of rainfall, but with the advent of the new empire, Tepiltzin had believed Tlaloc's influence would have been lessened since modern farming techniques were now the norm. Nevertheless, the Tlaloc faction was an important part of the Triple Alliance, and their demands would not be denied.

Isabel started sobbing as Carmencita stood up and offered her some tissue paper to wipe her tears away. Tepiltzin looked away as he sat there thinking about what to do. To use his influence to prevent the sacrifice of Isabel's son would precipitate a transgression against the priests of the rain god. If Tlaloc was offended, then the empire would be embroiled in an inner turmoil. The offensive against the United States was scheduled to resume as soon as Tlaloc's avatar was reborn. Without the proper sacrifices, the rain god might not even manifest himself and that would be even worse for all of them.

Just before she sat down again, Carmencita tapped her son's shoulder. "Isabel came here to ask for our help. I told her that we will do whatever we could."

Tepiltzin glanced at his mother before turning to look at Isabel. "Nenetl, I can understand your feelings as a mother to your boy. You have to realize that many people in the empire would consider it an honor to have their child chosen as a sacrifice to the rain god. Your son will live happily in the afterlife. My uncle, the avatar of Xipe Totec, has had visions of Tlaloc's realm and he says it is the best place for anyone to go after they had passed their final death. It is a paradise of light rains and water gardens for him to play in for the rest of eternity. He will be very happy there."

Isabel started crying again as she clutched the wad of wet tissues in her hands. "P-please do something! M-my son is a-all I have. He isn't ready for this. I am begging you. Could you maybe ask the high priests of Tlaloc and see if they could choose somebody else? Please, anybody but my son!"

Tepiltzin looked down at the red brick flooring of the house. "This will be very hard. I do know Tlaloc uses dreams and visions to guide his priests, just like Xipe Totec and Huitzilopochtli. If he has personally chosen your son then there is a reason why. The temple of the rain god in Teotihuacan will be completed soon and to be chosen as one of the inaugural sacrifices, well I think a lot of other parents would jump at the chance for that."

"Not me! Not me!" Isabel said. "We were neighbors once. We've known each other since we were kids. I never asked you for anything, Tepiltzin. Please, I am begging you to save my son. If he is sacrificed, there's no reason for me to go on living either."

Carmencita looked at her son with slight contempt. "Mi hijo, you cannot know the anguish of a mother when she loses a son. I've known Isabel's family long before you were even born. I'm sure you can come up with something to solve this problem."

Tepiltzin frowned as he looked at his mother. "But Mama, the priests of Tlaloc are the third power in the empire, I cannot just go over to them and tell them they shouldn't be doing this. The Triple Alliance might unravel!"

Carmencita snorted in disgust as she looked away from him. "You are just like your father, always making excuses instead of doing the right thing. I think it's better I talk to your uncle instead. I'm sure he will put a stop to this."

Tepiltzin had a sudden flash of anger as he almost stood up. This is what he hated every time he visited his mother. She would always force him to do something. "Mama, don't do that! If you go to Uncle Tlazopilli, you will make things even worse!"

Carmencita glanced away from him in slight condescension. "You think I can't get this done? Your uncle, the great avatar of Xipe Totec, is my brother. He won't say no to me. He never has."

Tepiltzin threw his arms up in aggravation. "Alright, let me handle this! I'll see what I can do."

Isabel cried out as she knelt down on the floor at his feet. "Oh thank you, Tepiltzin! I am so lucky I have you as a friend! I will be forever in your debt if you could find a way to spare my son's life!"

Tepiltzin stood up as he took Isabel by her shoulders and made her stand up as well. "Don't cry anymore. I will see what I can do. You must remember that this is a very delicate matter and there is a good chance I might fail."

Carmencita took out a cigarette from a metal case and placed it in her mouth. Then she reached for her gold lighter lying on a side table. "Make sure you don't fail. The family honor is at stake. If you're such a powerful high priest, this should be easy for you."

As Tepiltzin hugged Isabel, he glanced briefly at his mother. He had daggers in his eyes.

Chipahua was already on his third cup of coffee when Tepiltzin came over into the dining room and joined him. The young acolyte noticed his superior seemed to be in a troubled mood as Tepiltzin quietly began to spoon some food onto his plate. He had heard a little bit of crying and screaming coming from the courtyard and wondered what it was about.

Tepiltzin began to eat, but the problem that had been thrust onto him had killed his appetite. He put down the fork and sighed.

"Is everything okay?" Chipahua said.

Tepiltzin leaned back on the chair and tapped his fingers on the old wooden table. "I thought it would be a good day today but now I have another problem. How well do you know the priests in Tlaloc's temple in Teotihuacan?"

"I've spoken to the high priest there a few times though I do not know him personally," Chipahua said. "Their acolytes I know very well. We've had lunch together a number of times. Why do you ask?"

"How many times have they sacrificed at the temple of the rain god here in Tenochtitlan?"

"I'm sure they have sacrificed tens of thousands of children already," Chipahua said. "I've been to a few of them during my training days."

"How many children are scheduled for the inaugural sacrifice in the temple at Teotihuacan when it's finally completed?"

"I'm not sure," Chipahua said. "If I were to guess, it would be at least a thousand children on the first day, then a few hundred more on the succeeding days until Tlaloc's avatar has been reborn."

Tepiltzin nodded as he collated the information. "If one of the chosen children were to be substituted by another child, do you think the priests would notice it?"

"I do know the high priest examines them carefully just before they walk up the steps of the pyramid," Chipahua said. "Then they are led up by the acolytes as the sacrificial ritual begins. Are you planning to trick them or something like that?"

Tepiltzin nodded. "Yes, something like that."

18. A Model Family

Kansas

Charles Eason was always a believer. His father, a minister, had taught him that the only thing that mattered was the Bible, and he had to memorize the first three gospels by the time he was twelve years old. Charles was nervous when he stood in front of his father and began to recite the passages word for word. His father had his own personal Bible out and stood in front of him as he made sure that each and every word was said exactly as it was written. Every time Charles got a word wrong, he received a hard slap in the face, and by the time he had recited all three gospels of Matthew, Mark and Luke, his cheeks were swollen purple and he had blood oozing out from his split lip. His father then took out a white handkerchief and began wiping the blood off his son's face, telling him that he needed to get it right, because Charles would be retaking the test again the week after. On the second try, Charles did get everything right. His father placed his hand over the child's head and told him he was ready. It was the day when Charles finally understood what it was that meant to be a man of god, simply because he knew his father was right after all. Years later, when his father was on his deathbed in the hospital, he made his only son swear on his soul that he would always abide in the teachings of the Lord. Charles wept like a baby as his father let out a gurgle and died, and he vowed to continue on his legacy. It was the last time he ever cried.

When he finally started his own family, Charles had a dream. He would raise as many children as he could, and he would pass on the teachings of his father. It was his faith in the wisdom of the Lord that would serve as a spiritual bulwark against any sort of adversity that life would throw at him, and he was fully confident the holy book had all the answers. Then he encountered the biggest obstacle of all: his wife Lisa was unable to bear him any children. He had thought about divorcing her, but that would have gone against his religion. It was nothing more than one of God's tests, and he knew he would not fail it. There had to be another way. Not long after, Charles and Lisa began adopting needy children. The acceptance of orphans served a dual purpose. First, it allowed them to rear a large family they could teach and pass on their faith, and second, it gave them a good source of income, since the state was willing to pay them to take care of the children. By the time of the Glooming, Charles and Lisa had a large brood of ten foster kids living with them in Lexington.

Not long after the pagan gods had returned, Charles heeded the words of the great Pastor Erik Burnley and his Rock of God Church. He quickly got their possessions together and moved the entire family over to the McPherson compound for a few weeks, before finally settling in an abandoned house given to them by the church at the outskirts of Dodge City. Charles was completely devoted to his newly adopted church and was soon chosen to head the morality council in the city when the state declared its independence. He had been so diligent in his work, he was soon given another assignment to serve as assistant to the camp commander for the undesirables in Camp Purgatory, over at Fort Leavenworth. Charles hated the place because of the prisoners in it. He felt that any unbeliever was a fool and he would sometimes take out his frustrations by beating on them. After his request to be transferred back to Dodge was approved, Charles did find a number of children in the camp to be most eligible for adoption. Since the undesirables had no rights, he merely picked the ones he wanted and told the guards to take them away and put them in his car. A few of the parents protested and they were naturally dealt with. Since the prisoners refused to believe in the Lord's truth, there was no recourse but to take their children away because there was still some hope of turning the kids around to the church's point of view, he reasoned.

Charles had been back for several months now and he was enjoying the life he led. The fact that the Lord hadn't returned made him a little worried, but Pastor Erik's soothing voice on the radio alleviated his concerns. The Lord would come back when he was ready, in the meantime, one still had to live the life written in the holy book. The children that had been recently adopted had now adjusted to his exacting standards, so there was still hope their souls would ultimately be saved. He just needed to keep them on the right path until the eventual return of Jesus Christ.

It was now time for Sunday dinner, so Charles stood in front of the full length mirror in the master bedroom of the house as he made some last minute adjustments to his tie. It had been a family tradition handed down by his father that the family would be dressed in their Sunday best when they sat down for dinner. They had all attended church services and the children then went to Bible study in the afternoon. Now it was time for a feast to commemorate the end of another week as they all waited for the Second Coming of the Lord.

There was a knock on the door. Charles combed his hair before answering. "Come in."

His oldest boy, seventeen year old Eli, poked his red head through the doorway, "Mother says dinner is ready."

Charles kept looking at himself in the mirror. He wasn't quite six feet, but he was tall enough. Blue eyes behind wire rimmed glasses and his hazelnut brown hair was beginning to turn grey. "Get the other kids to their places, I'll be along shortly."

"Yes, father."

Charles put on his coat as he heard a parade of footsteps going down the wooden stairs. He made sure the second floor was quiet before opening the door and walking down to the dining room. The house had evidently been occupied by a wealthy Asian family forced out as soon as Kansas seceded. It had an old colonial style common back during the frontier days of the town. Their closest neighbor was a mile away and it would take Charles half an hour just to commute to work at the city center. He preferred the solitude, since his children would not be distracted by their peers, allowing them to focus on their homeschooling and their faith.

When he made it into the living room, all twelve of his children stood up. As he slowly walked over to the head of the table, Charles glanced at each and every one of them to make sure not a ribbon or tie was out of place. All the boys were dressed in their little suits and all the girls wore white and blue dresses. Charles pushed his chair back with a slight squeak and sat down. The moment he took the cloth napkin from the table and placed it on his lap, the children began sitting down, according to their respective places. Within minutes, nobody said a word as the children merely stared at their gleaming white ceramic plates as the steaming bowls of food sitting on the table remained untouched. One of the younger boys tilted his head up slightly but soon looked downwards again when he saw Charles looking at him intently.

Lisa walked into the room as she carried a large serving dish with two whole chickens from the oven. She placed it on the table in front of her husband before taking off her apron and placing it on top of a nearby cabinet. Then she readjusted her dress before sitting down beside him.

Charles frowned as he stared at the pair of roasted chickens on the table. "Why did you cook only two? There are twelve of us. It won't be enough."

"We're out of ration slips for meat and poultry," Lisa said. "Sorry, but I was so busy with the laundry and their school syllabus, I forgot to tell you about it."

Charles's backhanded slap caught her right on the cheek. It wasn't a hard blow, but all the kids heard it. One of the younger girls gasped before she realized it and immediately looked back down on her plate, along with the others. Lisa rubbed her reddish cheek for a few seconds as she looked out into the window and kept staring into the night.

The silence was broken when Charles clasped his hands together in prayer. "Well, I guess this will have to do. Some of us will not be having a full plate, but that is nothing compared to what the Lord endured when he was fasting to save us all." He turned to look at a twelve year old boy who was sitting at the far end of the table. "Wesley, I believe it is your turn to say grace. I think the one with Paul in Acts ought to be appropriate for this evening."

Wesley had freckles on his cheeks and was a bit on the pudgy side. He figured he would get only a small piece of meat, since he had failed his Bible memory test just a few days before and had a broken tooth to prove it. Wesley clasped his hands together and closed his eyes as he tried to remember the exact words to the verse. "When he had thus spoken, he took bread and gave thanks to God in—"

The boy's prayer recitation was interrupted by a loud crash coming from outside of the house. Everybody looked at each other in surprise. One of the younger girls thought it was Jesus finally coming back as she clenched her eyes shut and prayed even harder. Charles frowned as he got up from his chair and angrily threw the napkin on top of his still empty plate. *Who could it be at this time of the night?* he thought.

Charles walked over to the window and looked outside. He soon noticed that his car was burning. A high sheet of flame was roaring on top of the hood. The only thing around them was endless stretches of grass and farmland, so they surely would have heard a car coming in since everything was so quiet. A seething anger began grow in his head as Charles started to make his way towards the back door in the kitchen. He was head of the morality council in this entire county and if anyone dared play a trick like this on him there would be hell to pay. The back door had a large glass window above the door knob and he noticed a teenage girl standing outside, near the old stone well. He fumbled the lock as his hands kept shaking with a combination of rage and impatience. If that girl had torched his truck, he would exact a very strict punishment on her, whoever she was.

When he finally got the back door opened and pushed the screen door aside, Lisa ran up behind him. "Who is it?" she said.

"Stay here and make sure the kids don't eat the food," Charles said tersely as he threw back the screen door and walked out past the back porch with his fists clenched. His steps were slow and deliberate as he got closer to the girl. "Hey, you! Did you set my car on fire?"

The girl had reddish brown hair and she seemed supremely confident in herself as she just stood there with her arms crossed. "No, it wasn't me. One of my friends did it."

Charles stood a few feet away from her and looked around. White hot feelings of anger and barely suppressed outrage were boiling inside of him. The lens of his glasses was nearly steamed over despite the cold night air. "Where are these friends of yours? Don't you punks know who I am?"

The girl nodded. "I know who you are. I also know you have my brother. His name is Timmy and he's around seven by now. If you hand him over to me I'll make sure you won't get hurt."

"What are you talking about, you little jezebel?" Charles hissed. Who did this young punk think she is? He would show her just who she was messing with! "I run the morality council in this entire area! I can have you put in prison just on my say so! What's your name and who are your parents?"

"My name's Tara and you don't know about my parents," she said. "My brother Timmy is here, the records from Wichita said so. I'm asking you one more time to give him back to me."

Charles couldn't believe what he was hearing. "W-what? How did you get access to the council databases? They're restricted!"

Tara shook her head. She wasn't telling him anything. "That's for me to know and for you to find out."

Charles had his hands out as he moved forward to try and grab her. "Why you—"

Just before he could get his hands on her, he sensed some sort passing blur, as if a presence suddenly appeared at his left side, right where the night was darkest. As he turned slowly to his left, Charles noticed he was standing right next to some sort of pale skinned creature. It was something he might have seen when he sneaked off and watched one of those horror movies in the drive–in theatre all those years ago. Only this time it was real. Charles stifled a scream as Patrick Gyle placed a clawed hand on his shoulder and threw him down onto the ground.

Lisa had started screaming as soon as she saw some sort of naked, white hairless demon standing over her husband. The older kids got up from the dinner table and they all started running into the kitchen to see what was going on. The younger kids were still too scared to even get up but as Lisa's screaming continued, the spell Charles had over them broke and they all joined in with their adopted siblings as they crowded the kitchen to look outside.

Tara glanced at Gyle standing over Charles as she walked past them and headed towards the opened back door. "Keep him covered for me, willya?"

Gyle nodded silently as he glared at the man lying near his feet.

Tara walked up into the kitchen as she brushed past Lisa, who just stood there dumbfounded. The kids all moved backwards as they silently stared back at her. Tara looked at the younger kid's faces but she didn't notice Timmy among them. After a minute, she soon recognized an eight-year old kid with dark hair standing near the doorway that led to the dining room. It was Tyler Olsen alright.

She walked up to the wide eyed little boy. Timmy's old playmate. She was so glad to see him. But where was her brother? "Tyler? It's me, Tara. Remember the trailer park back in Phoenix? We were neighbors and you were my brother's playmate. My brother Timmy. Remember?"

Tyler's mouth dropped before he ran up to her and hugged her as he started crying. "Tara! Oh my god! D-did you see my parents?"

Tara hugged him for a bit, then gently pulled him away from her before leading him into the dining room. The other kids were too busy watching Gyle outside so it was just the two of them in the hall. She knelt down slightly so they were in eye contact. "I'm sorry, but your mom is gone. Your dad is hurt, but he's safe over the Federal border. I can take him to you if you want."

"Y-yes, please," the boy sobbed. "I-I hate it here. They force me to read the Bible and they b-beat me up. Take me away p-please. I wanna g-go back to my d-dad."

Tara nodded. "I will, Tyler. I have to find Timmy first. Where is he?"

Tyler started crying even harder. "They b-beat him u-up! He didn't wa-want to follow them so they beat him up bad!"

Tara's heart started to pound, it felt like it was about to burst from her chest. Oh god, was her brother hurt? She hoped he would still be alright. Maybe they put him to bed upstairs or something? "Wh-what? Where is he? Tyler, please tell me where he is!"

The boy just kept bawling as he pointed to the side door, it lead out to where a small hill was. "They put him out th-there!"

Tara quickly got up and sprinted to the side door. The doorknob had one of those twist locks so she just shifted it counterclockwise and got it open. She could hear her pounding breath as she ran out into the night once more, the only illumination was coming from the house behind her. *Did they tie him up to keep him up there?* she thought as she ran up the base of the small hill. Tara was thinking there was maybe some sort of shack or structure that held her brother prisoner as her strides slowed for a bit as she made her way up. The hill had patches of grass and a tall, skeletal tree was right on top of it. When she got up near the top, she noticed that the raven was there as it perched on something. It looked like a vertical stone slab sticking out of the ground.

"I'm sorry," the raven said.

Tara knelt down as her heart sank. Her breathing came in shallow gasps. A sudden tidal wave of unbearable pain crested inside of her and was about to drown her soul. Deep inside, she knew what it was. She shook her head rapidly from side to side, thinking it couldn't be real. It had to be just a dream she could wake up from. "No. No. No."

Tyler made his way up to the hill, it took him a few minutes. The little boy's leather shoes were caked with dirt as he stood behind her. His tears had dried and he was calm. "T-Timmy had a lot of guts. He didn't listen to them and didn't want to eat. He would call out to you every time they hit him, and they hit him a lot. Then one day my foster dad hit him too hard and too many times. Timmy just didn't wake up. T-they buried him up here."

Tara didn't say anything as tears rolled down her cheeks, her heart a tightly coiled ball of pain.

19. A Parliament of Owls

Alabama

Everyone was on high alert as the ship entered the great sunken forest. The captain had unveiled a harpoon cannon mounted right at the center in the bow of the upper deck. The gun was a massive Kongsberg 90mm breech-loading cannon that had been imported from Iceland and had several rolls of cable attached to the harpoon. The warhead looked like a giant dart sticking out of a cylindrical metal cannon. He had ordered that two men were to man it at all times the moment the outskirts of the forest came into view. Several swivel mounted searchlights were also attached along the railings of the upper deck to provide extra illumination at night.

Tyrone Gatlin stood in the pilot room as he manned the ship's wheel while the deck lights helped to see through the pitch black darkness ahead. He checked his watch and it was getting close to midnight, the witching hour. Captain Pillinger was sitting on his high mounted chair just behind his right shoulder. As Tyrone looked out at the huge swath of half sunken trees ahead of them, he couldn't help but marvel at the unnatural, flooded landscape. It was as if a magical forest of gargantuan, mutant trees had suddenly appeared in the bayous, right after the rains had caused a massive deluge that sunk most of the southern states. He remembered driving along the well-maintained highways near Talladega Springs just a few years ago. Now all that he was seeing was totally alien, it was as if they were in a completely different world.

The dark waters around them must have been at least twenty or even thirty feet deep, and that would make the gnarled trees along the waterways as tall as sixty or even eighty feet high if the land wasn't flooded over. There was no way that ordinary trees could have grown in less than a year into the giant oaks that surrounded them, with branches that were the size of concrete building columns. There was something bizarre about the whole forest, it was as if some god had pulled it out of a nightmare and placed it smack dab in the middle of the entire state, as to what its purpose was, he had no idea.

All the men that were out on the decks were fully armed with assorted hunting and semi-automatic rifles. A few of them had night vision goggles as they stared out into the darkness. The searchlights had been swaying back and forth as they ran their bright white beams along the opaque water, hoping to catch a glimpse of their quarry, the elusive and monstrous great horned serpent, the Sint-Holo. A few men on the lower decks had placed plastic buckets of fish pieces, blood and assorted entrails to throw them into the water as bait to bring out the great snake into the open. Chumming had been declared illegal in the state years ago, but since there was no longer any means of enforcing the law, every single idea was now in use. The smell coming from the bait buckets were awful, so the men who did the chumming had worn handkerchiefs over their mouths and noses.

One man absentmindedly placed a small wooden crate in front of the wheel house, right beside the forward window. Captain Pillinger immediately noticed it as he got up from his chair and started cursing at the man who placed it there. The hunter just shrugged as he came back and picked up the crate, then he carried it back down the stairs and out of sight.

"Stupid dumbass," Pillinger hissed out loud. "Putting that crate right in front of the wheel house. What a dipshit!"

Tyrone glanced over at the captain. "What was in that crate?"

Pillinger just snorted as he climbed back on his high chair. "What do you think? It's a box full of dynamite."

Tyrone exhaled slowly. He was somewhat relieved that JJ Glanton, the first officer, didn't accuse him of taking anything from the captain's cabin. It was clear Pillinger had obviously taken him under his wing, and he didn't want to jeopardize that trust. It was the voice of the being inside the locked box in the captain's quarters that sent shivers down his spine. The unknown creature said that the entire ship was cursed, and it was heading on a journey of doom. Tyrone was getting mixed feelings since the god in his dreams told him he must take part in this journey in order to fulfill something that was needed. What that was, Tyrone had no idea. The voice in the box had asked to be freed, but Tyrone was reluctant to break the trust of the captain. He had a feeling he would have to free whatever was inside that box, but he just couldn't bring himself to disobey the directive of his superior.

A sudden bump underneath the ship's hull jolted him and Tyrone nearly jumped. Several of the men leaned over the railings to see what it was. The harpoon team swiveled their weapon, hoping to get that perfect shot, while the ones attending the searchlights tried to get a bead on whatever was in the water.

"False alarm!" A voice from the lower deck shouted. "Just a sunken log!"

Pillinger got up and poked his head out of the open window. "Get some poles and push the damn thing outta the way! Make sure it steers clear of the paddlewheel!"

Several people shouted back to affirm the order.

Pillinger turned to look at Tyrone. "We'll be going around these waterways for up to a week until we find that big 'ol snake. If we don't find it by then, I'll take us south to the other sunken forest that sprouted up near Okefenokee. I can let you off on the way there when we get close to Columbus. Of course, if you change your mind, you can stick with us. We can use you. Don't worry about Glanton, I know he hates you, but I can deal with him."

Tyrone smiled at him. "Thanks for the offer, Captain. But I think my god or whatever it is that's talking to me in my dreams would want me to continue on to Macon."

One of the men operating the searchlights swiveled to his right and pointed at the water below. "There! Over there! I saw something!"

"Five degrees starboard, Tyrone," Pillinger said as he looked out of the side window.

Along the sides of the lower deck there were several spinning reels with cables of 100-pound monofilament and piano wire. These cables ended with shark hooks and were trawling the water with pieces of meat on their tips. Two of the reels began to spin rapidly as several hunters grabbed hand hooks after putting on their heavy gloves. One of the men poured some water from a plastic bottle over the reels in order to prevent them from overheating. As the spin on the lines began to slow, one of the bigger men started to reel the lines back in. It was a slow process, as whatever had took the bait was fighting to stay in the water, but with two heavy-duty lines, it would just be a matter of time until they brought it to the surface.

Tyrone had to tiptoe in order to look past the captain's shoulder as he tried to see what was happening from the pilot house. He noticed Glanton coming over to the lower deck, along with two other hunters as they got various fishing tools ready for whatever was in the water. Two of the searchlights were now pointed at the side of the ship as they illuminated the brown colored water below.

After a few tense moments, the water right near the starboard side began to churn as something was being pulled up to the surface. Tyrone's eyes opened wide in a mixture of excitement and disbelief as a cat-like head surfaced from the water. The head of the creature looked like some sort of panther, roaring with frustration as the hooks embedded in its mouth slowly pulled it up into the deck of the *Nimrod.* As the steel wires pulled the front part of its cat-like body past the waterline, Tyrone could see that it had webbed front paws, like that of a large seal. The creature was thrashing in the water as it kept trying to force its way back down, but the wires were acting like hangmen's nooses as it slowly pulled the monster up by its mouth.

"Shoot the damn thing before you get it on the deck!" Pillinger shouted at the men below.

One of the men in the lower deck carefully aimed his Winchester Model 70 at the ribcage of the struggling beast and fired from a range of less than five feet. Almost immediately, the creature's body went limp as it hung by its mouth on the two wires. A loud cheer went up from the crowd that had gathered on both upper and lower decks.

Pillinger cupped his hands for another shout. "Make sure the damn thing's dead!"

One of the men on the lower deck started laughing. "Oh, it's dead alright! Mac hit it right in its heart. One shot too. Yeehaw!"

Pillinger shook his head as he turned away from the window and sat back on his captain's chair once more. "Stupid idiots, a lot of these boys never hunted these things before and they sure are overconfident right now," he muttered.

Tyrone had a big grin on his face as he kept looking through the window at what was happening below. Even though he didn't do much other than steer the boat, the excitement was infectious. "What is that thing they just caught? I never seen anything like it before."

Pillinger shrugged. It wasn't new to him. "Those things are called water panthers. The Indian name for 'em is mishipeshu, I think. They started appearing along these parts soon after the floods sunk everything out here. Its hide is a pretty good water insulator and it's gonna fetch a pretty sum when we get back to port."

Tyrone shook his head in disbelief. "That's incredible. And I thought I seen everything."

As the men lowered the animal onto the deck, one of the men grabbed the first wire reel to keep it steady while a second man took out a pair of wire cutters. The moment the first line was snapped off, the water panther opened its eyes and in a split-second, sunk its teeth into the throat of the man nearest to it. Everyone on the deck was frozen in shock as the creature tore through the man's windpipe and the helpless victim fell onto the wooden deck, blood gushing from the fatal wound. The man who had been holding the wire tried to back away, but the water panther was able to bite him in his thigh and wouldn't let go. As the wounded man screamed for help, the mishipeshu began shaking its head while biting down as it crushed the screaming man's pelvic bone. Some of the other crewmen were able to react quickly as they aimed their weapons and began firing at the still-living creature. Several dozen rounds of 5.56mm bullets tore into the water panther, but they failed to penetrate the beast's thick hide. One man fired a shotgun at it, but the water panther just shrugged off the pellets as if they were thrown rocks. Another man took out a Smith & Wesson .44 Magnum revolver from his belt holster and fired it at the skull of the mishipeshu at point blank range. The creature shuddered for a second before slumping back onto the deck once more.

Pillinger ran out of the wheel house and was halfway down the stairs when they finally took it down. "You goddamn idiots! I told you to make sure it was dead before you got it on the deck!"

Glanton used his heavy gloves to help pry the dead creature's jaws from the still screaming man's thigh. Two more crewmen picked up a foldable stretcher and placed the injured man on it before they turned and headed for the saloon. The other men just stood there, silent with both shame and fear.

Pillinger made it all the way to the lower deck as he stood over the corpse of the creature as well as its first victim. The wooden floor was now slick with human and monster blood. The captain pointed at the corpse with its throat torn out. "Take a good look at it, you idiots! This is what happens when you get careless. Now I just lost one man and another is down!"

One of the men stepped forward. He was one of the younger ones, and a recent recruit out of Mobile. His dark brown beard was quite sparse. "Captain, you never told us that these things would be this dangerous."

Glanton took a step forward until he was beside the young protester. "Watch your mouth, boy! This is the captain's ship and out here, he runs things!"

Pillinger glared at the young crewman. "I told you this was going to be dangerous and you had to be careful! What did you expect to find out here, a couple of crocs and some catfish? I told y'all we were gonna go for some big game hunting!"

Another man stepped forward. He was an older man, heavily tanned, with graying hair and a balding head underneath his beaten-up baseball cap. "I'm sorry but I'm out, Captain. I ain't doing no more hunting and fishing. This place is way too damn dangerous. I'm sorry, suh."

Pillinger placed his hands on his thick hips. He was desperately trying to control his temper. "We ain't going back to port until we get more hides piled up on this deck. I got a contract with my backers to get the great horned snake and we ain't leaving here until we do. You've been given a berth and you're eating from my larder. This means you gotta do the work if you want to stay onboard. If you ain't gonna do the work you signed up for, you can dive right into them black waters and swim back to Mobile for all I care. If you're staying on this ship, you will do that task you're getting paid for. I will not have any cowards on this here ship."

The young protestor was evidently emboldened when the older man sided with him and he threw his rifle down on the blood soaked deck. "I quit. I'll stay inside the bar, but I ain't gonna stay out here and be a sitting duck for the monsters that are all around us," he said softly as he turned around and started to walk towards the saloon.

Pillinger drew his Redhawk pistol and shot the young man at the back of the head. The top part of the man's skull was blown clean off and landed in the water. The captain turned around and faced the crowd as he kept his gun on the ready. "Anybody else?"

Nobody said anything. One of the men turned and began vomiting over the side of the boat. Pillinger looked up at the crowd on the upper deck to see if there was any dissent up there. The men on the above deck above seemed impassive as they continued to stare silently back at him.

Tyrone's hands were trembling as he noticed the captain and Glanton talking to each other. He saw two other men coming back out with an empty stretcher from the saloon and took the second dead man off of the deck and out of sight. Three other men began using skinning knives to cut open the carcass of the water panther. As Tyrone wiped the sweat off of his forehead, he noticed something in the corner of his eye.

All the attention and the searchlights were focused on the starboard side, where the crew had caught the water panther. As Tyrone stared at the other side from the port window, he noticed something strange. The tree line at the opposite side of the waterway seemed to be moving. As he squinted his eyes to get a closer look, he realized that the captain had left his binoculars on the table beside the ship's wheel. Tyrone grabbed at the binoculars and used their magnification to get a closer look. As the details on the other side came into focus, he gasped.

The branches of the great oak trees in the tree line were teeming with creatures. Tyrone thought they were large owls at first, but as he kept focusing the binoculars for a more detailed look, he realized that they could not have been ordinary animals at all. The creatures were large enough to be the size of men. They had large, owl-like triple beaks with two lower mandibles, and their eyes were burning brightly with a reddish glow. Tyrone wasn't sure if he could make out any hands but the creatures had large wingspans, like pterodactyls. He couldn't see the extent of their lower torsos until one of the creatures moved slightly and he noticed it had bear-like lower limbs underneath its thick feathers.

Pillinger opened the door behind him and stepped inside. "What are you looking at over there?"

Tyrone was speechless. He handed the binoculars over to him and just pointed to the tree line. His gaping mouth just couldn't find the words to say anything.

Pillinger looked through the binoculars for a brief second. His hands trembled as he nearly dropped the field glasses. He pushed Tyrone aside and pressed the fire alarm button. The incessant ringing began almost immediately. "Everybody, look out! We got incoming!"

The creatures began launching themselves into the air as soon as the alarm sounded. Half of the crew was still on the other side of the ship and they were caught completely by surprise. Several of the owl creatures landed on the upper deck and began to attack everybody close to them. One of the men manning the harpoon cannon tried to swivel it to face the port side, but one of the monsters pounced on top of him and sent him falling down into the water. Another man looked up and his face was instantly engulfed by a massive claw as the creature carried up its struggling victim and they disappeared into the night. Several others grabbed their rifles and began firing into the air, but their panicked shooting didn't hit anything as the owl monsters swopped down on them and began tearing into their bodies with barbed beaks and six-inch long claws.

Pillinger locked the rear door of the pilot house as he placed a block of wood in place to bar it. He turned to look at Tyrone. "Pull up the shutters, we're sitting ducks in here!"

Tyrone was able to mentally recover his wits as he focused on the task at hand. He opened up the port window and grabbed at the latch just above the top frame. The steel shutters came loose and he pulled them down until the entire window was covered and he locked them in place. Just as he turned to open up the bow window, one of the owl creatures smashed the glass on the pane into a million pieces as it tried to wedge its massive head through. Tyrone fell backwards onto the floor of the cabin as he narrowly avoided the barbed beak trying to take off a huge chunk of his flesh.

Pillinger drew his revolver and fired. The bullet hit the creature's eye and it bellowed in screeching pain before withdrawing its head back out into the darkness. Tyrone got up and grabbed onto the base of the shutter before bringing it down and twisted the lock at the bottom of the frame. Pillinger was able to pull down the shutters on the starboard window and was able to get it locked too.

Another monster landed just behind the door of the wheel house and tried to smash its way through. The wooden bar that jammed the entryway cracked and splintered from the force of the blows and the door started to sag, but it held. Tyrone grabbed his shotgun and fired from his hip. The first shot bore multiple pellet holes in the door. Tyrone pumped another shell into the gun's chamber and fired again. The second shot went through the glass porthole of the door and hit the creature at the top of its head. The monster made a shrill scream before launching itself into the night.

The crew members that were able to react in time made it inside of the ship. Glanton's group was able to run inside the saloon. As the creatures attempted to go through the front doors, they were met by a hail of bullets and shotgun pellets and they had to beat a hasty retreat. One of the men who stood too close to one of the large windows in the main hall had his back ripped open when one of the creatures smashed through the window and tore into him with its beak. The creature tried to pull him through the broken panes but Glanton grabbed the screaming man's head. Both man and beast engaged in a brutal tug of war, until another man emptied his pistol at the monster and it let its victim go before flying off. Most of the men on the upper deck were able to get inside quickly as they stayed in the corridors, ready to fire at any creature that attempted to go through the narrow confines of the passageways.

It was the crews that were still out in the open decks who suffered the most casualties. At least three men who were manning the searchlights were instantly attacked from above as the creatures pounced on them. One man had his chest ripped open as his monstrous assailant used its powerful beak to rapidly slice through his ribcage to get at his still beating heart and rip it out. Another man had his skull crushed as one of the monsters used both its rear claws like a battering ram as it drove its victim headfirst onto the floorboards, its impact was so forceful, it cracked the wooden deck. The third man simply had his head torn off by another owl creature as it swooped by without even stopping. The fourth man who was manning another searchlight saw it all happen, just as he narrowly avoided another monster flying towards him by jumping from the upper deck and into the water. As he tried to swim towards the other side of the boat, something beneath the water caught his foot and he was pulled under, leaving a small trail of bubbles and froth in his wake.

The steel shutter on the port side window of the pilot house began to bulge inwards as one of the owl creatures tried to tear into it. Tyrone was trying to reload his Remington shotgun, but his trembling hands kept fumbling the shells and he couldn't get it into the loading slot. Pillinger waited until the lower part of the shutter gave way. The moment he saw the beak tearing its way through, he pointed his Redhawk just inches away and fired. The noise was deafening as the only thing Tyrone could hear was an incessant ringing that blocked out everything else. The creature instantly pulled back its large head and left the broken shutters just hanging there.

Tyrone's ears were starting to hurt as he finally got a shell into the loading port of the shotgun. He followed it up with another. Then he tried a third time but the slot was stuck. It was most probably full. Pillinger just kept his eye on the broken part of the window, his revolver at the ready.

Almost as soon as it started, the battle stopped. The sounds of gunfire and screaming gradually died down again. All that could be heard now was the monotonous sound of the diesel pistons powering the paddlewheels of the ship. Most of the men were dazed and silent, while a few of the wounded let out groans of pain. This time, nobody cheered.

As Tyrone's hearing started to come back, he looked at his watch and blinked several times in surprise. From start to finish, the whole battle lasted less than six minutes.

20. The Omega Fellowship

New Mexico

The small convoy of two dark painted sport utility vehicles finally stopped near the base of Cerro Pelon. It was late afternoon and the drive had been a long one. They had started the journey from the southern edges of Missouri, then skirted near the southern border of Kansas as they passed through northern Oklahoma before finally making it into New Mexico. Law and order had pretty much broken down in this part of the country and many of them were heavily armed. They had passed through a number of military checkpoints and were warned that they would be entering dangerous territory, but at least one person in the group felt the risk was worth it, and since he was the one in charge, they continued on. The whole trip had lasted two days and barely anyone had slept.

Ethan Quinn opened the rear door of the dark blue Chevrolet Suburban and stepped down onto the sandy ground. He let out a small groan as he stood on tip toes and stretched his back. It had been a long journey and he was sore and exhausted, but the real work was about to begin. The son of an A-list Hollywood actor and a supermodel mother, Ethan was born privileged and he could have easily gotten into showbiz with his good looks and natural athleticism. Instead, he spurned the trappings of fame and preferred an academic life of research. Even though he had an independent spirit, he still used his family's money and influence to get into Harvard as he worked on his Master's degree in anthropology. Ethan had been working on a number of archaeological digs in the southwest when the Glooming began. He spent the next few months trying to find his parents during the evacuation of Los Angeles. It took awhile for the government to track him down and to convince him that he was needed.

FBI Special Agent Lawrence Johnson stepped out from the SUV's front seat and looked around. He was dressed in khakis and carried an AR-15 rifle. "Where are we?"

Ethan looked up at the mountain as he adjusted his sunglasses. The sun would be setting soon and it would get cold in a hurry. "That mountain there is called Cerro Pelon. We're about fifteen miles west of Wagon Mound."

Johnson shook his head as he checked his rifle. "I've never been to this part of the country."

Ethan grinned as he walked over beside him. "I've always liked the desert, not a lot of people around and it's very, very quiet. Working out here in the dig sites, doing research on the Pueblo Indian settlements, those times gave me a great sense of peace and well being."

Three more FBI agents exited the second SUV behind them. Two men and a woman. Like Johnson, they all wore dark sunglasses, khaki hunting clothes and were carrying guns. At first glance, an untrained eye would have mistaken them for a hunting party, but their semi-automatic rifles and military body armor were clearly not meant for shooting animals. They spread out in a small perimeter near the cars as they wanted to make sure that there weren't any threats around.

Johnson sighed. He thought this whole thing was a wild goose chase. "As far as I know, the front lines against the Aztecs are nonexistent ever since they pushed into Dallas. We might even be behind enemy lines, nobody from the government has reported in this area."

Ethan continued to stare out into the distance. "I wouldn't worry too much. Based on the last reports I got, I doubt we'll be encountering any Aztec war parties."

"What makes you so sure?"

Ethan rubbed the stubble on his chin. He needed a shave. "Just the way they operate. Every time they conquer something, they take a lot of prisoners and bring them back to their cities for feasting and sacrifices. The ancient Aztecs didn't conquer and hold territory, they would have their neighbors swear fealty to them and exact tribute. The ones who resisted would have their people taken as war booty and sacrificed. I don't think the Aztecs want to come to this part of country either."

"Why not? Why wouldn't they annex this area? There's hardly anybody here to stop them," Johnson said.

"You answered your own question," Ethan said. "There's nobody here for them to take captive. This place has their own guardians."

Johnson stared at him. "What do you mean by that?"

"There was one report that stood out when I did research on this area," Ethan said. "After the Glooming, there were rumors of skin walkers being encountered here, you know, the people who could change their shapes, as well as other strange phenomena. There were no reports of Aztec encounters at all, it was as if they were avoiding the whole state with the exception of the large population centers like Albuquerque. I used to be part of an archaeological dig near Santa Fe, and I heard about an old man who lives near here. Many of the locals believe he's a sorcerer of some kind."

Johnson exhaled loudly. "Wait a minute, are you saying we went all the way here just to find some old Indian who you think is some sort of magic man?"

Ethan nodded. "Yup, that's exactly why we're here."

Johnson looked away. "You're as crazy as that Professor Dane was. I thought he was completely off his rocker, then I saw him bring in a demon that got the president back to us. In all my years in the bureau, I thought I had seen everything."

"I can sympathize with you. I saw the video too," Ethan said. "After the secretary of defense personally recruited me into this task force, everything's got a whole lot weirder. I studied under Dr. Dane and took many courses with him. I even served as his graduate assistant for a few months when I worked on my master's thesis."

Johnson ran a gloved hand along his close-cropped, curly hair. "So what do you think this old Indian is gonna do for us? I've followed hundreds of leads in the past few months and we're no closer to finding a cure for the president, nor do we have any idea as to what happened with the professor and Detective Mendoza."

"I know you think this is just another lead to follow up," Ethan said. "I really think this old man can help us. We've gone through a lot of so-called people claiming that they're wizards and all that and we pretty much concluded that they were fakes, but I think this guy is the real thing."

"What makes you so sure this guy isn't a fake like the others we already interviewed?"

Ethan smirked. "Just a hunch. That's all I can say."

Johnson rolled his eyes. Nobody saw it since he was wearing sunglasses. "We'll I hope we find him soon, I got another half dozen so-called magicians to follow up with when we get back east—"

The female FBI agent pointed near the summit of the mountain. "Up there! I spotted someone."

Johnson pulled out a pair of binoculars from his khaki hunting vest and started to scan the mountain. "Yeah, I think there's someone up there alright."

Ethan took out his backpack that had been sitting in the backseat of the SUV. "Yeah, he's right were they said he would be. He must be meditating up on that mountain. I'm going up there to meet him, you guys stay here."

"Wait," Johnson said. "You're a highly valued asset on this task force, I can't let you go up there without an armed escort."

Ethan started making his way up the base of the mountain. "As I recall, Secretary Arctor said I was in charge of this team, right? I'm ordering you all to stay here and do not attempt to shoot at him. I'm just going up there for a little chat."

Johnson muttered a cruse under his breath as he watched the younger man make his way up the dusty slope.

It wasn't a hard climb, but by the time Ethan had made it to where the old man was, night had already fallen. The old man was sitting cross-legged near the mouth of a small, shallow cave. He wore an old buttoned shirt and faded jeans. His long, silvery hair was tied back in a pony tail. Deep wrinkles crisscrossed his brown face. The old man seemed to be asleep as his eyes were closed. There was a small ring of stones a few feet in front of him.

Ethan sat down opposite to him. He wasn't quite sure if it was the right thing to do to call out the old man. Perhaps it was better to wait. Ethan had thought about loudly clearing his throat to make him notice, then decided not to because it might just piss the guy off.

After what seemed to be a long time, the old man opened his eyes and stared at him. "Welcome, Ethan Quinn. You had come a long way just to find me. I am called El Brujo."

Ethan smiled slightly. Brujo was Spanish for shaman or sorcerer. The fact that the old man knew his name was a good sign. "El Brujo is it? I have come here on behalf of the government of the United States. We need your help."

El Brujo smiled. His yellow teeth had large gaps in between them. "At last, the leaders of our nation have begun to realize the danger we are all in. I have already instructed the Chosen One in the ways of knowledge and power. If there is one who can help, then it will be her."

Ethan's eyes narrowed. "I'm sorry, the Chosen One? Who is this person?"

"Some of you may still consider her as a child," El Brujo said. "She was chosen by the trickster and she was able to thwart the rebirth of Okeus with the help of her friends, of course."

Ethan vaguely remembered the names on the transcript in which the demon Dantalion had described a young girl who had helped save Manhattan. He tried to remember the exact name. It was on the tip of his tongue. "Sarah? Or was it Lara?"

El Brujo made a short laugh. "Her name is Tara."

Ethan nodded. Now he remembered. "Right, Tara Weiss. That was her name. Sorry about that. Where can I find her?"

El Brujo didn't answer. For a long while they just stared at each other in the twilit darkness. Then Ethan heard a flapping of wings and a raven landed on a small boulder nearby. The young archeologist wondered why a bird like that would suddenly just land right beside them, then he recalled what the old man had just said.

Ethan turned and stared at the bird. "Are you Raven, the trickster god?"

The little black bird shifted its head from side to side. "Oh, I like this guy, he catches on quick."

Ethan's heart jumped but he was somehow able to keep his composure. "You are the trickster, aren't you?"

"More or less," the raven said. "Now what do you want?"

Ethan shifted his sitting position so he was able to look at both the bird and the old man without having to twist his torso. "I'll get right to the point. El Brujo here told me to find Tara Weiss. She is the key to helping us out. So could you tell me where she's at?"

"She's indisposed," the raven said. "She has come to realize the fate of her brother and she is in mourning."

"Is there maybe a way I can talk to her?" Ethan said. "The country is in a really bad state right now and we desperately need her help."

"The bird just told you she's depressed right now," a low, guttural voice that came from the shallow cave said. "Can't you take a hint?"

Ethan squinted his eyes as he stared into the darkened cave. Something man-like walked out and stood behind the old shaman. It was tall and lanky, with long sinewy arms that ended in razor sharp claws. Its skin was deathly white with rugged leathery ridges. A creature with glowing red eyes stared back at him. Ethan was able to control his fear as he continued to sit, but beads of sweat began to form on his forehead despite the cold night.

Patrick Gyle stayed near the edge of the cave. He was fairly certain the armed men below couldn't see him at this angle. "What government agency are you with?"

Ethan's mouth trembled for a bit before he was able to fully calm down. His response came a minute later. "Officially, we're part of the Department of Defense. Our unofficial name is Task Force Omega. We've been tasked to find a way to deal with these pagan gods and demons that have now manifested themselves. I'm Ethan Quinn, by the way."

"El Brujo said your name already," Gyle said. "Tara needs some time to grieve. She searched for her brother for a long time and it's been only recently that she found out he was dead. I need some time to talk to her."

Ethan looked down on the sandy ground. "I'm sorry to hear that. I hope she feels better soon."

Gyle crouched down. "So what's the sitrep?"

Ethan sensed that this pale thing that was talking to him might be named in the transcript report as well, but because his mind was racing in every direction, he couldn't come up with the exact information. *Might as well answer its questions and maybe I can find out later who he is,* he thought. "The Aztecs broke though our lines and US Army North has taken a lot of casualties. The enemy hasn't exploited the situation because we believe they are still sacrificing those captives that they took, and so the front is quiet once more. If they come at us again then we have no defense. We tried to nuke them, but each and every delivery system has failed to detonate against them. It's just a personal theory of mine, but I think the Aztec gods can somehow prevent nuclear chain reactions from happening."

Gyle nodded. "So we're almost at the endgame then. If we don't do something to stop them now, we're done for."

Ethan nodded. "That's about it."

"They must have a weakness," Gyle mused. "There must be a way to bring the fight over to them, or at least, get them to the negotiating table and stop this war."

"There's another problem," Ethan said. "My former mentor, Dr. Paul Dane, was able to rescue the president from the Kansas separatists, but now the commander in chief has been possessed by some sort of malevolent spirit. Dr. Dane was able to conjure up a demon and this monster took him away. We don't know if he's alive or dead, and I think he's the only one who can cure the president."

"I have heard whispers of Paul Dane amongst the spirits," El Brujo said. "A good man, and one who has the knowledge on how to proceed."

Gyle turned and looked at the black bird sitting on a rock. "Do you know where this Dr. Dane is?"

"Yeah," the raven said. "He was exiled to the Planes of Punishment for awhile, but his girlfriend saved him. I think they are now traveling across the Styx to hook up with your old friend, Atrahasis."

Despite his fatigue, Ethan's eyes were wide open. First he met a real life shaman, then a talking bird who could very well be a god, then some sort of demon-like creature came into the scene, and now they were talking about the man who had survived the great deluge and of other worlds. He felt like a kid in a candy store. He had so many questions, but he knew he had to stay focused with the task at hand. "So Dr. Dane is alive? That's great news! Is there anything I or the government can do to help you guys?"

Gyle turned and looked at Ethan. "Where is the president now?"

"He's being cared for at Camp David," Ethan said.

Gyle crossed his arms as he contemplated the next bit. "Okay, I'll go get Tara and we'll head over to Atrahasis. From there, we'll get to Dr. Dane and his girlfriend and let them know about the president."

"I can set up a helicopter convoy if you'll let me know where the meet up point is," Ethan said.

Gyle shook his head. "We don't need that. Just get back to Camp David and let them know we're coming. I don't want to have to fight my way through all those surprised guards."

"Okay, you got it," Ethan said to him before turning to face the raven. "If I could ask, why did you decide to help us?"

The raven ran its beak along its feathered torso. "A number of reasons, I guess. One of them is that I don't like all the gods bullying humanity like this. I prefer to join in with the underdogs because it's more fun that way. I also like Tara. I think she's charmingly naïve at times, but she's also a very strong girl. The best reason of all is I'm just bored."

"Not all the other gods are against us," El Brujo said. "The Great Spirit has made an alliance with Ahone and the Master of Breath. The three of them have vowed to resist the attempts by the Lords of the Night to venture any further into their sacred lands. The spirits have told me that another shaman is to be chosen, but he is in the flooded lands and has yet to find his spirit guide. It might be worthwhile to seek this man out, for the gods have told me he is the key in defeating the Aztec plans of conquest."

Gyle looked at the old shaman. "Does he have a name?"

El Brujo looked out into the night. "The spirits haven't told me his name.

I suspect it is because he has not yet completed his first journey. The Master of Breath watches over him. The spirits say that he must be taken to the Hall of the Slain, where he is to meet a boy from across the seas. This boy has the missing piece that can bring about an enormous change against the Aztecs."

Gyle looked confused. "Hall of the Slain?"

"That's another word for Valhalla," Ethan said. "This boy he must meet should be there if I heard this right."

"You are correct," El Brujo said.

Gyle looked at the bird again. "Valhalla? Isn't that where we left Atrahasis the last time?"

"No, Atrahasis is in Dilmun," the raven said. "Valhalla is getting kinda crowded too. That young kid El Brujo was talking about brought a lot of people over there."

"Okay," Gyle said. "So how do we get this other shaman into Valhalla then?"

"You don't," El Brujo said. "We must not interfere with his journey. He must make the choice to accept his spirit guide and see through the mists of time. Only if he chooses his fate will he be able to journey into the Spirit World and into the halls of Valhalla."

"What if he chooses not to be a shaman?" Ethan asked.

"Then things could get really complicated," the raven said. "But I'll see what I can do."

"So we have to depend on a guy who may or may not do the right thing, only he doesn't know the stakes involved," Gyle said. "And we can't directly influence him. Why can't things just be simple?"

The raven looked up at him. "They can be, but where's the fun in that?"

Gyle snorted in disgust. "Somehow I can feel that this is all just fun and games to you, Trickster. I can see why Tara is pissed off at you."

The raven said nothing. The people at the base of the mountain began pointing their flashlights near where they were meeting. Ethan's walkie-talkie started to squawk. The young archeologist realized he was supposed to check in with the ground team below every two hours, but the conversation they were having was so fascinating that he had forgotten about the time.

Ethan slowly got up and stretched his legs. "Okay, I think I got the picture. I'll get down this mountain before my FBI escort decides to make their way up here." He looked at Gyle. "I forgot to ask your name."

Gyle kept near the mouth of the cave so the roving flashlights wouldn't notice him. "It's Patrick Gyle. I'm sure they have a file on me."

"Okay, got it. See you guys soon. Goodbye," Ethan said as he turned around and started walking down the winding path. He had a feeling most of the people in the task force wouldn't believe what he had just heard, but he needed to do his best to convince them otherwise.

The cold desert wind whipped through her hair as she stood near the dried riverbed. She had stopped crying hours ago. She looked up and saw the desert moon as it illuminated the night sky, and wondered if there was anything she could have done differently. Then she looked down at where the upturned van was. Over a year had passed and it was still there. It had been Larry's van until it was taken by that renegade cop Josh. She had been a passenger and had traveled with them. She watched them both die. She wanted to return to this spot for a reason. This was where she finally made the conscious decision to try and save the country from the supernatural forces destroying it. The trickster had been her spirit guide ever since they met at that deserted strip mall back in Phoenix. She couldn't help but relive the past choices she made, which ultimately led up to this.

Tara Weiss let out a deep breath as she stared at the swaying grass. When she realized her little brother was dead, she couldn't get over her grief. Timmy was the one person she cared about, and now he was gone. Not long after they left Kansas, she felt an inner rage growing inside of her. She wanted to lash out, use everything in her power to kill those responsible for Timmy's death. She wanted to personally kill her dad and then use a rock to pound Charles Eason's face in. Her feelings would shift from unbearable sadness to white hot anger in a matter of seconds. She demanded that the raven bring her back to Phoenix so she could kill her father, but then changed her mind a few seconds later. That was when she realized she needed to be alone, so she asked the trickster to transport her back to the grasslands, where the van was.

Her stomach started to growl but Tara ignored it. Time flowed differently in the spirit lands and she never felt hungry or fatigued when she was over there. The moment she came back to the real world, she felt like she needed to sleep the whole day and her stomach was ravenous. A part of her figured it might be better off to just go back to the Otherworlds and stay there for good. Timmy was gone and she had no real reason for living on earth any longer.

"If you're hungry, I could catch a rabbit and roast it on a stick," a voice behind her said. "I learned that in survival training when I was a Marine. Or I could raid one of the houses in Kansas again, like what we did before."

Tara turned. Standing behind her was Gyle. He was near the old fire pit used by the skin walkers when she encountered them the last time she was here.

She looked away and stared out into the horizon. "Did you talk to El Brujo?"

Gyle walked up and stood beside her. "Yes. There was another man who showed up. He said he was part of some government task force to help fight the gods. He told me the situation has gotten worse. The Aztecs are currently busy doing their sacrifices, but they'll be back real soon. If we're gonna try and defeat them, we have to get started right now."

Tara looked down and slowly shook her head. "What does it matter what we do? I tried to do what was right and my brother died anyway. What's the point of it all? Everybody dies sooner or later, so it just feels so stupid to even keep trying."

"Look, I know it hurts losing someone you cared about," Gyle said. "An entire company of men I was with were killed by the Babylonians in Iraq. The reason we go on is because there are other people than can still be saved. The ones that died, we can't let them die in vain either."

"We don't even know if we are saving anybody," Tara said softly. "We don't even know if what we're doing amounts to anything at all."

"Your actions did save people," Gyle said. "Remember that camp in Fort Leavenworth? You saved thousands of lives there. We took out that camp and freed all the prisoners and they made it back to Federal lines. You reunited that Olsen kid with his dad. So searching for your brother wasn't ineffectual, some good did come out of it."

Tara's face was a stone mask of melancholy. "I don't wanna do this anymore. Let somebody else save the world. I'm just not strong enough."

"You were chosen for a reason, Tara. The trickster chose you. You're a lot stronger than you think."

Tara grimaced. "Well I don't want it! Don't you see? All I ever wanted to do was to just take care of my brother! I didn't want to be this superhero going around and saving the world! Why me? Why me!"

"Because you're special," Gyle said. "Think about it. Of all the people who could have done things, you did so much more. You've traveled across other dimensions that most people just dream of. You've talked to gods and tricked them. You beat evil wizards. You have done so much. If there was still a national news media, you'd be a worldwide sensation. The entire country is depending on you now."

"But I never wanted any of this."

"There's an old saying that heroes are made by popular demand," Gyle said. "Nobody ever sets out to be a hero, at least the real ones don't. A true hero doesn't discover him or herself until later on. If you look back at everything you've accomplished, I can say that you've earned that badge. You can't blame yourself for your brother. You couldn't have known what would have happened."

Tara bit her lip. In the end, he was right. She couldn't have known that her brother would have gone with the Olsens. She thought Timmy would stick around the trailer park to wait for her. Blaming the trickster wasn't right either. She consciously chose to get on the van with Larry. She deliberately chose to continue the journey with Josh. She made the decision to meet El Brujo and learn the ways of power. It was her choices and hers alone that determined her own fate. The country was crumbling and if she chose to stay away from the upcoming fight she would cause the loss of countless lives, just as her decision to leave her brother behind led to his death.

It was at that moment that she felt a tingling sensation at the back of her neck. As if there was some sort of nearby presence other than Gyle nearby. Tara looked around but she saw nothing. As she scanned through the tall grass she sensed a small figure at the corner of her eye, just to the side of her field of vision. When she quickly turned it was gone. As she dug through the memories of her mind, she knew who it was. It had to be. Timmy.

Gyle noticed that she seemed lethargic, almost gloomy. Then Tara's demeanor became agitated, it was as if she saw something, but his own enhanced senses were telling him that there was no one else around, other than the crickets. He looked at her. "Are you alright?"

Tara nodded. She had been waiting for a sign and she got it. It was as if she was made whole again. The feelings of loss and frustration began to ebb away from her inner core. It wasn't quite a direct contact, more like a feeling. That was all she needed for now. "Timmy. I sensed him for bit."

"Your brother? Did he say anything?"

Tara made a slight smile. "Sort of. I think a part of him is in me now. I guess if I need some extra encouragement, I think he'll be the one to give it to me."

Gyle rubbed the back of his bald, leathery head. He didn't get it, but she seemed to be feeling a lot better now. "Okay, well you seem in a good mood for the first time in awhile. So what's your decision? Do you want to help me or stay on the sidelines?"

"I'm not sure. But I know what Timmy would do," Tara said softly. "Even in the playground he was a fighter, and he would always win against other boys the same age as him. If he was around he would tell me to fight. I think that's what I'll do too."

21. The Rain God

Teotihuacan

It was the day of the official inauguration of the majestic temple of Tlaloc, and the dark clouds above the city had hung low in anticipation of a massive torrent of rain. For several days the festivities had been ongoing, and it was now about to climax at a fever pitch. Huge crowds of people thronged the main temple plaza. The representative high priests and avatars of Xipe Totec and Huitzilopochtli from the imperial capital of Tenochtitlan were present, as they observed the ceremonies from their own respective temples. This was the day that the avatar of Tlaloc would reveal himself, so that the triumvirate leadership that held sway over the Aztec world would finally be complete.

The ceremony was to be the final ritual before the next offensive against the Americans would begin. While Tlaloc was a minor player in the Triple Alliance of the gods, his power brought about the constant rains that inundated much of the Gulf of Mexico. His control over the weather was integral in allowing the dreaded tzitzimimeh star demons to be deployed in support of the Aztec armies. With a never-ending army of reincarnated warriors, storms that covered the sun and their demonic shock troops, the Aztec military was invincible against the might of the most powerful nation on earth. The imperial leadership was even contemplating a possible campaign further north, towards the frozen lands, once the United States was dealt with. A second campaign southwards, to crush the newly resurgent

Incas, was also planned. The possibilities were endless. The signs were good. It was a great time to be an Aztec.

Tepiltzin scratched his nose before adjusting the mask over his face. It was fortunate that the ritual costumes involving the rain god centered on the use of masks, for he needed to hide his face. He was wearing the heron headdress on the top of his head and a feathered white tunic over his loincloth. It was the standard uniform of the litter bearers. Tepiltzin was standing in an alleyway behind the west plaza, less than a hundred yards from the new temple. The side streets were mostly deserted, as practically the whole city was observing the festivities as they lined up along the Avenue of the Dead. If he was going to pull this off, then the timing had to be perfect. Tepiltzin turned and walked around a large wooden crate that had been placed along the sides of the alley. He knocked twice on the top of the box before pushing it open.

Inside the box was a nine year-old boy. The child was sitting on a stool and he was constantly adjusting his headdress since it was so itchy. The boy's costume was very similar to what Tepiltzin was wearing, except for the fact that the child's tunic was in a deep blue color and he wore no mask. The boy looked up at him and smiled.

Tepiltzin smiled back. "How are you doing?"

The boy shrugged. "It's a little hot in here, but I am ready to do my duty in honor of the rain god."

Tepiltzin grinned and patted him lightly on the head. "Do not worry, the procession will be here soon. Make sure you put on your cloak before I take you out of the box. Remember, if someone asks, your name is Atl."

The boy nodded as he took the black cloak which was sitting in the base of the box. Tepiltzin closed the crate once more before making sure nobody noticed them. No one did.

Tepiltzin sighed as he walked over to the edge of the alley. The crowds had their backs turned towards him as they sang along with the musicians and dancers who made their way down the avenue. It had been sheer luck that his assistant Chipahua was able to find a family with a boy who was the same age and had a passing resemblance to Isabel's son Atl. When Tepiltzin met them and told them what an honor it would be for their son to be sacrificed to the rain god, they were more than enthusiastic and willingly gave their boy to him. The substitute had fully understood what he would be doing, so all Tepiltzin had to do now was to make the switch and he would be able to bring the real Atl back to his mother in Tenochtitlan.

As the procession of Eagle Knights finally passed, Tepiltzin could see the litter bearers carrying the sacrificial children as they slowly made their way along the avenue. He quickly ran back to where the box was and opened it. The substitute Atl quickly put on the cloak so it covered his entire body, hiding his costume. Tepiltzin picked the boy up and took him out of the crate. As he held the boy's hand, the high priest of Xipe Totec calmly walked out of the alleyway and started to mingle with the crowds that lined the boulevard.

Tepiltzin slowly made his way on a parallel course as he walked towards the incoming procession of litter bearers, just staying behind the front of the throng of onlookers. His steps were deliberate as he made sure the boy was right behind him as they weaved through the crowd. He needed to find his assistant Chipahua, who was the front litter bearer of the real Atl.

The litters were essentially wooden platforms with small chairs on them. The children that were sitting on the chairs were decked out in the same costumes that the substitute boy was wearing. Tepiltzin could see quite a few of the children were crying and holding out their hands, begging anyone to help them. Many people in the crowd were encouraging them to continue. One set of parents were walking alongside their daughter who was up on one of the litters and they were encouraging her to cry even harder, as they kept teasing her that they would take her back. According to custom, the more tears they cried, the better it would be, for Tlaloc's powers would be enhanced by their symbolic crying. Many in the crowd would shout out insults and jeers to discourage the children even further, to break their spirit so that more tears would flow.

Tepiltzin turned to look at the boy he was leading. The substitute didn't seem fazed at all by what was going on. The high priest had a momentary lapse of confidence as he sensed that the child might be too eager to be sacrificed and might just give the game up for him. Just as he contemplated slapping the boy to make him cry, he heard a low whistle coming from one of the litters.

As he turned back to look at the procession, he immediately noticed Chipahua alongside of him. His assistant had slowed down in order to make sure Tepiltzin would notice. Chipahua started to put his litter down in order to get Atl off from the chair that he was sitting on, but the rear bearer immediately shouted that they needed to keep moving. Chipahua tried to say that there was a pebble in his shoe, but a Tlaloc junior priest who was nearby began to approach them. Tepiltzin waved his assistant away as that part of the procession started moving again.

Tepiltzin silently cursed to himself. The junior priests of the rain god were around and he would not be able to make the switch while the procession was ongoing. There were too many people watching. The only other way was when the procession finally made it to the base of the majestic temple. He would have to make a more direct approach if he was going to do that. Clasping the substitute boy's hand even tighter, he crossed the avenue once the last of the litter bearers passed him, and they both started using the deserted alleyways to get ahead of the procession.

As the two of them ran up past a side street that ended near the side of the temple of Tlaloc, Tepiltzin noticed a junior priest standing near the side entrance. This side of the pyramid was in shadow since the top of the temple had blocked out the sky. The Tlaloc priest was evidently the one in charge of leading the children up the steps of the pyramid. He was wearing a stiff, sleeveless black shirt with elaborate designs and had a small wooden club tied to his belt. There was no one else around.

Tepiltzin crouched down as he pushed the substitute to the side of the wall. "Stay here," he whispered.

The boy sensed something was wrong but he dutifully nodded. Tepiltzin waited until the priest's attention was turned towards the incoming procession as he slowly made his way behind him. Just as he got to the back of the priest of Tlaloc, Tepiltzin took out a flint knife from beneath his shirt, grabbed the target's forehead and plunged it at the back of his neck. The priest started convulsing as Tepiltzin tore off his mask while pushing the dagger further into the hapless man's throat. He could hear the crunching of cartilage as the flint blade tore through the neck bones. Gurgling crimson, the man finally drowned in his own blood.

Tepiltzin used all of his strength as he dragged the bloody corpse to the side alley. Quickly taking off his own clothes, he put on the dead man's shirt and metallic armbands. The sounds of the procession were getting closer. They were nearly there. Tepiltzin hissed as the fumbled with the dead man's pearl necklace as he put it on his neck. He ran over to where the Tlaloc mask was lying on the ground before picking it up and placing it over his face, just as the lead litter bearers made it to the base of the temple pyramid.

He gestured at the boy to follow him as he slowly walked out to the front part of the temple. His hands and arms were covered in blood, but he hoped that the crowd wouldn't notice it since it would be looking like that once the sacrifices would begin anyway. The sounds of trumpets and drums were constant, as a group of four priests came out of the base entrance of the pyramid. Tepiltzin knew enough of how the rituals would work as he began gesturing at the litter bearers to place their platforms on the ground.

One of the junior priests who was overseeing the procession walked slowly over to him. He pointed at Tepiltzin's bloody arms. "What happened to you?"

Tepiltzin just shrugged as he began to usher the children who were lining up in front of him. "One of the spectators tried to attack me while I was standing near the side of the temple. I took care of him."

The junior priest tried to glance over at the side of the pyramid but he couldn't see anything from his angle. "What? Who attacked you? Are you hurt?"

"No," Tepiltzin said as he gently pushed another child up the steps. "This was his blood. I threw him on the side of the alley. I'll ask a crew to clean it up once the ceremony is finished. Don't worry, I'll take care of everything."

Even though they both wore masks that resembled the goggle-eyed rain god, the other priest stared at him intently. "You don't seem very familiar to me. Are you part of the batch from Tenochtitlan?"

Tepiltzin nodded as he pushed another reluctant child up the first of the stone steps. "Yes, High Priest Eleuia initiated me himself several months ago, but then he sent me on an errand to the city of El Tajin. I only recently returned."

The other priest was taken aback. "That is strange, I have been serving as High Priest Eleuia's secretary these past few months and he never told me about it. Nevertheless, I shall ask him about it once this ceremony is finished. Tell me, what was this errand that he tasked you to do?"

Tepiltzin noticed that Isabel's boy Atl was next in line. He gestured at the trembling child to come forward. "I was tasked to find a willing sacrifice for the rain god and I did find one," he said to the other priest as Atl stood in front of him. Tepiltzin looked at the crying child to make sure he was the right one before pointing to the back of the line. "Go to the rear of the line," he said to the boy.

The junior priest placed his hand on Tepiltzin's shoulder. "Why did you do that?"

Tepiltzin pretended not to mind as he gestured at the substitute boy to come over to him. The child was calm as he walked over and stood in front of them. "This is the boy I was tasked to find. Go on up child," he said to the boy.

The junior priest shook his head as he gestured for another priest to come over. "This is highly irregular. This other priest will take over as a guide for the children. You need to go with me to the inner temple area and wait for the high priest there. I need to report this to Eleuia, but only until the ceremony is over."

"Very well," Tepiltzin said as he let the second priest take over. As he started to accompany the junior priest to the side of the pyramid, he glanced to the rear of the line and noticed Chipahua taking the real Atl away. His assistant had been able to get to the boy and had placed a cloak over him as they melded back into the crowd. Since there were no shouts of alarm, Tepiltzin concluded the ruse must have been successful. The children's body count would be the same. All he had to do now was to get away as well.

The junior priest was walking alongside of him as they made it to the side of the temple. "Where is the body of the man who attacked you?"

"Right over there," Tepiltzin said as he pointed to the nearby alley. As the junior priest started to move past him, he took out his flint knife and plunged it into the back of the Tlaloc acolyte. The junior priest cried out as he tried to twist away. Tepiltzin tried to push the knife in deeper but the moment it hit the other man's spine, the fragile flint blade snapped in two, leaving most of the pointed part of the dagger in the man's back. Tepiltzin cursed as he used his weight to bring his victim down. The junior priest kept screaming as he tried to draw his own blade while the two of them thrashed about on the ground.

The acolyte of Tlaloc was able to pull his own knife out from beneath his tattered robes and he tried to stab Tepiltzin's side. The high priest of Xipe Totec saw the flash of the blade and he was able to grab onto the other man's hand just as the knife was mere inches away from his ribcage. Tepiltzin grimaced as part of his hand that was holding back the knife had begun to bleed as he had grabbed part of the razor sharp blade. The other priest was hurting as he tried to bring his other hand up but Tepiltzin was able to wedge it underneath his own body. With one arm free, Tepiltzin elbowed the other man in the face several times until he let go of the blade. The junior high priest's mask had fallen away and it revealed his bloody face. Tepiltzin was able to get on top of the other man as he used both his hands and began choking the junior priest's throat. Tepiltzin was exhausted, but a last desperate surge of adrenaline seeped into his arms as he used all of his strength to push his thumbs down, right into the other man's windpipe and crushed it. The acolyte began to choke and within minutes, was soon lying still.

Tepiltzin took deep breaths as he slowly got up and looked around. The alleyway was still deserted and his victim's screams were drowned out by the crowds who were cheering at the child sacrifices occurring up in the temple summit. His right hand had a deep cut from the other man's knife and he had bruises all over his body, but otherwise he was alright. Tepiltzin dragged the second corpse and placed it on top of the first one. Noticing a pile of unused baskets, he placed them on top of the bodies to cover them up. There was no time to properly dispose of them, but at least it would give him some time since a casual observer probably wouldn't notice anything strange if he walked by.

As he limped his way down the alley, he noticed an old, discarded feather cloak lying on the ground nearby. It was torn and dirty, but he picked it up and placed it over his body anyway. By the time he was close to the temple of Xipe Totec, the sounds of revelry were a distant cacophony of unintelligible noises. A part of him regretted the murder of the two priests, but if he had failed in this then he would never hear the end of it from his mother.

When he finally made it to the almost deserted first floor of the temple of Xipe Totec, Chipahua was there along with Atl. His assistant was sitting in an old, blue colored Volkswagen Beetle and had started its engines as soon as he came into view. Tepiltzin smiled at the young boy who was still trembling in the backseat, before opening up the passenger door and he sat down with a heavy sigh.

Chipahua looked at the blood on his master's body. "Are you okay?"

"Yes," Tepiltzin said softly as he closed the car door. "Let's head back to Tenochtitlan as fast as possible. I feel there will be hell to pay over this."

Yaotl raised his cup of pulque as he faced his friends. "To the newest recruits of the Eagle Knight Regiment, us!"

Along with his two other friends, they all downed their cups of fermented agave sap in unison. Night had fallen over the city, and most of the crowds had dispersed. Everyone had waited for the rains to begin after the last child was sacrificed to Tlaloc, but for some strange reason, the clouds over the city had dispersed soon after. There had been rumors of some sort of desecration that had affected the rituals, but nothing definite had been announced. The high priests had declared the day's ceremonies had been completed, and more rituals were scheduled for the next day. The remaining patrons for the bars in the area were now the soldiers, as they finally received a break from their ceremonial guard duties. Yaotl and his friends were celebrating their acceptance into the elite Eagle Knights Regiment. Their training was to begin in earnest as soon as the festivities were over, but they were all hoping to forgo any additional time spent in the rear lines. As young men, they feared the war against the Americans would be over by the time they finished their training.

Achcauhtli was the youngest in the group at eighteen years of age. He could barely control himself as he swallowed his fifth drink of the night. He started coughing as he used his free hand to support himself on the bar counter. "Ahh, this pulque is stronger than normal, I think."

Yaotl winked at the bartender as he poured another round for them. "What if I told you that I had them add some tequila into the pulque? Would that make you feel better, yes?"

Ichtaca grinned and wagged a finger at Yaotl. At over six feet four inches, he was the tallest in the group. "You animal! How did you get a bottle of tequila? I thought there weren't any left?"

Yaotl laughed as he raised his cup once more. "If one has money, there's always a way!"

A booming voice came from the entrance of the bar. "All of you, cease this disgraceful display immediately!"

The three young warriors turned. Standing near the entrance were four Eagle Knights in full costume, their feathered uniforms seemed subdued in the night. Yaotl noticed they weren't equipped with shields, but they did carry pistols and clubs strapped to their belt holsters.

Ichtaca placed his cup on the bar counter before lurching forward on a few steps. "What can we do for you, fellow eagle warriors?"

One of the Eagle Knights stepped forward as he placed his hand near his pistol. "Which one of you is Yaotl, of the Obsidian Knife?"

Yaotl stepped forward until he was beside his big friend. "I am."

"We need you to come with us," the first Eagle Knight said. "You are wanted for questioning."

Yaotl frowned as he crossed his arms over his chest. "What for?"

The Eagle Knight shook his head. "That is not for me to say. We have orders to bring you to the temple of Xipe Totec by any means possible. You will either accompany us voluntarily, or we will force you to do so."

Ichtaca tilted his head as he whispered in Yaotl's ear. His breath smelled of alcohol and agave. "They don't look so tough. You want me to take the first two and you and Achcauhtli take care of the rest?"

Despite downing several tequila laced cups of pulque, Yaotl was still somewhat sober. He sensed something ominous in the air. "No, this sounds serious. Stay here and I'll catch up with you later."

Ichtaca shook his head violently. "No! We are friends! We fought together and we have fun together! I shall stand by your side!"

Achcauhtli staggered forward until he was beside his two friends. "Me too!"

Yaotl shrugged as he stared back at the Eagle Knights. "Do you have any objections if I bring my drunken friends along?"

The Eagle Knight kept a straight face. "None, as long as they behave themselves."

In their intoxicated state, the walk to the temple of Xipe Totec took longer than usual. Two of the Eagle Knights led the way as Yaotl and his friends would sometimes meander back and forth as they headed to the base of the temple, while the two remaining knights prodded them forward from the rear. The night seemed strangely silent, as if the gods refused to even let the wind blow.

By the time they had made it into the temple's inner hallway, the effects of the drinks had dissipated from Yaotl's body. His two other friends were still somewhat tipsy, but he already had a growing sense of foreboding. Something was going on and they were suspecting him, but of what, he had no idea. As they walked up the inner stairs, Yaotl had stopped talking as he pondered what it was that was so important that it would involve him.

When the three young recruits entered the grand inner hall of the temple, they all gasped in surprise. Standing before them on the raised platform were the two avatars of Xipe Totec and Huitzilopochtli, along with High Priest Eleuia, who was the leader of the Tlaloc faction. Standing beside the leaders of the empire was High Priest Coaxoch, the avowed enemy of Yaotl's brother, Tepiltzin. Their superior, Commander Huemac, was also present, along with a full squad of his Eagle Knights.

The three youths were pushed by the Eagle Knight guards behind them as they alternately stumbled and staggered until they were only a few feet away from the platform. Ichtaca and Achcauhtli began to sober up in a hurry as they instantly bowed to the assembled leaders on the stone stage. Yaotl hesitated at first, but he shifted his stance as he made his bow of respect to everyone except the current high priest of Xipe Totec, Coaxoch.

Tlazopilli, the avatar to Xipe Totec, was wearing a golden skin suit and held an ornate staff, his face painted in red and yellow. Yaotl knew it was his uncle, but he sensed the avatar was only half there, it was as if two beings shared the single body standing before him. Ixtli, the avatar of Huitzilopochtli, was painted entirely in blue and wearing his customary feathered headdress and loincloth. To Yaotl, he seemed to be the most distant as the avatar of the patron war god of the Aztecs didn't seem too concerned about what was happening, he continued to stare out into the tall windows of the room. Eleuia was wearing the goggle-eyed, fanged mask of the rain god, and Yaotl couldn't discern what he was thinking.

Coaxoch was also carrying a nearly identical staff that Tlazopilli had, but it looked to be of lower quality. The three youths instantly turned to look at him as he pounded the floor with the staff to get everyone's attention. "There has been a grave violation of the temple of Tlaloc. The rituals that were supposed to bring forth the avatar of the rain god have been desecrated and he is very angry. Two priests of Tlaloc have been murdered in cold blood, and one of his chosen children was stolen today. This is the most heinous of crimes and the perpetrator will be brought to justice!"

Yaotl's heart started pounding. So the rumors about the failure of today's ritual were indeed true. Something had happened. Why would they be brought here? Unless…

Eleuia raised his arms high up in the air. "We beseech thee, oh god of rain, please forgive us for spoiling the ritual that was to bring your spirit into one of our own. We ask for your forgiveness and for your patience, for we shall try again!"

Tlazopilli pointed to his nephew. "Yaotl, you are a promising young man. You have been recruited to the Eagle Knights, a very prestigious faction of our warriors. Your best days are ahead of you. We are of the same family, and you are of my blood. I must tell you our family name has been dishonored. Your brother who is my nephew, High Priest Tepiltzin, is under suspicion of causing the grievous sacrilege that has stopped us from calling forth the avatar of Tlaloc. You must help us, you must answer when we ask you if you know the whereabouts of your brother."

Yaotl's mouth trembled. "M-my brother? He did all of this? B-but that's impossible!"

"Liar!" Coaxoch hissed as he stepped forward until he was less than a foot away from the youth. "Your brother Tepiltzin has been lying to us from the very beginning! He lied to your own uncle, the avatar of Xipe Totec, about a traitor within, when all the while it was actually him! He stole one of the children destined for sacrifice and killed two priests of Tlaloc, he is the despoiler of the empire!"

Yaotl turned to face his former servant. His face was flushed with rage. "I don't believe you! You have always been trying to undermine my brother and I bet you are making false accusations just to discredit him!"

Coaxoch grimaced. "I have witnesses! Your brother's personal assistant was seen in the city today, and Tepiltzin was supposed to be present for the ceremony in his full regalia, but he was nowhere to be found!"

Yaotl snorted. "That is all circumstantial, it doesn't prove a thing!"

"As soon as the murder was reported to the garrison, we did a search throughout the city," Commander Huemac said. "We found costumes that supposedly belonged to the litter bearers for the sacrifice, but we couldn't identify who wore them."

"One of my acolytes reported that one of the supervising priests where the sacrifices were to be received was not the same person assigned to the task," High Priest Eleuia said. "It was a different man and unknown to us. He murdered the priest assigned to that duty, and he engineered a way to take the child sacrifice away from the procession. He disappeared before we had a chance to question him."

Yaotl threw his arms up in frustration. "That still doesn't prove my brother was that man."

Coaxoch's voice continued to drip with menace. "Listen, you young fool. When I questioned the witness, he described the exact height, voice and mannerisms of Tepiltzin, there is no doubt it was him!"

Yaotl stared back at him with slit eyes. "Did he actually see Tepiltzin's face?"

Coaxoch shook his head. "No, it was covered with a mask. But his description of the voice and mannerisms match your brother's! There is no denying that!"

Yaotl placed his hands on his hips and sneered. "Just because you say so doesn't make it true."

Coaxoch moved another step forward until his face was mere inches away from Yaotl's. "If your brother is so innocent, then why is he not here to defend himself then? Only the guilty run away! I accuse not just your brother, but I also accuse you of helping him. You scum are one and the same, you are a serpent, just like Tepiltzin!"

The lingering effects of the alcoholic drinks and his inflamed passions for defending his brother got the better of him. Yaotl's punch hit Coaxoch right on the high priest's nose and broke it, the unexpected blow staggered Coaxoch and he fell backwards into the stone floor of the temple. Caoxoch's staff rattled on the floor as two of the Eagle Knights reacted by grabbing a hold on Yaotl's arms and pulling him back. The other two youths were still somewhat inebriated and they instantly threw kicks and punches at the guards. Within seconds, more Eagle Knights leapt into the fray as the three youths were pushed back and Coaxoch was helped on his feet. Yaotl and his friends were soon held fast by the guards as their respective adrenaline surges began to die down.

"Enough," Tlazopilli said calmly. "Nephew Yaotl, you have made a serious violation by striking a high priest. You and your friends will face a severe punishment for that."

Yaotl raged as he struggled while being held by two guards. "He insulted me! He accused me and my brother without any real proof! This is not fair!"

"We must resolve this standoff so that we can continue the rituals to bring my god's avatar into the world," Eleuia said. "These two men are bitter enemies and I am not sure who is telling the truth right now."

Ixtli swayed his head back and forth as if in a trance. "Neither can I. Huitzilopochtli sees through my eyes, but even he cannot see towards the truth in this matter. A great void is all I can sense. Something is very confusing in all of this. It is as if the gods themselves might be at odds with each other, and they are actively clouding our collective judgment."

"Then we must choose the path that retains the peace between our factions," Tlazopilli said. "Both men have been dishonored. One is a young warrior and the other is a high priest. If word of this gets out, our empire will be divided by the accusations. The Triple Alliance must be maintained at all costs."

Coaxoch wiped the blood from his nose. "But I have been attacked. By a lesser warrior too! I demand justice and satisfaction! No one is allowed to strike a high priest!"

Yaotl shook a fist at him. "And I have been falsely accused of being a traitor, along with my brother! If you want a duel of honor, you've got it!"

"Stop!" Tlazopilli said as he raised his hand. "We cannot allow any bloodshed such as duels. This must be resolved peacefully and honorably. A warrior cannot challenge a priest to single combat, that would be unfair."

"This must be resolved quickly," Eleuia said. "Tlaloc's avatar must be brought forth without any delay."

"Let them play the game," Ixtli said softly.

Eleuia turned to look at the avatar of Huitzilopochtli. "What?"

Tlazopilli nodded as he realized the genius of the suggestion. "Yes, it is an excellent compromise. The game of ullamaliztli. The ball game. My high priest can choose his players. Both sides retain their honor."

Yaotl looked at his other friends and grinned. Yes. The game. Ullamaliztli was the classic ball game played by the ancient Aztecs. Two teams would face each other with the goal of putting a rubber ball through a vertical stone hoop. Players were not allowed to hold the ball with their hands- only elbows, knees, hips and the head were used. Yaotl and his friends played the game every chance they had and were very good at it. "I accept," he said. "My friends and I will play the game to restore our honor."

Coaxoch sensed a moment of opportunity. "Avatars and leaders, since I have been wronged, then I demand to choose my own players."

Tlazopilli glanced at his counterparts, who nodded in accession, before turning to face his high priest. "Your request is granted."

Coaxoch nearly smiled as he pointed to the man he wanted. "I choose …

Commander Huemac as my team captain."

All three youths gasped. Huemac was considered to be the best ullamaliztli player in the empire. It was said that if he wasn't a warrior, he would be the greatest champion to ever play the game. Achcauhtli and Ichtaca glanced nervously at Yaotl, but Tepiltzin's brother was not to be denied. Yaotl only nodded as he looked at Huemac, who remained impassive but signaled his acceptance to be the representative of the high priest.

"Then it is decided," Tlazopilli said. "The game is to be played at dawn tomorrow. Commander Huemac, remove the youths from the temple and have them rest and prepare. You should also do the same."

As he was being led out of the great chamber, Yaotl stole a glance at his enemy Coaxoch, who he noticed had a grim smile on his face. The young man knew he had already lost. After his brother, Yaotl practically worshipped Commander Huemac, it was one of the reasons he volunteered to join the Eagle Knights, to be led by a great warrior and hero of the empire. Huemac was also a good friend of Tepiltzin and no matter what the outcome was, Yaotl knew that he would be paying a terrible price for it. If he lost the game, then he and his friends would no doubt be sacrificed. Even if he was somehow able to win the game against the greatest player ever, he would be heartbroken to see Huemac being sacrificed just to protect his brother's honor. That was when he realized that deep inside his heart, he had sensed that his brother might be guilty after all. If his brother was indeed the guilty one, then how could he save his family's honor, yet still prevent the death of his idol and mentor?

22. The Forests of Eden

Otherworld

The three of them were standing at the beach, near the edge of the shore. Behind them was the small boat where the ferryman still stood, as he waited until he could once more venture across the seas of infinity. Paul Dane stood side by side with Valerie Mendoza as he looked around. Whether they were standing on an island or part of a continental landmass he wasn't so sure, but then again this was a place where anything was possible. It was daylight, but where the sun was located he just couldn't tell, it was as if the star was just over the horizon. Paul could see a vast forest out in the distance. He wasn't a botanist, but the plants seemed both oddly familiar, yet completely strange. It was as if the flowers and trees had yet to crossbreed with other plant species in order to produce the fruits and herbs as he knew them. The greenery were all still in their original, primordial state.

"This is where I leave you," the old man said as he stood in front of them. "The ferryman waits for me."

Valerie smiled faintly. She had grown used to being with him and considered the wanderer a friend. She had a distinct feeling she would see him again. "Where will you go from here?"

The old man smiled back. "Perhaps I shall journey to the upper realms. Where the contented spirits go. Then perhaps even to Irkalla, where some of my family dwells. Then after that, who knows? Perhaps I shall wander the wastes again."

Paul nodded. Irkalla was the name for the Sumerian underworld. A place somewhat akin to Hades of the Greek myths. "I wish you'd stay for awhile. There's so much more I can learn from you. I still have so many questions."

The old man laughed a little as he turned his scrawny head and gazed out at the bluish water along the shore. "I must be on the move, it gives me a purpose. I made a vow to myself to wander these plains forever until I can find the answers to which I seek."

Paul took his glasses off and placed them in his front shirt pocket. His vision was perfect in this other world. "I have a feeling that you'll never find those answers."

"Perhaps you are right," the old man said wistfully. "Though it gives me something to do. What is life without a purpose?"

Paul laughed. "Back in my time you'd be called an existentialist."

The old man seemed puzzled. "I am not familiar with that word."

"An existentialist is one who believes that life has no meaning," Paul said. "Yet one creates meaning by giving oneself a purpose in one's life."

"I see. That is one new word I have learned today," the old man said.

"The Righteous Sufferer," Paul said. "You're him, aren't you?"

"I have suffered in my life," the old man said. "Though again, I am not familiar with that title."

"It's an old Babylonian poem," Paul said. "About a man who becomes sick and loses everything. He asks the gods what he has done wrong to deserve such a fate. Later on, the Hebrews adapted it and sort of made their own version of it- except that instead of many gods, they just made it one. They called it the Book of Job."

"Yes, you can say that the poem is a reflection of my life story," the old man said. "It is a story that has been told many times by many people over the course of history. Such is the way with mankind, we create new stories from old ones and retell them in a slightly different way each time."

"The Book of Job is a timeless story," Valerie said. "I gotta ask though, is this all the work of one god or multiple gods?"

The old man shrugged. "Does it really matter in the end if all these gods are truly different beings or just different aspects of a single god? Does it really change anything?"

Valerie looked down on the white sand. "I guess not."

The old man turned and started to walk towards the small boat at the edge of the shore. "Then I shall leave you both to it. I am sure Urshanabi is getting restless just standing on his boat. He might try to leave so it's best that I go too. Farewell and I hope we shall meet again." With those words, the old man waded into the clear waters and then climbed into the boat. The ferryman began to paddle away and both were soon lost in the mists that surrounded the waters.

Valerie looked confused as she turned and looked at Paul. "Urshanabi? That was the name he called the boatman with. I thought that was Charon."

Paul shrugged. "Well, Urshanabi was a companion to Gilgamesh and he was the one who ferried that great hero across the underworld. The Sumerian ferryman has very similar traits to Charon so I guess it's a universal theme. They both could be the same person."

Valerie pointed towards the forest. "Well, we might as well get moving. He said there would be a friend waiting for us somewhere here."

They both held each other's hands as they started walking towards the distant forest. Paul was quiet as he kept thinking about his ordeal and he felt shameful about it. Despite all the knowledge about myths and legends that he had, Paul had felt totally powerless when he was trapped in the infernal city of Dis.

Valerie stole a glance at him as they continued walking. "You're more brooding than usual, Paul. Is everything okay?"

"I'm just mad at myself that I couldn't have broken out of that prison I was in," Paul said. "I mean, I'm thankful for what you did and all, but—"

"As a man, you felt that you should have been the one to rescue me, is that it?"

Paul sighed. "I guess that's it. I'm not saying that I think men are supposed to be stronger, it's just that I felt that I've let myself down more than anything. I mean, here I am, the great mythology professor, brought down by my own guilt. It's not something to be proud about."

Valerie nudged him slightly with her elbow. "It just goes to show that you're human, Paul. It proves that we all need someone to help us out every now and then. That's what the world ought to be about."

Paul clasped her hand even tighter. She was his guardian angel. Valerie was everything he could have asked for. "You're right. I owe you my life and my very soul, Val. I love you."

"And I love you."

For a long while, neither of them said anything further. They both were content just to be with each other as they walked along the base of the tallest mountain they had ever seen. The short grasslands were dotted with occasional shrubs and flowery trees. There were strange looking fruits that neither of them ate. The one peculiar thing about the Otherworlds was that they didn't feel the need to eat nor did they feel tired. The time of day didn't change as the shadows of the land stayed the same, it was as if the hours had stood still in this world, except that they were moving along on it. Paul wore a watch and as he looked at it, the hands on the dial had apparently stopped moving the moment the demon Dantalion had transported them into these planes.

As they moved through a small forest of coniferous trees, Paul soon realized that these very plants had been extinct for millions of years on earth. Small, knee high plants with oval leaves and grass that resembled overgrown bean sprouts attested to the primeval nature of this world. Paul smiled to himself as they kept on walking. Many of his colleagues in the scientific fields would have killed somebody just to have a chance to study all this lost greenery. They would have been envious as to what he was seeing now. Then he remembered the state of the world, and the fact that many of his colleagues might already be dead.

A light rain had started. Paul cried out in pleasant surprise as they both ran underneath a huge cedar tree overlooking a grassy clearing. As he ran his hand over Valerie's hair to brush the droplets of water away, he noticed that his hands didn't get wet as every single molecule of water slid off the skin of his palms and hit the wet grass below.

Valerie noticed his slight confusion. "The water doesn't seem to stick to our clothes. That's why they look and feel as if brand new. I was stuck in a world of mud before the Righteous Sufferer found me. Even though I was wallowing in all that muck, none of it stuck on my clothes or my body."

Paul shook his head and smiled. "It's strange, the rain affects the land, but not us."

Valerie nodded and smiled at him. Just as she was about to say something, she caught a movement in the corner of her eye. She turned and noticed a figure near the center of the clearing. She tapped Paul on the shoulder and pointed to where she saw it. "Look."

Paul twisted his head slightly. There was an old man wearing a bathrobe as he crouched down near a small stream. The robe that he was wearing looked modern and it looked like it had a sales tag still embedded in its collar. Paul took Valerie's hand and they both started walking towards him.

The old man stared at the stream for awhile, as if contemplating something. He had a white stubble on his chin and cheeks, and wisps of silvery strands on the top of his head. Just as Paul and Valerie got to within thirty feet of him, he noticed them as he stood up and smiled. Valerie could see that the old man had crooked yellow teeth.

Paul raised his hand in a gesture of peace. "Hi there. I'm Paul and this is Valerie. We came through a boat from the beach that was past the big mountain. The wanderer told us we would meet a friend of his here."

The old man nodded. "Yes, I have heard of you. My friend the raven god told me of your imminent arrival. I go by many names, but my current one is Atrahasis."

Paul's eyebrows shot up. "Atrahasis? Of the great flood?"

"Yes," the old man said.

Valerie looked at Paul as she stood beside him. "I'm sorry, do you know him?"

Paul nodded. "I know of him. He is the original Noah, of the flood. The Hebrews took the flood stories of the Sumerians and the Babylonians, and adapted the story to fit their own religion. In the original version, it is a decree by many of the gods to destroy mankind, but one of the gods took pity on one man and tasked him to preserve humanity. Atrahasis is the original one, though I think he went by another name."

The old man was impressed. "Yes, I was also known as Ziusudra. It has been such a long time ago and I have had so many names. Now I like to change my name every now and then. It keeps my mind fresh."

"If I could ask," Valerie said. "Where are we? This place seems so serene, so peaceful as compared to the hellish lands we just came from."

"You are in a land that is sometimes called Dilmun," Atrahasis said.

Valerie looked around and smiled. "It certainly is pleasant, like the garden of Eden."

Paul winked at her. "That's because it probably is. Dilmun was supposedly a historical place on earth, an actual land of prosperous, healthy people who traded with the Sumerians. There were other theories that it was an unearthly paradise, the home of the gods. The Hebrew concept of Eden may have been influenced by that myth."

Atrahasis clapped his hands. "Most impressive, Paul. Your knowledge of the ancient world is very good."

"It's an honor to meet you," Paul said. "Did you also mention the raven god? How did you get to know him and how does all this have to do with us?"

"The raven god is currently the mentor and guide to a few of my friends. They mentioned to me that you would make your way here soon and they would meet you. They told me that the ancient empire from the south of your lands is now threatening to engulf your world," Atrahasis said.

Paul glanced at Valerie. "That would be the Aztecs. Yes, it seems that before I was forcibly taken by a demon and sent out here, my government had warned me of an impending invasion by them. My guess is that it has started to happen while we were away."

Valerie frowned. "That's not good, we need to get back to earth then and do what we can to try and stop them."

"Your friends are of a similar mind," Atrahasis said. "All we should do is to wait until they arrive."

Paul nodded. "I hope the kids are alright. Hopefully those Aztecs haven't advanced as far up as the Midwest."

"The others will surely give you the latest information when you finally speak with them," Atrahasis said.

"Thank you. I'm glad we're not the only one in this fight," Paul said. "If I can ask, why have the gods come back like this? What do they want?"

The old man looked away for a moment, as if he was thinking about Paul's words. "It is very hard to discern the motivations of the gods. Their wants and needs are somewhat different than that of mortals. In my time they caused a great flood because they felt that there was too many of us and that we were making such a multitude of noises that it disturbed them to no end."

Valerie sighed. "I can't believe that the gods would just decide to kill off most of humanity just because we were making too much noise. It's such a silly motivation for genocide."

"The one main trait of all gods is that they are mysterious," Atrahasis said. "One cannot know what motivates them, for an immortal life bestows a different way of looking at the world and at the cosmos beyond."

"Yet they compel us to worship them and show them respect," Paul said angrily. "It isn't fair. Are we nothing more than cannon fodder to them? Just mere playthings to do with as they please?"

"I cannot give you the answer to that, I'm sorry," Atrahasis said. "My ruminations have given me some insight, but I do not know if it is the truth. What I can say is that perhaps the gods view us as their children and that they expect obedience and respect, just like a father would demand from his offspring. They created us and therefore our destinies are decided by their whims."

Valerie folded her arms over her chest. "Wow. Big freaking deal. If the gods are our parents then they have done a terrible job at it. They leave us alone for a long time, without any signs as to even whether they existed at all, and then bam! They come right back and throw all sorts of monsters and demons and kill an awful lot of people. What kind of parenting is that?"

Atrahasis looked at her solemnly. "Let me tell you a tale of the gods in my time. It is said that civilization was a gift from the gods. It was civilization that elevated mankind from the beasts of the land. With the advent of cities we were given prosperity, peace and luxurious living. But this blessing also had a curse- civilization would also bring about war, famine, disease and drought. The arts of beauty, music, pity and justice had their own counterparts in fear, terror, strife and deceit. All this was the gift of civilization, these things were all given to us, and once the gift was given, it could never be taken back. To the gods, all their gifts have the power to bless and to curse. Such is the way with all benefactions. One cannot have one without the other. We could not pick and choose what gifts could be bestowed upon us, we had to accept them all."

"I don't doubt the wisdom in your words, Atrahasis," Paul said. "Though despite our weaknesses, our present day world before the Glooming happened wasn't such a bad place to live in. Granted, we still had wars and there were people who were starving in some parts of the world, but the majority of us were living decently. The rule of law was followed by most nations and many of us had a great standard of living. Then all of a sudden the gods just decided to return, and now there's so much chaos and destruction. So many dead. So many wasted lives."

"The gods give, and the gods take away," Atrahasis said. "Human life is fragile and so is that of our achievements. It can all be ground to dust in a manner of a short season. In my time, it was our civilization that became our own undoing. It was our very gift that ultimately led to our destruction. My people were once prosperous, and then the salt in the earth rose up and ruined our crops. The cedar forests that we had cut down were no more, and the once fertile land became barren. The cities in the land between the rivers began to weaken and many people moved away. In the end, our nation had become so pitiful that it was conquered by other civilizations. Humanity is capable of making great accomplishments, yet it can all be undone. Such is the way of the world. I have seen it happen in countless civilizations."

"Of all the gifts the gods could have given us, eternal life would have been good. At least, we wouldn't have to die by the millions right now," Paul said.

"That is the one gift that the gods could never bestow upon humanity," Atrahasis said. "I am perhaps a rare exception but I feel that it is not much of a benefit. I have seen my loved ones grow old and die. I could not bear the thought of having to love someone since I know, deep in my heart, she would die and I would go on living. It would drive one mad if one thinks too deeply about it. A world full of immortals will be like Irkalla, the underworld- it shall be a grey and dreary place, one bereft of purpose or of hope. A great champion had once sought me out, just so that he could learn the secret of eternal life."

Paul looked at the old man. "Gilgamesh?"

"Yes," Atrahasis said. "His great companion Enkidu had died and he lamented his loss. He felt that if he could live forever then perhaps it would take some of the pain away. In the end, it was a futile quest for even when he found the plant that would give him eternal life, it was stolen from him by a serpent while he was asleep. He should have listened to the tavern keeper Siduri, she met him while he was searching for me. Siduri told him that it was better to enjoy the simple pleasures in life than to search for the unattainable. Little things such as holding the hands of your children, the embrace of one's wife, hearing the cries of the night creatures while in the comforts of your house, enjoying the pleasures of a simple meal. It is these things that matter. Humans have but short lives so it pays to live it to the fullest."

Valerie was listening intently. She let out a deep sigh right after the old man finished his speech. "Let me tell you what I think. The gods do this to us because they're afraid of us. They hate humanity. The gods are jealous because we live such short lives and the little things we do have more meaning than whatever it is that they do. We get to love for a short time, and we get to laugh and be happy for a short time, yeah. But the gods can't do any of that. All they can do is throw thunderbolts, or cast storms and kill people. They may have all that power, but they can't love each other the way we do. We don't need to live forever or have godlike powers to be loved and to love back. We can earn respect from other people just by doing good deeds. No god can say that about themselves. And that's why I'm going to keep fighting. Because even if my life is short, it's worth living."

Paul looked at her and smiled. He clasped her hand and gave her a kiss. "You know what, Val? That's the best attitude I've ever heard anyone proclaim during this whole crisis. The time I've spent with you has been as good or even better than I had when I was with Elizabeth. I've found the right person in my life. That I know for sure."

Valerie smiled at him and they both hugged each other for a long time. "We'll get through this, Paul. Once this is over, I'd love to raise a family with you."

Paul just smiled and kissed her forehead. He couldn't wait until this was all over. His old life with Elizabeth had been bliss, but it was now time to turn a new page. Valerie was the one he was waiting for. He knew that now.

As the two of them continued to hug each other, Patrick Gyle and Tara Weiss emerged from the edge of the forest and made their way towards them. Atrahasis immediately noticed as he stood up and looked in their direction with a wry smile on his face. Valerie noticed them as she pulled herself away from Paul and faced the two of them, her right hand on her hip holster. Paul saw the potential for hostility as he gently placed his hand above hers and winked at her a second time.

Gyle strode into the clearing with an air of supreme confidence. "You must be the two people that we were supposed to meet up with," he said. "I'm Patrick and this here's Tara."

Paul blinked a few times as he remembered the conversation he had when he summoned the demon that took them here. He looked at the pale creature with wonderment. "Patrick ... Gyle, right?"

Gyle nodded. "Correctamundo. I know the way I look freaks you out, but every gift has a price."

Paul nodded. "I agree, we were just talking about that." He looked at the teenage girl. "And you must be Tara, nice to finally meet you both."

"So you're supposedly the one who is supposed to help us?" Tara said. Then she pointed to Valerie. "Who is she?"

"Valerie Mendoza, NYPD," Valerie said. "I heard about you, Tara, you saved my life and I'd like to thank you for it."

Tara looked confused for a bit. "I did? When?"

"A demon told me you were able to stop some sort of Indian god from being born," Valerie said. "I was in the museum when a giant worm popped out from under the floor. It nearly killed me before it somehow disappeared. From what a demon told us, there was a boy who helped you. Where is he?"

"His name is Ilya, from Siberia. He got hurt rescuing me and he is being taken care of by the Fey in the faerie realms until he recovers," Tara said.

Paul could barely contain his giddiness. First he met the oldest man in the world, now they were talking about faeries. It was so much information to process. He could probably spend several lifetimes just talking to these people. Nevertheless, there was a job to do. "I hope he gets better soon then, we're going to need him. You'll have to forgive us, but we were trapped in Hell for a time. Could you both maybe give us an update as to what's going on back on earth?"

"I'll give you the long and short of it," Gyle said as a raven landed on top of a nearby shrub. "The Aztecs have broken through the southern borders. Most of Texas has now been absorbed by their empire along with lots of counties in the southwest. They have apparently stopped because they're busy sacrificing all their captive prisoners to their bloodthirsty gods. As soon as that's done they'll be moving north again, and this time there ain't no military in their way. The US government tried nukes but apparently they couldn't get them to detonate. The president, the one you rescued from the Kansas separatists, is also possessed by demons."

Paul said nothing at first. Then he glanced over at the black bird perched on the shrubbery. "You got anything to add?"

Valerie looked at Paul as if he was crazy. "Paul, that's a bird you're talking to."

"I may not have ears, but I can hear him good enough," the raven said to Valerie as the NYPD detective staggered back in awe.

Paul narrowed his eyes. So his guess was right. "So you are the trickster that everyone's been talking about. Tell me, since there are trickster gods in just about every culture, are you all one and the same, or a whole bunch of different beings with the same characteristics?"

"I could tell you the truth," the raven said. "But where's all the fun in that?"

Tara rolled her eyes. "Don't bother trying to ask it a direct question like that. You won't ever get a straight answer."

Paul smiled at her. There was something sad about Tara's demeanor, but he felt a kindred spirit when he looked at her. "I get it. That's why they're called tricksters after all. They have to live up to their godly reputation," he said.

Valerie pointed at the raven. "You're telling me that bird is some sort of … god?"

Tara crossed her arms and looked away. Paul could sense her petulant mood from her body language. Something was bothering her— she seemed to be resenting the trickster. "I think it's just a talking animal that thinks it's a god. Even if he is one, he's probably a pretty weak god since he didn't raise a finger to help when Ilya got hurt or when I was in danger!" she said.

The raven raised one of its claws up in the air as it stood on one leg. "Well, since I don't have any fingers, how can I raise one?"

Tara sneered. "Shut up."

Paul raised his hands up to try and calm everyone down. "Okay everyone, take it easy, this isn't getting us anywhere. Raven, how do these Aztec gods operate? Have they actually manifested themselves on earth?"

"Sort of," the raven said. "The Aztec gods channel their power through what you modern day people call avatars. These avatars are ordinary people that are imbued with a portion of their divinity and the Aztec gods see through them and give orders to their subordinates. That's how their empire is run."

Gyle stole an angry glance at the black bird. "Why didn't you tell us this before?"

The raven started to preen its left wing with its beak. "You never asked."

"Okay," Paul quickly said in order to interrupt a brewing conflict. "So I guess this means that if their avatars are human, they can be killed, thereby disrupting the operations of their empire, am I right?"

"It's certainly possible. Their avatars are in Tenochtitlan, though in the heart of their empire. Their powers get stronger the closer you get to them. I won't be able to transport you right into their city, I can only get us to the outskirts. From there, we have to walk to where their avatars reside. They are holed up in their mighty temples, and they are heavily guarded."

Gyle smiled as the fangs in his mouth became visible. "I can take care of those guards with no problem."

"The humans will be the least of your problems," the raven said. "The avatars themselves are pretty powerful, probably as powerful as you, Gyle. Let's not forget they have the star demons at their side in a mutual alliance."

Tara didn't like the sound of that. "Star demons?"

"I think the trickster means the tzitzimitl," Valerie said. "They are powerful creatures with fangs and claws. The ancient Aztecs even worshipped them as demigods. Female fertility goddesses who can be very dangerous to their enemies."

Paul nodded. "Okay, if these tzitzimitl are allied with them, then is there a way we can either get them to stop allying with the Aztecs or maybe find a way to neutralize them?"

"Well, the current Aztec empire that exists right now is calling itself the Triple Alliance for a reason," the raven said.

"Big deal," Paul said. "The ancient Aztec Empire also called itself the Triple Alliance. They were called that because the three Aztec city-states of Tenochtitlan, Texcoco and Tlacopan jointly ruled the empire together."

The raven shook its head rapidly from side to side. "This new Triple Alliance has a very different meaning. It's an alliance between three gods-Huitzilopochtli, Xipe Totec and Tlaloc. The two avatars of Huitzilopochtli and Xipe Totec are still waiting for the avatar of Tlaloc to manifest itself, but there has been a disruption of some sort. Once the avatar of Tlaloc is born, then this alliance will be invincible against any kind of attack for its power will be too great."

Valerie's heart started to jump. It felt just like the museum all over again. "Then we gotta do something! We need to attack quickly before Tlaloc can be reborn!"

"Hold on, Val," Paul said. "We need to know everything we can as to how Tlaloc's avatar got delayed and any weaknesses they might have before we go in."

"El Brujo said something about another shaman who needs to go on his vision quest somewhere in the Old South," Gyle said. "He said that that shaman holds the key to forcing a great change amongst the Aztecs. We have to wait until that man, whoever he is, assumes the title of shaman."

Paul rubbed his forehead. "A shaman? Which god is he a shaman to?"

"I think his god is called the Master of Breath, or something," Gyle said.

Paul nodded. "Okay, that's Esaugetuh Emissee, he's a Creek Indian god who was worshiped as their supreme creator. So if this god is using his shaman to effect a great change, then I guess we can assume that at least we have one god on our side, right?"

"Correctamundo," the raven said. "Hmm, looks like I'm getting the hang of this latest slang now."

"That's about all we know," Gyle said. "The problem is we don't know when this shaman is supposed to go on his vision quest or when this great change is supposed to happen."

Valerie sighed. "Oh, that's just great. So we are going in, half-blind into the lion's den, and we won't even know if this shaman is gonna pull his weight or not? This is a very risky operation- all sorts of things could go wrong."

"I don't like it either, but I'm guessing we may be running out of time. So that leaves us with no choice but to go ahead," Gyle said.

Paul looked at Gyle. "You mentioned that the president is possessed by a demon?"

"Yeah, that's what they told us," Gyle said to him. "He's being cared for over at Camp David, but unless someone is able to get that demon out of him, the country is in bad shape."

Paul turned his attention to the trickster. "You really can't tell us when this new shaman will be able to use his powers to help us?"

"Nope," the raven said. "As with what has transpired, you just need to have a little faith that the gods on your side will pull through."

Valerie shook her head. "I've got a bad feeling about this. It's way too risky to execute."

"You went into that museum without really knowing anything," the raven said to her. "And yet you were able to succeed."

"What we did in the museum really didn't matter much since it was Tara and her other friend who really fixed things in the end," Valerie said as she pointed to the teenager. "When all was said and done, a lot of cops were killed. For nothing."

"You were able to prevent that nuke from going off though, Val," Paul said to her. "So it wasn't all for nothing."

Valerie looked away. She didn't want to argue about it anymore. It brought on too many bad memories for her.

Paul pondered over the whole situation. A few of them were needed to exorcise the demon from the president. Another team needed to be deployed to the Aztec Empire to do battle against their godlike avatars. It would all depend on a mysterious shaman who had yet to reveal himself. There was a very high chance of failure, and they would all be facing certain death.

Atrahasis was quiet for the whole time as he sat listening to the arguments being bandied back and forth. As everyone else stopped talking, he felt that he needed to say something. "As with all things, there are times that one needs to rely on faith," he said softly as everyone turned to look at him. "One must have trust in one's fellow man, for only if you believe in each other will you be able to achieve a greater thing than what you would have done if you had acted alone."

Paul nodded. They had to act. "Okay, here is my suggestion. We split into two teams. One team goes to Camp David to get the president's demon out of him. The other team needs to head for Tenochtitlan to confront the Aztec avatars."

Valerie placed her hands on her hips as she looked at him. "Paul, you were able to summon that demon, so it's only logical that you head to Camp David to see what you can do about the president."

"I'm the one with the claws, so I'll be part of the team to head to the Aztecs," Gyle said softly. No one disagreed.

Paul turned to look at Tara. "Where would you like to go?"

Tara looked away and gave an indifferent shrug. "I dunno and I don't care."

"You need to stay safe," Gyle said to her. "You go with Professor Dane to Camp David."

Valerie glanced at Gyle. "I'm going with you. I know how to speak Nahuatl and I'm a cop. I can handle myself."

Paul let out a deep breath as he turned to look at Valerie. "Val, it's too dangerous. I think you ought to stick with me."

Valerie smiled as she stood next to him and gave Paul a big hug. "I have to do this, Paul. It makes the most sense for me to go to Tenochtitlan. You know it, and I know it. Don't worry, I was at the museum before and came out without a scratch, remember?"

Paul bit his lip. He couldn't lose her. Not now. Not after all they've been through. He knew it was a foregone conclusion she would be going to the lands of the Aztecs. She could pass off as an Aztec woman and he figured that as long as she stayed careful, she would hopefully be alright. "Okay, but take care of yourself out there," he said softly as he kissed her on the forehead. "Please come back to me."

Valerie smiled as she held out the jade Aztec necklace around her neck. "Don't you worry, I still have my mama's protective charm, remember?"

Tara put her hand up. "I think I could probably deal with the president. El Brujo taught me how to control my mind and spirit and all that."

Paul nodded to her. "Okay, I trust you. Since you were able to sabotage the avatar of Okeus, I'm sure you're more than capable of handling this."

"I'll probably get El Brujo to join me, just in case I need extra help," Tara said.

"Good idea," Paul said to her before turning his head to look at Valerie once more. "Looks like I'll be joining you in Tenochtitlan, Val."

Valerie smirked at him. "You sure you can handle it? You're not the physical type, Paul."

Paul snorted playfully. "Come on, I took on a Wendigo, which is pretty much like an avatar. I'm pretty sure I won't be a hindrance to you or to Patrick."

"So that leaves me," the raven said.

Paul twisted his head slightly as he stared down at the black bird. "Yes, that leaves you. Since trickster gods can change their shape, I'm pretty sure you can too, right?"

"Somewhat," the raven said. "What is it that you would want me to change into?"

Paul glanced at the others one by one and gave them all a wink before turning to look at the raven one more time. "There's a being I want you to assume. And one that I'm sure you'll get a kick out of."

The raven gave a loud caw that was almost like a sigh. "Something tells me I'm not gonna like this."

23. The Serpent of Vision

Alabama

Nobody slept since the attack two nights ago. The *Nimrod* had been heavily damaged, but the captain had insisted that they would continue on until they sighted the great horned serpent and killed it. The diesel engine that powered the paddlewheel was behaving erratically since it was damaged by the owl-men. The exhaust had begun to belch infrequently and the vibrations were becoming so noisy that anyone near the engines had to cover their ears. Two men had been reassigned to the engine room and they tried their best, but everyone could tell that the pistons were on their last legs. Eight-Ball Jackson was gone. He had either abandoned the ship during the attack, or he was killed and his body was carried off into the night. When the rest of the crew heard about it, there were hushed whispers that they needed to stage a mutiny in order to get the ship turned around and back to the nearest port. But ever since the captain had executed the last one who crossed him, no one dared to try anything. The ship's first officer, JJ Glanton, still had a small group of loyal friends, and they were the most heavily-armed among the crew. If anyone dared to try an uprising, they would have to get through him first.

Tyrone Gatlin could barely keep his eyes open as he stared out through the ruined front window of the pilot house. The late afternoon was overcast, and it looked like it was going to rain again soon. The air was muggy and droplets of water vapor stuck to his clothes, making him sweat even more. He was constantly making minute adjustments on the ship's wheel as he maneuvered the Nimrod around the massive trunks of half sunken trees. They were deep in the sunken forest, and the waterways would twist and branch out in many directions. This was his first time in ever piloting a boat, but even he knew that they were hopelessly lost. It was as if the sunken trees had swallowed them up and were never going to let them go. Whatever was in that box that the captain kept locked up in his room was right, the ship was cursed, and they were getting ever closer to their doom.

He looked out towards the upper deck just below him and he could see the captain standing at the bow, right beside the harpoon cannon. Captain Pillinger was using his binoculars to search the murky waters around him, but the rising mists kept obscuring any details. The remaining hunter crews were spread out along the sides of the upper deck as they leaned over the railings while using binoculars and scoped rifles to try and spot their quarry, so they could finally kill it and go home. Everyone was on edge, but the fatigue from all those sleepless nights was making them see things. Just yesterday, two hunters thought they finally spotted the great serpent and shouted at the captain to turn the ship hard to starboard, but as they got closer everyone realized it was just another sunken tree. The captain was filled with rage and he wanted to execute the two men on the spot, and it was only through Gatlin's timely intervention that the men's lives were spared. After that, no one dared to shout out an alarm unless they were absolutely sure.

Just as his eyes began to droop, Tyrone shook his head rapidly from the side to side in order to stay awake. He hadn't been dreaming about the Master of Breath, but that was only because he hadn't slept at all. The captain had ordered him to man the ship's wheel and he hadn't left the pilot house in nearly two days. Four large plastic bottles sitting in the corner near his legs were filled with yellow urine. The one time he had been able to go to the bathroom was when the captain mercifully took over the ship's wheel for a few minutes. Tyrone glanced over through the smashed-in side windows to see if he could get anyone's attention. If he could just get a cup of steaming coffee, then it would keep him going for another hour, at least. As he peered over the port side of the ship, that was when he saw something.

At first he thought it was just a floating log near a copse of sunken trees. Then it started moving as it undulated its cylindrical body through the muddy water. Tyrone blinked several times to make sure he wasn't dreaming. The creature was apparently swimming parallel to the ship, as to why, he had no idea. Either way, he wanted to get this over with. Tyrone began to turn the ship's wheel to his left as the ship started to turn portside.

Captain Pillinger turned and looked at him through the front window. "What in the hell are you doing?"

Tyrone gestured with his chin as he signaled the engine room to go to full speed. "Over there, I think I see it!"

Everyone started to look out over the decks as Tyrone maneuvered the ship into a much wider waterway. A few of the men started shouting and pointing at something in the water, less than thirty feet away from their front starboard side. As they got closer, the shouts turned into muted gasps of shock and awe. That was when Tyrone realized that they would need a bigger boat.

The great horned serpent reared its head above the water, and Tyrone guessed it must have been as big as a bulldozer. The front part was streamlined, with rows of fanged teeth that were the size of great swords along its wide mouth. Its glowing reptilian eyes must have measured several feet in diameter. Two gigantic curved horns grew from the side of its head, while a massive red crystal seemed to be imbedded on the top of its forehead. As the sea monster began to bring the full length of its gargantuan, snake-like body to the surface, everyone realized that it had practically encircled the ship. Men on every side of the boat could see that its coils in the waters surrounding the *Nimrod* had run around the entire length of the ship, as the creature seemed to be following its own tail. A deepening sense of dread began to permeate as many of the crew realized they had their work cut out for them.

The captain started to bellow as he readied the harpoon cannon. "I need another man here!"

One of Glanton's loyalists ran over, as he began assisting the captain in tying a cable just behind the head of the harpoon. Several of the men along the decks began firing their weapons, but Tyrone figured that it would be useless, a snake that big probably wouldn't even feel those tiny little bullets hitting its body.

Pillinger looked back at him. "Tyrone, just go straight ahead, steady now!"

Tyrone kept the ship's wheel stable as the *Nimrod* plowed forward, the ship's bow was now aimed directly at the serpent's head. Just as they got to within fifty feet, the creature submerged its head under the water sending out strong, undulating waves to rock the ship from side to side. Pillinger knew he had one chance as he could see the creature diving under the boat, but parts of its body was still submerging, just as they were finally in range.

Pillinger pressed the trigger as the firing mechanism impacted the cartridge. There was a loud bang as the harpoon was fired and it struck the back part of the snakelike body just as it submerged right in front of them. Almost immediately, the attached whale cable started unrolling along the deck. Pillinger quickly stepped back as his assistant began to reload the harpoon cannon while he made sure the winch that the cable was tied down to was secure on the ship's superstructure. For a full minute the cable kept discharging until it reached its maximum length, then the line became taut and stiffened.

There was a loud crash and all of sudden everyone was thrown backwards along the decks as the entire ship listed sideways. Tyrone was able to hang on to the ship's wheel as everything started to tilt to the right. Several of the crew started screaming. Glanton shouted at the men to grab some spears that were lying in the saloon. Even though the ship was running at full speed, the weight of the great serpent seemed to hold it in place as the right side of the paddlewheel kept revolving helplessly in the air. Pillinger cursed out loud as he struggled to mount another harpoon on the Kongsberg cannon.

The Sint-Holo raised its head high above the listing starboard side of the ship. Tyrone turned and he stared briefly into the creature's massive eyes before it lowered its head and bit into a terrified crewmember, tearing the hapless man in half and swallowing his upper body before diving back down into the churning waters once more. Several of the men fired their assault rifles, using full automatic bursts at the beast, but it didn't seem to have affected it. The creature's tail lashed out from the water at the aft part of the ship and smashed down onto the spinning paddlewheel and splintered it completely.

As the ship lurched back and became level once again, Tyrone knew they were done for. The paddlewheel was gone—there was no way they could move. He quickly turned and got out of the pilot house as he made his way down the stairs.

Glanton noticed and ran up to him as he was drawing his pistol. "Where the hell do you think you're going, boy?"

Tyrone didn't stop as he threw a fist at Glanton's surprised face. The ship's first officer took it right on the bridge of his nose and he fell back onto the deck, stunned. Tyrone ran past him and opened the door that led into the corridor. He kept his arms out as he steadied himself, just as the ship began to rock sideways as the monster underneath them began to wrap its massive body along the hull of the *Nimrod.*

Pillinger screamed out a curse as he aimed the harpoon at the serpent's cylindrical torso and fired once more. The massive dart embedded itself on the scaly body but the creature didn't even seem to feel it. The captain of the stricken ship turned as he opened a wooden crate nearby. Within the container was a set of antique 19th Century whaling harpoons, they were essentially barbed javelins that he had kept as a last ditch resort. Pillinger pulled one out from the crate and hefted it before tying its attached cable to his waistline. The creature was even bigger than he had remembered it, or had it grown larger somehow? Either way, he wasn't going to allow it to get the better of him this time.

Tyrone had finally gotten to the door of the captain's quarters as he fumbled for the key in his pocket. Just as he pulled out the key and was about to place it into the hole, the groaning ship once more tilted to the left and the key clattered away onto the deck and gone from sight. Tyrone cursed out loudly as he tried to kick the door open, but he quickly remembered it had been reinforced. He tried the door to an adjoining room and it opened.

As he went inside, Tyrone could see that the porthole in this room had been torn through when one of those owl creatures tried to force its way into the corridor. He braced himself and then started kicking where the crew had nailed some planks over the hole. His first kick loosened the nails in the patched side of the hull, while the second kick finally tore the whole thing loose just as the entire room he was in tilted sideways and a sliding cabinet pinned him near the side of the door. Tyrone cried out in pain as his ankle was twisted by the heavy wardrobe.

The serpent's coils had tightened around the ship's hull and the *Nimrod's* wooden superstructure began to break apart. A number of crewmen were screaming in terror while some of them leaped out into the water as they desperately tried to save themselves. As a few of the crew tried to swim towards the nearby trees, packs of smaller water creatures converged on them and started attacking. More than half a dozen men were pulled under the churning waters, never to be seen again.

Pillinger hung on until he was able to climb along the upper side of the listing ship. A man of his age would have already given up, but he was possessed by an interminable spirit of vengeance that somehow kept him going. As he finally pulled himself up and stood on what was once the left side of the ship, the creature turned its gargantuan head and stared at him for a long moment. Then the Sint-Holo tilted its head up and roared up into the sky.

As he prepared to throw the harpoon, Pillinger screamed out a final curse at the monster that had killed his son. It was a phrase he read from an old book about a white whale. It seemed fitting since the nightmare had become real. "From hell's heart, I stab at thee!"

The creature seemed to have acknowledged him as it paused its orgy of destruction and lowered its head right after he said it. Pillinger threw the harpoon and it embedded itself near the monster's left eyelid. The horned serpent made a massive bellow as it tilted its head down, back into the water. Pillinger had the wind knocked out of him as the cable around his waist tightened and it quickly dragged him into the churning depths.

Tyrone groaned as he was finally able to push back the cabinet and he squeezed himself through the gap. The room had now fully tilted ninety degrees and he could see the water rising as he glanced back at where the door was. He quickly climbed up until he passed through the hole on the side of the room and he was soon standing on the side of the ship's hull. He could still see the great serpent's coils slowly tearing the remaining parts of the hull that were still in one piece. Tyrone knew he didn't have much time as he glanced to his side and saw that the porthole that led into the captain's cabin was open.

Steeling himself, Tyrone tried to push his body through the narrow porthole as he led feet first. Just as he got his hips through and tried to slide downwards into the room, his shoulders instantly got stuck in the window. Tyrone let out another curse since his arms were raised over his head and he could no longer push himself through. His legs were left dangling in the air. Tyrone whimpered when he realized that he was stuck fast and couldn't get himself out of it. The constant crashing noises of the ship breaking apart made him even tenser as he realized that he could very well drown. *What a stupid way to die*, he thought. *Stuck halfway through a porthole in a sinking ship.*

Suddenly, the wood around the metal porthole that held him began to splinter and break apart. In less than a minute, the porthole fell from the wall and Tyrone landed in the captain's room. Tyrone got up as he pushed down on the now separated porthole and pulled it downwards past his ankles before kicking it away. A series of loud crashing noises hurled him to the side of the room as water began to seep in. Tyrone got back on his feet and looked around until he noticed the ornate wooden box underneath the writing desk. He quickly used both hands to pull it out.

"Ah, you have returned," the shrill voice that came from the box said.

Tyrone could barely catch his breath. "Look, I dunno where the key is, man! How do I get you outta there?"

"There is more than one way to open a locked box."

Tyrone glanced around him. There was a fire axe affixed to the side of the wall. Using both hands, he tore it loose from its fittings and started hacking away at the lock on the box. As the water started cascading around him, he heard an audible click on the lock as he pounded it for the eighth time. Dropping the axe, he fumbled with the lock, then flipped the top part of the box open. As he stared at what was inside of it, he doubled back in surprise.

Standing in the box was a small, humanlike creature. It seemed to resemble a two foot tall man, only it was covered in brown fur from head to toe. Its large brown eyes were like that of a mouse. It had a flat nose and a small mouth with white teeth.

Tyrone's mouth trembled, even as the cabin began to fill with water. "W-what are you?"

"We can talk about that later," the little creature said. "I can save you from the others in the water, but you must allow me to ride on your shoulders as I do not like getting wet."

Tyrone nodded meekly. He moved forward as the creature placed its tiny hands on his arms. He helped the little being up on his shoulders. "Now what?"

"Go out through the hole from whence you came," the creature said. "I hope you know how to swim."

Tyrone made his way carefully to the hole where the window was. As the water began filling the room, he was able to climb his way out along the side of the ship as the little furry creature hung on to the back of his neck. It was like carrying a big rat, but Tyrone had a feeling that the creature wasn't hostile so he decided to play along. He slid down to the edge of the waterline and stared out at the men being attacked in the water.

"Be not afraid," the creature whispered in his ear. "You have been chosen and therefore you will not be killed."

What was left of the hull shuddered again as the ship started to sink. Tyrone knew he had no choice. He slipped into the water as he made sure the creature was riding high at the back of his neck. Tyrone began to breaststroke slowly, keeping his head and shoulders above the water as he made his way towards the nearest line of trees, ignoring the screams of the dying men all around him.

By the time evening had fallen, Tyrone was able to cobble together a raft made from the wooden wreckage of the *Nimrod.* He had hoped that there would be some survivors, but he didn't find any. The small creature waited patiently as it sat on a tree branch, while he spent a few hours picking up floating planks of wood and lashing them together with some of the loose shark cables. The rains had begun by the time they had set out on the raft. Tyrone was cold and wet, but he knew it was better to go on than to spend the night where they were. He had learned that the creature called itself one of the bohpoli, his kind had begun to reoccupy the swamps and forests of the surrounding lands. When he tried to ask more questions, the creature merely stayed silent.

Tyrone stood in the center of the small raft as he occasionally used a barge pole to veer the craft away from the trees that popped up along the waterway. A mysterious current was propelling them ever deeper into the sunken forest. He looked down at the impish creature that sat in front of the raft. "Now that we're moving again, can I ask you something?"

"You may ask," the bohpoli said. "But I may not answer."

Tyrone shuddered as the cold night air blew by. His clothes were still dripping wet and he was afraid he would catch a cold. "Why did the Master of Breath choose me? I'm nobody special."

The creature turned and looked up at him. "That I do not know. All I can sense is that you have something in you."

Tyrone was confused. "Something in me? Like what?"

"I'm not quite sure. I can sense some great power in you. Like some spirit that is about to awaken, but for some reason it cannot yet do so."

Tyrone didn't understand any of it. He felt like a puppet on a string. "This is just weird. I'm doing things like I don't have any choice. I hate it. I could've been killed many times over already."

The bohpoli let out a shrill laugh. "Oh but you do have a choice, you have been making choices ever since you took the first step in this journey."

"Could've fooled me," Tyrone said blankly. "It feels like I'm just doing whatever you guys want. I'm just being used and there's nothing I can do 'bout it."

"Let me ask you, Tyrone Gatlin," the creature said. "Do you feel you owe your people?"

Tyrone frowned. "My people? You mean the African American community? I never really thought about it. I was too busy living my life you know?"

"What I meant is that do you feel that you owe the peoples of these lands? Would you be willing to fight to preserve the communities here?"

Tyrone looked out into the distance. Despite the darkness all around them, he was able to somewhat see the waters and obstacles ahead of him. It was as if he gained some sort of night vision, as the trees and the water seemed to give off some strange green bioluminescence. "I was in the Army. I tried to fight. In the end, it was no use against those Aztecs. Finally I just gave up and ran. I don't feel good about it."

"If you were given another chance, would you fight to defend the peoples here?"

"If there was a way I could fight those Aztecs on their terms, sure why not," Tyrone said wistfully. "I just hate to fight when it's hopeless."

"Then you shall be given that chance," the bohpoli said. "The Master of Breath has chosen you to be his champion."

"Well if I screw up, I hope he ain't gonna be too disappointed," Tyrone said. "I have a habit of screwing up."

The creature stood up and pointed at something just ahead of them. "Your test will come soon enough. And it may not be what you expect. If you succeed, you will become a medicine man among your people."

Tyrone squinted his eyes as he tried to look to where the bohpoli was pointing at. Up ahead of them was a huge mound. At first glance it looked like a gigantic beaver dam made up of tree logs and it was blocking the waterway directly ahead of them. Tyrone used his pole to try and steer the raft away but the current was too strong.

"Do not fight the path of water," the bohpoli said softly. "Let the power flow through you, and you shall prevail over the stronger enemy."

Tyrone placed the barge pole on the floor of the raft and decided to wait. Within minutes, they came upon the edge of the massive wood mound and the raft stopped in front of it. As he wondered what to do next, the mound suddenly shifted as if a massive earthquake hit. Tyrone staggered and nearly fell off the raft as several huge wooden logs rolled towards them and nearly toppled them over. Suddenly, the water behind them started to churn rapidly as Tyrone fell on his knees onto the lashed wooden planks, just as he turned to see what was causing it.

Tyrone's eyes opened wide as the head of the great horned serpent rose up from the water right behind them. He noticed that the body of Captain Pillinger was still hanging by an attached cable around its massive neck. The huge stone crystal that adorned the creature's head had begun to glow with a bluish fire. A strange feeling began to cascade all over his body, it was as if the light from the crystal on the giant snake head had provided some sort of energy that warmed his cold, clammy skin.

"This is the Sint-Holo," the bohpoli said. "The great horned serpent of these lands. When the gods had returned to the world, so did he. The Sint-Holo appears to those who have the gift, and it is through he those chosen are blessed."

A sense of calmness washed over Tyrone as he blinked several times to make sure he wasn't dreaming. "Please tell the serpent that I had no intention of hurting it. I was only traveling with those people because I had to."

The bohpoli nodded. "The horned serpent knows. Do not fear, for no man could ever harm it. Your foolish companions all chose their fate, just as you have chosen yours. It asks you now, what is it that you wish?"

Tyrone fell to his knees. "All I could ask is that if it could help me stop the threat of these Aztecs, help me find a way to fight them off, so that I can return to my family and we can have peace all over again. I am greatly ashamed I ran away. I don't wanna be known as a coward ever again."

The great serpent's head seemed to sway back and forth. The red crystal glowed a violet hue and it cast strange beams of light onto the waters. It opened its mouth as if to say something, but no words came out.

"The Sint-Holo understands," the little furry imp said. "It will give you the chance to right your wrongs. It will give you the opportunity to become a man of power, to learn your true place and your true calling."

Tyrone nodded meekly. "Yes, yes. Whatever it wants, I'm ready."

The bohpoli made its way until it stood beside him. "Then your path is now chosen. You will do battle with the Aztecs. The prize will be the lands all around you. If you fail, the Aztec will conquer all. If you succeed, then you will have fulfilled your chosen path."

Tyrone gritted his teeth as he stood up. "Just tell me what to do."

The bohpoli gestured at the murky water in front of them. "You must enter the water and swim to the other world. From there, you shall meet the boy who wields the black mirror. That child shall be your companion against the darkness of the Aztecs. Or you can forgo what you were destined for and forge an uncertain path in these forests. Choose your way."

Tyrone looked down at the black depths. He was never a good swimmer. He would probably drown if he jumped in. A part of him just wanted to give up, to run away. He had survived all this time, surely he would make it. He didn't have to be this medicine man that his god had wanted him to be, he could just be his own man. Then his thoughts strayed back to all the people who had died. From his friends in the Army who were most certainly dead, over to the families in Shreveport, like Monique and her two daughters- they would surely be killed too. If he walked away from all this right now, more people would die, and it would be because he turned away from the gift offered to him. It would be the easy way out if he truly wanted it.

He made his choice. Tyrone drew a deep breath and then dived headfirst into the muddy water. As he began swimming into the suffocating darkness, his ears started to pop as the water pressure increased. He could see a distant light somewhere down below so he used his hands to swim deeper. Within a few seconds, his lungs started to get painful as it screamed for fresh oxygen. The light at the bottom became more distinct. It was like a bluish white circle, a hole in the ground made of solid, glowing energy. Tyrone was starting to black out and he inadvertently swallowed some river water. He started to back away and panic as the stinking, brackish water partially filled his lungs. The pain was intense as he could no longer see around the corners of his eyes, but he somehow regained his composure and kept on swimming towards the glowing circle. He knew he was close to death's door now as the darkness had just about had him.

The last thing he remembered was touching the glowing circle. Then everything faded to black.

24. The Betrayer

Tenochtitlan

Chipahua placed the suitcases in the forward trunk of the Volkswagen and closed it before getting back into the driver's seat. It was still very early in the morning and the sun was about to rise. Checking the reading on the gas gauge, he hoped that the car would have enough fuel to make it to whatever destination that his master would command them to go to. His devotion to High Priest Tepiltzin was total. Out of all the other priests in the temple of Xipe Totec, he felt that the avatar's nephew had the best chance of becoming the ultimate successor and that he would have a better chance to ascend as well. To that end, he firmly believed the reasoning as to why the child needed to be spared from being sacrificed to Tlaloc. Tepiltzin had convinced him that the traitor was one of the high priests in Tlaloc's temple, and the rebirth of the rain god's avatar needed to be delayed.

Isabel and Tepiltzin emerged from a nearby house and walked towards the waiting car. Since they were on the outskirts of the city, there were practically no checkpoints once anyone went past the causeways and into the surrounding suburbs along the foothills. Tepiltzin figured that by the time the child's identity had been known and a search was conducted, both Isabel and her son Atl would be long gone.

Tepiltzin stared into the backseat of the car and noticed the little boy was fast asleep in the backseat. He turned to Isabel and gave her a letter envelope.

"Here, this is a signed pass with an official seal from the great temple. If any warrior or magistrate gives you any trouble, just show it to them and they will be forced to let you go."

Isabel had been at the ragged end of her nerves since the day before and now she was physically and mentally exhausted. She smiled slightly and hugged him. "Thank you, Ramon. For everything that you have done. I know your mother put you up to this, but nevertheless I am eternally grateful to you for saving the life of Atl."

Tepiltzin smiled back as he caressed her shoulders. He'd always liked her. "We've known each other for a long time, long before the return of the gods. You're like a family to me so I did it for that, not for my mother's sake."

Despite her fatigue, Isabel's lips began to tremble. She was ready to cry again. "I really don't know how I could thank you, if there was only some way I could repay you, but what you did was beyond any price."

Tepiltzin winked at her as he opened the passenger door of the car. "No need. I would have done this service for any other member of my family. Now, you need to go as far away as you can, I think it's better you even leave the empire. My suggestion is that you make it southwards and go past the Incas. Do not worry, we are still at peace with them, but I fear that once we have finished with the Americans to the north, the Incas will be next, so it's best to keep moving."

She clasped his hand tightly before she sat on the front seat of the car. "I will try. Once more, thank you, Ramon."

Tepiltzin closed the car door and leaned over on the window. "Chipahua, make sure you get her past the southern border, then come back here quickly, we still have much work to do."

Chipahua nodded as he started up the engine. It came to life after a loud bang and the car began to vibrate slightly. "Yes, master. See you in a few days."

As the car sped away, Tepiltzin adjusted his cloak and started making his way towards a nearby plaza. The sun was now beginning to rise above the hills. The days usually started like this. There would be a bright morning before the darkening of the skies just before noon, and then the heavy rains would begin by nightfall and their torrential downpours would last for the rest of the evening. He had heard that there was less rainfall in the nearby farmlands so that the harvests would not be flooded, such was the blessing of their gods. A small part of him regretted having to violate the sacrifice for Tlaloc in Teotihuacan, and he shuddered at the potential consequences of his act. Then again, he had already been lying to everybody ever since he dreamt of that boy, and of the prophecy of Tezcatlipoca. He wasn't afraid to die, but he figured he would at least finish off his hated rival Coaxoch in order to protect his family before the gods finally claimed him.

Tepiltzin walked through the streets and wandered in the local stone plaza for a bit. He needed some time to clear his mind and plan his next move. The morning sun had now cast its warming rays over the neighborhood and most of the city had begun to wake up. He noticed a plump, dark-skinned woman tending a small fire as she prepared some tortillas beside her food stall. He walked over and bought a plateful of huevos rancheros, the classical breakfast of Mexican rice, beans, eggs and tortillas smothered in a spicy red tomato sauce. He hadn't eaten since arriving late last night with Isabel's child in tow, so the mouthfuls of food were comforting for him.

An hour had passed by the time he got back to his home. He used a key to open the outer gate. No one had been in his house since he left it. Tepiltzin quickly went to his bedroom and opened up his safe. Seeing its contents hadn't been disturbed, he took out a flint knife he was sure would incriminate Coaxoch. Since he was given the authority to find and eliminate the so-called traitor, all he had to do now was to present his findings to Ixtli, the avatar of Huitzilopochtli.

Several loud knocks on the metal gate interrupted his train of thought. There was no doubt it would be the temple guards. What surprised him was how quickly they had come to take him. Tepiltzin looked at himself in the mirror and made sure his clothes were prim and proper before walking out of the house, carrying a leather pouch with the dagger in it.

A whole squad of warriors were waiting for him outside as he opened the gate.

The lead warrior bowed slightly as a token of respect. "High Priest Tepiltzin, I am here to escort you to the great temple. You have been summoned to appear before your avatar."

Tepiltzin nodded. Since the festival of Tlaloc had happened just yesterday, his uncle and his entourage must have journeyed all night to return to the capital. "Very well, let's go."

The warriors had cars. Tepiltzin rode in the backseat of a Chevrolet Silverado that still had Mexican Army markings on it. Even though they started to adopt many of the fighting styles of the ancient Aztecs, their warriors still made use of present-day technology when it came to certain things such as transportation. It took less than fifteen minutes to cross the causeway and the car had finally stopped near the frontal entrance to the great temple of Xipe Totec.

Tepiltzin was escorted by a group of four temple guards as he walked in between them. He was somewhat relieved that they were using the inner stairways. If they had gone up the stone steps along the outside of the pyramid, it would have been a public execution that awaited him. Then he realized that if they proved that he was a traitor, then his death would be done quietly and out of sight, since it would have caused a major scandal due to his exalted position within the temple hierarchy. The fact that the warriors who came for him did not put him in restraints still boded well to Tepiltzin, he had his evidence and could still bluff his way out of this. All he had to do now was to convince his uncle.

He was led into the main inner hall. The ceiling above him was at least thirty feet tall and the massive room was lit by burning stones on nearby braziers. Large stone columns had recently been added to help buttress the hall. In front of him was a raised stone platform and nearly all the high priests were standing there. Tepiltzin noticed that many of them had haggard faces, clear evidence of their hurried journey to return back to the capital. He was only slightly better rested than they were as he had spent all night in preparing for Isabel's escape from the empire.

The crowd of priests quietly parted in the middle as Tlazopilli, the avatar of Xipe Totec, strode forward and faced him. His uncle was painted in red from head to toe and wore a yellow feathered headdress. His loincloth was made of corn leaves and he carried an ornate wooden staff. "High Priest Tepiltzin, you have been summoned before me, and before my entire priesthood, to answer some very serious allegations that have been made against you. First, it has been said that you were in the holy city of Teotihuacan in disguise yesterday, during the festival to celebrate the rain god. Second, it has been said that you murdered several priests of Tlaloc, and that you abducted a child who had been chosen to be sacrificed that day. What do you have to say about these accusations?"

Tepiltzin made a quick glance at the crowd of priests. His uncle said that the entire priesthood was present, yet he didn't notice Coaxoch anywhere. That only meant that his rival must still be in Teotihuacan. Good, that meant that he could accuse Coaxoch of being the traitor, and his enemy would have no chance to defend himself today. "I adamantly deny these accusations against me. I had spent most of the day here, in the capital, in order to gather evidence as to the supposed traitor in the empire."

The other priests began to murmur amongst themselves, but his uncle was unmoved as he banged his staff on the floor to quiet the room. "Can you present any witnesses that state that they saw you here in the city all day yesterday?"

Tepiltzin nodded. "I can provide witnesses. I also demand that whoever has accused me of murder and deceit, to present himself and his evidence as to my guilt."

Tlazopilli raised his hand. "That will come in due time. Now, have you made any findings as to who this avatar of Tezcatlipoca might be?"

"Yes," Tepiltzin said as he drew out the flint knife from his leather pouch and placed it on a dais in front of the stage. "That is the dagger which belongs to the traitor. My visions had led me to that knife and I soon found out the identity of its owner. I accuse Coaxoch, high priest of Xipe Totec's temple in Teotihuacan, as the future avatar of the god Tezcatlipoca! May the Triple Alliance of gods damn his soul!"

Loud gasps of surprise came from the other priests as their murmurings once again started. Tlazopilli continued to stare back at his nephew without a hint of emotion on his face. Tepiltzin noticed some movement behind the crowd of priests. There was evidently something going on behind him that he couldn't see.

Tlazopilli struck the stone floor three times with his staff. "Tepiltzin, despite the fact that you were given authority to find this traitor, my visions have not been able to discern your true thoughts. As such, your recent actions have fallen under suspicion. We will find out if you are telling the truth soon enough. On the other hand, your accusation against High Priest Coaxoch is a grave matter. I am aware of your mutual hatred for each other and I will now state the truth. It was I who made Coaxoch antagonize you. I considered it a test to see if you were worthy of becoming a future avatar to succeed me."

Tepiltzin's eyes opened wide. He was speechless. His own uncle had set him up.

"Your recent actions have been very disturbing and have now threatened the stability of the Triple Alliance," Tlazopilli said. "We know for a fact your assistant Chipahua was one of the litter bearers of the child that you stole. One of the people in the crowd was using a video camera and we studied the footage of what he took during the procession in Teotihuacan yesterday. The fact that Chipahua is nowhere to be found has led me to conclude you may have indeed engineered yesterday's incident in the other city. For that, you have dishonored your priesthood and you have personally shamed me."

Tepiltzin shook his head. "No, no, Uncle Paco. I would never—"

"Silence!" Tlazopilli said menacingly. "You have debased my own house. I have carefully considered what I would do with you, but I sense that there is still hope for you. You are highly intelligent, but lack loyalty to the empire. I will purge you of your uncleanliness and I shall set you back on the right track. To that end, I must break you first."

A small band of musicians came out from behind the crowd of priests, as they walked off the side of the platform and positioned themselves near the far end of the hall. Almost immediately, the band began to play a traditional dancing tune with soft drumbeats and flutes. The crowd of high priests on the platform parted again, as Coaxoch emerged from behind them. He was wearing the flayed skin of a recent sacrifice as he started a rhythmic dance on the stage.

Tepiltzin had a confused look on his face as Coaxoch jumped off the platform and began to dance less than ten feet in front of him. The skin he was wearing had been freshly flayed and drops of blood began to fall on the stone floor. Tepiltzin narrowed his eyes as he stared at the flesh mask that Coaxoch was wearing. The features looked familiar to him. Wait, it couldn't be!

"Yaotl!" Tepiltzin screamed as he fell on his knees. He realized the awful truth. He sobbed as tears began to flow down his cheeks.

"Your brother was loyal to you," Tlazopilli said. "He even attacked Coaxoch after the latter accused you of the murders of the priests of Tlaloc. He was so loyal to you, he even played a game of ullamaliztli just to defend your honor. He played against the greatest player in the empire, Commander Huemac. And do you know what? Your brother won the game! He scored a goal against Huemac's team and singlehandedly defended your honor. He could not bear to see Huemac being sacrificed, so he instead demanded that he be sacrificed himself. Your brother's selfless devotion is the reason why I am not going to execute you."

Tepiltzin cried out in frustration as the pain of his loss shuddered through his body. Everything he cherished was gone. All that was good in the world had died with his brother. There would be no resurrection when it came to sacrifices, those souls would end up in the underworld forever. He realized that he had nothing left to live for.

"You feel that you have suffered a great loss today," Tlazopilli said. "You must think of this only as the next step on your way to becoming the high priest that I wanted you to be. In order to be devoted to Xipe Totec, one must let go of all attachments in this life. What better way to give your most valuable possession as a gift to Xipe Totec? For only when one has nothing will one truly be appreciative of one's god. Now you have nothing. Now you may begin again."

25. The Exorcists

Camp David

Secretary of Defense Mary Arctor drew a deep breath as she got out of the armored sport utility vehicle and stared at the front part of Laurel Lodge, one of the larger buildings in the camp. Originally designed for official meetings as well as dinners, the lodge had recently been modified to house the ailing president. The night air was chilly and everyone was wearing thick clothing. She could see a large contingent of armed soldiers along the driveway, just milling about in the shadows of the tall birch trees. Ominous thunderclaps could be heard in the distance, but so far there was no sign of rain.

Sheila Giraud got out of the other side of the car and walked over until she stood beside her superior. The foot-tall step lights situated along the edges of the driveways obscured everyone's upper bodies and faces. "What are all these men doing out here?"

Mary shook her head slightly. "I was about to ask the same thing."

FBI Special Agent Lawrence Johnson had already gotten out of the front seat of the car and stood in front of them as he pulled out his walkie-talkie. "I'm here outside of the lodge with the secretary of defense, what's going on?"

In less than a minute, Ethan Quinn ran over to them. He was wearing a heavy wool sweater underneath his leather jacket. He held out his hand to Mary. "Secretary Arctor, thanks for coming on such short notice."

Mary shook his hand. "What's going on, why are all these men out here?"

Ethan shrugged sheepishly. “I’m sorry, but I didn’t have enough time to organize things. When one of our subjects suddenly appeared, she demanded we clear out all the furniture in the building as quickly as possible. I had the Marines and Secret Service contingents here help us out. If you could please follow me.”

As they started walking up the driveway, Mary noticed that a number of heavy furniture pieces had been left on near the side of the walkways. Long mahogany tables, chairs, cabinets, even a pile of flags that had once adorned the presidential office had been placed outside.

Ethan pointed at a sofa as they got near the side entrance of the lodge. “That was the president’s favorite, and if he pulls through from this, I’m sure he’ll want it back.”

Mary placed a restraining hand on his elbow as she stopped in mid stride. “Hold up, you need to tell me everything as of right now.”

Ethan turned and faced them. “Sorry, I thought you wanted to get inside first since it’s a cold night. Anyway, here it is: one of the people that I reported who would be appearing here just showed up out of nowhere. She brought along that old Indian I was telling you about. Anyway, Secret Service were all over them as soon as they showed up and I had to do a lot of improvising to get them to stand down. When the situation calmed down, the subject told me that she needed to see the president and we needed to put him in a room where she could take a look at him.”

Mary instinctively buttoned up her coat as the chilled air wafted around them. “Wait, who is this subject you’re talking about?”

“Tara Weiss,” Ethan said. “She brought along that old shaman, and he goes by the name of El Brujo. I suggested that they might want to use the chapel for what they were going to do, but they insisted on a large room with nothing in it other than the president on his bed.” He pointed to the lodge. “The meeting room in this building was adequate, but they told me to get rid of everything else in it, so that’s how I got the men together. As you can see, they just finished moving everything out.”

Mary looked around. She had a feeling what was going to come next. “Who’s in command of the military?”

Ethan pointed to the door. "Captain Davis. He's right inside."

Mary walked up the side door and opened it. More than a dozen people were crowded in the kitchen as they tried to peer into the next room. There were camp staff, soldiers and Secret Service agents. One of the soldiers had rank bars on his shoulder pads and noticed the four of them come in. He quickly moved over to them.

Captain Davis made a salute. "Madame Secretary."

Mary acknowledged him with a curt bow. "I need you to get your men back to barracks, but keep them on standby. I also want you to clear this room. Only essential staff stays."

As the people started filling out through the side door, Sheila finally figured it out. "They're doing an exorcism, aren't they?"

The main lounge of the Laurel Lodge had been cleared of furniture, the only exception was the large bed in the center of the room. The president was lying on his back and his arms and legs were in plastic restraints that were tied down to the base of the bed. He was dressed in blue pajamas and it looked like he was sleeping soundly. The curtains covered over all the sliding glass doors and windows. All the lights were glaring brightly over the spartan floors and bare walls, which helped to intensify their illumination. A slow, rhythmic chanting came from El Brujo, as he sat crossed-legged on the floor while facing the president's bed. The old shaman continued to sing his mantra, as he used his fingers to pour fine colored grains of minerals over the elaborate sand painting that he was making at the foot of the bed.

Tara Weiss had been sitting beside the old shaman for several hours now. She remembered the tense faces of the Secret Service agents as they all pointed their guns at her, just as she casually walked up to where they had been keeping the president. They had pushed her down on the ground and were in the process of restraining her until Ethan came running over and intervened on her behalf. It took several hours of intense negotiations with the security personnel and the staff of the Executive Office until they finally relented to her demands. In the end, it was the First Lady who gave her permission to do what she wanted. The president's wife had read the confidential reports on her and realized she had come to help.

With her eyes closed, Tara could sense the invisible energies that were swirling around the room. El Brujo's chanting had summoned many of the benevolent spirits in the area. The Algonquin Indians called these spirits the Manitou. The old shaman was making sure that only the good spirits would be present, since the president himself radiated a sort of black energy that was the antithesis of their ritual. The coming battle would not be physical, but of a spiritual nature. During the time that she had been instructed to the ways of the other worlds, Tara could remember the teachings of her mentor. She had a distinct feeling all her lessons would now be put to the test.

As she alternately shifted from an awakened to a spiritual state, Tara heard a loud screech. She sensed that the demon inside the president's body was now preparing to fight as El Brujo's chants had broken through its outer defenses. When she opened her eyes, she saw that the bed had moved a few inches by itself as the frame was being dragged along the floor by some supernatural force.

El Brujo sensed the ebbing waves of defensive energy from the demon as his chants became louder. He had now finished the sand painting in front of him and he stared into it in order to try to discern the identity of the demon that they were fighting with. The brownish grains of sand in the painting began to change color into a bright red. Within a few seconds, a few fine grains had begun to float up into the air as if pulled up by an unknown, invisible hand. El Brujo narrowed his eyes as he stared directly into the painting on the floor, imbuing it with his own form of spiritual protection.

The wind outside began to pick up in intensity and the surrounding trees in the camp had begun to sway as the immediate air had swirled to gale force intensity. The noise from the howling winds had increased to the point where one had to shout just to be heard. The president let out a shrill scream as the bed he was lying in suddenly started to levitate in the air.

Tara's eyelids had begun to feel heavy and it was a struggle to keep her eyes open. It was as if something was trying to force them to close. She could sense a malevolent energy field coming from the floating bed in front of her. Just as she was about to break her concentration, she sensed the warm, allied spirit of El Brujo beside her. Tara quickly refocused her mind as her spiritual energy joined with that of her mentor's own essence, and they started to tear through the demon's hold.

The president arched his back as he tried to break free from his restraints. His eyes had gone completely white and he was shouting out unintelligible things that only creatures of the netherworld would understand.

As she kept up her focus on the energy surge, Tara could feel that they were close now. She had sensed it was her contribution was loosening the demon's hold over the president. Just a little bit more effort and all would be well—

"Why'd you leave me, Tara?"

Tara opened her mouth in shock as she turned. Standing on the far side of the room was Timmy, her little brother. He was wearing his favorite Buster Rocket t-shirt and the loose jeans she bought for him at the discount store with her own savings. She had helped out her friend Crissy on her newspaper route and Tara delivered some papers by hand, even though she didn't have a bicycle. She remembered going to the discount store with her brother, as she helped Timmy try on all the used pants for a boy his age. They finally settled on a pair of slightly torn jeans, even though it was somewhat too big for his waistline. Tara figured he would grow into it eventually. Then again, it was the only pair of pants that came close to fitting him.

Timmy held out his hand. "Why'd you leave? We could still be together!"

Tara's mouth trembled as tears started to form over her eyes. "Timmy, please forgive me!"

Timmy opened his mouth. It was full of blood and started to drip down his chin. "Why?"

Tara's body began to shake uncontrollably. Her little brother was right. She killed him. It was all her fault. It was her selfishness that sealed his fate. If she only had more courage to endure the abuse from her dad, then everything would have been alright. Her hands covered her face as she started to cry. She was nothing. She didn't deserve to live while so many others had died.

Just as she was about to let go, something inside of her began to stir. Tara immediately sensed something wasn't right. She was not looking at her brother at all. As her essence reached out into the room, she surmised the little boy she was looking at wasn't real, he was a test. It really wasn't Timmy. No, it was the demon. As she started to draw her shattered reality back together, she glanced back at the spot where her brother had been standing.

Timmy was no longer there.

That was it. The demon was tempting her. It had tried to break her will by delving into her subconscious, and to draw out the guilt that lay buried deep within the recesses of her mind. She had somehow become aware of it and was now able to refocuses her concentration. As her thoughts returned to clarity once more, Tara could sense that El Brujo was silently congratulating her. She had passed the test.

The president began to make a choking noise as his head and neck was almost vertical. The restraints were holding his limbs fast but it looked like his neck was contorted and stretched. Then a strange grey mist began to pour out of his gaping mouth. Within a few minutes, a man-sized dark cloud hovered over the bed as it crashed back down onto the floor of the room.

The mist began to coalesce until a human-like outline could vaguely be seen inside of it. The voice that it uttered had a strange, harmonious quality combined with a brutal sounding baritone. "Who dares to disturb me from my task?"

Tara knew what it was now. In the demon's desperate attempts to sway her, she had learned of its true name. "You are Ronove, Earl of Hell. Your task has ended. Begone, and return to the infernal realm that you were summoned from."

The demon hissed at her. "You think you can banish me just like that? You are but a weak little girl. I can crush you with my great hands like a matchstick!"

Tara's look was serene as she knew it was powerless now. "You have done all you could and failed. Stop wasting everyone's time and go!"

The demon made a loud bellow. "We shall meet again, Tara Weiss! The next time I shall have your soul!"

Suddenly, there was a blinding white light that engulfed the entire room, followed quickly by a loud, deafening bang. It was as if a bolt of lightning had manifested itself indoors and detonated.

When Tara opened her eyes, she was lying on the floor as medical teams and Secret Service agents started to rush inside the room. Paramedics surrounded the bed as they tried to find out the condition of the head of state. El Brujo had been standing over her and started to help her up. As she looked around, she noticed Ethan and two well-dressed women approaching her.

The president was sitting upright on the bed. "I'm alright, goddamn it! Just get these restraints off of me."

El Brujo clasped Tara's elbow and he smiled at her. "You have done well, my child. You are now a true being of power and you are no longer my pupil. In fact, you are now more powerful than I could have ever hoped to be."

Tara smiled back. Deep inside her heart, she knew she had some help, and she had a very good idea who it was.

26. Intrusion of the Profane

Otherworld

Tyrone Gatlin opened his eyes to a light blue sky. He could see twinkling shafts of light across the heavens, streaking by like falling stars. He blinked several times to make sure he wasn't dreaming. He felt the dry clothes over his skin and it took him a few seconds to recalibrate his sense of reality. After a few minutes, he sat up and looked around. He was sitting along the slopes of a small, grassy hill. A stream with clear flowing water was running along the base of the mound. He neither felt cold nor warmth, and he wasn't tired either. Across the horizon was a massive wooden wall hundreds of feet high, with millions of overlapping metal shields covering the top of it. Where in the hell was he?

"Pretty impressive isn't it? I was quite gobsmacked the first time I came here," a voice behind him said.

Tyrone turned his head. Standing behind him was a young boy of about twelve or thirteen. He wore jeans and had a blue hooded sweater on. The kid smiled at him. Tyrone quickly stood up and tried to wipe away the grass stains on his clothes, only to realize there weren't any.

The boy nodded. "Yeah, no need for that. Your clothes can't get dirty out here."

Tyrone was still somewhat confused. "Who are you?"

The boy moved forward and held out his hand. "Steve Symonds. You must be the shaman I've been waiting for."

Tyrone shook the boy's hand. "You don't sound American with that accent of yours. You, like Australian or somethin'?"

"I'm from England," Steve said. "And you are?"

"Tyrone Gatlin. From Georgia."

Steve smirked. "Right. Now that our introductions are complete, we got a bit of work to do, yeah?"

Tyrone rubbed his forehead. He was mystified at what was happening. "Wait, from what I remember I was swimming under the bayou towards a circle of light and now all of a sudden I'm here? Where are we?"

"Right," Steve said. "From the top then. You are in what we call Valhalla. This was once the domain of the valkyries, you know those Norse angels who take the best Vikings who died and brought them up here to get ready for the final battle. I think it was called Ragnarok."

"Okay, but I was sort of following the Master of Breath who I was worshipping, only he's an American Indian god," Tyrone said. "Isn't this place like in Europe? What does this have to do with what I'm supposed to do?"

The boy took out a small black mirror from underneath his hoodie. It was circular, and seemed to be made of polished obsidian. "It was because of this. It's called the mirror of Tezcatlipoca and I took it from an old wizard that tried to kill me and my sister. I've somehow become attuned to it and I started to have strange dreams about it."

Tyrone was intrigued. "What sort of dreams? I got dreams of my own too that led me here."

"There was sort of a man in the mirror, he had black skin, but not like yours," Steve said. "I mean his skin was black as the night, quite unnatural. He spoke to me and he said he needed to be released in the temple of his enemy. When I asked him how I could do that, he said I needed to wait for the man with the power. That's where you come in, mate. He described you."

Tyrone was shocked. "Me? For reals? This is just so unbelievable. Now that I'm here, what are we supposed to do next?"

Steve looked away as he held the mirror in front of him. "Well, I guess now we need to go to the temple of his enemy and get things started."

Tyrone put his hands up. "Wait a minute, we're just supposed to go like right now? H-how do we get ready and all that?"

Steve closed his eyes as he started to focus on the mirror. "That was all he told me. Let's get started. I'm sure we can make things up as we go."

Suddenly, the mirror had begun to sparkle as a black mist began emanating from it. Tyrone shouted at Steve to wait, but the dark vapors quickly surrounded them both before suddenly collapsing in on itself. Within a few seconds, they had both vanished, it was as if the hillside had never been disturbed.

Xochimanca Causeway

Patli frowned as he sipped his cup of coffee while staring out the window. The young warrior had been designated as the commander of the night watch guarding the main road towards the center of the capital city of Tenochtitlan. The guard house was a one room shack hastily built beside the causeway. He hated guard duty, for it meant doing nothing since the travelers heading into the city were always cooperative when challenged by the sentries. Even worse was the evening shift, and he had to struggle to stay awake. The coffee he was drinking was stale since the pot hadn't been cleaned in weeks and the old coffee grounds had pretty much been robbed of their flavor. If only he hadn't forgotten to take some coffee with him.

Zipactonal was sitting beside the rickety old table in the middle of the small guardhouse, he was playing some cards when he noticed Patli sighing while looking out towards the darkened, empty street. "Do you want to play a game with us?" he asked.

Patli turned. Zipactonal was a young recruit, just a year younger than him and he hardly ever complained. The older warrior sitting across from him was Iuitl, a veteran of several campaigns against the Americans. Iuitl hardly said a word and would stare back at them blankly when asked a question. Patli had heard that Iuitl had been resurrected several times already after being killed, and it looked like he had lost any trace of emotions or the memory of his family. Patli hoped he would not turn out like that when he would finally participate in the coming campaign.

After seeing just how silly playing a game with those two would turn out, Patli just looked away. "No, thank you. I think I would rather stare at an empty road than play a boring card game with the likes of you two."

Zipactonal shrugged as he started shuffling the cards again. The commander was right, Iuitl played the game like a robot. "Okay, it's up to you if—"

Patli interrupted him. "Shh! I heard something!"

Zipactonal looked up at him. "What? I don't hear anything."

Patli looked out into the roadway. The sounds of distant drumming and flutes could be heard. As the minutes passed the music became louder. As Patli picked up his macuahuitl from the nearby table, he could see three figures coming up on the road beside them.

"On the alert, someone's coming up through the causeway," Patli said as he carried the Aztec sword with him while he walked out towards the checkpoint.

Zipactonal rolled his eyes. This was just going to be another routine check. He got up and holstered his pistol before going out of the guardhouse. Iuitl said nothing as he followed. As the three guards stood behind the barrier pole, the figures soon came into view from the other side. When they saw who it was, Patli and Zipactonal's eyes opened wide in total awe. Only Iuitl's face remained impassive.

Coming towards them was a large, light furred coyote that seemed to be walking upright. As the animal came closer, they saw that it had human-like arms, with hands that were playing the flute it was carrying. Right behind the creature were two humans, a pale-skinned, grey haired man and a woman with a scar across her face. The two were wearing heavy robes that covered their bodies and they were banging on small leather drums.

All three guards instantly knew who it was. It had been fated by the high priests of the empire that the gods would soon return in their actual forms. So far, the Aztec deities only spoke through their avatars, but now an actual, living god had returned to his people in the flesh. Among the Aztec pantheon was the animal god Huehuecoyotl, the old, old coyote. He was the god of music, dance and unbridled sexuality. Now he had suddenly arrived, walking towards them this very minute.

Patli instantly fell on his knees as the old coyote stood in front of him while playing a tune on its flute. "Hail, Huehuecoyotl! The old, old coyote has returned to us!"

Huehuecoyotl took the flute from its mouth while his assistants kept on drumming. "I have returned! I give you blessed tidings this evening!"

Zipactonal quickly fell on his knees as well. Only Iuitl stood upright. "Whatever you command, o' old coyote, we will obey!"

"Since I have just returned, I need to go see my brother Huitzilopochtli," Coyote said. "Can you give me directions to his temple?"

Patli quickly got up as he manually raised the barrier pole. "I can do better than that, old coyote, I shall escort you to the grand temple myself!"

The coyote god seemed disinterested, but then quickly nodded and howled at the moon above. "Very well, lead the way, but only you and my followers shall go."

Paul Dane smiled to himself as he made a quick glance at Valerie Mendoza while the two of them followed behind the coyote. His drumbeats were off key, but the others didn't seem to notice. The plan was working beautifully so far. Once they were in the temple, they could deal with the avatar of Huitzilopochtli before facing the avatar of Xipe Totec in another pyramid. It wasn't a sound strategy, but it was all they had.

Valerie noticed Paul's glance as she walked silently with him. It was a good thing those guards hadn't tried to search them. He knew that underneath her robes she had a Heckler & Koch MP5SD6 sub-machinegun. It had a folding stock and a built-in suppressor for silent kills. Her Glock pistol was in her hip holster and that had a suppressor as well. Since her drum had a sling, she had one hand gripping her pistol, while the other continued to pound the drum as the coyote god talked to the guards. Paul could see that she had been tense the whole time while the trickster was talking to the guards, but now she relaxed as they made it through the checkpoint.

In the dark waters beside the causeway, Patrick Gyle's pale head bobbed above the waves. His original plan was to take out the guards so that Paul and the others would get through. Now it looked like the alternate plan was working so he used his long, sinewy arms to swim forward as he headed towards the embankment near the temple grounds.

Temple of Xipe Totec

A continual wave of defeat and despair coursed through his body. He had lost his title of high priest and he had lost the one person he so cherished in this life. Tepiltzin bawled as the metal shackles on his arms restrained him. Once his treachery was exposed, they had him chained to one of the stone columns in the inner hall of the temple. For what seemed like hours, he was forced to witness his enemy Coaxoch's ritual dancing while wearing the skin of his flayed brother. His own uncle, the avatar of his god, had betrayed him. Coaxoch was now the designated successor to become the future avatar of Xipe Totec. Tepiltzin wondered what sort of things he could have done differently. If only he could have done this, or have done that, then maybe his brother would still be alive. The unending thoughts of lost possibilities gnawed at his very being. All he wanted to do now was to die.

The braziers continued to cast a yellowish hue across the great hall as Tlazopilli entered the area once more. Following right behind the avatar was Coaxoch, still wearing Yaotl's flayed skin as he had vowed to keep wearing it until it dried and naturally flaked away. Coaxoch stood on the stone platform as Tlazopilli made his way to where his nephew was.

Tepiltzin could see that the avatar was standing right in front of him. A sudden feeling of rage coursed through him, making the chains on his shackles rattle slightly. Even then he knew it was useless, so he averted his tired eyes to look at the ceiling while saying nothing.

Tlazopilli crossed his arms and frowned. "I am very disappointed in you, Ramon. It has been hours, yet you are still defiant. Your brother is gone because it had to be done. You had to be punished. You should be thanking me for sparing your life since Coaxoch over there wanted to wear your skin as well. You are very, very ungrateful to me, your own uncle."

"He was my brother!" Tepiltzin bellowed. "You all hated him, but I loved him! Then you took him away from me! I curse you, uncle! Damn the Aztec Empire! Damn you all!"

Coaxoch laughed as he started dancing on the stone platform. This was the best day of his life so far. His enemy was defeated and now he had the inside track to become the next avatar. It was all so easy. He was just about to say something that would insult Tepiltzin when he sensed some sort of movement at the corner of his eye. As he turned his head towards the side of the stage, he let out a surprised yelp before jumping off of it.

A great black cloud had suddenly materialized out of nowhere as it appeared on the far side of the stone platform. It was a swirling mist, like a vertical whirlpool of dark energy. The whole temple began to shake as if an earthquake had hit. Tlazopilli was in complete shock as he just stood there. He had been unable to foresee what was happening. Coaxoch ran over and stood beside him as both men were petrified with fear and awe.

Less than a minute later, a black man and a young, fair-haired boy suddenly emerged from the swirling portal and stood on top of the stage. Coaxoch cried out in surprise. Tlazopilli placed his hands on his temples to see if his god could sense who the two strangers were.

Tyrone was still feeling disorientated as his legs wobbled and his head spun. "Whoa, that was some trip."

Steve had traveled across worlds before and he instantly adjusted as he looked around. "Blimey, this whole place is bloody mental!"

Tlazopilli scowled as he slapped Coaxoch's shoulder. "Infidel intruders! Alert the guards!"

Coaxoch sprinted towards the doors so he could call for reinforcements. Tlazopilli held out his hand as an invisible force grabbed his wooden staff lying on a far table and brought it towards him. He was an avatar of the Flayed One, and whoever these interlopers were, they would be facing his full wrath as the godlike powers of Xipe Totec coursed through him.

Temple of Huitzilopochtli

Patli had led them to the lower entrance of the temple pyramid. As they passed through the main foyer and into the basement holding area, more than a dozen temple guards were there. At first, all the men were speechless as they just stared at the coyote god. Within less than a minute, their training took over and they reverted back to their professional ways.

The officer of the guard took a step forward and bowed slightly to Coyote. "Huehuecoyotl, news of your return is now being heard across the city. We are now in the process of waking up our temple priests to see if they could rouse the avatar of Huitzilopochtli so that he may see you this late evening. Please bear with us."

"Thank you for that," Coyote said. "Can we go up now towards the main inner hall so we can wait there?"

The officer was apologetic. "I'm sorry, but your assistants must wait here for they cannot accompany you up in the great hall."

"Oh dear," Coyote said. "That is not convenient for me. I demand that my followers go with me. I … need their drumbeats to concentrate."

The officer shook his head. "I am sorry, but we must insist your followers stay here." He snapped his fingers as two other guards started moving towards them. "We must also search them as a precautionary measure."

Paul couldn't speak Nahuatl so he had a hard time trying to follow the conversation. The moment he saw the guards starting to approach them, he knew the game was up. Just as one of the guards stood in front of him and made a gesture for him to raise his robes, Paul pulled out a Taser gun from beneath his garments and fired it at point blank range. The guard stood stiffly as he started to convulse before falling backwards to the stone floor.

Valerie instantly drew her suppressed Glock and started firing. The officer and two other guards were shot in the chest and they went down. The other guards in the other side of the holding area instantly took cover, as Valerie grabbed Paul and pushed him until they were both behind a stack of crates. One of the guards drew his macuahuitl sword from the scabbard on his back and charged at Coyote, who instantly leapt out of the way. Another guard drew his pistol and shot a surprised Patli in the chest. Patli fell down into the stone flooring and started to cough up blood. Valerie jumped up and shot another guard in his shoulder before dropping back into cover again.

With lightning speed, Gyle sprinted through the entrance and began to attack the remaining guards. He would make rapid leaps from one end of the room to the other, using his claws to slice through bare flesh to tear out their innards. One of the guards fired multiple rounds into the air, hoping to hit him as he jumped, but Gyle easily got to him first as he shoved his arm through the hapless man's chest. Within less than two minutes it was over. The three of them stood over a room full of corpses as Gyle wiped the blood off his arms before standing beside them.

"Jesus," Paul said softly as he surveyed the carnage around him. The stench of blood and excrement was potent. "You're a one man army."

"We need to move," Gyle said tersely. "I'm sure the shots fired were heard all over this place."

Valerie nodded as she readied her MP5 sub-machinegun. "Lead the way."

It was a long climb up to the upper part of the inner temple. Paul was trying to catch his breath as Gyle and Coyote effortlessly went over a hundred stories up in a mere two minutes. Valerie was in better shape, but she still had a hard time catching up with the leading pair. Every time a priest or a guard would try to descend down the stairs, Gyle would make short work of them. By the time Paul and Valerie got to the main landing of the inner temple, they had to walk over dozens of corpses.

Gyle and Coyote waited at the sides of the main entrance to the great hall as Paul and Valerie staggered over to them. Paul was breathing heavily, his lungs strained from the marathon climb up the narrow stone steps. Valerie's shins were aching as she leaned on a wall to steady herself.

"I just remembered," Paul said in between breaths. "Legends state that the idol of Huitzilopochtli would talk to his people. They carried the idol from their ancestral lands for a long time and endured many hardships, until the talking statue told them where to build their city, and then the legend of the Aztecs was born. So I think a lot of his power might come from the statue.

That means if you come across any idol, destroy it."

"Got it," Gyle said as he stood in front of the wooden double doors. He took a step backwards before kicking it with all his might. The two-inch thick doors instantly buckled and collapsed inwards. The way was open.

As the four of them ran inside, Ixtli was standing on the middle of the stone platform as he faced them. The avatar of Huitzilopochtli was painted entirely in blue, with a purple feathered headdress on the top of his head. He was holding a small atlatl shaped like a serpent. His eyes were glowing bright orange and he pointed at Coyote. "You are not the true Huehuecoyotl. You are an imposter and you have defiled my temple by bringing these intruders here."

Coyote walked forward as he stood close to one of the columns that braced the roof of the great hall. "How do you know that I'm not the real one?"

Ixtli sneered. "Huehuecoyotl would never betray his brother gods to these infidels!"

"Maybe I would," Coyote said. "Especially if I have good reason to do so."

Ixtli roared as he made a throwing motion with the atlatl at the trickster. Coyote instantly ducked behind the stone column. A javelin made of pure energy instantly materialized on the spear thrower, was thrown and struck the pillar. The column was instantly shattered in a cloud of dust. Valerie gasped. Another spear made of light began to form on the atlatl that Ixtli carried.

Gyle knew it was now or never. Like a blur, he sprinted towards the avatar, hoping to cut him in half with his claws before he could bring that weapon to bear on his companions. Just as he was about to get close to Ixtli, something leapt out at him from the other side of the hall and threw him into a stone pillar. The stone column had cracked, but did not give way as Gyle landed sideways into it. As he quickly got up and looked around, a tzitzimitl demon stood just a few feet away from him as it licked the blood from its own claws.

As he rubbed the sides of his torso, Gyle felt a stinging pain. He looked at his hand and it was covered in blood. His blood.

Temple of Xipe Totec

The two cascading waves of energy were in opposition as they crashed against each other and shook the temple's foundations to its very core. Steve was on one knee as his trembling arms could barely keep the black mirror up in front of him. The wall of black energy that surrounded the mirror was slowly dissipating against the furious onslaught of Tlazopilli's lightning based attacks. The avatar of Xipe Totec was unleashing furious currents of white hot power that continued to expand as the support columns in the middle of the great hall started to buckle. Sensing that victory was soon at hand, Tlazopilli grimaced as he focused his attacks on the boy. Once the protective forces around the mirror were stripped away, he would take great pleasure in personally sacrificing that kid to the Flayed One.

Steve gritted his teeth as the pain in his arms became unbearable. His whole body was being steadily pushed backwards by the sheer power that was being thrown against him. He made a quick glance at Tyrone, who was huddled behind a support pillar. "You have to do it now! I can't bloody keep this up!"

Tyrone threw his arms up and shook his head as the winds caused by the opposing forces were hurling all sorts of dust and materials around them. "I dunno what I'm supposed to do!"

Steve turned his head and used his chin to gesture at the former high priest being held captive at the far side of the hall. "Get over to him! Free him quickly!"

Tyrone had to squint his eyes as the gale force winds in the room kept him rooted to the column where he took cover at. He got up and started making his way to where the other man was bound. Tyrone could only make one step at a time as he moved close to the ground so as not to be blown backwards by the concussive forces that swirled around him. The pace was slow and it was like trying to walk across a sea of molasses. It was so tempting to just give up and cower behind one of the far columns, but he had a feeling that if they lost, it would be a fate worse than death for the both of them. He heard the boy scream out in pain but Steve was able to miraculously hold on as Tyrone finally got close to the bound man.

Tepiltzin could only watch helplessly as he struggled against the chains that held him fast on the column. The black man that had slowly made his way towards him was obviously going to free him, but what he would do after that, he had no idea.

Just as Tyrone got his hands on the chains that were binding the renegade high priest, Coaxoch tackled him from behind and both began to wrestle on the floor. Even though he had alerted the guards, Coaxoch had a feeling the avatar would need help, so he ran back into the room, just in time before the force storm had blocked the others from entering. He had been hiding behind one of the stone pillars and waited until one of the intruders tried to free his enemy Tepiltzin. The moment he saw the intruder get close to his captive, he made his move and intercepted him.

Tyrone cried out as his hands slipped as he tried to pull away from Coaxoch, the flayed skin suit was waxy and it easily slipped off so he couldn't get a grip on it. Tyrone saw the flint blade coming out from its sheath as Coaxoch tried to plunge it into his shoulder, but he was able to hold onto the high priest's wrists and the point of the blade stopped at less than an inch from his body. Coaxoch cursed as he used all his weight to bear down and push the knife in, but Tyrone twisted the blade so its point became parallel to his chest just as Coaxoch plunged it down. The fragile flint blade snapped in two as its flattened end was forced on Tyrone's chest. Tyrone twisted sideways and rolled over until he got on top of the struggling priest as he pulled out the Gerber knife from his boot. Now it was Coaxoch's turn to panic and scream as the blade plunged into his throat. Blood started to gush from the high priest's mouth as the sharp edges of the steel blade tore through his artery. In less than a minute, Tyrone could feel the other man's strength ebbing away. Just as Coaxoch died, Tyrone felt something within himself. It was like a seed in his soul that began to grow. When he looked up at Tepiltzin, he knew what he had to do.

The swirling, chaotic forces in the room no longer seemed to affect him as Tyrone got up and stood to his full height. He walked up to Tepiltzin until their faces were only inches away from each other. Tyrone opened his mouth and vomited out a black mist that swirled in front of the captive's face.

Tepiltzin now realized what the mysterious dream about the boy meant. The god of the smoking mirror had been here since the very beginning. He had been biding his time, just waiting for the right moment to strike back against the other gods that had banished him from his people. Now he would show them his supreme power. Just as Xipe Totec and Huitzilopochtli chose their avatars with which to reign on earth, so would the god of the smoking mirror. Now he understood it all. Tepiltzin opened his mouth and breathed in the dark vapors. The black mist swirled in his lungs and then the transformation had begun.

Tlazopilli grinned with satisfaction as the boy in front of him cried out and fell sideways to the floor. A few more minutes and he would finally overcome the remaining defenses of that accursed mirror and shatter it. Then he would bide his time with that boy and learn all he could about how the child could have possessed such a powerful artifact. The avatar of Xipe Totec knew the significance of that mirror and it would be the final nail in the night god's coffin once he was able to destroy it.

"Destroying my mirror will grant you nothing," a voice beside him said. "Your Triple Alliance will cease to exist as of now."

Tlazopilli's eyes went wide as he turned his head. Standing beside him was Tepiltzin, but his nephew had somehow been transformed into a being with jet black skin, far darker than the color of night. The avatar of Xipe Totec was stupefied as he stared back at the newly born avatar of Tezcatlipoca.

Tepiltzin opened his mouth to reveal rows of razor sharp teeth. He roared as he bit into his uncle's throat, sending a gushing torrent of blood onto the stone floor in front of them. Tlazopilli's lightning staff dropped onto the floor and began to transform itself into a solid ball of energy that crackled and became as bright as the sun. The dying avatar of Xipe Totec fell onto the floor as his nephew continued to bite into his flesh.

Tyrone let out a deep breath as he turned and ran over to where Steve was lying. As he knelt down and checked to see if the boy was still alive, Steve opened his eyes and gave him a wink. "Goddamn it kid, I thought you was dead," Tyrone said.

Steve grinned as he stood up. Both of them could barely see as the glowing sphere of power was starting to engulf the whole room. "We need to get out of here," the boy said as he looked into the mirror that he had been holding.

Tyrone nodded as he held up his hands to shield his eyes from the ever expanding wave of blinding white energy heading towards them. "I ain't saying no to that!"

Steve was exhausted but he used the remaining reserves of his willpower and concentrated on the black mirror. If he didn't do it now, they would be dead. Suddenly, the black mist began to emanate from the mirror once more and surrounded them. Less than a second after that, they were gone.

Temple of Huitzilopochtli

Gyle had finally met his match. The tzitzimitl's claws narrowly missed him as they tore chunks out of the wall where he had been standing in front of less than a second before. They both moved so quickly it was like watching two blurred figures that dodged each other's attacks. Gyle was certain his own clawed hands had connected against the demon, but the tzitzimitl didn't react as if it even felt any pain. A piece of Gyle's shoulder was already lying on the floor when the star demon bit into him and tore a chunk of flesh out from his body. Gyle was hurt, but he kept at it, hoping for a weakness to reveal itself before it was too late.

Ixtli continued to hurl lightning bolts from his atlatl at the trickster god, but Coyote continued to jump around from one end of the room to another as portions of the hall was slowly being ground to dust by the force of the explosions. The avatar of the war god Huitzilopochtli was getting frustrated at his enemies, so his attacks were steadily increasing in intensity.

Valerie hid behind one of the columns as she fired another short burst from her MP5 at the entrance of the great hall. She had fired several rounds at the avatar, but the bullets seemed to just harmlessly bounce off Ixtli's body. The remaining temple guards and priests tried to force their way into the room so she concentrated on them instead. Valerie would sprint from column to column, making sure that she was behind cover against both the reinforcements coming from the entrance and the lightning attacks coming from the central platform.

Paul was ready to cry out in frustration as he crouched behind one of the stone pillars for cover. He never felt so useless in his life. The others were busy fighting and he wasn't up to it. As he tried to think at what he could do to help, he spotted a three foot tall stone idol of Huitzilopochtli sitting in an alcove at the far side of the hall. He remembered the creation myths of the city, when the Aztecs were nothing more than a wandering tribe. They had been carrying a talking idol of their war god that finally led them to a swampland in the middle of the lake. From there, the small tribe began their ascent to dominate this part of the world. Paul sensed the idol might be the key.

The moment Coyote started jumping to the other side of the hall, Paul made his move as he started running towards the location of the small statue. He made sure to move only when the avatar finished his attack. It took less than a minute, and Paul was now standing behind the last column. Now he had to run out into the open and make a grab for the idol. He waited until Ixtli fired another lightning bolt at Coyote, then he started sprinting towards the wall where the alcove was.

The tzitzimitl instantly sensed Paul's intentions. It quickly kicked Gyle away and lunged at the mythology professor. Gyle was able to recover quickly and caught up with the demon just as it clawed Paul's back. Gyle tackled the tzitzimitl from behind and drove it into part of a nearby wall.

Paul cried out in agony as he fell face down onto the stone floor. It felt like his back had been ripped wide open. Blood began to seep down his lower back as he was momentarily blinded by flashing pain. His hands trembled as he got up to his knees and stared at the stone idol just a few feet above.

Valerie was reloading when he heard the scream. She turned and saw Paul trying desperately to get back up. "Paul!' she screamed as she started running towards him.

The tzitzimitl elbowed Gyle in the face as it tore away from him. With the speed of a lightning bolt, the demon dashed forward, holding out its claws to rip open the man who dared to attempt the destruction of the holy idol.

Valerie got there first. Just as she got in between the demon and Paul, she pulled out her Glock pistol and fired several rounds at the demon's face. The tzitzimitl lashed out in rage, concentrating on her as its claws tore through her chest. Valerie's eyes opened wide as she started to spit out blood and fell backwards.

"Noo!" Paul cried out and pulled her away, just as Gyle got to them and threw the tzitzimitl into the other side of the hall before leaping after it. Paul gently placed Valerie on her back as he cradled her head in his arms.

Valerie began to cough up more blood, but she was able to slight smile slightly as she looked up at him. She reached up and lightly touched his chest, right where his heart was, before slumping back down. Then she closed her eyes forever. Paul screamed out in pure unadulterated anguish. The one person that truly mattered in his life, the woman who saved him from an eternity trapped in Hell, was gone.

Gyle was doing his best to keep the demon away from the others but it was like trying to hold onto a snarling tiger. The tzitzimitl kept tearing into him and ripped at his left arm, nearly severing it. Gyle used his own fangs and bit into the demon's throat and cut off the spinal column, as the monster's head was torn off. The demon kicked him away as it stood up and then reattached its own head. "Paul," he bellowed as he stood to block its way. "I can't keep this up, do it!"

Paul fought through his tears of loss as he stood up. He just wanted to die with her. His life didn't matter anymore, but Gyle's cries of desperation took hold and reignited his sense of duty. These Aztecs had to be stopped. If he failed, then Valerie gave her life up for nothing. His wobbly knees could barely support himself as he wrapped his hands around the idol and removed it from the pedestal. The stone statue was surprisingly light as he held it above his head and threw it down onto the floor. The idol was smashed into a million pieces.

Ixtli let out a cry as his powers started to fluctuate, his control over the energies coursing through his body was lost. The lightning bolt on his atlatl suddenly overloaded and exploded in his hand, severing it. Coyote sensed his chance as he leapt up and kicked the avatar in the chest, sending him flying backwards into the central support column. Ixtli collided with the stone pillar and shattered it as his body began to burn from the inside out, as the internal energies in his aura had made it unstable. Then the entire building began to buckle as a chain reaction had started, just as other parts of the braces that held it in place began to collapse.

Gyle knew he wasn't going to make it. He had lost too much blood, and the snarling demon in front of him was going to kill everybody else if he let it get away from him. He could see the rear support column was not that far. One more ought to do it. The demon hissed before it lunged at him. This time, instead of dodging the tzitzimitl attack, Gyle only pushed it slightly away and redirected the creature's momentum as they both were hurled sideways into the remaining support column. The demon began ripping out his stomach as Gyle smashed the pillar with all his remaining strength and it finally gave way.

The entire pyramid groaned as its apex collapsed in on itself. The outer temple at the top of the structure caved in, and the four upper sides imploded. Huge blocks of falling stone started bursting through the ceiling of the great hall. The remaining priests tried to run down the stairs but many of them were crushed as the inner stairwell gave way. Corridors within the interior of the pyramid crumbled inwards, sealing many of the rooms inside.

Paul was wailing as he cradled Valerie in his arms. The trickster suddenly appeared behind him. "We need to go," Coyote said as the ceiling began to fall all around them in a tremendous crash of stone and dust.

Seeing that Paul wasn't responding, Coyote grabbed him by his shoulder and pulled him away. Paul cried out just as a vertical rip in the air opened up behind them and the trickster pulled him through. Paul hung onto Valerie's body and was pulled into the black hole, just as a huge block of stone smashed right into the spot where they had been.

27. Ouroboros

Georgia

As soon as the rowboat touched the shore, Tyrone Gatlin stood up and walked up to dry land. The late afternoon sun had cast giant shadows over the monstrous, looming trees that blanketed the horizon. All the areas in the Old South were like this now: flooded landscapes, with bayous and waterways, big and small islands in between. It would take a new kind of human being to live in these parts. He was lucky it hadn't rained all day, but he sensed the storm clouds would arrive by early evening.

The old store was still standing there, right where he remembered it. His grandparents first started building the place. Then his father, still in his teens, had steadily expanded it, adding new sections in, until it was as big as one of those department stores in the malls. One of the big chain stores had just opened up at the far end of town when he left, and business was steadily getting worse, but his daddy always believed that they would hold on, no matter what.

Tyrone stood in front of the building. His father said those words to him a long time ago. All of the windows in the store had now been boarded up with rickety, warped plywood and rusted nails. Most of the paint had peeled off and the air conditioning units on the flattened roof had rusted away into oblivion. At least his family was luckier than most, as he turned and surveyed the edge of the water where the other side of the street used to be. The daily deluge of rain had pretty much wiped out everything else, but his daddy's store was still standing.

He tried the rusted doorknob and it opened with an ear-piercing creak. Right after he stepped inside, he could hear the sounds of rats scurrying about in the darkness. Tyrone looked around and he could see nothing but rusting, empty shelves that stretched out into the dim recesses of the store. He could hear the crackling of broken glass as he stepped over assorted bits of trash and other refuse. The smell in the inside was a combination of rusted metal, dried river muck and animal droppings. The white marble counter where the cash register used to be was cracked and a layer of dust had painted it to the color of ashen grey. The old stool where his parents would take turns watching over the place was still there, but the upholstery had been eaten away by vermin. The only bits of light that shone through were from the opened door and the cracks where the plywood had broken off.

Tyrone heard the sound of a shotgun being pumped as he turned to his left. Standing at the far side of the deli section was the silhouette of a woman. She moved forward for a bit so she could get into optimum range with the old Mossberg 500 that she carried in her arms. Tyrone saw the wrinkles underneath her dark brown eyes. Her thick black braided hair hung loosely over her shoulders as she got to within twenty feet of him. Tyrone recognized her pouting face as she glared back at him with pure, unadulterated contempt. Yes, it was his sister all right.

"Laila? Is that you?" he asked.

She turned the shotgun so the barrel wasn't aiming at him directly anymore. "You picked a hell of a time to come back, Tyrone."

Tyrone took a deep breath. "What happened here?"

Laila snorted. "What do you think happened? The Glooming happened. While you were away, it just kept on raining and it never stopped. Daddy waited for you to come back but you never did."

Tyrone looked away. "I told him I was joining the Army. And I did."

The rage in her voice was palpable. "He depended on you! He needed you! He was an old man, but you left him because you didn't wanna work here. Now he's dead."

Tyrone's mouth dropped open. "Daddy's dead?"

"He drowned," Laila said softly as her free hand pointed to the outside.

"He was out there, helping the others, when a huge wave of water just came in and swept them all away. Momma had a heart attack and now she can't get outta bed. So many people are dead, and you weren't around."

Tyrone slumped as he leaned on the edge of the counter by the door. The rotting wood made a loud creak, but it didn't give way. "I tried to ask to go on leave, but they wouldn't let me. It was a national emergency. The Aztecs were comin' and we had to do somethin'."

Laila shook her head slowly. She wanted to cry, but the past year had already hardened her. "You can keep telling youself that. As for me, I blame you for what happened to daddy and momma."

Tyrone sighed. There was no point in arguing with her. "If you blame me for everything, fine. But I'm here now."

She snorted a second time. "Lotta good that does now."

Tyrone looked around. "What happened to the store? The flooding didn't touch it cuz our grandaddy saw fit to build on high ground, that's why he bought this lot in town, it had the highest elevation."

"All this came later," Laila said. "After the floods and the dying, people were starving and all that. Then the Klan came along and took whatever they could. They still out there. They come in every now and then in them fast boats and they take what they can. If anyone tries to fight them, they die. You ain't gonna last long out here, Tyrone. There's so few of us left. I'm only stayin' cuz of my son, he too young to go anywhere."

Tyrone straightened up. She could sense something different about him. It was like he had some sort of power within him. "Well, all that's gonna change, starting now," he said to her as he held out the gris-gris that he wore around his neck. "I went on a vision quest. Saw so many things y'all just wouldn't believe. The Master of Breath chose me as his shaman."

Laila's eyes narrowed. She was wary but still intrigued. "Shaman? What's that?"

Tyrone smiled faintly. "It's a special kind of man, someone who talks to spirits and has traveled across many worlds. If the Klan comes back, they be in for a big surprise."

Brooklyn

Valerie Mendoza's funeral was held in Cypress Hills Cemetery. A small police honor guard led by Lieutenant Joe Pascorelli wrapped the American flag and gave it to her mother, Josefina, while two bagpipers played Amazing Grace and Lochaber No More. Dr. Paul Dane stood alongside her mother as he held the hands of Kim and Troy Desmond, his newly adopted children. The President of the United States was present, along with Commissioner Donovan of the NYPD. Secretary of State Mary Arctor and her staff were able to attend as well. Patrick Gyle had been officially listed as missing in action, as in accordance to his own wishes.

As the funeral rites finally ended and everyone started heading to their cars, Paul looked out into the peaceful meadows and the surrounding tombstones. The day seemed sunnier than usual. Kim and Troy had already gone ahead back to the apartment as they were escorted by a few cops. He didn't want them to linger here. It was better for them to move on with life as quickly as possible, he figured. There already was too much death in the world for them to have to worry about another one.

Paul sighed. He had heard from the trickster that the new shaman had been able to help neutralize the faction of Xipe Totec in his own temple, just as they were doing battle against the avatar of Huitzilopochtli. With the apparent demise of the two avatars, the Aztec Empire was thrown into turmoil. America had won a reprieve, at the very least. There was still a lot of work to do. There were renegade Aztec war bands still crossing the porous border to take captives. But without their leaders, there would be no major invasion. The country now had some precious time to look for a more permanent solution.

A wrinkled brown hand took him by the elbow. It was Josefina. "Don't grieve too long, your country needs you."

Paul smiled slightly as he stared into her deep brown eyes. In many ways, Valerie's mother reminded him of her. "I miss her. She renewed my life when I thought it was lost. I thought we were destined to be together forever. If only things could have turned out differently."

Josefina nodded. "Do not worry, she is in a better place. Valerie wanted to be a cop more than anything else in her life. She died fighting for what she believed in."

He held his hand over hers. "Thank you, Mama Josefina. I would like you to live with us. The two kids are very fond of you and I owe you so much because you took care of them while Val and I were somewhere else."

"Muchas gracias," Josefina said. "We are one family now. Let us head back to the apartment so that I can start cooking for the kids."

Paul nodded. "Okay, go ahead. I'll join you in a bit. I just wanted to hang around for a little while longer."

As she walked away, Paul turned around and stared out past the row of white headstones. Her mother was right, Valerie just wouldn't have gone out any other way. As he recalled the brief but happy times they had together, he felt something in his pocket. As Paul pulled it out and stared at it, he quickly realized it was Valerie's Aztec necklace. Then it hit him. She had secretly placed it in his clothes as a token of good luck. Did she know she wasn't going to make it? Or did the necklace actually afford some sort type of protection and she had willfully placed it in his possession as a way to save him?

Tears began to stream down his face. He had kept his composure throughout the funeral but now he just couldn't take it anymore. Paul fell on his knees and started to weep.

Otherworld

The wind blew her long, reddish brown hair around in all sorts of different directions, but she didn't bother to put it back in place. The rolling, grassy hills that surrounded Valhalla seemed peaceful, almost heavenly. The overcast day seemed constant and night would never come. There was a magical calmness to the place as Tara Weiss stared out into the vast distance. She figured it would be a great spot to hang around in, but with all she experienced, it would become boring in no time.

"Hi," a voice beside her said.

She turned. Standing near her was Steve Symonds, the 13 year old from England. Tara stared at him for a bit before looking back out and enjoying the pale skies above them. He was sort of handsome, but he was also two years younger than she was.

Steve laughed a little. She was ignoring him. That was a good sign. "I'm Steve by the way," he said.

Tara kept looking away. She wasn't in the mood but she didn't want to tell him that. At least, not yet. "I know who you are. Everybody's been talking about you."

Steve grinned sheepishly. So it looked like his reputation preceded him. "I know who you are as well, you're Tara. You did a lot for people too."

Tara made a slight shrug. "Okay, I guess we have that in common."

Steve looked down at the grass on his feet. "I was wondering, what are your plans? Will you be going back to earth anytime soon?"

"I will be … sooner or later," Tara said wistfully. "I need to look up a friend first. I promised him I would help him find his mother."

"What's his name?"

"Ilya," Tara said. "He's in the faerie realms. He got hurt saving me and I'm going to see if he's well enough to travel now."

Steve nodded. He knew the faeries all too well. "I would be careful around those Fey, they have a habit of deceit, if you know what I mean."

"I know," Tara said softly.

Steve turned around. She didn't seem to be in a good mood, maybe he would chat with her later. Just as he started to walk away, he turned his head one more time. "What will you do after you help him then?"

Tara closed her eyes for a bit before she answered him. "I'm going to go look for my brother. Even though his physical body is gone, I know he's out here somewhere. The worlds that we can travel throughout here are like, infinite. I know I can find him. I can feel it in my heart."

Coming Soon:

Mortuorum Luctum

Wrath of the Old Gods

Book IV

Join John Triptych's mailing list for the latest news, exclusive discounts, and FREE books!

It's FREE to join in and you can unsubscribe at any time!
http://eepurl.com/bK-xGn

J Triptych Publishing

Spellbinding literary entertainment at an affordable price!

Crime Thrillers:

The Expatriate Underworld Series: John Triptych's gritty, no-holds barred exploration of South East Asia's expatriate underworld, a sordid society in which one man is determined to succeed at any cost. Recommended for mature readers.

The Opener (Book 1)
The Loader (Book 2)

The Amoralist Series: John Triptych returns to the thriller genre with a new series that focuses on a highly unique assassin who travels the world for all manner of whims and murder.

A Man of Leisure (Book 1)
Savage Wanderings (Book 2)

Science Fiction and Mythology:

Wrath of the Old Gods Series: The entire world is thrown into turmoil as the ancient gods of myth and legend return. An epic, post-apocalyptic series with multiple characters, mythical beings, and world spanning adventures.

The Glooming (Book 1)
Canticum Tenebris (Book 2)
A World Darkly (Book 3)
And more to come!

Wrath of the Old Gods Young Adult Series: A complete and standalone series for young adults that ties in with the main Wrath of the Old Gods series. This trilogy centers on a young British boy and of his quest to save his country from supernatural forces.

Pagan Apocalypse (Book 1.5)
The Fomorians (Book 2.5)
Eye of Balor (Book 3.5)

Look for these books in e-book and paperback formats via the internet or by request at your local bookstore!

www.ingramcontent.com/pod-product-compliance
Lightning Source LLC
Chambersburg PA
CBHW021439240626
47153CB00001B/217
* 9 7 8 6 2 1 9 5 3 3 2 5 6 *